THE OPEN PORTAL

CONQUEST OF THE VEIL

BOOK ONE

MICHAEL SCOTT CLIFTON

Books by
MICHAEL SCOTT CLIFTON

The Treasure Hunt Club

The Janus Witch

Conquest of the Veil Series
The Open Portal

(Coming Spring 2020)
Escape From Wheel

Book Liftoff
1209 South Main Street
PMB 126
Lindale, Texas 75771

Interior's book design by Champagne Book Design
Cover design by Simply Defined Art

Library of Congress Control Number Data
Clifton, Michael Scott
The Open Portal / Michael Scott Clifton
Magical Realism / Fiction.
Dragons & Mythical Creatures / Fantasy / Fiction.
3. Paranormal / Fantasy / Fiction
BISAC: FIC061000 FICTION / Magical Realism
FIC009120 FICTION / Fantasy / Dragons & Mythical Creatures.
2019937533

ISBN: 978-1-947946-44-6 (Kindle Direct Publishing Soft Cover)

www.michaelscottclifton.com
www.bookliftoff.com

DEDICATION

"To my wife Melanie.
My ever present partner in everything I do."

*"There was the Door to which I found no key; There was the Veil
through which I might see"*
Edward Fitzgerald

℘ROLOGUE

The Empire of Meredith: One Thousand Years Ago

ENDRILS OF BLACK SMOKE ROSE IN THE EARLY MORNING AIR. Huddled within a thicket of vegetation, Larson Crump watched, his heart pounding, while the manor house slowly burned to the ground. Greedy, licking flames consumed the once grand structure, and with a groan of tortured wood, the southeastern corner of the manor collapsed in a shower of flame and sparks.

Above the noise and tumult of the raging fire, a scream rang out, and Crump jammed a fist in his mouth to stifle a whimpering cry. With great trepidation, he managed to force his quaking hands to part the thick screen of leaves, and despite the need for caution, a moan escaped his lips at the sight. There, against the backdrop of the burning manor, Lady Sonja stood stripped naked and struggling in the grasp of...*creatures* straight from his worst nightmares! Beneath a set of small piggish eyes, the brutish beasts possessed wicked, yellow tusks jutting from their lower jaws. Waddles of pinkish-gray flesh framed their necks, the boar-like heads attached to a squat torso of powerful arms and legs.

Crump returned his attention to Lady Sonja and groaned at the sight of the long, bloody slashes that marred her breasts, the streaks of crimson painting her ribs and abdomen. His eyes widened when Lady Sonja's husband, Lord Will, was brought forward and forced to stand beside his wife. Face battered and bruised, he fought with the nightmarish creatures to assist his wife. Amused grunts and squeals erupted from the beasts, and they rained blow after blow until fresh blood ran down the lord's face and head.

There was a stir among the throng of manlike beasts, and they parted to provide passage for two figures. From his vantage point, Crump could see a couple, a man and woman, strut through the brutish creatures and up to the manor's veranda. Ink-black hair fell to the woman's waist, and even from a distance, he could see she possessed a terrible beauty. The man, slightly taller than the woman, wore sharp features and a cruel smile.

When the couple turned to face the grunting man-beasts, Crump saw their eyes for the first time. Black as a bottomless pit, they oozed a malevolency so potent, Crump's legs trembled, and his hair stood on end.

Sorcery! The dark magic filled the air to such an extent Crump felt it assault his senses, like some ill breeze portending disaster.

From the veranda, the sorceress turned and held a small, round object high above her head for all the assembled creatures to see. Loud squeals and snorts boiled into the air until the enchantress held up her hand for silence.

"The orb is ours! It is now *our* time and *our* destiny! We shall be the Masters, and they," she said, a cruel finger pointed at Will and Sonja, "shall be the ones who serve us! We will kill all who oppose us!"

Lowering the orb to cradle it in her hands, the sorceress turned to Sonja. "Before you die, I want you to know *your* Artifact, *your* creation made our ascension to power possible." Lady Sonja flinched at the words as if struck by a hammer. Fresh despair spread across her tear-streaked face.

Laughing, the sorceress gestured, and Lord Will was thrown into the mass of man-beasts. Raw screams tore from Lady Sonja's throat at the sight of her husband torn to bloody pieces.

The violent sight and sound overwhelmed Crump's senses.

Gorge rose in his throat and what little remained in his stomach spewed out. Mercifully, the screams came to an abrupt end. Crump sank to the ground and wept, his thin shoulders shaking.

He wiped his eyes and tried to make sense of what happened. His friends, the Lord of the Manor...*all dead!* He alone survived and only because he had spent half the night in the bushes with a belly flux. When the creatures attacked, there had been no outcry, no alarm raised—almost as if the entire staff was drugged or ensorcelled by some dark magic.

All but Crump.

Fresh shrieks bruised the air when Lady Sonja's turn came to be given to the creatures. Her desperate cries rose into the early morning light and pierced Crump's soul like a dagger.

He turned and fled.

CHAPTER 1

East Texas—Present day

*B*RRRING!

Even before the last notes of the lunch bell faded, classroom doors flew open, and students exploded into the hallways of Spring Hill High School.

Mona Parker found herself carried along like a leaf in a river as she unsuccessfully tried to navigate a course to her locker. Finally, she reached the intersection of two hallways and found a quiet eddy as students rushed past her to the cafeteria. Once the flow abated somewhat, she backtracked to her locker. Opening it, she removed a brown paper bag containing her lunch, along with a large, hardbound book. She stuffed her backpack into the cubbyhole, closed the door, and hurried to her favorite location to eat lunch.

She burst out of the glass doors from the high school and turned a corner leading to the student commons area. With a sigh of relief, she spied her coveted table still unoccupied. Her eyes darted left and right to see if anyone else might beat her to it.

No other students in sight.

Mona rushed to the table and threw her book and bagged lunch down with breathless abandon.

Success!

At first glance, the outdoor picnic table didn't seem to have any visible attributes to lend itself as a desirable lunch location.

Covered in a crisscross veneer of ugly blue polyurethane, it was uncomfortable to sit on, and depending on the season—fall, winter, or spring—it either never seemed to get enough sunlight or too much. However, this particular table possessed one thing Mona found valuable above all else.

A perfect view.

On cue, a slender boy with a lunch tray in hand walked up to another picnic table directly across the commons area from Mona. He set his lunch down, and several friends joined him moments later.

With a happy sigh, Mona arranged her book—a large illustrated edition on antique clocks—in front of her. She found the book in the nonfiction section of the school library, and while she had absolutely no interest in clocks, the book, with its oversize, large-print format, propped up easily on the table. Moving the spine of the book like a gunsight to zero in on a target, Mona finally positioned it perfectly so when she looked up above the spine of the book, her quarry came into view.

Brock Stanton.

Brock's blue eyes flashed while he chatted with his friends, and Mona felt her heart beat faster when he smiled at some comment. She *met* him over a month ago when they accidentally bumped into each other. Coming from different directions in the always crowded hallways, Mona turned a corner and ran right into Brock. She dropped her books, and he picked them up and apologized. Best of all, he displayed the same gorgeous smile before he turned and left.

Mona had a crush on him ever since.

Quite by accident, she discovered later that Brock and his friends often frequented the same table at lunch. Since then, she and her trusty antique clock book were fixtures at the picnic table across from him.

Although she had not spoken or even crossed paths again with Brock, Mona loved to peek at him over her book and fantasize about being his girlfriend. In her happy dreams, they traveled to exotic and romantic locations with breathtaking backdrops from which to kiss and hold each other.

Walking hand-in-hand on the dazzling white sand of a secluded Bermuda beach just as the sun is setting. Check!

A Colorado ski lodge with the gorgeous snowcapped Rocky Mountains in the background. With arms wrapped around each other, they watch their breath billow out to comingle in white clouds. Check!

An intimate Paris bistro sipping an espresso together while a white aproned maître d' hovers nearby smiling at the lovely couple. Check!

Sharing a delicious chilled shrimp cocktail, their—

"Well, well, what do we have here?" A voice intruded on Mona's dreamy meanderings.

Startled, Mona looked up. Eyes shaded with her hand in the bright December sunlight, Mona's pleasant fantasies came to an abrupt halt. Her heart sank, and despite the unusually mild day, a chill ran down her spine.

Lady Anne Golightly stood beside her, hands on slim hips, a predatory smile on her face—like a cat preparing to pounce on a mouse. Silky blonde hair cascaded past her shoulders, while glacial blue eyes regarded Mona with no small amount of contempt.

Mona gulped, a cold knot of fear growing in her stomach.

As a freshman four years earlier, she had been in the snack bar line at lunch, a rare thing since she usually had no money. The long, conga line of students shuffled along at a snail's pace, when Lady Anne and her coterie of friends burst into the snack bar. With laughs and snorts, they stepped in front of Mona, like her place was theirs for the taking and her no more substantial than a ghost. When Mona objected loudly enough to attract one of the coaches on cafeteria duty, he made Lady Anne and her friends go to the end of the line. As she walked by Mona, Lady Anne fixed her with cold, hate-filled eyes.

It was the last day of *normal* high school life for Mona.

Since then, Mona became Lady Anne's special project.

Dead rats found in her school locker.

Photoshopped images of her face on a naked, grotesquely obese woman shared on all Lady Anne's social media sites.

A continuous series of text messages that described in graphic detail various parts of Mona's anatomy.

Opening her P.E. locker and discovering her P.E. clothes had been urinated on.

At first, Mona tried to fight back by going to the Principal, Mr. Garrett, but no proof could ever be found directly tying Lady Anne to the harassment. In fact, it served no purpose other than to make the acts worse and more frequent. Lady Anne's father, president of the largest bank in Longview and a member of some standing in the community, made the investigation difficult. Mona suspected Mr. Garrett was reluctant to pursue the matter, and to her dismay, he soon quietly dropped the matter.

Desperate, Mona finally turned to her foster parents, Bud and Elaine Baker, and tearfully asked for help. With feet propped up on a rickety and stained coffee table, Bud drained the last of his Coors Light, belched, and said. "Why are you such a pantywaist whiner? Suck it up!"

Elaine dismissed Mona's problems with a wave of her hand. "Bud's right. You can't expect to get along with everyone at school. Honestly, you're almost eighteen. You'd think you would be mature enough to handle such minor problems by now."

With that, the Bakers promptly turned their attention back to the cage-fighting event on television.

Mona never mentioned it to them again.

Since then, Mona avoided Lady Anne and tried to keep a low

profile. Job number one became staying out of her crosshairs. While it didn't stop the harassment, she found it lessened somewhat. Now, Lady Anne's acts of cruelty came in ebbs and flows.

Today was a flow day.

Hand trailing over the top of Mona's propped up book, Lady Anne made a slow circuit of the table before coming to a stop behind her. She bent and peered over Mona's shoulder—which put her gaze directly on Brock.

"Something tells me you aren't reading your book," Lady Anne breathed in her ear. "What's the matter? The pictures not big enough for you?"

Snickering erupted from several of Lady Anne's friends. Like sharks, they sensed blood in the water. They appeared out of nowhere to form a semicircle around Lady Anne, eyes aglow in eager anticipation.

Lady Anne stood and tapped her lips as if deep in thought. She paced back and forth, then moved in front of Mona to block her vision of Brock. With a sudden movement, she whirled and placed both hands on the table, her face inches from Mona.

"I think you are interested in something besides your pathetic book." With a glance over her shoulder, a twisted sneer appeared on Lady Anne's face. "I think it's those boys over there." Mona's breath froze in her throat.

No, no, no, oh please God, no! Please don't—

Lady Anne interrupted Mona's silent pleading. She purred, "The problem is...which one are you *really* interested in."

Wearing skin-tight leggings and a short skirt, Lady Anne's shapely posterior jutted directly at Brock and his friends while she spoke to Mona. It made quite an impression, and the boys' attention riveted on her.

"*Eeny meeny miny moe,*" Lady Anne intoned as she pointed her finger at each boy in turn. "I think it is...*you!*" With a dramatic sweep of her hand, she gestured at Brock.

All color drained from Mona's face, and she found it hard to breathe. This reaction sealed her fate, and Lady Anne gleefully skipped across the space between the tables and returned moments later, arm-in-arm with Brock.

Her head spinning at the sudden turn of events, Mona couldn't believe the nightmare unfolding before her eyes.

Lady Anne pointed a slim, manicured finger at Mona. "Brock, I believe you have a secret admirer." Hoots and snorts erupted from all sides, including Brock's friends, who had joined the crowd around Mona.

His friends laughing at him caused Brock to react like he'd been scalded. His face turned red, and he stepped back from Mona.

"That's a bunch of crap! I don't even know who she is!" His protest served only to make the howls of laugh louder.

Mona's eyes filled with tears at Brock's reaction.

"Why, Brock, I think you are mistaken," Lady Anne exclaimed with a puzzled look. "Why else would Mona spend the past month mooning at you every day over this book?" She knocked it over, the multicolored pictures of old clocks flapping in the breeze.

Mona closed her eyes, a silent groan on her lips. Lady Anne knew...had *known* for at least a month that she came here to secretly gaze at Brock. Then she waited for the perfect moment to spring her trap.

She dug fingernails into her hands and desperately tried to stem the flow of tears that threatened to erupt at any moment.

How could I have been so stupid, stupid, stupid!

"I think the *only* proper thing to do would be to ask Mona out right here and right now!"

Lady Anne leaped on top of the table and waved her arms

like a carnival barker. She cried out to the circle of a dozen or more students, "Don't you agree? Brock needs to ask Mona out!"

Lady Anne turned to face Mona and Brock and chanted, "*Ask Mona out! Ask Mona out!*" Within seconds, the assembled students picked up the chant and soon it echoed throughout the commons area.

Brock's face turned purple. He whirled on Mona and spat, "Look, you dirty little bitch! Stop spying on me and leave me alone!"

He spun, pushed his way through the knot of spectators, and stalked off. The show over, students drifted away in ones and twos, giggling and pointing at Mona. Soon, only Lady Anne remained. A ragged silence, like the aftermath of a storm, filled the air. Mona stared dully at the pages of antique clocks fluttering in the light breeze.

She felt nothing.

She felt empty.

She felt *dead*.

Lady Anne moved and seated herself next to Mona. She whispered in her ear, "You *are* a dirty little bitch, but I would add an *ugly* little bitch as well."

Numb, Lady Anne's words barely registered with Mona. Finally, she mumbled, "Please leave me alone. Why won't you leave me alone?" This elicited a derisive snort from Lady Anne.

"Oh, Mona. Leave you alone? Of course not. What would be the fun in that?"

"Why? Why not?" Mona pleaded. "You have everything and I'm...I'm a nobody. Why can't you ignore me and act like I don't exist? Everyone else does."

Lady Anne stood and smoothed her skirt. She picked at a piece of lint on her blouse, then looked down at Mona, her expression hard.

"Because people like *me* are supposed to pick on people like *you*. You're the garbage in the garbage disposal, Mona. All you're good for is to be ground up and flushed down the drain. That's all your miserable life means to me."

With a smirk, Lady Anne added, "Well, I'd love to stay and chat some more with you *girlfriend*, but speaking of life, I have to get back to mine. *Ta!*" She blew Mona a kiss and skipped off.

Moments passed before Mona finally stirred. The tears that earlier threatened to gush from her eyes were gone. Instead, she felt nothing but helpless futility. Cornered like a rabbit, she had no way to escape, no way to stop Lady Anne's predacious bullying.

She stood and picked up her lunch and book. Her mouth tasted like ashes, and she dropped the brown sack in the nearest trash. Like a robot on autopilot, Mona walked to the media center, turned in her library book, and after a few minutes of aimless wandering, found herself alone in the girl's bathroom.

She twisted the cold water knob, cupped some water into her hands, and splashed her face. The shock of the cold water brought her mind back into focus, and she looked at herself in the mirror above the sink.

Frizzy brown hair spread like foam around a narrow face. Her cheekbones were shallow, angular planes, giving her a pinched expression, like she wore shoes a size too small. Her raptor-shaped nose, long and slightly hooked, had a pair of black-frame glasses perched on it. Brown eyes, puffy and red, stared back at Mona from behind the spectacles. Her pasty-white complexion resembled a minefield littered with angry red spots of acne.

Mona stepped a few paces back so the rest of her body would come into view.

She wore blue jeans and a long-sleeved blouse and sweater, which covered skinny, birdlike arms and legs. Her bra size, 32A, hadn't changed since seventh grade, and even now, at almost 18 years of age, Mona more closely resembled an adolescent girl than a woman.

I'm unremarkable.

I'm plain and colorless as water.

I'm a nobody.

"I hate my life," Mona whispered to the image in the mirror. "Do you hear me? I HATE MY LIFE!" she screeched.

The tears she had earlier banished now came back with a vengeance. Mona stumbled into a stall and shut and bolted the door. Hugging herself, she leaned against the wall and sobbed.

Mona's misery so completely consumed her, she lost all sense of time. When at last she managed to stop crying and look at her phone, she realized lunch was over—her next class had already started fifteen minutes earlier.

She staggered out of the stall. Unable to bear seeing herself again in the mirror, Mona averted her gaze to the cold, concrete floor as she splashed water for a second time on her face. While she dried her face with paper towels, she couldn't help recall how happy she had been when enmeshed in her daydreams of Brock...and how quickly Lady Anne turned her happiness into humiliation. She learned a valuable lesson.

Dreams were a dangerous thing.

CHAPTER 2

PRINCE TALMUND EDWARD MEREDITH BROODED.

Astride his winged mount, the heir to the Meredithian Throne and Empire observed the approaching storm north of the Veil.

His thoughts, like the advancing tempest, were dark and angry. The Veil always affected him in such fashion. More than a thousand years now since its creation, the malignant barrier still stood, despite the vigorous efforts of the Empire to destroy it.

Every attempt a failure.

As always, there was no substance, no physical evidence of where the boundary lay. One could look right through it—see leaves moving or a flight of birds in the air—yet a slight shimmer gave the only clue to its existence. Despite this clarity, the Veil boundary remained impenetrable as mountain granite to soldiers of the Empire. Only the scum of the wicked sorceress, Marlinda, had the ability to pass unencumbered through it.

A Blood Prince and Heir, the young prince's surname came from the planet Meredith itself, the tradition passed down by the founding Kings and Queens of old. Yet despite this linage and the combined successes and knowledge of his forebears, none provided the key to erase the monstrosity which had trapped generations of men, women, and children. The enchanted barrier became a testament to his ancestors' futility, a dark stain even the passage of time could not erase.

Near dusk, the wind began to pick up. Tal stirred and viewed the dark clouds with eager anticipation, the heat lightning dancing through the black billows.

It won't be long now.

A rider approached and observed the young prince with a bemused expression.

Tal's spectator carefully looked him up and down. He noted the lanky and muscular physique and how easily the young prince lounged on the horse—as if born for the saddle. A strong chin jutted from a chiseled visage—a hint of the stubborn nature the observer knew only too well the Blood Prince possessed. Piercing green eyes viewed the coming tempest with raptor-like intensity. The rider shook his head. Those eyes…too aged by far for one yet to see twenty-one summers.

"Do not be so impatient, Tal. The storm will soon be upon us."

The young prince started and turned toward the horseman. His eyes widened in recognition, and a snort erupted from him.

"Easy for you to say, Bozar, since you are responsible for my post in this backwater province. At least I can look forward to riding a storm horse in a *real* squall."

White teeth flashed in the thickening gloom. Bozar Ali Shehem, the *Eldred* or First Advisor to the Prince, smiled at Tal's frustration.

"Were you not so impulsive, so ready to march into danger at a moment's notice, perhaps the Queen would not have listened so closely to my suggestion."

Tal pounded the pommel of his saddle. "So my mother's solution is to place me far away from the action? To stand idle while the Veil filth murder and plunder? I should be leading attacks against the raiders and protecting our citizens. Instead, I sit here in the least populated province in the Empire, *where nothing ever happens!"*

Unfazed, Bozar replied, "Excellent! You can put your free time to good use and reflect on your past reckless actions. Perhaps you'll come to the same conclusion I have repeatedly pointed out—the need to use better judgment and *think* before your wild charges into battle."

The First Advisor's smile grew wider.

"And *here* you will have plenty of time to gather your thoughts."

CHAPTER 3

ISERABLE, MONA LAY ON THE BED AND STARED AT THE CEILING.

"What's wrong, Sis."

Startled, Mona sat up. Her younger brother, Joe, peered at her from the door of her small bedroom, concern in his eyes. He leaned on crutches, the late afternoon light from the bedroom window glinting off the metal braces supporting each of his legs.

"How do you do that? Sneaking up on people, I mean."

"You mean how do I manage to move around without so much as a *clink* or a *clank*? It's a gift."

Joe stepped into the room and closed the door behind him. He pulled a chair beside Mona's bed, laid the crutches on the ground, and dropped into the seat.

"You haven't said a word since you got home from school… and you still haven't answered my question. What's wrong?"

Mona didn't want to re-live the lunchtime humiliation she experienced at the hands of Lady Anne, but she knew if she denied anything, Joe would instantly sniff out the lie. They had survived together through five different foster families—the past six years with Elaine and Bud Baker—and their ability to read each other's thoughts and moods was uncanny.

Their biological parents—*meth-heads* according to Elaine and Bud—hadn't been in the picture since Mona turned four and Joe a baby. Child Protective Services removed them from their care when a 911 call resulted in Joe being rushed to the hospital.

There, the doctors discovered Joe had a damaged spine—which their parents claimed resulted from a fall out of his crib.

They never saw their mother and father again.

These years together in all manner of environments served to create a tight and unbreakable bond. They shared everything, and Mona could no more hide anything from Joe than he could from her.

With a sigh, Mona related what happened at lunch, pausing only when Joe interrupted to ask questions. When she finished, tears came to her eyes again. Knees clasped to her chest, she rocked back and forth on the bed and willed herself not to break down in front of her brother.

"That bitch! That sick, twisted bitch!" Joe exploded. His face red, he struggled to his feet. Joe held on to the back of the chair for support and pointed a finger shaking with rage at Mona. "She's gone too far! You can't let her get away this! You have to report her!"

Mona wiped her eyes with the back of her hand and looked at her brother. Even with a face flushed with anger, it was easy to see he had inherited all the looks in the family. Tall for his age despite his twisted legs, Joe's blue eyes flashed from a handsome face crowned by thick brown hair. Unusually mature and intelligent for a thirteen-year old eighth grader, he normally exercised better self-control and judgment than Mona.

But he didn't know Lady Anne Golightly.

"I've already tried. I went to Mr. Garrett. I told him, and I told Bud and Elaine too. You know all this."

"Then try again! *Lady* Anne," Joe spat, "needs a kick in her rich, pretentious ass!"

Joe only cursed in front of Mona when extremely upset, and she knew it would do no good to try and reason with him until he calmed down. Finally, he sat down again, and although still angry, he managed to regain some semblance of control over his emotions.

"It's not right, Sis. She has bullied and harassed you since the ninth grade. It *has* to stop! If you won't tell anyone, I'm going to!"

Panic coursed through Mona. "No! It will only make things worse for me. Please don't tell anyone, Joe," Mona pleaded.

Before Joe could respond, Bud's gruff voice called from the den on the other side of the house.

"Preacher's here!"

Thankful for the distraction, Mona leapt up, grabbed her sweater and purse, and headed for the door. While she waited for Joe, she scanned his face. *Would he really tell someone about Lady Anne?*

Joe pushed himself up from the chair, then grabbed his crutches and moved next to Mona. "This isn't over, Sis." He opened the door and moved past her.

Mona closed her eyes in dismay, then turned and followed.

CHAPTER 4

TAL'S STARE BORED INTO HIS FIRST ADVISOR.

Tall and thin, his *Eldred's* dark, intelligent eyes—a match for his ebony skin—calmly met and matched the young prince's gaze. A thicket of tightly curled black hair, now populated with pockets of grey, crowned his head.

Disgusted, Tal refused to be baited into a reply. Instead, he turned his attention to the men he would ride with. Experienced winged cavalrymen, they were all part of an elite group of *Storm Riders* that patrolled this quadrant of the Veil. Pleased, he studied his own storm mount.

A magnificent creature of a tawny-brown color, the steed's slim flanks sloped toward muscular legs, while the graceful neck and mane merged with its deep chest and shoulders. The wings gave him pause in his observation. Now folded, the great wings flanked his legs and sprouted from either side of the equine's shoulder bones. Heavily muscled, each feathered appendage extended outward almost ten paces when fully employed in flight. Smaller, nubile wings, located just above the hooves of each leg, acted like rudders for directional control.

Around him, all the cavalrymen were similarly mounted on storm horses. Each steed wore a *qurille,* a thin apron of incredibly light but almost impenetrable chain mail which covered the horse's chest, abdomen, withers, and large joints where wing and shoulder met. This protected the horse's underside from arrows, javelins, and any other object hurled or shot.

Similarly light, the saddle had a strip of hooked and scaled reptilian skin—provided by giant swamp-dwelling pythons—sewn down the middle and sides. The seat and inside legs of each cavalryman's pants were stitched with wiry wool, thus adhering the pants firmly to the snake's skin on the saddle. This made the unhorsing of a rider while in flight a rarity, whether in the heat of battle or during treacherous winds produced by storms.

Tal's hair whipped about his face and neck in the freshening breeze. He tied the shoulder length, auburn hair with his Warrior's Traces, a braided rawhide woven with small lodestone beads. Each bead represented a kill of a Veil raider. Even though practically a teenager by the Empire's reckoning, his Warrior's Traces lay heavy with numerous beads. He fingered the lodestones.

One way or the other, he would add to their number soon...very soon.

Tal turned. "Do you remember my first encounter with the Veil raiders?" His First Advisor nodded.

The young prince continued. "I recall you had taken me on a routine inspection of one of the outlying garrisons. While there, the alert went out a small hamlet had been overrun. We accompanied the garrison's soldiers and caught the foul scum in the midst of their pillaging."

Tal's hand tightened on his sword hilt. "There, I encountered one of Marlinda's melded creatures—my first. Even after I cleaved the beast in half, it continued to snap and claw at me."

The young prince shook his head. "I'd heard the stories, of course, but I was barely of age. To see such a sight shocked me. Little did I know I'd only scratched the surface of the horrors I would see." He nudged his horse closer to Bozar. "The worst was yet to come."

"Barely a year later, we joined another engagement against

the Dark Queen's marauders. This time, a larger village had been attacked. In the ensuing battle, I charged into a cottage and found a woman backed into a corner. Her assailant was cloven-hooved with horns like a bull. When I attacked the creature, the woman tried to stop me. Still, I managed to run the beast through and slay it. The poor woman screamed and screamed..."

The young prince paused, his throat tight with emotion.

"Tal, don't—" Bozar began, then stopped when Tal raised his hand.

"When I turned the beast over, it wore a human face—the face of the woman's son. He had been captured in a raid but a few years earlier. Before I could stop her, the boy's mother pulled a paring knife from her apron and plunged it through her heart... and now both—mother and son—lay dead at my feet."

Tal's eyes smoldered. "And yet here I am, exiled to the farthest reaches of the Empire, while Marlinda's abominations continue to rend and destroy. While raiders continue to take captives destined as fodder for her breeding pits." He stabbed a finger at Bozar. "And you helped put me here!"

Face twisted in anger, Tal clenched and unclenched his fists.

Bozar sighed. "You cannot save the world in one night, Tal, regardless of your location."

The young prince spat, "If the Creator is good, he will send Veil raiders for me to slay tonight."

"The Creator does not revel in the destruction and vengeance of man," Bozar admonished.

"So you have told me many times, my *Eldred.*"

"And so I shall again," his First Advisor shot back. "But since we are on remembrances, recall *why* you are here. You are increasingly reckless. Such behavior leads to careless action. The Veil needs no more shedding of royal blood," he said, a pointed reference to Tal's father.

Tal flushed at Bozar's words.

"My father died in defense of men, women, and children who were fleeing the Veil filth! Who among us would not do the same?"

"I loved your father like a brother, just as I love you. I would have gladly died in his place. But his pride and stubbornness led directly to his death—*an unnecessary death*—at the hands of the Dark Queen's minions."

The First Advisor's obvious concern moved Tal. In truth, he loved this gentle and wise man who filled the void in his life after his father's death. Many times, his quiet patience deterred Tal from wild and hasty acts. Bozar also interceded for him on more than one occasion with his mother, Celestria—the reigning Queen of Meredith—when news of his youthful indiscretions reached her ears. No doubt she would never have let him near the Veil but for Bozar persuading her as the Heir, his knowledge and experience of the enchanted border must be part of his formal education.

With a deep breath, he turned and faced the First Advisor. "Once again, you are right, my *Eldred.*"

Bozar smiled and inclined his head toward his young charge.

Twilight darkness descended on the horsemen. The first fat drops of rain spattered about Tal's head and shoulders. A tall figure with graying hair detached himself from a column of horses and trotted down the line. With a formal bow, Bowen Banebolt, the commander of the garrison of storm riders, spoke. "It shall not be long now, Sire. We will wait until the storm breaks and then ride. Marlinda's filth like to raid on nights such as this."

"When was the last raid in this area, Lord Banebolt?"

"Over two years ago, Sire. They came in from the Veil about five leagues south of the Watch Tower. We engaged them before they could escape through the barrier and killed all but a handful.

Since then, they have only raided at night and often when aided by stormy weather. Tonight we will ride at a higher alert, just in case."

Hopeful, Tal said, "Perhaps our hunt shall be productive then."

Banebolt nodded and scanned the roiling, black clouds in the evening's last light. Within moments, the storm broke upon them, the rain and wind blowing wildly. Forks of lightning punctuated the darkness, followed by *cracks* of thunder.

"It is time to begin our patrol, Sire," Banebolt shouted over the deluge. He wheeled his horse around and bellowed orders.

One by one, the columns of winged cavalry broke apart and took flight. Tal joined Bozar on the outer wedge of the formation, and with a mighty beat of wings, his horse soared into the air. A savage thrill coursed through Tal when the ground fell away and the wild ride into the stormy night commenced.

A ruthless gleam appeared in his eyes. *Sooner or later raiders will issue from the accursed enchanted boundary.*

And I'll be there to kill them all.

CHAPTER 5

ILL PROCTOR, OR BROTHER BILL AS HIS PARISHIONERS affectionately called him, stood just inside the front door of the Baker's house. A huge, hulking man, his head barely cleared the doorframe without having to stoop. A reddish beard shot with grey covered his grinning face. When combined with his thick, red hair, Brother Bill more closely resembled a Viking berserker than the pastor of The Cornerstone Full Gospel Church.

"How you kids doing?" the big man boomed.

At the sight of Brother Bill's friendly face, Mona's tension and fear melted away. She marched over to him and announced, "We're doing fine."

A huge paw reached down and hugged Mona. Looking up, Brother Bill quipped, "How about you, 88?"

A huge NASCAR fan, the big preacher's boyhood hero was the late Dale Earnhardt. The first time he saw Joe at church, the boy was scooting rapidly along in his motorized wheelchair. Brother Bill promptly dubbed him 88 after Dale Earnhardt's son, Dale Earnhardt Jr., and the nickname stuck ever since.

Joe's grin covered his face from ear to ear. "Hey, Brother Bill!"

"Bring 'em back at nine o'clock?" the big man asked, an eye cocked at Bud.

Seated in his lounger, a drift of empty beer cans at his feet, Bud waved a beefy hand. "Sure, Preacher." He stifled a belch, then picked up the remote and began to channel surf.

The church van idled in the weed-infested gravel driveway next to the Baker's doublewide mobile home. Several junked cars stood sentinel a short distance away, surrounded by a thick growth of brown, frost-killed weeds and vines. Mona, Joe, and Brother Bill tromped through the ankle-high growth, the *crunch* of dead grass marking their passage.

Thankfully, Joe remained silent about Mona's experience at school, and she felt herself unwind as the van pulled into the church parking lot. Although early in the evening, only a faint glow remained on the horizon as the weak December light quickly faded.

With other teenagers, they spent the next couple of hours packing shoeboxes and gorging on pizza. The boxes were meant for Operation Christmas Child, which sent diverse items, from basic toiletries to toys, to impoverished children across the world. Mona and Joe's youth group spent the past month gathering supplies and money from the church and community to fill the shoeboxes.

Finished at last, Mona, Joe, and Brother Bill studied the stacked pyramid of boxes ready for shipment. The other teens had already left, leaving them as the only youth left. The pastor's wife, Barbara, busy cleaning up the empty pizza boxes, looked up and commented, "My, so many."

The big preacher rubbed his hands. "Yep. It looks like we did okay. We'll ship more shoeboxes than we did last year, and there will be a few more happy kids in the world this Christmas."

Brother Bill pulled an envelope from his pocket. "While we are on the subject of happy, this is for you, Mona."

Bewildered, Mona took the envelope and stared at it.

"Go ahead. Open it," Brother Bill urged. Across the room, Barbara paused to watch.

Mona broke the seal and took out five twenty-dollar bills. *One hundred dollars!*

"Wh-what's this for?" she whispered.

"You remember when Mrs. Burke was gone a month visiting her daughter and her new grandbaby? You took her place in the church nursery during services. This is to pay you for filling in."

Mona shook her head. "But I just volunteered. I didn't know the church paid anyone for that. Th-thank you."

"No thanks, necessary. You helped out when we needed someone in the nursery, and now you have a little Christmas money."

Joe squeezed Mona's shoulder. "Way to go, Sis."

Mona placed the money in the small purse she carried. Her gaze crossed the table laden with the shoeboxes, and she hesitated. Like everyone else, she watched the video produced by the Operation Christmas Child ministry. Indelibly etched in her mind were the scenes of small children, some dressed in nothing more than rags, grinning while they held up their shoeboxes full of simple toys and necessities like they were made of gold. The powerful images, even now, tugged at her heart.

Slowly, she removed the envelope from her purse and handed it back to the big preacher.

"I've got plenty, Brother Bill. Can you use this to make a few more kids happy?"

The big man paused, then finally took the envelope. "Sure we can, Mona. Why don't you and Joe go wait in the van for me, and I'll take you home?"

After Mona and Joe left, Barbara marched over and put her arm around Bill's thick waist. Unlike her burly husband, Barbara's petite stature barely came to his shoulder. He glanced down at her with moist eyes.

"You big softie," she said. "You know the nursery worker is a volunteer position."

With a chuckle, Brother Bill swiped his eyes with the back of his hand. "Just wanted to do a little something for Mona and Joe. The Good Lord knows the Bakers certainly won't."

Barbara patted his arm. "Well, I'd say you succeeded. Mona looked very happy at the prospect of helping a few more children."

"Yeah. She's a great kid, isn't she? I wish we could do more for her and Joe."

Brother Bill gave Barbara a final hug, then trudged out. Moments later, he loaded Mona and Joe up in the van, and they headed back to the Baker's.

After he dropped them off, Brother Bill's thoughts returned to Mona. She had little in the way of material possessions. Her foster parents provided her and Joe with little more than food and a roof over their heads. Mona's clothes, shoes, and even her handbag were secondhand. The hundred dollars he tried to give her would be like a king's ransom to her. Yet she still gave it back to help others.

Brother Bill felt his eyes grow damp once again. The same thought percolated over and over in his mind.

The world would be a better place if it had more Mona Parkers in it.

CHAPTER 6

BESIDE THE VEIL, ROLF BURKE WAITED IMPATIENTLY ON HIS MOUNT for clearance through the portal.

He scowled at the sight of the raiders scattered about him. No doubt it would take half the day just to get them in some semblance of order, and the other half to march them through the wormhole.

Known as *Razor* to both friend and foe alike, he long ago acquired the nickname because of his fondness for sharp objects. When a young and a barely blooded raider, he had killed an older and larger man in a tavern fight. Rolf no longer remembered what the disagreement was about, but he *did* remember whipping his foot-long dagger around and through his antagonist's neck. The sharpness of his blade was such it passed through the marauder's neck without so much as a ripple of tissue.

His adversary's head toppled off his shoulders and onto the floor. The body stayed erect a moment longer, blood spurting from severed arteries before it joined the head on the floor. The rough patrons of the tavern looked on in astonishment, with none realizing the head had been severed until it had rolled off the raider's neck.

The nickname Razor stuck ever since.

Since then, Rolf took part in many successful incursions. Rising steadily through the ranks, he now commanded his own *horde* of raiders. He prided himself on detail and the absolute cohesion of his marauders...and he *never* failed to lead a successful raid through the Veil.

Tonight, he was determined to continue that streak.

However, this particular mission would, in all probability, not go as smoothly as those in the past. His cursed luck drew him the duty to lead a training raid of a green and mostly inexperienced *horde*. A typical *horde* consisted of at least three hundred raiders, with one hundred of the marauders on horse. Boarogs made up most of the rest, mixed with a handful of Marlinda's *specialty* creations, and finally, a few Dark Brothers.

Razor snorted in frustration. *Hordes* were built to strike fast, grab plunder and captives, and then beat a retreat to safety through the Veil. Surveying the motley group assembled before him, he knew this concept would be sorely tested tonight. The Boarogs assigned to him were new and never blooded in a raid, with the men on horseback equally inexperienced...all green as a willow in springtime.

He gagged when a breeze brought him the foul odor of the assembled Boarog. It smelled like they rolled around in their own shit, and then, still not content, wallowed around some more in a putrid carcass. He once owned a dog that did the same thing. It couldn't resist rolling in anything rancid.

He killed the dog.

Razor pinched his nostrils in an attempt to block the thick stench and wished he could do the same to the beastly creatures. Killing a few would certainly make the air sweeter.

Boarogs—the most successful of Marlinda's dark creations— were the product of magically melding man and boar. The faces of these man-beasts resembled a boar with jagged yellow tusks protruding from their lower jaw—along with an ugly disposition to match. Small, piggish eyes peered out from a heavily ridged brow. Their bodies, squat with a thick torso attached to short, powerful legs, also included heavily muscled arms. Noted for their notoriously short tempers, the brutes could quickly turn on one another if not closely watched and controlled.

While most of Marlinda's *experiments* were sterile, the Boarog had the singular advantage of being fertile, with most of their females capable of multiple births. This produced an endless supply of the beasts.

Despite their smell and nasty dispositions, Razor valued the melded creatures. Although witless as a clod of dirt, they more than made up for this deficiency with their fierce and savage fighting ability. However, what he really prized above all else about the man-beasts was another of their characteristics.

They were expendable.

No one cared if one or a hundred Boarog died in a raid—least of all the brutish beasts themselves. He could use them in any way he saw fit, with a fresh batch straight from the breeding pits ready to take the place of the fallen.

A fickle puff of wind brought the foul smell of the assembled man-creatures back to Razor's nose again. Cursing and gagging, he turned away and rode his mount upwind of the beastly host. He stopped near a cowled Dark Brother serving as Leash Master to several shape-shifting lycanthropes. The Dark Brothers, along to supply defensive magic in protection of the *horde*, also controlled Marlinda's *special* creatures.

An involuntary shudder shook Razor at the sight of the *specials*. Two appeared to be centaur-like creatures. Poorly healed sutures formed a jagged pattern where the torso of a man melded with the main body of a horse. Another man waved unusually long and supple *arms*. Where his arms should have joined the shoulder joints, a snake's coiled body was attached. Instead of hands, the heads of serpents bobbed and weaved, forked tongues flicking in and out.

A trio of ogres rounded out the party of *specials*. Each stood over ten hands tall, with gray-green skin stretched across thickly muscled arms and legs. Saber-like incisors, yellowed and sharp, erupted like stalactites from their upper jaws. A thick ridge of bone sloped from the ogres' forehead, terminating at coal-black eyes. Hands the size of blacksmith anvils gripped massive clubs resting on their shoulders. Their fingers twitched as if their eagerness for pulping living flesh could barely be contained. They cast insolent looks at the *horde* leader while they lounged against a tree.

Razor eyed the giants with no small amount of uneasiness. When it came to an evil disposition, he believed the huge creatures to be more than a match for the Boarog. With a wrinkle of his nose, he added smell to the list.

The veteran raider shook his head. When properly trained and under the direction of an experienced Dark Brother, Marlinda's creatures of meld and magic could be an effective and fearsome force. The ones under his command tonight were neither well trained nor well controlled. Even the Leash Master struggled to bring the shape shifters to heel.

A prescription for disaster.

At the end of the cursory inspection of his host, Razor decided the most immediate problem were the werewolves. Even while their Leash Master struggled to control them, they continued to shift between man and beast. One in particular appeared more difficult to control than the others. A canine snout sprouted and receded in quick succession from the creature's face. It snarled from behind wicked, flesh-rending teeth. Wolf-like ears, thick fur, and sharp claws suddenly appeared before the lycanthrope's Leash Master managed to regain control.

Another bad sign.

The last thing he needed was out-of-control werewolves wreaking havoc among his own *horde*. Disgusted, Razor dismounted and strode to the Leash Master. "Control your charges, damn you, or I'll find someone who can!"

Red-faced, the Leash Master turned and spat, "Who do you think you are to speak to me in such fashion? We are chosen to our Order by Marlinda herself. It is not for low-born scum like you to tell me how to do my job!"

A whisper of unsheathed steel was the Leash Master's only warning. In an instant, a dagger pricked his throat.

"I have killed men for less," Razor whispered in his ear.

"You—you go too far!" protested the Dark Brother in a shaky, high-pitched squeal.

"Really? I don't think I go far enough." The dagger pressed harder against the Leash Master's throat to produce a thin trickle of blood.

"Now, let us come to an understanding," Razor continued. "You will control these beasts, or I swear I will kill you myself and feed you to them piece by piece."

The cowl fell back to reveal a shaved scalp. A youthful face, eyes bulging, stared at the *horde* leader. His brother sorcerers stood nearby and, observing the scene, moved to help their comrade.

Razor barked, "Colley, Winston!"

Two riders detached themselves from the mounted raiders and galloped toward the confrontation. Crossbows cocked, they stopped in front of the Dark Brothers and aimed bolts directly at them.

"Would you like these two skewered or diced, *Horde* Leader?" asked the larger of the two riders.

Razor turned to the pair. "Do you fools have anything to add to our little chat?"

Faces ashen, the Dark Brothers vigorously shook their heads. They tripped over one another in their haste to back away, the crossbows of Colley and Winston trained on their every step.

Jaw clenched, Razor shoved the Leash Master from him and signaled his men to lower their crossbows. The sorcerer ran to his brethren, hand at his throat. The veteran raider spat at the trio, then marched to an empty wagon and vaulted into its bed. He stood to face the *horde*.

"Now listen you pack of green, barely weaned scum!" he roared, "We raid tonight, and I'll be damned if any man or beast among you doesn't pull his own weight! I'll brook no excuses, and I'll cut down anyone who even hints of cowardice should we come to battle. You will follow my orders, and you will follow them without hesitation, or I will kill you where you stand!"

Razor studied his assembly. The ogres now stood erect, insolent looks gone from their faces. In their place was a new look, and one he knew well—*fear*. He surveyed the rest of his raiders, pleased to see every face riveted on him. A grim smile appeared on his face. Respect was something you earned among veteran campaigners and raiders. Fear, however, became a great substitute for respect when experience was lacking. He almost hoped for one of his marauders to turn tail at the first sign of trouble. After he cut down the man or beastly creature, it would erase any doubt he meant business.

And with this green and untested pack, an execution might be just what I need.

At least he had his core group of officers to lead this motley crew, especially Colley and Winston. They knew life and death often depended on his experience once outside the enchanted boundary and into the Empire's territory. They would see his orders carried out or die trying.

The horde leader jumped off the wagon and remounted his horse. He barked, "Now, form up by ranks. We will go through the portal in orderly fashion and by the book. Squad leaders, take your positions and make sure these motherless bastards don't run each other over when we pass through." He wheeled his horse around and galloped to the head of the pack, while squad leaders cursed and struggled to get their columns into a semblance of order.

The debarkation point of the portal resembled a simple arch of stone with lodestones located in each of the four directions. Approximately twenty hands high by fifty wide, it allowed a column of fifteen mounted raiders to ride abreast into the portal, or twenty men or Boarog marching alongside to pass through. A clear void appeared on the other side of the arch—no sound, color, or movement issued from this abyss.

At the gate, Razor nodded at Muurch, the *Gatemaster*. A veteran of the Veil, the stooped and aged Dark Brother, unlike many of his brethren, affected no airs of superiority and went about his task with quiet and unflappable efficiency. More than once, he had saved Razor's skin when he shifted portal exit locations contaminated by a nearby Watch Tower, to allow the raid leader and his host to escape the pursuit of Meredithian forces. Although Muurch simply did his job and would do the same for any *horde*, Razor afforded him something he spared few others.

Respect.

Muurch returned Razor's bow, then turned his attention to a spherical object mounted on a waist high pedestal. The Artifact or mechanism connected Muurch to the Veil and allowed for the formation of the portals. At the Gatemaster's touch, a glowing ball of greenish-yellow light appeared. The smell of ozone filled the air, and lightning arced outward from the core.

Without turning from the radiant globe, Muurch spoke to Razor. "The weather will be stormy where you will exit the Veil. Expect rain with wind, lightning, and thunder. It should last most of the night, more than enough time for completion of the raid.

As usual, I will attempt to place you far enough from the nearest Watch Tower to escape detection but near enough to your target so the distance is not unreasonable."

Muurch motioned to an assistant, who handed Razor a familiar Artifact attached to a necklace of thin metal links. The *horde* leader accepted the object, slipped the chain over his head, and then tucked it inside his jerkin. The Artifact, a brass object with rings his fingers slipped through, was essential for their success—if not their survival. Its magic, triggered by the pressure of gripping it, opened a doorway and allowed their return through the Veil.

At the Gatemaster's signal, Razor moved toward the portal, the rest of the *horde* close behind. Where once nothing but empty space appeared, a cloudy murkiness swirled in a counterclockwise motion beneath the arch of stone. An uneasy murmur arose from the inexperienced raiders. Having never been through a portal before, the fear of the unknown gripped them.

Razor turned his horse around and shot a steely glance at the *horde*. Immediately, the muttering stopped. He held his gaze for a few moments, then motioned the columns forward through the portal.

When the veteran raider entered the twirling mist, the usual feeling of disorientation came over him, and he wondered how many of his marauders would soil themselves before they exited the gateway. Regardless, green or not, they would become Veil warriors tonight.

He licked his lips and looked forward to the coming raid.

CHAPTER 7

AFTER BROTHER BILL DROPPED THEM OFF, MONA TOOK A BATH and went directly to bed. Her routine—unchanged for the past four years—continued unbroken, and she prayed the same desperate prayer.

Please God, please help me. Please make Lady Anne stop. I-I don't think I can take much more.

Then, thoroughly drained by the day's events, Mona fell fast asleep moments after her head hit the pillow.

Hours later, she awoke with a start. Heart pounding, she sat up and wondered if she was having a panic attack. With a hand pressed to her chest, she threw off the covers and padded to the bathroom. A small glass rested on the sink, and Mona filled it with water. She carried the glass back to her bed. After a moment's hesitation, she reached under the mattress and pulled out a plastic pill container.

Light from a street lamp filtered through her window, and she held the bottle aloft to study it. Half-filled, it contained a mix of Bud's back pain medicine and Elaine's sleeping pills. Over the past year, she had managed to pilfer one or two at a time, and the Bakers never noticed their absence.

The pills represented her escape clause—the final solution to Lady Anne. Instead of unending misery and hopelessness, she could have peace…if she wanted it.

Mona clutched the container to her chest. *"Just in case,"* she murmured, *"just in case."*

Mona caught a glitter out of the corner of her eye. She turned her head—and gasped. Dust motes, disturbed by her passage, floated in the weak shaft of light. But these tiny particles sparkled like gold flakes that grew brighter and brighter. The glittering specks coalesced into a whirlpool of tiny sparkles of light, which slowly began to rotate. Scrabbling for her glasses on the bedside table, she jammed them on.

The shiny lights were still there!

Mona pushed the glasses up her nose and rubbed her eyes. When she looked again, a muted scream escaped from her lips.

Below her—where the solid comfort of the floor should be—black emptiness stretched as far as the eye could see, punctuated only by millions upon millions of miniature pinpoints of light.

Her bed floated weightless among the stars in the deep void of space!

She scrambled backwards until her spine ground against the familiar security of the headboard. Eyes wide, she clutched the bedsheets to her chin.

A single point of light separated itself from the others and moved toward Mona. It grew larger and larger until she could make out a tiny figure traveling toward her from a great distance. Finally, a man materialized out of the void and stepped in her direction with a long, even stride.

The *man* reached Mona's bed and looked down at her. Bedsheets held even tighter, she attempted to shrink away from the stranger.

Mouth slack, she stared. Of medium height and build, her visitor appeared to be in his early to mid-60's. Crow's feet etched his eyes, and he wore a simple white cotton shirt and faded blue jeans. A thatch of thick gray hair crowned his head, while a well-trimmed goatee framed his mouth. A pair of piercing blue eyes peered at Mona from beneath a bushy set of eyebrows.

"What's wrong with you? You look like you've seen a ghost," the stranger quipped in what vaguely resembled a clipped British accent.

"Huh? Wh-what?" Mona gargled.

Her visitor rolled his eyes. "They told me you were bright. Why do I *always* get the dullards?"

"Dullards?"

"You know. Dim-witted, slow, low IQ—"

"I know what it means!" Mona blurted, her cheeks burning.

"Oh, good. I wasn't looking forward to elaborating on every word in the English language."

The peculiar circumstances of the man's arrival forgotten, Mona threw her bed sheets down into her lap.

"Look, you—whoever you are—you can't talk—"

"The name's Finkle. Thaddeus Finkle."

Thoroughly incensed, Mona pointed at him. "I don't care who you are or what your name is, it's no excuse for being rude!"

A thin smile played across Finkle's face. "Well done. I knew sterner stuff existed in you somewhere…and you're going to need it. So, let's start over, shall we?"

He bowed in exaggerated fashion. "Thaddeus Finkle—you may call me Mr. Finkle—at your pleasure, Mona."

He pulled his arm from behind his back. Clutched in his hand was her pill bottle. He frowned. "This is a bad idea…a *very* bad idea." With a flourish of his palm, the bottle disappeared to be replaced by a bouquet of long stemmed red roses. Their heavy fragrance filled the air.

Mr. Finkle thrust them at Mona. "Consider this a sweeter smelling alternative."

Eyes wide, Mona stuttered, "My…medicine! How did you know—"

"—And I think we both know you have no need of this *medicine*."

Mona lapsed into silence, shame warming her face. After a moment's hesitation, she took the roses and placed them in her lap. "Th-thanks."

Mr. Finkle clapped his hands. "Good! Now that we have all the droll niceties out of the way, we can get down to business."

Mona's mouth worked soundlessly, while she tried to process the sudden succession of events—which started with the simple act of getting a late night drink of water.

Mr. Finkle shook his head. "You look like the village idiot whose mother dropped him on his head. Please tell me you aren't going to start to drool as well."

"Wait. *Wait!* What business are you talking about? How did you get into my bedroom, and who...*what are you?*"

Mr. Finkle mumbled in irritation and twitched his hand. A chair materialized from the darkness and he sat in it next to the bed. "I should think the *who* or *what* I am is obvious."

Mona threw up her arms. "Look, I don't know what you're talking about."

Mr. Finkle sighed. "Very well."

He stood and gazed at Mona. "I am an angel. In fact, I have been assigned to be *your* angel."

Mona cocked her head. "You? An angel? I don't believe it!"

Mr. Finkle pursed his lips. "And why not?"

"*Hmmm,* let's see. How about you don't look like an angel, and angels aren't bad-mannered and rude like you."

"An expert on angels now are you? I had no idea my client was so knowledgeable. Very well. If I *must.*"

He stepped away and snapped his fingers. Enormous white wings suddenly sprouted from his back. Robes of gleaming white replaced his shirt and jeans, and a bright halo appeared above his head. Eyes closed and hands clasped as if in prayer, Mr. Finkle held his pose for several moments. Finally, he cracked an eye open. "Satisfied? Can I change out of this ridiculous appearance?"

Startled by the sudden transformation, Mona nodded. In an instant, he appeared once again in his comfortable shirt and jeans. "Now, can we finally get down to business?"

"I guess we can—if you tell me what *business* you're talking about."

The angel rolled his eyes. Speaking slowly as if to a child, he said, *"The. Answer. To. Your. Prayers."*

Mona's nostrils flared. She was tired of being treated like a mindless idiot.

"No thanks," she snapped. "If you're the answer to my prayers, then I'll just wait for an upgrade. I'm sure whatever the return policy is in Heaven, I would certainly qualify since you are a defective angel."

Mr. Finkle crossed his arms and studied Mona like some new species of recently discovered insect. "I assure you I am eminently qualified to handle your case."

"Thanks, but no thanks."

"Do you want something done about Lady Anne or not?"

"I don't—Huh? You know about her?"

"Of course. You are my client, and I have studied every aspect of your life. I know *everything* about you."

Hope sprang onto Mona's face. "Then make her leave me alone!"

Mr. Finkle quickly raised his hand. "Prayers are rarely answered in the way and fashion you would like. You are not Aladdin, and I am not a genie. You can't simply make three wishes and have them answered. There is a cost to answered prayer, and you would do well to remember this in the days, weeks, and years to come."

Mr. Finkle bowed for a second time. "Until we meet again."

He walked away, his figure shrinking until once again, it

became a pinpoint of light to merge with the other myriad twin-kling stars.

"Wait! When will that be?" Mona cried before Mr. Finkle to-tally disappeared in the spinning cartwheel of light.

"Soon, Mona," the angel's disembodied voice replied.

"Very soon."

CHAPTER 8

L EVI LEDBETTER EYED THE BLACK, ROILING CLOUDS.

He hurried to the barn where his children were securing the barn doors and shutters against the coming storm. He made it only halfway when heavy drops of rain began to fall, scattered at first, and then in earnest. By the time he reached the barn's interior, he was drenched. Shaking the rain from his hat and slicker, he spied his offspring laughing at him.

"You look like a drowned rat, Papa," his daughter Ellie said.

"Well, next time, you and your brothers can lead the cows back to pasture," he sputtered, unable to keep the smile off his face.

Ellie playfully stuck her tongue out at her father. *She's practically grown up now.*

A bit of sadness touched his thoughts. *Where has the time gone?* Just yesterday she bounced on his knee and screamed for joy. Now his little girl had transformed into a young woman. Slender, with honey brown hair and clear blue eyes, her figure filled out a dress in in all the right places—despite her repeated complaints it wasn't nearly fast enough. Yes, the boys would soon be calling on the Ledbetter household with a wearisome regularity.

Levi's oldest son, Caleb, brought him out of his reverie. "Papa, we finished cleaning the barn for tomorrow's milking."

Levi and his family milked over a hundred cows every morning and evening. Most of the milk, along with meat from butchered cattle, went to the Storm Rider garrison stationed ten leagues south of his farm. This provided his family with a comfortable living. Although the Veil border was dangerous—as any fool knew—he took proper precautions. With the garrison nearby, and a Watch Tower only five leagues away, they were as safe as one could be along the enchanted perimeter.

Caleb walked over to Levi, a look of concern in his blue eyes. A spitting image of Levi at Caleb's age, the boy had already grown tall and muscular. Untidy sandy blonde hair spilled into his eyes, and he had a deep, even tan from a life spent working outdoors. No doubt when the time came, his son would not lack for his choice of girls.

"All right, Caleb, I've seen that look before. Out with it. What's wrong?"

"It's Juniper. She is ready to calve, but something is wrong. I don't think her calf is turned right. Can I stay and help deliver it? Pulpit says we may have to pull the calf out by hand, otherwise both may die."

When Juniper's mother rejected the calf and refused to allow her to nurse, Caleb bottle fed her every day until she was old enough to forage on her own. Aware of his son's affinity with animals, especially Juniper, Levi knew if anything happened to her, he would be crushed.

"I'll talk to your mother about it. She claims you pick at your food because you're more concerned with the animals than you are with yourself."

At Caleb's crestfallen look, Levi hastily added, "However, I think I can talk her into it."

Caleb's face lit up. "Thanks, Papa!"

"I'll stay with the boy," a deep voice called from the back of the barn.

Moments later, the gangly figure of John "Pulpit" Fedders rose from where he had been examining Juniper. Although John was his given name, he acquired the nickname, *Pulpit* from the Ledbetter children—due in no small part to his propensity to *lecture* on anything and everything he thought of import.

A Monk of the Order of the White, Pulpit's long hair—the color of freshly fallen snow—cascaded past his shoulders, while pale blue peered from beneath bleached eyebrows. Levi knew that when White Monks completed their training, all members of the Order eventually took on the appearance of albinos.

When Pulpit showed up looking for work two years ago, Levi's initial instinct was to send him on his way, even though he needed another hand. Levi feared the strenuous farm work would prove to be too difficult for the young monk. However, Pulpit seemed far older than his youthful countenance—particularly his eyes—which made him appear both older and younger at the same time. This puzzled Levi to the extent he decided to take a chance and hire him. The monk proved to be a hard worker and competent hand, and Levi never regretted his decision.

During Pulpit's tenure at the Ledbetter farm, he freely shared with Levi and his family the basic tenants, beliefs, and practices of his Order. As pacifists, members of the Order of the White believed in service to their fellow citizens. They would not lift a finger to defend themselves, even if attacked or assaulted. The Monks tended toward academics, and many were teachers—with some even being powerful practitioners and instructors of magic.

Monks like Pulpit, when initiated into the Order, went on individual missions to cities, villages, farms, and even households. They were not *sent* in the sense they were directed to this place or that. Rather, each Monk decided the direction they would go, when to stop, how to serve, and how long they would stay. It was something they would *know* when they got there.

Members of the Order would not take money—a source of constant regret with Levi. Pulpit worked only for food and lodging. Like his brother Monks, he depended on the providential nature of the people he lived and worked among. Each time Levi tried to pay Pulpit, he politely refused. A strong believer in a day's wages for a day's work, the dairy farmer always felt guilty—like he was taking advantage of the monk.

Levi even tried to give Pulpit tools and a horse in lieu of wages...then discovered the White Monks could own no material possessions, save for the clothes on their back, the shoes on their feet, and one other unique tool—their *haloub*. The monks wore the magical Artifact—a small knobbed baton—thrust through a belt or sash at their waist. All members of the Order of the White were trained in the proficiency of its use, and the *haloub* served as both a defensive and offensive weapon.

At first, this seemed at odds with the pacifism of the Monks. However, Levi discovered they pursued one more very important mission—one which formed the basis of their Order.

The obliteration of the Dark Arts.

Monks—who would avoid ant hills so not to accidentally step upon an ant—would not hesitate to kill any man, beast, or creature who carried the stench of dark magic or evil. This stark dichotomy between the gentle, peaceful nature of the Monks and their merciless attitude toward practitioners of the dark arts was unshakable. The White Brethren possessed an uncanny ability to sense the stain of the black arts. Stories were legend of members of the Order launching sudden attacks against agents of the Veil in villages and towns...individuals the local inhabitants *thought* were normal citizens.

This penchant attracted Monks to the borderland in large numbers. So, when Pulpit showed up at Levi Ledbetter's doorstep, he wasn't particularly surprised, nor was Pulpit the first

White Monk to offer his services.

"If Pulpit is going to be here, can I stay too, Papa?" an excited voice called from the hayloft above. Seconds later, a young boy of ten vaulted from the loft to the ladder, then scrambled down to stand breathlessly next to Pulpit.

"I want to see Juniper's calf! I'll stay out of the way, Papa. Besides, Pulpit says I will need to learn how calves are born if I am going to help on the farm."

The Monk chuckled and ruffled the boy's hair. "I said *someday*, Samuel Ledbetter, not necessarily tonight."

"But why can't I stay?" Samuel persisted. "Pulpit says all the time the sooner a task is started, the sooner it is finished. Can't I begin to learn tonight?"

Levi tried to stifle a grin. "Enough!" he roared. "It seems the boy has taken your words to heart, Pulpit."

Pulpit chuckled. "Aye. I have always said he's a fast learner. Pray he would be as quick to carry out his chores."

Levi motioned with his hand. "Come. We must get to supper before your mother thinks we mean to eat it out here. And you," he said, finger pointed at Samuel. "If you eat all on your plate and keep to your best behavior, then I *may* let you come back to the barn with Caleb and Pulpit."

Samuel let out a whoop. "I'll eat everything, Papa, and I'll even help Mama clear the dishes!"

"Understand you can't stay the whole night," Levi warned. "However, we'll see about you remaining until bedtime. Now, let's go eat supper before it gets cold."

***

The Ledbetter family sprinted through the rain to the two-story house across from the barn. Last to leave was Pulpit.

A premonition, cold and prickly, suddenly crawled up his neck, and he turned and looked. A damp breeze blew across his face, and Pulpit suppressed a shiver. He caressed his *haloub*, then shoved the magical implement tighter into his belt.

With a last look, the monk ran through the rain to the farmhouse.

CHAPTER 9

"WHAT? THE BITCH SAID WHAT?"

"Watch your language young lady, or I'll add more days to your detention!"

Lady Anne stood before the desk of the assistant principal, Stacy Jones. A diminutive woman, Jones more than made up for her lack of stature with a steely determination.

Lady Anne clenched her teeth. "Oh. I'm *so* sorry, Ms. Jones. Where are my manners?" In a syrupy sweet voice, she asked, "Mona said I frightened her last week?"

"No, not Mona but her brother, Joe…and the description he used is *bullied,* not *frightened.* He told the counselor at the Jr. High, who in turn referred the matter to me."

Jones studied some papers in an open folder. "Quite an impressive young man. He downloaded the school policy on bullying, completed the form that triggered this investigation, and managed to list in detail a number of incidents which indicate a long-term pattern of harassment."

Lady Anne's lip curled. Before she could stop herself, she blurted, "That's bullshit—I mean that's a bunch of crap! Her brother is lying."

"Really? Then what's this?" Jones turned the computer monitor around and clicked her mouse to play a clip of video footage. It showed Mona in the commons area surrounded by Lady Anne and her friends. A short time later, the video stream revealed Lady Anne leaping onto the table. She felt the blood rush from her face.

Satisfied she had seen enough, Jones clicked off the video. "We archive security camera footage for several months. I'm sure if I searched some more and talked to your friends, I'd be able to document other incidents like this."

Lady Anne recovered quickly. She sat down and leaned forward with both elbows on Jone's desk. "Why, Ms. Jones. I don't know *what* you're talking about…and I want to talk to my father. *Now!*"

A thin smile played across Jones's face.

"Already have. I have a meeting set for later this morning with your father. In the meantime." Jones scribbled on a pad of paper, then ripped off the sheet and thrust it into Lady Anne's hands. "You are to report to Coach Briles in Detention Hall and give him this."

Lady Anne stared at the paper in her hands, cheeks flushed. "You-you can't do this to me."

Unperturbed, Jones continued. "You have five days detention. More if you are absent or misbehave while in D-Hall. And Ms. Golightly?"

"What?" Lady Anne snarled.

"It goes without saying, if this poor girl suffers from any further incidents—is harassed in any way—you will be up for more serious charges, and I will push for your placement in Alternative School."

Lady Anne grabbed her purse and kicked her chair out of the way. It fell to the floor with a *bang*. She stalked out of Jones's office and didn't spare a backward glance.

Furious, Lady Anne spun left and stalked to the student parking lot. She stopped at a silver BMW sports coupe. A click of her key fob unlocked it, and she slid into the bucket seat. She fished inside the glove compartment and removed a baggie with several neatly rolled joints. Buzzing the car window partially down, she lit one up, took a deep hit, and plotted her revenge.

Muttering to herself, Lady Anne was so preoccupied, she didn't see a figure come up to her window and rap on it.

Startled, Lady Anne dropped the joint in her lap. "Shit!"

Desperately, she groped for the joint before it burned a hole in the expensive leather seat. She finally looked up to see a familiar face.

"Johnny! You almost made me pee in my pants!"

A sardonic grin on his face, Johnny Luna opened the door and slipped into the passenger seat next to Lady Anne. He took off his jacket which revealed tattoos crawling up both arms. Short, black hair crowned his head, razor-cut so patterns of lines and stars appeared close to his scalp. The red t-shirt he wore exposed a thick, bull-like neck nestled between wide, muscular shoulders. A broad face with dark eyes apprised Lady Anne while she took another hit.

"Hey, that must be good shit."

"You ought to know, Johnny…especially since I bought it from you."

"One more happy customer," he smirked.

Lady Anne handed the joint to Johnny. She studied him as he took a drag. "What are you doing here?"

"Me? I just got to school and saw you get into your car."

Lady Anne rolled her eyes. "You'll be like what? Fifty years old when you graduate? You have to actually *attend* school to graduate."

Johnny made a rude noise. He took one last hit and handed the joint back to Lady Anne. "You sound like my old man. I can make more in one month running dope than he can at the rendering plant in an entire year…and I get to keep all my fingers, unlike a lot of the *mojados* he works with. Graduating from this pisspot school ain't high on my list of things to do."

A persistent chirp came from Lady Anne's cell. She glanced at the screen and discovered she had already received three texts from her mother and four from her father. She silenced the phone. *I'll deal with them later.*

A plan formed in her mind. She asked, "So, you have no interest in graduating?"

Johnny's head swung toward Lady Anne. He studied her for a long moment. "That's what I said. Why?"

"Because I have a business proposition for you, which, if successful, might get you kicked out of school."

She reached for her purse and took out her wallet, then spread five one hundred dollar bills on the BMW's console.

"I can give you five hundred dollars now and another five hundred when the job's done."

Johnny stared at the money. He looked up, his expression hard, eyes narrowed into thin slits. "What's going on? No one lays out this kind of money unless they want something illegal done—like breaking a few arms and legs."

An innocent smile played across Lady Anne's lips.

"I don't want you to hurt anyone, Johnny—not physically anyway. But I do want you to scare someone for me. I want her scared so badly she'll have nightmares for the rest of her life. I have a plan if you think you're up for it."

Johnny regarded Lady Anne a few moments longer. He finally scooped up the five bills. "Okay. Let's hear it. If I don't like your *plan*, I'll just give you the money back…minus a hundred bucks. My time is valuable."

Lady Anne laughed and waved at the money. "Of course." She then spent the next fifteen minutes sketching out her plan. Johnny listened silently for the most part and asked few questions. When she finished, he shook his head.

"You rich bitches are all alike. You think you can buy anyone and anything."

"Why, Johnny," Lady Anne purred, "I don't believe I've ever received such a wonderful compliment—and a *yes* that you'll do it."

She adjusted the BMW's mirror and checked her lipstick and makeup. The act thrust her breasts forward as she sat up, and she was rewarded with the sight of Johnny staring. She undid a button on her blouse to reveal more of her cleavage.

Time to set the hook.

"And, of course, if you pull this off, I will be *ever* so grateful."

Johnny's gaze traveled slowly from Lady Anne's breasts to her face.

He locked his eyes on hers.

"Consider it done."

CHAPTER 10

RAZOR EMERGED FIRST FROM THE PORTAL, TO BE GREETED BY darkness, blowing wind, and rain.

Lightning flashed, followed by deafening claps of thunder. The raid leader muttered words of power, and a small lodestone ring glowed briefly on his hand. When he passed the ring over his eyes, his night vision sharpened to the clarity of broad daylight. At the same time, the rain sleeting in his face abated. Not for the first time, Razor thought the magical tool worth its weight in lodestones. His officers and the Dark Brothers carried similar Artifacts.

While not able to provide the rest of the *horde* with the same Artifacts, the Dark Brothers did generate a magical spell that gave the rest of the raiders better night vision. Although not as potent as Razor's Artifact, it at least kept the mass of men and man-beasts from marching over one another. No such protection from the rain existed for them, however. Razor quietly celebrated this fact, with the hope some of the stench from the Boarog would be washed away.

He pushed the thought aside and scanned the countryside. He spied no threats and signaled the first company through the portal. Half an hour later, the entire *horde* was assembled outside the portal.

He shouted over the wind and rain. "We are now outside of the Veil! Since this is a training mission, our target is an isolated farm approximately three leagues northwest of here. There is little in the way of spoils, so the shares normally earned from a raid are suspended."

Shares—plunder obtained in a raid—were doled out after a successful incursion. Raid leaders like Razor received the largest share, followed by officers and the rank and file. The Boarog got nothing, of course, except captives thrown to them too old or infirm to be of value. Healthy men and women were highly prized by Marlinda and destined for the breeding pits for her cruel experiments in permutations. The Dark King and Queen were most generous to raiders who brought back scores of captives. Such a system made Razor a very wealthy man.

A general muttering greeted this announcement as Razor knew it would. His mouth twisted. "Shut your pestilent lips! Not one of you save my officers have been bloodied in even a single raid! When you earn the right by blood and experience, you might, and I said *might* mind you, be offered shares! Count yourselves lucky if you return tonight, alive and whole, through the Veil!"

He barked orders to his lieutenants, then rode a short distance from the *horde* before he wheeled around to address them a final time.

"Remember what I said before we entered the portal. *Obey my orders without question!*"

His long sword swished from its scabbard, and the *horde* leader fixed the trio of Dark Brothers with a steely glare.

"Each of you has a job to do. If any among you fail to carry out a task to my satisfaction, I will cut you down on the spot. Pray I do not have to make an example of any of you."

The terror reflected in the Dark Brothers eyes caused Razor to smile. *Fear could indeed be a great equalizer when experience is lacking.*

The sorcerers would obey him without question, of that he

had no doubt. Whether or not they were up to the task continued to be problematic. The werewolves persisted in periodic shape shifts, despite the Leash Master's best efforts. The Veil Queen's *specials* still appeared disoriented, and the Dark Brothers struggled to control them as well. The lycanthropes, however, remained his greatest concern.

He signaled to Colley, his second-in-command. "I want three of your best bowman with silver-tipped arrows trained on the shape shifters at all times. If they so much as piss without my permission, I want them to sprout so many arrows, the fletching's will make them look more fowl than werewolves."

Colley nodded. "Aye, though I'll be hard-pressed to find three competent bowmen. We'll be lucky to find even one who won't soil his pants the first time one of the shape shifters looks at him with more than passing interest in its eyes."

"Do whatever you have to do to prevent them from causing problems," Razor warned. "When I was on only my third raid out from the Veil, I saw a lycanthrope shift to a werewolf with no warning. One minute it appeared a normal man, the next it was tearing out its Leash Master's throat. By the time our *Horde* Leader managed to kill the beast, it had savaged and slaughtered a score of raiders. I'll not have that repeated tonight!"

"Understood, *Horde* Leader. I will kill them myself if need be."

Razor breathed easier. Colley was as solid a second-in-command as he could have hoped for. In time, no doubt, Colley would lead a *horde* himself. If he said he would kill the werewolves should they become a threat, then it was a deed already done.

He signaled to the *horde*, and they moved off into the storm-wracked night.

CHAPTER 11

ONA AWOKE THE NEXT DAY, RELIEVED TO SEE BRIGHT SUNSHINE streaming through her window, the solid walls and floor of her bedroom revealed in its light.

She stretched and yawned—then the memory of the previous night rumbled through her mind. She leaped out of bed and thrust her hand under the mattress. Her fist closed on the pills, and she pulled them out. A gasp escaped from her lips.

The bottle was empty...except for a single rose petal resting inside.

Heart hammering, her conviction that last night's surreal experience must have been a vivid dream evaporated.

Shaken, she whispered, "No."

Her mind raced with thoughts of a dozen possibilities on how the drugs could have disappeared. She finally settled on the most disturbing possibility of all.

Mr. Finkle must be real. It's all real!

Mona quickly banished such a preposterous notion. More troubling to her was the prospect *Joe* might have discovered her cache and thrown the pills away. Shame colored her cheeks. Her brother knew her better than anyone. He *must* have taken them.

Thoughts of Mr. Finkle now a distant concern, Mona went to the small bathroom and brushed her teeth. She eyed herself in the cracked mirror. Surprised at her calm expression, it dawned on her the disappearance of the pill hoard had lifted a weight off her shoulders. Never convinced she could have attempted an overdose anyway, a sense of relief filled her.

A smile tugged at the corner of her lips. The school bus would be here soon, but Mona allowed herself a moment of respite. Perhaps there *were* times when all was okay with the world, when nothing waited to threaten her.

She just *knew* today would to be a good day!

The Christmas holidays approached, and the next few weeks passed by in peaceful and uneventful fashion—a welcome relief for Mona. She didn't run into Lady Anne at school, nor was she harassed by any of her friends. Even though Mona constantly scanned the hallways, cafeteria, and school grounds for her tormentor, she never caught sight of her...almost like Lady Anne had dropped out of sight. A thread of worry wriggled in the back of her mind on how such a visible and social creature like Lady Anne could suddenly fall off the radar. However, she decided to let it go and enjoy the reprieve while she could.

Joe seemed in high spirits and asked her about school, particularly about Lady Anne. When Mona told her brother about the bully's strange absence, he nodded, a huge grin on his face.

Even the Bakers seemed to be caught up in the Christmas spirit and took Mona and Joe to *Texas Roadhouse* for dinner one night. Other than fast food, burgers, and pizza, going out to eat at an actual sit-down restaurant was something their foster parents rarely indulged in.

Best of all, there were no more *visits* from Mr. Finkle. Although convinced she must have been caught in the throes of an intense dream—her *Angel* a figment of her imagination—the images still appeared crystal clear in Mona's mind. Since logic and reason told her none of what she thought she had seen and experienced was possible, she put the matter out of her mind.

She hadn't given serious thought to Mr. Finkle since.

The nearer the holidays and semester break drew, the slower the days seemed to crawl by. Restless, Mona was ready for school to be out so academics could be put aside for a few blissful weeks. Doodling on a piece of notebook paper in her English IV class, she jumped when the intercom in class crackled to life.

"Mona Parker, please come to the main high school office."

Mona gathered her books and with hall pass in hand, hurried out of the classroom. A chill ran down her spine. *What's going on?* She *never* got called to the office. The drowsy, routine day evaporated and suddenly became unpredictable. Unable to help herself, she found herself casting nervous glances at corners and blind spots in the hallways.

At the office, Mona walked up to the reception kiosk that fronted the lobby of the large room. She recognized the high school receptionist, Gloria Bynum, tapping on her computer. Although barely five feet in height, Mrs. Bynum possessed an over-sized smile, which she flashed at Mona. She stood and waved her over, a slip of paper in her hand.

"Mona, I have a message from Elaine Baker."

The block of ice in her stomach began to melt. Occasionally, Elaine or Bud would leave her a message—most of the time consisting of instructions to watch Joe because the Bakers wouldn't be home when they got off the bus. Of course, texting her would be much easier than leaving a note with the school office, but Elaine and Bud refused to pay for text services on their cell phones.

Mrs. Bynum handed Mona the message. *"Do not take the school bus. Instead, wait after school for your foster parents to come pick you and your brother up."*

Mona scanned the note while Mrs. Bynum signed her hall pass and handed it back.

"Have a good day, Mona."

She nodded and, relieved, hurried back to class.

The rest of the day proved uneventful. Before she knew it, the final bell rang. *School's out,* her mind shouted with glee. Mona tossed her books in her backpack, then joined the throngs of students streaming out of the high school.

Joe's campus, Spring Hill Jr. High, was located adjacent to the high school, with a single, one-way street separating the two campuses. As Mona emerged from school, a cacophony of honks and rumbling from dozens of cars greeted her. The line of vehicles—all waiting to exit—stretched the entire length of the boulevard. Mona knew it was fruitless to attempt to cross the street through the heavy traffic, so she found a concrete bench facing the busy road and sat down to wait for Joe.

The day was cold and overcast, and the weak December sunlight struggled to break through the thin mantle of clouds. Mona pulled her coat tighter as the traffic dwindled. She scanned the crosswalk leading from the Jr. High and spotted Joe's familiar figure cruising toward her. As he drew closer, Mona frowned. Normally, Joe zipped about in a motorized wheelchair, but instead, he was in his old wheelchair, arms churning to propel himself along. She hefted her backpack and hurried to meet her brother.

"What's going on? Where's your other wheelchair?" she demanded.

Joe, face flushed from the exertion, grinned at Mona. "The battery is dead. I didn't want to wait for it to charge up, so I just used my backup."

Knowing her impatient brother well, Mona rolled her eyes. "Well when Elaine and Bud get here, they're going to ask you the same thing."

"So let 'em ask. Besides, Bud doesn't care as long as he doesn't have to push me. Anyway, we're going to have walk home."

"What? The message said we were supposed to wait for them to pick us up."

"Plans have changed. I got called to the office right at the end of school and given this note." Joe handed the slip of paper to Mona. "It says the Bakers have some errands to run, and we should take the bus home."

After a quick scan of the message, Mona stomped her foot. "The buses have already left! How are we supposed to get home?"

"We do it the old-fashioned way. We walk—or rather, *you* walk and *push* me," Joe said with a wink.

Mona threw her hands up. "Great! Just great!" After a moment's hesitation, she whipped out her phone and considered calling the Bakers.

Joe tapped her on the arm. "I wouldn't do that. If Elaine and Bud are at Walmart, they'll just get pissed off."

"Okay. Whatever!" Mona snapped. She shoved the phone back in her purse and considered their options. The wind picked up, and she shivered, the cold breeze penetrating her coat. *They couldn't just stand around forever.*

"Look, like I said, let's just walk home. It's only a mile or so, and we've done it before," Joe said, exasperation creeping into his voice.

"Yes, but instead of using your motorized wheelchair, *I* have to push you," Mona shot back.

Joe's face, already ruddy in the cold air, turned a darker shade of red. "Sorry I'm so much trouble. I can do it myself!" Joe pivoted and propelled himself toward the crosswalk.

Mona sighed and ran after her brother. She caught up with him, and grabbed the handles of the wheelchair, forcing him to stop. She bent over and wrapped her arms around him. "I'm sorry, Joe. I didn't mean it that way. You know I don't mind pushing you."

The anger melted away from Joe's face, to be replaced with one of frustration. He looked up, tears in his eyes.

"I know, Sis. It's just—I *want* to be able to do it myself, and I don't *want* you or anyone else to have to help me. I wish I could walk like everyone else. I wish…" his voice trailed off, and he shook his head. "Never mind. It's stupid to hope for something that's never going to happen."

Mona held him tighter. "It's okay. I understand. I'm so proud of you and what you have already overcome. What *I* wish is that I could get you to understand you are so much more than a pair of legs."

Mona tapped Joe on the head. "If I had half your brainpower, I'd be a millionaire by the time I'm thirty."

A grin blossomed on her brother's face, and Mona hugged him again. She stood up and gripped the handles of the wheelchair. "Let's go home."

Intent on getting out of the cold, Mona pushed Joe along at a brisk pace. They passed the last car left on the once crowded street, which stood parked beside the curb.

A red Corvette.

CHAPTER 12

LEVI BELCHED AND RUBBED HIS STOMACH. HE FLASHED HIS WIFE, Constance, a smile. "Great supper."

He stood and peered out the window. Lightning and thunder continued to flash and boom outside. "Doesn't look like this is going to let up anytime soon."

"Pulpit and I are going back to the barn now," Caleb announced.

Constance looked up from clearing the dishes off the table. "You sit right back down," she stated firmly. "I prepared a pie for dessert, and it hasn't been served it yet."

"But, Mother, Juniper is going to calve at any minute. If we aren't there to help, she and the calf could die!" Caleb protested.

"It's all right, Constance," Levi said. "Ellie can bring them their dessert later. Juniper's calf may not wait for the pie."

Caleb looked at his father with relief. Before his mother could object further, he grabbed an oilskin slicker from a peg on the wall, opened the door, and sprinted out into the rain. Pulpit followed close on his heels.

"I'm going too!" Samuel declared and jumped up to get his own small raincoat to trail after his older brother.

Constance, hands on hips, barred his way. "You stop right this instant! You aren't going anywhere until we finish eating, and that includes dessert."

"But, Mother, Papa said I could help with Juniper too!" Constance flashed a look at Levi...one he knew all too well.

"Er, now look, Samuel. I said you could go *after* we finished eating. Now sit down and take that piece of pie. And remember, I said you could only stay until your bedtime."

He risked a glance at his wife to see if this placated her. Arms crossed, mouth pursed, she returned his look with a steely expression. A sigh escaped his lips. *Apparently not.*

"The boy lives on a dairy farm," Levi said. "How is he to learn about dairy cattle if he is shut up in this house?"

Constance waved her arms. "He is only ten years old! Must he run off in the rain to see things he no doubt will see many times later on when he is older?"

She opened her mouth to add another comment, then decided the better of it. *"Fine.* Samuel, you can watch Pulpit and Caleb. However," she turned and pointed at her husband, *"you* will stay up with Samuel if he has nightmares because something went wrong with Juniper's delivery. Come, Ellie. We have dishes to wash." Constance huffed back to the kitchen with her daughter in tow.

"Whoopee!" cried Samuel, doing a little dance at the table.

"You better hope I don't have to sleep in the barn with Juniper tonight," Levi quipped. "Now be sure you put your slicker on tight. When your sister brings the pie out for Caleb and Pulpit, you can stay until they finish eating it. When Ellie comes back, you come back with her. Is that understood?"

"Yes, Sir!" Samuel shouted and ran out the door to the barn.

With a sigh, Levi picked up the few dishes left on the table and went to the kitchen to help his wife and daughter with the dishes. Perhaps if he was very helpful, she would forget this night's events.

Hopefully, sooner than she normally did.

Tal had no trouble seeing in the blackness of the night and pounding rain.

He peered at the ground far below him and searched for anything out of the ordinary. Artifacts carried by the Storm Riders allowed them to see regardless of weather or darkness. The magical objects also shielded them from the rain—the wind-driven drops simply fell around the Storm Riders, not on them. Tal, as a Prince of the Blood, inherited advantages all the nobly-born shared, including excellent vision, whether night or day. Few on Meredith could match him in terms of raw power, whether it be in physical strength or the weaving of magic.

Bozar often warned him, however, that these hereditary advantages were no substitute for patience, prudence, and intellect. His advisor claimed these advantages could work against him if they gave him false confidence or caused him to act in a foolish manner. Sound advice, indeed, but still, Tal struggled daily against the very impulsive nature Bozar warned against.

Bolts of lightning flashed through the sky, followed immediately by claps of thunder. Vicious updrafts and downdrafts pulled at Tal's mount and the rest of the Storm Riders. The winged horses compensated easily enough, although not enough to eliminate the wind shear. This constant rise and fall exhilarated Tal, and he was suitably impressed by the prowess of his mount to navigate in the raging storm. He resumed his scan of the landscape below and observed scattered trees, thick forest, and rolling hills. North in the distance, the topmost spire of a Watch Tower stretched upward into the rain-drenched night.

A voice appeared in Tal's ear. "We will continue north for another few leagues, Sire, and then swing south toward the next Watch Tower." A communication Artifact—in the form of a lodestone bracelet on his wrist—allowed him to speak and be heard by any of the Storm Riders, as well as to be spoken to himself. Contact with the skin was all the magical object needed in order for him to hear with absolute clarity.

"What lies to the North, Lord Banebolt?" Tal asked.

"Nothing immediately, Sire, except a few scattered farms and a nearby dairy that supplies us with meat and milk. However, it is farther North and West than our usual search pattern."

Outside the normal search pattern. Something clicked in Tal's mind. "Lord Banebolt, don't the cursed Veil raiders constantly change their raid patterns? Could they have spies with knowledge of your patrol area?"

"Of course, Sire. But with such scant pickings, it is unlikely they would risk an incursion for so little reward."

Tal chewed this over in his mind a few minutes more. Abruptly, he came to a decision. "Lord Banebolt, humor me and let us fly as far as the dairy farm."

"As you wish, Sire."

He issued orders, and the formation of Storm Riders swung westward.

The first indication of trouble came when Razor's outriders came back with news that cattle—dairy cattle by the look of them—were pastured less than a league from the main body of the *horde*. The lead scout hesitated before finishing his report, and the raid leader had a sinking sensation it wasn't good news.

"Out with it! Finish your report!" Razor demanded.

"One of the shape shifters is close to the herd. It appears to be stalking the cattle."

Razor cursed and sawed the reins. He galloped back to where the Dark Brothers, including the Leash Master, plodded over a small hill with the rest of the marauders. Coming to a stop so sudden it threw wet clods of dirt from the horse's hooves on the Dark Brothers, Razor leapt from his horse. He grabbed the young sorcerer by his robes, ripped him from the saddle, and held him thrashing in the air.

"Where are your charges?" he screamed. Spittle sprayed on the terrified face of the magus. "Only two shape shifters follow behind you. You are one short!"

The Leash Master gurgled, unable to speak from the pressure at his throat. With his eyes bulging and tongue blue, the veteran raider finally eased the pressure and allowed him to find his voice.

"I-I sent one ahead to sc-scout, *Horde* Leader," he gasped.

"By whose orders?" Razor demanded.

"No-no one, *Horde* Leader. Standard procedure calls for at least one lycanthrope to range ahead on a raid." The terrible expression on Razor's face caused the young sorcerer's face to drain of all color.

Razor's fingers curled once more around the gibbering Leash Master's throat. He longed to rip the fool's head from his shoulders and stuff it down his bloody neck. But if he killed the magus, any chance to recall the renegade shape shifter would be lost.

With an effort that cost every bit of his self-control, Razor loosened his grip. Holding the Leash Master's face just inches from his own, he shrieked, *"Call the werewolf back!"*

He flung the Dark Brother away from him. The sorcerer staggered backward, tripped on his own feet, and fell in the mud.

"Now, damn you!"

The sorcerer managed to regain his footing, then grasped

a bag tied to a leather thong around his neck. Made of a hoary material with tiny lodestones sewn into the fabric, it contained hair and fingernail clippings from each of the lycanthropes and was the means by which they were controlled. The young magus grasped the bag and chanted. A silvery glow emanated from the satchel. Brow furrowed in intense concentration, perspiration mixed with rain trickled down his forehead while he continued to chant.

Finally, the Dark Brother stopped. The blood emptied from his face. Trembling, he whispered, "It...it isn't working."

Razor quickly signaled Colley. "Kill the shape shifter! Take what men you need and see to it immediately." Colley waved a salute and rode off.

"You-you can't do that!" the Leash Master blurted before he could stop himself. "I-I mean they are the Dark Queen's creatures, and it takes years to train them."

A knife appeared in the raid leader's hand. With a blur of motion, he sliced off the sorcerer's right ear and held the dripping trophy before his astonished eyes.

Ignoring the screams, Razor pulled him close and whispered, *"It would seem the training is incomplete."*

The *Horde* leader kicked the Leash Master away from him. "Count yourself lucky if you lose no more body parts tonight. Control the remaining lycanthropes, or you are a dead man! Do you understand me?" Hand clutched to the side of his head, blood dripped through the sorcerer's fingers. With a whimper, he nodded.

"Good!" Razor paused before remounting his horse and turned to face the shape shifters behind the Leash Master. Partially transformed, the creatures were covered in coarse fur and stood on two feet. Muzzles full of sharp canines thrust from their faces, while red-rimmed eyes followed his every move.

The raid leader tossed the severed ear to them. "Fetch." The nearest werewolf leapt into the air to catch and swallow the grisly trophy all in one motion.

Razor smiled at the Dark Brothers. "*Hmmm.* I guess they are good for something after all."

CHAPTER 13

P ER LADY ANNE'S INSTRUCTIONS, JOHNNY WAITED IN HIS CAR AT the end of the street while cars disgorged from both campuses.

The road dead-ended less than a hundred yards from the crosswalk—a perfect place to observe the comings and goings of anyone leaving the junior high or high school. As Lady Anne predicted, the road became a deserted strip of asphalt just fifteen minutes after school let out.

The plan devised by his curvaceous conspirator was simple— wait for Parker and her 'crip brother to cross the street, then bear down on them in the 'Vette at a high rate of speed. At the last minute, he would screech to a stop. Basically, he needed to scare the shit out of Parker and send the appropriate message.

Never mess with Lady Anne Golightly.

Bored, he lit up a cigarette and fantasized about the promise made to him by Lady Anne should he deliver on *really* frightening the skinny bitch. He decided there on the spot Parker and her brother would need a fresh change of underwear when he got through with them.

He rolled the window down a crack for the cigarette smoke to escape. Johnny caressed the console. Four years earlier, he rescued the rusting '69 Corvette from a junkyard and worked nonstop on its restoration ever since. It pretty much represented the only honest labor done in his entire life. Any money he earned, legitimately or otherwise, went into the 'Vette's restoration. A car built when muscle cars ruled the road, the Corvette was the baddest set of wheels in town. Everybody knew Johnny's car; therefore, everybody knew Johnny.

Lost in his thoughts, he almost missed Mona pushing her brother across the intersection. He flicked the cigarette out the window and turned the ignition.

The 'Vette roared to life.

Hunched over the wheel, he punched the accelerator, and the powerful car sprang forward. Having determined beforehand where he would need to hit the brakes and stop before he hit Parker, a white spray-painted X appeared on the asphalt ahead. The marker inched closer and closer to Parker in his mind every time he thought of Lady Anne's promise.

The sportscar thundered down the street. Mona and Joe looked up, eyes wide, fear evident on both their faces.

Johnny grinned. *You ain't seen nothing yet.*

He mashed down harder on the accelerator. Tires screeching, the 'Vette leaped forward with a fresh burst of speed.

Legs pumping and arms straining, Mona pushed her brother's wheelchair as fast as she could across the intersection.

Out of the corner of his eye, Johnny caught sight of Lady Anne perched on the hood of her car in the deserted lot. From her vantage point, she had a birds-eye view of the show. Surrounded by a group of friends, they clapped and cheered when he buzzed by them.

His car rocketed closer and closer. The point of no return—the spray-painted X—suddenly appeared on the hard blacktop, and Johnny hit the brakes hard. The 'Vette slowed down…but not nearly enough.

What?

A high-pitched squeal pierced the air, and the scorched smell of burning brakes filled the car's interior. With dread realization, Johnny knew the accelerator he thought he had fixed was stuck again—and at a wide-open throttle!

Desperately, he pulled the emergency brake, and the car shivered and slowed down. However, a split second later, the back wheels of the 'Vette struck some loose gravel on the road. The car fishtailed, and Johnny spun the wheel hard to try and compensate. The maneuver failed, and the powerful vehicle drifted out of control.

Mona watched everything as though in slow motion as she struggled to push Joe to safety. Despite her best efforts, Mona knew they weren't going to make it.

We're going to die.

Fear and adrenaline coursed through Mona, and she managed one final, desperate push. The wheelchair shot across the road and rolled to safely to the other side.

This final lunge caused Mona to stumble and lose her balance. Frantic, she attempted to regain her footing. With a look over her shoulder, she gasped at the sight of the fishtailing 'Vette. The back-end of the muscle car swerved toward Mona. She screamed and put her hands up—then she was flying through the air.

A meaty *crump* announced the car's impact. Johnny overcompensated again, and lost complete control of the car. The Corvette slid hard into the curb, bounced and became airborne. Like a missile, it twisted and flew in a parabolic arc over Lady Anne and her gaggle of friends, to crash into the parking lot. It rolled over once, then twice, before it finally came to a stop...upside down.

Pain filled Mona. The ground came to meet her, and she struck her head sharply on the hard, unyielding tarmac of the road. A last thought streaked through her mind before she blacked out.

Did Joe make it to safety?

CHAPTER 14

RAIN DRIPPED FROM THE WEREWOLF'S MUZZLE TO JOIN ROPEY strands of saliva clinging to the beast's lower jaw. Lightning flashes exposed three-inch fangs which gleamed white in the reflected light.

The beast stood to its full height of over seven feet and sniffed the air as it stalked the fat cattle. After undergoing numerous minor shape shifts since exiting the portal—each transmogrification costing it energy—ravenous hunger now drove the were-beast with single-minded determination. When summoned by the Master, hunger won out over the compulsion to obey.

A fat yearling munched grass at the edge of the herd, and the werewolf crept closer. The storm's treacherous winds shifted suddenly, which brought the beast's scent to the cattle. Nervous lowing ensued, and the herd bull, a huge and muscular three-thousand-pound animal, stopped grazing and lifted its massive head. The bull snorted, pawed the ground, and shook its horns.

At the sight of the yearling trotting away, the werewolf snarled in frustration and leaped up to pursue the young bovine. The bull bellowed, lowered its head and charged, sharp horns pointed at the lycanthrope. With a sideward leap to avoid being gored, the werewolf aimed a savage blow at the bull's exposed neck. Armed with long, razor-sharp claws, the lycanthrope's paw scored a direct hit on the thick neck. Ragged, bloody gashes appeared as the claws ripped through hide and flesh. With a bellow, the bull wheeled around with a dexterity that caught the werewolf by surprise. Unable to dodge aside in time, the bull gored the lycanthrope from groin to abdomen. The shape shifter howled in agony and wrenched free of the horns. The terrible wounds began to heal immediately. Filled with blind rage, the werewolf renewed its attack.

Colley and four raiders rode onto the titanic struggle between the two creatures. The deafening noise created by the bellows, howls, and panicky lowing of over a hundred dairy cattle reverberated in the air. The *horde's* second-in-command immediately ordered his men to dismount, spread out, and form a rough circle around the werewolf. Each were armed with crossbows and silver-tipped bolts.

Colley cursed. "Kill that damn shape shifter before he wakes the entire countryside!" With little confidence in the *best* men he picked, he snorted, "Be careful you don't shoot each other."

The second-in-command shouted over the noise of the storm and the savage battle, "Aim for the heart or the head."

Colley held no hope his archers would come close to this feat, even armed with crossbows. On a clear day with no rain or wind, these inexperienced fools would find it difficult to hit a stationary target, much less a moving one. Instead, he would use them to distract the were-beast while he snuck up on it and put a silver-tipped arrow through its pestilent heart. He just hoped none of them got killed in the process.

Colley moved into position.

He viewed the titanic struggle with professional interest. Were the shape shifter a mortal creature, the herd bull would have long ago won the battle. Instead, the werewolf seemed oblivious to the horrible wounds inflicted by the bovine's horns. In fact, it appeared to Colley the were-beast took punishment it could have easily avoided just to get close enough to savage its huge adversary. Ragged, bloody slashes ran up and down the bull's flanks and neck, blood pouring from these copious wounds. Despite their injuries, neither beast slowed down. Indeed, each fresh wound seemed to enrage them even more.

Colley knew he had to end this soon before the entire countryside became aware of their presence. If not for the intense storm masking the noise of the epic struggle, the alarm would already have been raised.

Crossbows snapped when two of the raiders, eager to get off a good shot, prematurely released bolts at the werewolf. One hit the bull in its meaty rump, while the other sailed harmlessly overhead and almost skewered an archer opposite the lycanthrope. The huge bovine bellowed and turned to engage this new threat. The shape shifter dropped and crouched to the ground, feral eyes probing the direction the arrows came from.

Any chance to catch the werewolf unawares was now lost.

"Shoot!" Colley screamed. "Shoot the shape shifter!" Sprinting, he pulled his longbow from its case and nocked an arrow as he ran.

The werewolf, on all fours, streaked toward the archer who overshot his mark. Struggling to crank his crossbow for another shot, he looked up to see the were-beast bearing down on him. Momentarily frozen at the terrible vision, the raider dropped the crossbow and ran. Before he had taken two steps, the werewolf caught him. With a snarl, the beast ripped out his throat.

Gurgling and drowning in his own blood, the archer dropped like a stone. Gore dripped from the lycanthrope's muzzle as it looked for another victim. Colley's men, witness to the graphic death of their comrade, lost all semblance of discipline. They fired bolts indiscriminately while they edged farther and farther away from the shape shifter.

"Aim, damn you!" Colley screamed. "You are *wasting* the silver-tipped arrows!" If his men heard him, they gave no indication of it and continued to fire wildly.

With a howl, the werewolf charged the nearest archer. To his credit, after seeing the result of running, the raider held his ground and aimed the crossbow before releasing the bolt. The lycanthrope leaped, and the missile slammed into the beast's chest.

The shape shifter crumpled onto the muddy ground.

Colley's men stood and cheered when they saw the werewolf fall. Moments later, the cheers turned to moans when the beast picked itself up off the ground and plucked the bolt from its chest.

Colley cursed at the sight. *The archer had squandered all of his silver-tipped arrows—the werewolf had been struck by a plain arrow!* Even now, the wound closed and appeared almost completely healed.

Having used all the profane words he knew, Colley made up new ones when the were-beast launched itself at the nearest raider. The archer's scream ended in mid-shriek when the lycanthrope ripped his head completely off his shoulders. Hot blood sprayed from torn arteries to mix with the downpour. Covered in bloody gore, the werewolf lifted its muzzle to the dark, rain-drenched sky and bayed.

This proved to be too much for the surviving raiders. With gibbering moans, they dropped their weapons and sprinted for their horses. None made it halfway before the were-beast fell among them to end their lives in a spray of blood and torn appendages.

Distracted, the shape shifter forgot about the bull. The bull, however, remained focused on the werewolf. Maddened by its wounds and the smell of gore, the huge bovine charged while the lycanthrope ripped the archers to pieces. The ground shook as the massive beast bore down on the shape shifter. With no chance to react, the shape shifter didn't see the bull until hit at full charge.

Cartwheeling high into the air, the werewolf slammed into ground and for the first time, lay still. The lycanthrope's hooved adversary snorted and pawed the ground, waiting for the prone body to move.

Colley took this all in while he scrambled to get in position for a good shot. With the shape shifter lying motionless on the ground, he hesitated. He did not want to draw the unwanted attention of the maddened bovine, but he had to be certain the were-beast was dead.

Before he could decide what to do next, the werewolf decided things for him.

Without warning, it rolled over and leaped on the bull's back. The lycanthrope seized the bovine's neck with razor-sharp claws and sank its fangs into the thick flesh. Bellowing in pain, the bull bucked in an attempt to dislodge the werewolf. The wild motion made it impossible to get off a clean shot, and Colley ground his teeth in frustration. Repeated savage blows rained on the side of the bull's head. Each landed with such ferocity, Colley could hear the meaty *thump* above the noise of the storm.

Stunned, the bull finally went down to its knees, the werewolf rolling off to keep from being crushed. The lycanthrope stood and bayed in triumph before it moved in to tear out the dazed animal's exposed throat. This provided a momentary silhouette of the were-beast.

It was all Colley needed.

The *twang* of his longbow sounded, the silver-tipped arrow finding the werewolf's heart. The lycanthrope looked down at the shaft protruding from its chest.

A moment of silence filled the air, broken only by the hissing rain and the groggy snorts of the bull while the beast attempted to regain its feet. Then the werewolf began to convulse and thrash. Smoke issued from the arrow in its chest, a few wisps at first, then billowing clouds. The shape shifter's body spasmed, and the curling smoke made it difficult for Colley to see. Finally, the oily fog cleared, and Colley knelt to examine the beast's remains. A charred and greasy outline burnt into the grass was the only vestige left of the werewolf.

The veteran raider sank cross-legged onto the wet grass, spent from his exertions. Dully, he became aware of the ground shaking beneath him.

He looked up.

The herd of cattle, wild-eyed, stampeded toward him. Led by the badly injured bull, strips of hide flapped on the beast's back, blood from numerous wounds streaking the bovine's sides.

Spurred into action, Colley jumped to his feet, vaulted over the pasture's fence, and sprinted to his horse. He just made it to the saddle when a tremendous crash echoed in the wet air. The panicked cattle reduced the fence to kindling and now bore down on him. Bent low in the saddle, he urged the horse to full speed and raced away. Once at a safe distance, he reined in his mount.

The dairy herd angled away from him and disappeared into the rainy night. Colley slumped in relief, great ragged breaths exploding from his lungs. Finally, he hitched the reins and started back to the *horde*.

He made it less than a league when he ran into the first of the raiding party's outriders. The main body of marauders appeared a short time later. Colley spotted Razor, and he rode up and gave his report. The raid leader remained silent at the bad news. Finally, Colley asked, "What are your orders?"

The *horde* leader swore and slammed his fist onto the saddle. "We have no choice! We ride for the dairy at once. If the alarm hasn't been raised, it soon will be. Our only luck on this wretched night is the storm. The wind, rain, and thunder may have drowned out the sounds of this disaster. Leave at once and see to it the farm is surrounded. Allow no one to escape. We *will* have something to show for this night's work, even if it is a single pail of milk! Now go!"

Colley nodded, then raced away to carry out Razor's orders. He shouted, and a column of raiders peeled off to join him.

As they sped for the farm, he couldn't shake the feeling that the night's misadventures were only just beginning.

CHAPTER 15

ARKNESS ENVELOPED MONA, HER THOUGHTS AND MEMORIES A jumbled soup.

Am I dead?

She felt no pain and could see nothing. Silence surrounded her. Throughout this confusion, she heard a voice call out to her, faint at first, but it grew stronger as she strove to locate its source.

"Mona, come here," it commanded.

A brilliant spear of light pierced the murky shadows of her mind, and like a swimmer striving for the safety of the shore, Mona drove herself toward the light. Brighter and brighter, the light beckoned as she struggled to reach it. Without warning, the gloom melted away, and she found herself in view of a familiar sight.

Caldwell Park—the city park located near Bud and Elaine's house.

The sun sparkled brightly, birds sang in the trees, and a warm breeze caressed her cheeks. The pleasant tinkle of water from a fountain came to her ears. With a start, Mona discovered she sat on a bench inside the park. The place appeared deserted except for a lone individual seated across from her. She peered closer at the man who busied himself feeding pigeons bread from a brown paper bag. With a gasp, Mona immediately recognized the face.

Mr. Finkle!

Her angel stood and brushed crumbs off his shirt and pants. The pigeons scattered, and he quickly traversed the short distance to sit beside Mona.

He waved a hand at the flapping birds. "Pigeons. Useless fowl, good only for the numerous and artful ways they spread their excrement."

Mona stared open-mouthed at Mr. Finkle.

After a few more moments of uncomfortable silence, Mr. Finkle drummed his fingers on the wooden bench.

"Very well. Fowl are birds. You know what birds are, don't you? Creatures with feathers? Excrement is poop as in bird feces. Perhaps you recognize the word in the childish vernacular as 'Number Two—"

"I KNOW WHAT IT MEANS!" Mona screeched.

"Then why must you give me the lobotomy stare again?"

"Are you kidding? Is this a joke? *I just got run over by a car!*"

"Technically, you weren't run over. You were merely struck a glancing blow by the rear end of a 1969 Corvette. In fact—"

"Stop it! Stop it right now! What am I doing here?"

Mr. Finkle spread his hands. "Why, Mona, I told you we would meet again soon. Didn't you believe me?"

"That's it? *That's* your explanation? I have to get hit by a car for us to meet?"

A sudden thought struck Mona, and she leaped to her feet.

"Oh my God! Joe! Is he—"

"Unharmed and in the pink of health," Mr. Finkle quickly assured her.

"So, he's okay?" Mona persisted. Fear for her brother drove all other thoughts from her mind.

Mr. Finkle nodded. He patted her arm and gently pulled her back onto the bench.

"A lot has happened to you and in a short period of time. My impatience often leads to a bedside manner that makes me seem indifferent or uncaring to your plight. However, I *do* care...I care with a depth and intensity which makes the brightest star appear dim in comparison."

Huh?

The abrupt change in Mr. Finkle stunned Mona. She cocked her head and studied him anew. However, she could detect nothing false or insincere in his manner or body language.

"So, why am I here, Mr. Finkle? Why is all this—this *crap* happening to me?"

Mr. Finkle sighed, then took her hand and squeezed. "Why did you say you hated your life?"

The unexpected question left Mona speechless. Unwanted memories came rushing back with a white hot intensity. Her cheeks burned with hurt and humiliation at the picture of Brock, face purple with anger, calling her a dirty bitch while Lady Anne and her friends laughed. Tears rolled down her cheeks.

"Because I'm tired of being invisible, a ghost nobody sees or hears," Mona whispered. "I'm tired of having dreams that will never, *ever* come true. But most of all, I'm tired of being lonely. I can't help thinking, *this is my life...and it is as good as it's going to get.*"

Mr. Finkle produced a spotless white handkerchief and handed it to her. "Ah, but you see, you are wrong, Mona. You are here because your life *does* matter. You are the key to a chain of events which began millennia ago."

Mona dabbed her eyes, face creased in confusion. "I don't understand. I'm plain vanilla, Mr. Finkle. I have no special talents. How could I possibly be part of anything important?"

"Now, *that's* a very good question, and one which absolutely must be answered."

A smile spread across Mr. Finkle's face. "And Mona? You know the best part of all?"

"What?" Mona asked sniffling.

"It is the stuff dreams are made of."

CHAPTER 16

"PULL THE ROPE TIGHT, CALEB."

Satisfied the rope was secure around Juniper's head, Pulpit added, "I'm going to attempt to turn the calf and pull it out."

Pulpit plunged his hands inside the cow and grunted. He struggled to turn the breeched calf into the proper birth position. Moments later, the calf emerged, feet first. Pulling steadily on the legs until completely out of Juniper's body, Pulpit laid the wet, glistening body on the hay-strewn ground.

It lay motionless, pink nose tinged blue.

"Caleb, give me the cloth hanging by the stall!"

Caleb ran, grabbed the fabric, and threw it to Pulpit. The monk caught it in midair, then rubbed the cloth over the calf's mouth and nostrils to clear them of mucus and fluids. He blew vigorously into the newborn's face and massaged its chest and throat. The calf twitched and began to suck air into its lungs. A *bleat* issued from its mouth, and the calf struggled to its feet. On unsteady, wobbly legs, it was nuzzled by Juniper.

Samuel jumped up and down. "Hooray for Pulpit! Hooray for Juniper!" he brayed.

Caleb wore a wide smile as he moved the calf inside the stall with Juniper. He watched it nurse while Juniper licked and nuzzled her calf. Finally, he went over to where Pulpit was washing his hands and arms in a basin of clean water.

He clapped the monk on the back. "That was great, Pulpit!

How did you know to blow—"

Pulpit's body suddenly went rigid under his hand.

"What's the matter?" Caleb asked.

The white monk held his hand up. Even Samuel, still jumping up and down, stopped and stood quietly at Pulpit's signal.

Then they heard it.

A wolf's howl came faintly through the open doors of the barn during a lull in the storm. The monk reacted as if stung.

"Shut and bolt the barn door!" Caleb hesitated, and Pulpit barked, *"Do it now!"* His voice had an edge of urgency Caleb had never heard before, and he scrambled to obey.

"Samuel, help me shut and bolt the windows and shutters. You can start with the loft." Samuel swarmed up the ladder, fear and uncertainty playing across his face.

Moments later, another howl, stronger this time, came through one of the few open windows. This caused Pulpit to redouble his efforts. Finally, all the doors and windows to the barn were shut and bolted.

"Wha—What is it Pulpit?" Caleb asked again, beads of sweat on his lip.

The monk gripped Caleb by the shoulders. "Listen to me. You must do what I tell you—without hesitation and without question. Do you understand?"

"Yes, but…but why?"

"The howl we heard did not come from a normal wolf. It came from a lycanthrope. *A werewolf!* It is close by, and they move at incredible speed. The shape shifters don't travel alone. There is a good chance raiders are close by."

Caleb's face drained of all color. *"Ra-raiders? Were-werewolves?"* he stammered. Suddenly, comprehension dawned on him.

"Papa, Mama, Ellie! We have to warn them!" he shouted and ran for the barn door.

Pulpit moved to block his way. "We don't know where the raiders or werewolf are. Even now, they could be outside. Your father is a smart and resourceful man. If he heard the wolf howl, he will come to the same conclusion I have."

Caleb shook his head. "But we don't know for sure. We have to warn them!" He tried to push past the monk.

"No. I will not let you pass. I will not let you put yourself in danger."

Caleb redoubled his efforts to get by Pulpit. The white monk grabbed his wrist and twisted until Caleb went to his knees in pain. He blinked at the forceful reaction of the normally gentle monk.

"Let me go! I have to warn them!"

"Listen to me!" Pulpit said, urgency in his voice. "If there are Veil raiders out there, you will never reach the house to warn *anyone*. Worse, they will use you to bait your family and try to draw them out. Is this what you want? To endanger the rest of your family? *Think!*"

Pulpit released him. Caleb rubbed his wrist, then paced back and forth. He stopped and jaw clenched, pointed at the monk. "Even if you are right, what do we do? We can't just wait here."

"We are safe for now," the monk replied. "However, we must plan for escape in case the raiders try to break in. Although stoutly built, the barn is not Warded like the house. If they are determined—and the marauders are *always* determined—they will get in."

Pulpit paced about the structure and examined the barn's structure. Made of stout oak timbers, the walls would not be easy to breach, while the floor was paved in dressed stone. He stopped at a large iron grate recessed into the floor. The grate covered a culvert that wastewater drained into. When the day's milking was done, the floor was hosed down, and the dirty water flowed into the grate, through the drain, and out to a ditch some two hundred paces from the barn. Since over a hundred cows were milked daily, it took a large volume of water to hose and clean out the barn. By necessity, the drain pipe and grate were large.

Pulpit considered for a minute before he motioned Caleb and Samuel over. "It will be a tight fit, but I believe you can make it."

Caleb's expression blanched. "You mean...you want us to crawl through the drain pipe?"

"Only if need be," Pulpit replied. "Only if necessary."

Dazed, Caleb shook his head. "So, what do we do now?"

The white monk pulled the *haloub* from his belt. He sat and faced the barn doors.

"We wait."

Tal shook his head in disappointment.

The detour to the isolated farm proved to be a waste of time. He opened his mouth to tell Lord Banebolt to resume their normal patrol...then closed it when he spied a strange sight. In the distance, cattle—dairy cattle by the look of them—stampeded in a direction roughly away from the dairy farmstead.

His eyes lit up, and Tal waved at the herd. "Lord Banebolt, what do you make of that?"

The garrison commander followed Tal's arm. "It looks like a spooked herd of cattle, Sire."

"What could have agitated them so?"

"The storm might have caused it, Sire." Banebolt frowned. "However...it does seem passing strange."

Tal needed no more. Already he turned his mount to pass over the herd. Moments later, Banebolt and Bozar followed close on his horse's wings until directly over the stampede.

Tal pointed at an enormous bull at the head of the cattle's mad rush. "Look!" he cried.

Banebolt spit an oath when he spotted what the young prince pointed at—the bull's flayed and mutilated neck and back. "Those wounds could not have been caused by any normal creature."

Bozar gestured at a crossbow bolt protruding from the herd bull's rump. "Nor could that shaft have been shot by any *creature* other than one with two legs."

Heart racing, Tal clamped a hand on his sword hilt. "How much farther to the farmstead?"

"Just a few leagues, Sire," Banebolt replied.

"Then we must make haste."

With a shout, Tal urged his mount on, and mighty wings beat the air. The storm horse surged and turned into the blustery wind and sheeting rain.

Tal reached up and fingered his lodestone beads, a savage smile on his face.

I can't wait to see how many I will add tonight.

CHAPTER 17

"LET ME SHOW YOU SOMETHING."

Mr. Finkle gestured, and Mona followed him to the fountain. A trio of catch basins composed the fountain, with the smallest at the top and largest at the bottom. Water burbled merrily as it cascaded from bowl to bowl and into a circular, brick-lined basin. Sunlight glinted off coins tossed into the shallow pool.

Mr. Finkle snapped his fingers. "Observe."

The bright sunshine dimmed, and evening fell. The fountain collapsed, each tier melting like candle wax until only the basin remained. The water within formed a smooth, quiet pool. The coins moved, their glimmering shapes flowing like quicksilver. Within moments, the still water resembled a giant pinwheel galaxy, its billions of stars displayed with a warm luminescence.

Mr. Finkle pointed to a star which flared brighter than the others. "The Earth's solar system. As you can see, it is located on one of the outer spiral arms of the Milky Way Galaxy."

He motioned again, and another star flared, this time on a band of stars opposite the other side of the galaxy from Earth.

"The solar system of Meredith, a planet the virtual twin of Earth. It's sun, axial tilt, rotational speed, and size and mass are remarkably similar. A day is 28 hours in length, and a year is composed of 350 days."

Mr. Finkle turned to face Mona. "So, what do you think of Meredith?"

"Um, I guess it sounds a lot like here."

"Quite similar. In fact, one could say Meredith is a parallel planet located in a parallel solar system. There *is* one very important difference, however."

He tapped the side of his nose. "Do you know what that difference is?"

Mona shrugged and shook her head. *It feels like I'm back at class in school.*

A wide smile creased Mr. Finkle's face. "Meredith is a planet of *magic*!

Mona studied Mr. Finkle. *He can't be serious.* Finally, she asked, "Magic? You mean like pulling a rabbit out of a hat?'

The angel sniffed. "Of course not. I mean the kind of magic you read about in fairy tales where force and matter are manipulated, not some parlor trick."

Mona shook her head. "I don't believe you. Everybody knows there's no such thing as *real* magic."

Mr. Finkle frowned. "Well, I would think my very presence and all you have seen me do are proof enough *ordinary* has been thrown out the window...but so be it. Since you need more convincing—"

He stepped up onto the elevated brick that circled the fountain's pool of water. The angel held out his hand. "Let's go."

After a moment's hesitation, Mona grasped Mr. Finkle's hand. He pulled her up to join him at the water's edge.

"When I count to three, we will both step into the water. Do *not* let go of my hand." Mona nodded and tightened her grip.

"One, two, three, *go!*"

With a deep breath, she stepped into the shallow water.

And kept going.

Rather than the cement floor of the basin, they both continued to fall as if a chasm opened beneath their feet. Mona screamed and clutched Mr. Finkle's hand with desperate abandon. Within seconds, the stars in their millions and billions flashed by in a kaleidoscope of winking brilliance to merge into a solid mass of light. Her scream ebbed away, and Mona gazed in wonder at the cosmos.

After a few moments, the cosmic display rushed by at a slower pace. Soon, individual stars reappeared. One in particular grew larger and larger. As they drew nearer, the star grew into a yellow sun. Geysers of superhot plasma boiled from the gaseous surface as they whizzed by. Planets, some gas giants, others little more than spherical, pock-marked asteroids, soon appeared.

One planet, different from the rest, appeared before them. Blue oceans covered the surface, broken only by large land masses, while white clouds scudded across the lower reaches of its atmosphere.

Mona gasped. *It looks like Earth…except the continents are different shapes!*

The parallel Earth rushed toward them as they continued to travel at breakneck speed. A prickle of concern started to tingle down Mona's spine. Seconds later, they streaked into the atmosphere, the wind whistling by like a hurricane. A land mass appeared, but they flashed toward it so quickly, Mona only caught a glimpse of the countryside. It revealed a verdant land of rivers, lakes, and forests, with plains, valleys, and mountains.

The solid surface rushed to meet them, and with impact imminent, Mona screamed again and clawed at Mr. Finkle. With a twitch of his hand, they stopped and hung motionless in the air.

"We have arrived," Mr. Finkle announced.

"Welcome to Meredith, Mona."

CHAPTER 18

"ARE YOUR MEN IN POSITION?" RAZOR ASKED.

"We have the house, barn, and outbuildings surrounded, *Horde* Leader," Colley replied.

"Good! It seems we have surprised them, despite every effort to alert the entire countryside."

Motioning a Dark Brother forward, Razor asked, "What of the defenses?"

No family within a hundred leagues of the Veil would dare live in any house or structure not warded with some sort of defensive magic…a fact Razor had long been aware of.

The Dark brother took a pouch from within the folds of his robes, opened the bag, and took out a handful of what appeared to be sand. The sorcerer tossed the grit into the air and whispered words of power. A bright, ambient light glowed from the powder, and it streaked toward the farm's structures. Moments later, various areas on the farmhouse and outbuildings glowed blue.

"The farmhouse is well-warded, *Horde* Leader. However, there are no wards on the barn and only a few on the other structures I can detect. In addition, strangle vine has been planted around the house."

"Excellent! You will, of course, be able to disable the wards?"

The Dark Brother hesitated. "With time we should be able to, *Horde* leader."

Razor's expression darkened. He had tolerated the mage's excuses long enough.

"I see. Then I suggest you begin as soon as possible. Oh, and *should* you take too long, your ears will join those of your brother sorcerer in the bellies of the shape shifters."

Even with the advantage of charmed night vision, the darkness of the night and blowing rain made it difficult to see. However, Razor could see the Dark Brother's complexion pale.

"It-it will be done, *Horde* leader," he stammered.

A light came from an open door in the farmhouse, and a figure ran out into the storm toward the barn. A piercing scream followed moments later. Razor immediately wheeled his horse around toward the sound. Pinned to the ground by two of the Boarogs, a young girl struggled to free herself. When he drew closer, the looks of her rounded figure revealed her to be not a girl but a young woman. Razor nodded in satisfaction.

The first catch of the night!

The door of the farmhouse opened again. Squeals and grunts erupted from the Boarog, and several hurled spears at the figure silhouetted in the light. The javelins missed badly and thudded into the walls. More of the man-beasts tossed spears as the figure retreated and slammed the door shut.

A commotion erupted next to the farmhouse while the spears still quivered in the wall. A pair of Boarog wandered too close to the farmhouse porch and stepped into a patch of strangle vine planted there. Tendrils flowed up and around the creatures and encircled their bodies. With squeals of fear, they struggled to free themselves. The tendrils constricted, and their bones broke with sharp *snaps*.

The squeals abruptly stopped.

The lifeless eyes of the Boarog bulged from their heads, tongues protruding from their mouths. The strangle vine shuddered and dropped the crushed bodies to the ground.

Razor's nostrils flared. "Idiots!" he roared. "Who gave the

order to attack?"

The raid leader flung himself off his horse and tossed the reins to a nearby subordinate. He ignored the pair of dead Boarog at his feet and raged, "We could have captured the whole family without a struggle. Now they are warned!"

Razor hurried over to the girl, who still struggled to free herself from the grasp of the beast men.

"Hold her up," he ordered. "And bring a lamp. I want her family to see this!"

Lifted to her feet, the girl faced the *horde* leader. He nodded with approval at the fear reflected in her eyes. He grunted and motioned the Boarog to turn her around to face the farmhouse.

"Call out."

In reply, the girl twisted and spat in his face. Casually, Razor backhanded her. Gasping in pain, the young woman remained silent.

"Call out to your family," he repeated. He received nothing but a glower.

Razor sighed and motioned to the beastly creatures. They pulled the girl's rain slicker off to leave her shivering in the deluge.

Once again, he demanded, "Call out."

The girl remained silent and stood dripping in the downpour. Impatient, Razor pulled her close and asked, "What is your name?"

"El-Ellie," she stammered.

"Well, Ellie, you can either obey me and cry out, or I'll force you to do it another way."

He motioned to the Boarog. They held her roughly while the raid leader turned to face the girl. Smiling, he fondled her breasts. She whimpered and closed her eyes.

The *horde* leader laughed. "Oh, we haven't got to the best

part yet."

He straightened and grasped the front of the girl's blouse. With a sharp motion, he wrenched it off to expose her bodice. His captive gasped, breasts heaving.

"*Appeal to your family!*" Razor snarled.

Lips trembling, tears mixed with rain coursed down the girl's cheeks. Despite her terror, she remained mute. A small part of Razor admired her courage, but admiration or not, he had a job to do.

He jerked his dagger from its sheath, then grasped the young woman's bodice and quickly sawed off the straps. He jerked the bodice free and threw it into the mud. Her breath came out in explosive gasps as her breasts fell free. Razor took a moment to admire the girl's full bosom, while his men hooted in appreciation at the sight. The Boarog also joined in, their grunts filling the wet air.

Razor let the commotion continue for a few moments, then chopped his hand. The raiders fell silent. Merciless eyes bored into the girl. "Cry out. Appeal to your family."

Ellie struggled to cover herself, eyes filled with tears of fear and shame. "Pl-please," she whispered.

"You can end all this by simply calling out to your family."

"I-I can't. Please, just take me and leave."

"Oh, I certainly plan to do that. But I'm afraid I'll need more from this raid tonight than a single girl. *Now, cry out!*" Razor barked.

"No!" Ellie shrieked. "I won't do it!"

"Suit yourself. A pity."

Razor used his dagger to slowly trace an imaginary line from her flat belly to her breasts. Ellie redoubled her futile struggle, but the Boarog held her firmly. The knife stopped at the vein pulsing in her neck.

Razor smiled. "Careful. My blade might slip."

Ellie sobbed and ceased to struggle. Razor repeated the dagger's path, the flat of the blade dragged across the length of her body. Finally, the raid leader held the sharp knife-edge before her eyes. He moved it side to side, her eyes, wide as saucers, following the dagger's path.

"Do you know what they call me?" Trembling, Ellie shook her head.

"I have an interesting nickname due to some indiscretions in my youth. I am called *Razor* due to the keenness of my knife."

Razor moved the dagger so that light from the lantern reflected off the blade. "Would you like for me to demonstrate it on you?"

Ellie shook her head vigorously. The raid leader clutched his captive's hand and placed the sharp edge below the first digit of her little finger.

"I'll start with this, then carve off one piece at a time. When I'm finished, I'll move on to the next finger." He grabbed her hair and pulled her face inches from his. "Now, once I begin, I like to finish the job I've started. It will be too late to do as I asked then, because your screams will already be so loud, you'll be heard for leagues...*I guarantee it.*"

He gave her hair a last painful jerk. *"Now cry out!"* He moved the blade and pantomimed a sawing motion. Ellie's shrieks echoed in raw, full-throated panic.

Razor smiled in satisfaction. *Nothing like a good scream to capture a family's attention.*

He turned to face the farmhouse and waited.

CHAPTER 19

ONA WAITED FOR HER HEART TO STOP JACKHAMMERING.

"This-this is Meredith?" she managed to blurt.

Mr. Finkle nodded. He flicked his hand, and once again they hurtled through the air. A mountain range rushed to meet them, and they rose effortlessly over its jagged, snowcapped peaks. They descended to the other side, where Mona discovered a spacious body of water surrounded on three sides by the lower reaches of the mountain. A river emptied from the deep aquamarine blue of the lake, and flowed past a large city situated on the water's edge. An island sprouted from the middle of the lake and glittered like a jewel.

The city spread throughout a series of foothills, with trees, flowers, and colorful houses sprawled throughout its expanse. A long bridge or causeway connected the islet to the city.

They drifted lower, and a much clearer view of the island appeared. A castle occupied the middle of the isle. Elegant turrets stretched skyward from the stronghold, while pennants flapped from the ramparts. Squares of quarried rock formed the battlements, a soft ambient blue glowing from the dressed stone.

Cobbled service roads led from gates inset into the thick walls. Gardens, trees, flowers, and fountains filled the grounds around the castle. The sun, low in the horizon, cast golden rays across the island and the fortress-citadel resting upon it. Pinnacled turrets with banners fluttering, combined with the warm light to form a scene that reminded Mona of the opening credits of a

Disney movie.

"It's beautiful," she breathed.

"What you are looking at is Lodestone Palace, the ancestral home to the kings and queens of Meredith," Mr. Finkle said. "The metropolis you saw earlier is Meredith City, which is the capital of the Empire."

"Come. Let's meet some citizens."

Once again, they rocketed through the air. The city and palace rapidly shrank from view, which left Mona with a sense of disappointment. *It is so lovely.* What would it be like to stroll across the castle grounds or perhaps, throw a pebble into the lake and watch the ripples spread across the water's placid surface?

Soon, they were over farmland, the familiar quilt-patch sections of crops clearly visible from their birds-eye view. Mr. Finkle zeroed in on a farmhouse, and as they drew closer, Mona saw a number of figures moving about. They stopped in the air, and Mona got a clear view of the inhabitants. Her mouth dropped open.

They looked ordinary—just like regular humans!

A woman sat in a chair on the porch mending what appeared to be a pair of pants, while two small children, a boy and a girl, played at her feet. A man strolled in from the barn, a handful of bulbous plants like beets or potatoes clutched in one hand. He placed them in a basket next to the woman, then took a colorful kerchief and wiped his face. Soon, they all filed into the farmstead.

Mr. Finkle eyed Mona. "You look disappointed. What did you expect?"

Mona squirmed. "Ah, I don't know. Maybe something with tentacles or a big head with a bulging braincase? The last thing I expected to see is *normal* people."

A dry chuckle erupted from the angel. "Appearances can be

deceiving. Meredith and its people are anything but *normal*. Let's go."

This time, a snap of Mr. Finkle's fingers transported them instantly to another location, where they hung suspended in midair. Curious, Mona looked around. Below them lay a pastoral scene of thick grasses and scattered colonies of colorful wildflowers. A series of low, rolling hills stretched before them into the horizon. Thick stands of hardwood trees stood interspersed across the landscape, broken here and there by fields like the one beneath their feet.

Slowly, they descended until, with a gentle *bump*, Mona's feet touched solid ground. The air was alive with the clicks and buzzes of insects, while birds whistled and chirped from their perches in the dense stands of trees and bushes.

Mona looked around, the scene similar to the piney woods in East Texas where she had grown up. "This looks rather...*ordinary*."

"Yes, it does," Mr. Finkle answered. "But as I indicated earlier, things aren't always how they appear. For example, take a few steps forward and reach out."

Puzzled, Mona did as he asked. She stretched out her fingers—until stopped by an invisible barrier. With a yelp, she jumped back, hand clutched to her chest.

"Wh-what happened?"

With a grim smile, Mr. Finkle replied, "What you felt is called the Veil. Essentially a wall of magic, it has partitioned a huge territory from the Empire of Meredith. An object known as the *orb* controls it. This small, spherical object can fit in the palm of your hand, and it can open portals—doorways if you will—through the enchanted barrier. Those who possess this magical Artifact control passage through the Veil."

Mona blinked. *A wall of magic?*

Hesitant, she took a step forward, arms stretched before her like a blind man. Her hands again came in contact with the invisible barrier, and she moved them up and down. The barrier, smooth and seamless, had the consistency of glass. She decided to test it and pushed hard.

The effort produced no noticeable effect.

The Veil's surface did not bend or give. Face pressed forward just inches from where her hands rested on the magical wall, Mona strained to see anything that would give evidence of the barrier right there in front of her.

Nothing. She could see nothing.

On the other side, leaves waved in the gentle breeze, and birds flew through the air. Mona could hear the normal cacophony of animal and insect sounds traveling unimpeded through the Veil.

Mystified, Mona turned to Mr. Finkle. "You say this Veil is a *wall* or barrier, yet I can see everything on the other side. I feel the wind on my face, and I can even hear the birds and insects. A wall would block all of this."

"Ah, yes, but you see, this is no *normal* barrier. As I said, it is a creation of magic. Among the Veil's unique characteristics are that soulless creatures and inorganic matter—wind, rain, birds, and other animals, for instance—pass freely through."

Mona chewed on her lip while she absorbed this information. "Soooo—humans, like those on Meredith—cannot pass through the Veil unless this Orb thing is used?"

"Correct."

Brow creased, Mona tried to process everything Mr. Finkle revealed about the enchanted boundary. Her senses seemed to contradict themselves. Her eyes could see no obstruction, her ears heard normal animal and insect sounds with no impediment, and her skin felt the soft caress of the breeze passing unhindered through the enchanted barrier. Yet her hands felt a solid, unyielding surface, like a wall of poured concrete. A sudden thought struck her.

"What about the people within this wall? What if they want, you know, to get out and go someplace else?"

Mr. Finkle shook his head. "Ah, yes. What indeed, Mona. What happens to them?" Brushing grass burrs from his pants, Mr. Finkle stepped next to Mona and grasped her hand.

"Come. It's time to go home."

CHAPTER 20

THROUGH A WELL-CONCEALED EYE SLIT IN A SECOND STORY ROOM OF the farmhouse, Levi witnessed the brutalization of his daughter.

Numb, his heart pounded in his throat, and hot tears ran down his face. He racked his brain but could think of no way to save Ellie which didn't put the rest of his family at risk. These thoughts competed with worry about Caleb and Samuel in the barn. *What happened to them? Were they safe? How long before they too were discovered?*

It all happened so fast! Ellie left the house running for the barn, and the next minute, her screams filled the air. When he rushed out the door, a trio of spears greeted him, the shafts sprouting from the walls like mushrooms after a rain. He retreated quickly back inside, bolted the door, and secured the house. Then he sent Constance, wide-eyed and weeping, upstairs. He wouldn't let her look outside, nor answer repeated pleas to tell her what was happening to Ellie and the boys.

He prayed she followed his last words, "Bolt the door and do not open it for anyone but me!"

Levi crossed the room to a closet, opened the door to reveal several crossbows secured to pegs on the wall. He retrieved one, along with a quiver of bolts, and went back to the spy hole.

He leaned against the solid wall, eyes closed. *"Pulpit is a Monk of the White Order. Caleb and Samuel are in safe hands. If anyone can get them out of this, he can,"* he mumbled to the air.

He couldn't bring himself to offer such false assurance for Ellie.

If the raiders took her through the Veil, horrors greater than death awaited her there. He couldn't let that happen. Death would be a merciful alternative.

Levi stared at the crossbow, comprehension of what he must do dawning on him. *"No!"* he screamed. He threw the weapon across the room, where it clattered onto the floor. Head in his hands, he sobbed.

His beautiful little girl captured by these monsters…and in time, would herself be transformed into a monster. This couldn't happen. No matter what, it must not be allowed to happen.

Ellie's scream ripped Levi from his thoughts. He knew what he had to do. On unsteady feet, he retrieved the weapon.

He pushed open the eye slit and saw his daughter stripped naked to the waist, a large raider holding a knife to her.

Levi cranked the crossbow and loaded a bolt in it. Sliding the spy hole wider, he squinted and centered the shaft onto Ellie's chest. Tears filled his eyes, and he shook uncontrollably. Forced to stop, the dairy farmer wiped his hands on his shirt and took aim again. Try as he might, he couldn't pull the trigger. Deep ragged breaths filled his lungs.

He sighted the weapon again.

Images came unbidden to his mind while he tried to aim. *Ellie as a baby laughing and gurgling. Ellie, a young girl in a new dress Constance made for her. She had been so proud of that dress.* Levi shook his head and tried to clear his mind. Rage began to creep into his thoughts. *The Veil raiders would pay for what they were doing to his daughter—for the decision they forced him to make!*

Hatred clouded his thoughts until he could stand it no longer. With a scream of fury, he took aim and fired. The bolt flew straight and true to bury itself in the neck of one of the beast-men holding

Ellie. The foul creature slumped to the ground, blood pumping from its wound.

The crossbow slipped from Levi's hand and dropped to the floor. "I couldn't do it," he whispered. "I just couldn't do it." The thud of spears and arrows thudded into the wall. He ignored them and sat, head down, tears forming a puddle by his feet.

The rain drummed against the roof, and the storm raged into the night.

In the barn, Pulpit gave Caleb last-minute instructions.

His worst fears materialized when a large force of Veil raiders surrounded the barn and farmhouse. He was profoundly glad the noise of the storm dampened most of Ellie's screaming. Had Caleb clearly heard his sister's desperate cries, he would have been forced to knock the boy out to prevent him from going to her aid.

"You know where the Watch Tower is. Once you and Samuel crawl out of the drainage pipe, make for it straightaway. You know what to do once you get there?"

Caleb nodded. Everyone living in the Veil zone, old and young alike, knew what to do when raiders attacked, and all knew how to activate a Watch Tower.

"Good. The fastest way to get there is to follow the Kings Road, which parallels the Watch Tower. The raiders will be reluctant to show themselves on an open thoroughfare, but you can be sure they will have someone watching it. Stay close to the road but stay off of it and *out of sight*."

With that, Pulpit took his *haloub* and twisted its knobby head counterclockwise. The baton immediately telescoped to a staff six hands in length. A *hum* pulsed from the magical Artifact. The monk held it over the heavy grate and touched the staff's tip against the grill. Thick, rusty screws holding the grate in place rattled and shook. A tortured screech filled the air, and the screws began to turn. The protesting bolts continued to twist and then popped out of the grill. Pulpit lifted the heavy grate and placed it beside the now open drain pipe.

Caleb looked at the dark hole and frowned. "I don't know. It looks awfully small, even for Samuel. I don't think I'll be able to crawl through it."

"Don't worry," the monk assured him. "I am going to make you, shall we say, *extra slippery*. You and Samuel will have no problem moving through it and out into the ditch."

"What about you? You can't stay here. The raiders will kill you if they find you."

"Don't worry about me…and I don't plan on being killed. I'll follow you eventually, after I slow down any pursuit."

Samuel, silent the entire time Pulpit gave Caleb instructions, walked up to the monk and put his small hand in his.

"Do you promise?" he asked, eyes wide. "Do you promise you will follow and not get killed?"

Pulpit smiled at the boy, then swept him up in his arms. "I promise, Little Man. Besides, we still have Juniper and her calf to look after, don't we?" Samuel nodded, lower lip trembling. The monk gave the little boy a final squeeze and lowered him back to the ground.

"You go first and lead the way. When you get to the end of the drainage pipe, take a peek to make sure there are no raiders around, okay?"

Samuel nodded, knuckling tears from his eyes. Pulpit touched the boy on the head, shoulders, and feet with the *haloub*. A light shimmered and enveloped his small body. The light cascaded over the boy's skin, like the march of thousands of crawling ants. Within seconds, the glow disappeared, and Pulpit repeated the process with Caleb.

"The spell is temporary and will last only a quarter hour. Any longer, the Veil mages will immediately sense it and trace the path of your escape. Once the spell dissipates, even a skilled mage will have difficulty following the trail of magic. No doubt, they will detect the magic anyway, but this way buys us time."

The monk dropped to his knees and pushed the bright tip of his staff into the dark opening. He studied the drain pipe, the air ripe with the reek of cow feces and urine. The cylinder formed an elbow before disappearing into the darkness. He nodded.

"Down you go," the monk said and lowered Samuel into the dank opening. The little boy dropped to the bottom of the drain and moved easily about.

Samuel looked up, a grin on his face. "Hey, this is easy!"

The monk sighed in relief. "Good, Little Man. Be sure to wait for your brother. He'll be right behind you." He turned to Caleb and lowered him through the opening.

Caleb slipped down into the drainage pipe. He reached the bottom and looked up at Pulpit. "Remember—you promised."

The monk knelt beside the opening and grinned. "I am a Monk of the Order of the White. I would be defrocked and banned from the Order if I broke a vow. Besides, I plan to set some diversions for these children of darkness before I follow after you." A grave expression replaced the grin. "Make haste for the Watch Tower. Your life and that of others may depend upon it."

"I will not fail, Pulpit, I swear it!" The monk nodded, reassured by the determined set of the boy's jaw. "I'll see you at the Watch Tower." Caleb slithered down into the drain and joined his brother.

Pulpit pushed the *haloub* down as far as he could into the dim opening. The light revealed both brothers scuttling away. Eventually their images faded, and they were completely swallowed in darkness.

CHAPTER 21

THE TRIP BACK SEEMED MUCH QUICKER, AND MONA WATCHED WITH regret as Meredith's blue sphere receded to become lost within the stygian blackness of space. Moments later, she found herself on the park bench, blinking in the bright sunlight.

"What do you think of Meredith?"

Mona spied Mr. Finkle next to her, head cocked. His pale-blue eyes bored through her—as if her response would be sifted and weighed on a scale that could have only one acceptable answer. In a flash, all the disparate pieces came together. An almost audible *click* resounded in Mona's mind, and she experienced a clarity of what this was all about.

I am being chosen. But for what?

A current of energy—comprising equal parts fear and adrenaline—coursed up her spine.

"A be-beautiful place. Kinda like Earth," Mona stammered. Heart pounding, she stood and faced the angel. "Look, I think I know where you are going with this, but you have the wrong person. I've already told you I don't have any special abilities or talents. There's a reason I'm always the last person picked for a team. I just want to go home and back to Joe."

Mr. Finkle wiggled his finger. "I couldn't disagree more. In fact, you are the *perfect* choice for what I have in mind."

Mona opened her mouth, but the angel quickly raised a hand to forestall any comment. "Why did you give the money back? Why didn't you keep the one hundred dollars?"

The question took Mona by surprise, and it took a moment to gather her wits. "I don't know. Why are—"

"Answer the question, Mona. *Why* did you give the money back to Brother Bill?"

His persistence caused images to flood into her mind, like some internal dam had broken. The Operation Christmas Child ministry provided a video that included pictures of small children, some in rags, some naked, and some displaying obvious signs of disease and malnutrition. These depictions scrolled through her mind's eye. Yet the smiles on their faces while they held simple toys and commodities—the things she and everyone else took for granted—could light up an entire room.

Other images, unbidden, appeared in her mind. In her World Geography class, the teacher played a YouTube video which displayed a gigantic dump in the Philippine city of Manila. In the clip, ragged families lived on the edge of a massive landfill and scoured the refuse for anything of value they could find and sell. Filthy scarves were tied around their faces to block the incredible stench arising from garbage rotting in the tropical heat. As they moved about, clouds of flies were disturbed in numbers so vast, when they rose into the air, they blackened the sky.

Tears leaked from Mona's eyes. "I always thought my life is so unfair. I mean, look at me. I'm scrawny and plain. I struggle to make B's in school, so it's not like I can fall back on my brains. I'm not popular and don't have many friends, so I guess my sparkling personality can be marked off the list too. My brother has been in a wheelchair since he was a baby, and we haven't seen our parents in years—I don't even know if they are still alive."

Mona hung her head. "I spend most of my life being invisible," she whispered. "*Nobody sees me.* At school, I can walk into and out of a room, and my classmates act like I'm not even there. And you know why?" A sob escaped from her lips. "Because I'm so insignificant I'm not even worth a second glance. The *only* time I'm noticed is when I provide a show for Lady Anne and her friends."

Mona collapsed on the bench and buried her face in her hands. Mr. Finkle remained silent, his face creased in sadness.

Finally, Mona regained enough of her composure to sit up. Sniffling, she knuckled her eyes with the back of her hand. "You picked the wrong person. Believe me, I'm the last person on Earth anyone would want."

The angel shook his head. "Again, I disagree. Your life is valued in ways you cannot begin to comprehend or measure."

Mr. Finkle positioned himself to gaze directly into her eyes. "And you still haven't answered the question. Why not keep the money? What possible reason could you have to give it back?"

Mona couldn't hold his stare and dropped her eyes. "When I first saw the YouTube video of those poor families in the Philippines, it actually gave my ego a boost. To know there are people worse off than me in the world—it gave me a kind of perverse comfort to know I wasn't at the bottom of the pile."

Tears returned to her eyes. "Can you imagine how low someone has to sink to feel such a thing? To *think* that way? And to see those smiling children in the ministry video holding Dollar Store items like they were priceless jewels? How I could feel anything but compassion for *anyone* suffering in such staggering poverty— it makes me so sick to my stomach, I want to throw up every time I think about it."

Mona sat up and managed to take a deep breath. "So to answer your question, I gave the money back because it could bring some happiness and a little hope into the world. I'd like to say it came entirely from my heart, but to be honest, I did it to rid myself of guilt—to feel better about myself."

With a harsh laugh, Mona crossed her arms. "Not exactly

hero material, huh, Mr. Finkle? That's why you have the wrong person."

With a sigh, her angel leaned back. "You see yourself—you *measure* yourself—through the eyes of the world. But what you don't see, and what I recognize quite clearly, is your compassion and fortitude. You consider your life meaningless, but you don't realize how rare it is to think of others—and not just yourself."

He stood and placed a hand on her shoulder. "You've had a hard life and, in its course, been forced to suffer pain and humiliation. One might even say you have been tried through a crucible of fire. But despite your perceptions, here you are still in one piece...and these experiences have only served to purify and make you stronger."

"I don't feel stronger," Mona sniffled.

With a wry smile, Mr. Finkle put his arm around Mona.

"Strength is often measured in very different terms. In the heat of battle, why do some men lose courage and flee while others, facing certain death, stay and fight? What causes someone to risk their own life to jump into a raging river and attempt to save someone who is drowning? You see, no one can be certain of their reaction until a situation presents itself."

Mr. Finkle tapped his forehead. "However, I think there are ways to tell. I believe it is in the small things that tell volumes about character and heart...like giving back money to enrich the lives of a few impoverished children."

Mr. Finkle took Mona's hand and placed it on her chest. "You have the heart of a lion, the capacity of which you have barely begun to scratch. I see this with absolute clarity—even if you do not."

The angel's words soothed Mona's raw emotions. For the first time, a spark, a tiny ray of hope, flared in her heart.

"What if you could make a difference which affects not just a handful of children, but the lives of hundreds of thousands, if not millions, of people?"

Mona's hands flew to her mouth. *He must be joking.* But when she glanced at him, no humor or flippancy appeared in his expression.

He's serious!

Again, the connections suddenly snapped together—the flying trip to Meredith and to the invisible barrier called the Veil—none of it coincidental but designed to help Mona make a decision and to answer the very question he asked now.

"This is about Meredith, isn't it? It's about the magical wall and the people who are trapped behind it, right?

Mr. Finkle inclined his head.

"But what I don't understand is, *why me?* There must be others who would be better choices for this-this—*whatever* you have in mind."

"If that were so, we wouldn't be having this conversation."

"This is crazy! I need to know more—"

Mr. Finkle raised his hands to cut her off. "I can tell you no more other than what you have already surmised. You have been chosen for this task, and you must freely accept—or reject it—based on what has been revealed to you. To say more would unduly influence your choice."

"You mean, if I knew more, I wouldn't just say no, I'd say *hell* no!"

Her angel shrugged. "If it were so simple and easy, I would have told you. But nothing about your choice is simple. I *can* tell you that."

Mr. Finkle folded his arms. "I told you Meredith was the stuff dreams were made of. But with dreams there are also horrors. On Meredith, beauty and wonder exist that even your most fervent imagination can scarce comprehend. There also exists evil of such black malevolency, your worst nightmares would seem pleasant experiences in comparison."

An emphatic *no* hovered on her lips. But…what if he knew something she didn't? What if she, Mona Parker, despite all evidence to the contrary, contained within her something which made her special? Something that set her apart?

Her thoughts drifted back to Meredith and the beauty of Lodestone Castle. A tug appeared in her heart as if, somehow, this was meant to be. She shook her head to dissuade the thought, but all it accomplished was to make the feeling more acute.

"What happens if I say no?"

Lips pressed tight, Mr. Finkle replied, "You go back to your old life. Nothing changes."

Nothing changes.

The same miserable existence.

The more Mona thought about it, the more it left a bitter taste in her mouth.

"What if I say yes?"

For the first time Mr. Finkle hesitated. Finally, he said, "Then you leave your old life to start a new one. I wish I could tell you more, but I have been forbidden. However, make no mistake. Your life *will* be placed in danger. There *are* no assurances I can give you."

Mona nodded. "But you said I could make a difference. Did you mean it?"

Mr. Finkle took a step toward Mona and pulled her to her feet. "Oh, most assuredly. On that you can be certain."

A calm Mona never experienced before descended upon her. Her angel—even though at times rude and disdainful—could offer a warmth and comfort when he wanted to. With great reluctance, she pushed away and looked him in the eye.

"Then I say yes…provided Joe is taken care of." The thought

of not seeing Joe—perhaps ever again—pierced Mona's heart. "Will he be okay?"

"I give you my word. His future is a bright one."

A happiness bloomed within her. Joe would be okay and have a great life to look forward to. Any remaining vestige of doubt in Mona's decision dissipated.

"I'm ready. What happens now?"

No sooner did the words leave her mouth than the park darkened. A sound like a distant wind rustled through the air. Mr. Finkle lost focus as though he were melting right before her eyes. The park and all within it disintegrated. Like wind-driven sand, the remaining particles swirled away. Where the park once stood, billions of stars and galaxies winked in the black void of space.

A great weariness overcame Mona, and her eyelids grew heavy. Moments before she could no longer hold them open, a voice cut through the void with bell-like clarity.

"Remember what lies within you is far greater than what lies on the outside. Trust your heart, Mona, and it will guide you through the doubts and dangers to come. Always trust your heart…"

Darkness overtook her, and Mona slept.

CHAPTER 22

RAZOR WATCHED THE BOAROG GO DOWN WITH THE BOLT IN ITS throat as dispassionately as he might observe a bug being stepped on. Not moving an inch, he stood unconcerned he might be the next target.

"Archers!" he barked. Arrows flew toward the direction of the eye slit the bolt came from. He sheathed his dagger and roughly pulled the girl toward him.

Face inches from the girl's nose, he growled, "It seems we will have to do this the hard way. Bind her!" he ordered and shoved her back to the Boarog. While contemplating his next move, a Dark Brother approached him.

"*Horde* Leader. We have detected the use of an enchantment from within the barn."

"What strength?" All magic left a scent because it always left residue. This signature could be used to identify not only how powerful the magic, but how formidable the user was. *Know your enemy*—the first of many hard lessons the veteran raider learned during his early forays through the Veil, and one he never forgot.

The Dark Brother hesitated. "It-it is difficult to say, *Horde* Leader."

The veteran raider took a step toward the sorcerer, a black look on his face.

"Bu-but, after consulting with my fellow Brothers, we believe it is magic associated with a Monk of the White Order," the mage added hastily.

Razor pursed his lips. *Interesting.* The White Monks were not uncommon on the Veil. Although fierce fighters and fanatic in their pursuit to extinguish anything that issued from the Veil, the threat of a single monk hardly ranked as a matter of concern. Of course, he didn't entirely trust the judgment of the fool of a Dark Brother, but if it was their best guess, so be it.

However, he would take no chances.

He signaled to the cowled magus. "Send the ogres to break into the barn. Then I want the wards nullified on the farmhouse." Bowing, the Dark Brother hurried off with the ogres in tow. Razor remounted and waited.

Boom! Boom!

The rain-filled night reverberated with the sound of massive clubs punishing the shuttered doors. Tendons on trunk-sized arms stood in sharp relief, while each ogre took a turn pounding away. Rather than shattering into a thousand splinters, however, the clubs bounced off the thick wood. The ogres' frustrated growls filled the air.

With an oath, the raid leader trotted over and glared down at the sorcerer. "What's wrong now? You said no ward existed on this outbuilding!"

"Something is wrong, *Horde* Leader," the Dark Brother answered. "We should have broken through by now. The door must have been reinforced by the monk inside."

Razor bent low in the saddle and grabbed a fistful of the mage's robe. "Then do something about it!" he snarled.

Pale, the Dark Brother gibbered, "We-we will, *Horde* Leader. It will ju-just take a little more time."

The veteran raider released his grip, and the Dark Brother scuttled back to the ogres. The massive creatures redoubled their efforts with vicious determination.

The *crack* of enormous clubs hammering wood resumed.

Inside the barn, Pulpit smiled in satisfaction.

He reinforced the barn doors with a simple spell the Veil mages could easily unravel. Yet, from the sounds of it, they were going to do it the hard way by beating the entrance to pieces. Even with the spell to reinforce the doors' integrity, they would not hold for long. However, it did buy Caleb and Samuel precious time to escape to the nearest Watch Tower. By the time the boards were reduced to kindling, the two brothers would be well on their way. No sooner did this thought flash through his mind, when a fissure appeared through the broken planks.

Time to leave.

He ran to the drain and held the *haloub* high above him. He rolled the staff back and forth in his hands, a cascade of sparkling light erupting from its tip to fall about his head and shoulders. It tickled and itched and a chuckle escaped his lips. Slowly, his image became ethereal and vaporous. Pulpit's ghost image floated toward the dank opening and sank into the drain.

The monk paused and pointed his wraithlike *haloub* at the heavy grate. The grill rose silently, rotated, and positioned itself over the drain. With a *clank*, it dropped onto the hole. Screws floated over to the grate, sank, and with a raspy squealing, spun to refasten the metal grill back into place. Pulpit nodded before he flowed down the culvert and to the mouth of the drainage ditch.

Try figuring this one out, you dark-hearted bastards.

Razor waited impatiently while the ogres continued to batter the thick boards. After what seemed an hour but actually took less than half that, the doors finally fell inward with a *crash*. The ogres, bent over from their exertions, gulped in great lungsful of air.

The raid leader signaled for a squad of Boarog to move forward, while the Dark Brothers stood ready for any magical surprises. When nothing happened, he ordered a complete search. The inspection revealed an empty building. The veteran raider ground his teeth and gestured to the sorcerers who stood nearby, perplexed.

"There was someone in this barn, and I want to know how they got out without being spotted!" The mages bobbed their heads and attempted to trace the magic. While they worked, Colley gestured for Razor to follow him to the milking area of the barn.

His second-in-command pointed at the floor. "Look. There are fresh scratches on the grate and screws. In addition, the floor around the drain has been disturbed."

A feral grin split Razor's face. "You have sharp eyes...and you've saved us a great deal of time. Over here!" he roared at the Dark Brothers still poking about the other side of the dairy.

When they arrived, he asked, "Is this the bolt hole?" The mages scurried around the grille mumbling to themselves. Finally, they conferenced and the boldest of them cautiously approached Razor.

"It smells of magic, *Horde* Leader. The monk, and possibly others, have used this sewer to escape."

"How? It appears too small for even a child."

The Dark Brother shrugged. "There are spells to affect size and space that can ease passage through tight areas. Undoubtedly, the monk was clever enough to use one of them."

Razor mulled this over. In his experience, Monks of the White Order did not flee from Veil marauders but sought them out... usually with deadly consequences. To escape was not an option— unless they had a higher priority. When his raiders attacked, there might have been others with the monk. A thought suddenly occurred to him.

"Colley, bring me the map!" His lieutenant dug a waterproof map from a pouch at his belt and handed it to the *Horde* Leader. A quick perusal of the chart confirmed his worst fears.

He swore. "They are making for the Watch Tower five leagues southeast of here!"

Razor barked orders. "Winston, take a squad of horsemen and make for the Kings Road. It is the most direct route to the Watch Tower. The cursed monk is protecting someone, and I am certain he will use it. Cut them off before they get there!"

He pointed at the Leash Master. "You! Release a shape shifter to hunt them down. I want them dead!" Finally, he gestured to the other Dark Brothers. "I want one of the ogres to follow behind on the Kings Road. The Monk may double back to throw off the pursuit. If so, I want him and whoever is with him to find an unpleasant surprise awaiting them."

Winston cleared his throat. "I understand killing the monk, but if we can capture his charges, shouldn't we take them alive?"

A reasonable question, and if this raid were taking place under reasonable circumstances, Razor would have said yes. Healthy captives, after all, were their stock in trade. However, nothing on this night had gone according to plan—just one disastrous incident after another.

Red-hot anger boiled deep within him. "No," he growled. "Kill them. Kill them all."

Colley waited until the horsemen galloped off, followed closely by the werewolf and ogre. "What do we do now?" he asked.

"Give orders to depart and head for our rendezvous point," Razor replied.

"We are headed home."

CHAPTER 23

MONA DRIFTED IN A FOG.

There were no colors to brighten this nether existence—no black or white, only various shadows of gray. Although Mona could *see* in a fashion, she neither felt nor saw her solid physical body, yet she possessed a form of consciousness because she *knew* she was Mona Parker. She still possessed her thoughts and identity. This provided her with no small comfort while she continued her aimless drift. Her thoughts turned to Joe and Brother Bill. *Would they miss her? Would Lady Anne Golightly and Johnny Luna be punished for what they did to her?*

Thaddeus Finkle's wonderful, strange, and even terrible descriptions of Meredith thundered through her mind.

It is the stuff dreams are made of.

With dreams there are also horrors.

On Meredith, there will be beauty and wonder.

You will find evil of such black malevolency that your worst nightmares would seem pleasant experiences in comparison.

However, what Mr. Finkle *didn't* say concerned her the most. He divulged few if any details about what was to come or what would happen to her. More importantly, he gave no clues as to the role she would play. As she continued to drift in the leaden nothingness, she realized this wasn't completely true. He *did* give her one nugget, one simple guide.

Trust your heart. Always trust your heart.

The fog began to swirl faster and faster. Caught up in the

current, she moved toward a large whirlpool made up of the grayish mist. Closer and closer she came to the swirling edge. Suddenly, the vortex grabbed her and drew her into it. She whipped round and round, drawn deeper into the sucking orifice. At some point, she moved so quickly everything that became blurred. Pulled lower, darkness fell about her until it was pitch black.

She panicked. *I'm falling!*

Then...murky emptiness with no beginning and no end.

The deep throb of a headache brought Mona back to consciousness.

Slowly, she tried to open her eyes, but they seemed to be glued shut. This made the pounding even worse. Finally, she cracked open her left eye and after a moment, the right. She paused and tried to focus her vision. The effort set off such a drumbeat of agony, she immediately squeezed them shut. Tears dribbled down Mona's cheeks, while she waited for the pain in her head to subside.

With deep, even breaths so as not to jumpstart the orchestra in her head again, she cautiously tried to open her eyes. She had less trouble this time, and her head hurt only marginally worse than before. Afraid to move, Mona was content to gaze at what lie directly above her.

A canopy of a rich, colorful material hung from posts above her head. With care, she rotated her vision to the left and then the right. She discovered she lay in an enormous bed, a thick quilt pulled up to her chin. The bedstead extended several feet past the end of her toes, the width almost matched by its length. She tilted her chin a fraction to view more of her surroundings, which set off a fresh round of stabbing pain in her skull. She screwed her eyes shut, her breath exploding in hiccups of agony. The pain eventually subsided, and she risked a crack in her eyelids again. Little discomfort accompanied the act, and, emboldened, Mona continued her observations. Songbirds twittered in the distance.

Could there be an open window nearby?

Mona forced herself to remain still, fearful any movement would cause the pain to return. Finally, she gathered her courage and attempted to turn her head. The discomfort that greeted her this time was a subtle ache, not the searing agony she had experienced before. Sunlight bathed one side of the room, although she dared not move her head far enough to spot the source of the sun's rays. A sofa covered in handsome leather sat close to her bed, while richly upholstered chairs and a matched pair of stools stood near the sofa.

Where am I?

Mona twisted to face the other side of the room. Two massive doors stood sentinel some twenty feet across from her. Ten feet in height and filigreed with highly burnished metal, large intricate tapestries hung on the wall beside each door. Paintings of various scenes decorated the wall on either side of the tapestries. A delicate vanity, embossed with precious gems and gold leaf, was located a short distance from the bed.

Mona's curiosity, already piqued, began to gallop.

Her thoughts raced. *Where am I? Definitely not a hospital room.*

While possible she could be in the grips of a vivid hallucination—maybe brought on by the impact with Johnny Luna's car—she didn't think any of this could be a fevered vision.

If true, there could be only one explanation.

This is all real.

Alone, she occupied a strange bed in a strange room filled with furniture which looked like it cost more than Bud and

Elaine's entire house. What's more, something seemed out of kilter about everything. It felt...*alien*. An icy tingle crawled up her spine.

Maybe this isn't Earth?

Her nostrils flared from a sharp intake of breath.

I'm on Meredith!

Adrenaline coursed through her. Unable to stay in bed a moment longer, she struggled to prop herself up on her elbows. The waves of pain returned with a vengeance, but Mona gritted her teeth and refused to collapse back onto the pillow. Eventually, the throb subsided. She placed both hands beneath her and struggled to sit up. The blinding agony was so intense this time, Mona thought she might pass out. She fought the waves of nausea until the pounding in her temple began to fade.

Mona surveyed the entire room. Bright sunlight streamed through large open windows on her left, and the delicious scent of flowers laced the air. Thick carpet covered the floor from wall to wall, with the exception of a tiled area on the floor adjacent to a flagstone fireplace. The hearth lay directly in front of her bed against a wall with two large, cased openings on either side. More luxurious furniture was scattered throughout the room, which looked to Mona like it could put any Park Avenue penthouse in New York City to shame.

The unmistakable warble of running water came to her ears. Careful not to unleash fresh waves of pain in her head, she craned her neck but couldn't locate the source of the sound. The tinkle of water made Mona uncomfortably aware of the pressure in her bladder. She tried to ignore it, fearful if she tried to stand, the drumbeat would start all over again. Finally, she could wait no longer. Gingerly, she slid her legs out from under the bed sheets and onto the floor—not daring to stand up completely.

So far so good.

Mona pushed herself off the bed and slowly stood up. Although only a dull throb returned, she experienced a slight dizziness. She waited until the bout of vertigo passed and then shuffled from her bed in search of a bathroom. Her body had a clumsy, strange feel about it as though her arms and legs were not in full cooperation with her brain. Mona shrugged off the feeling and reasoned it must be the natural result of being struck by a car.

She moved past the fireplace to continue her search for the bathroom. She stopped suddenly and stared at the source of the running water...a sunken pool located in the middle of the floor. Water cascaded from a fluted urn to bubble merrily back into the circular basin. Water plants floated in a display of flowers in various shades of red, pink, and white. A flash of movement caught her eye, and Mona leaned closer. Large, multicolored fish swam lazily in the water.

Sunlight streamed from a vaulted ceiling high above her head. Constructed of clear glass, natural light illuminated the entire area. Although the effect was stunning, she didn't linger, her bladder even more insistent. Spying a doorway a short distance from the fountain, Mona trudged toward it.

She reached the entrance to discover a wide hallway with exits on either side. On the right were two sets of sliding doors with polished golden handles. Mona pushed the first set apart, and they separated easily. She sucked in a breath at the sight of a walk-in closet larger than her entire room at the Baker's. Gowns hung from a double set of clothes racks located on either side. The wardrobe was so enormous, ample space existed to walk *between* each clothes rack.

Mona ran her hand over the fabric of a beautiful dress. Black with long flared sleeves, the hem stretched to floor length. A thin silver chain wound below the bodice and wrapped around the waist. She selected another dress, this one a brown baroque color.

Long-sleeved as well, the dress belled outward to the floor, the heavy fabric stiff and covered in a rich embroidery. Crisscrossed with gold lace, the bodice plunged to a scandalous depth.

A cursory inspection revealed similar gowns, although curiously, no pants. The clothes reminded Mona of what someone would wear to a costume ball.

The next set of doors revealed another sizeable closet filled with multiple tiers of shoes. Footwear, from dainty shoes to soft leather boots, lined the walls by the hundreds. Mona blinked at such opulence, then closed the doors and hurried toward the exit at the end of the hall.

She burst through the doorway and almost stumbled into a large sunken tub. Twenty feet in diameter and three feet deep, steps led down into the bath, a gold railing mounted on the floor to help with getting in and out. Best of all, Mona spotted the unmistakable shape of a toilet. It looked old-fashioned, but all she cared was if it worked.

Mona made a beeline for the commode and caught movement out of the corner of her eye. Startled, she glanced over her shoulder and spied a woman staring at her.

Mona screamed.

The throbbing returned with an eruption so vicious, it drove her to her knees. Curled in a fetal position on the floor, she moaned and held her head until the pain subsided. After several minutes, she managed to struggle to her knees and peek over the polished marble surface of a long, low cabinet.

As she peeped through the various bottles and brushes arranged on the cabinet, Mona caught the strange woman peering at her again. She struggled to her feet, while the woman did the same—aping her every move. Shock turned to puzzlement at such outlandish behavior.

Why is she mimicking me?

Realization suddenly struck home. Behind the vanity, a mirror covered the wall from floor to ceiling.

That's me! It's my own reflection!

Hand to her mouth, Mona took a step back, the image in the mirror doing the same. Her head pounded anew, and she felt faint. A small bench sat next to the vanity, and Mona collapsed on it, thoroughly confused.

How can the face looking back at me be the same person? It can't be me. It-it's impossible!

The few details Mr. Finkle shared with her contained no hint of any of this. *Maybe I'm hallucinating after all, and the knock on my head has produced weird illusions. Maybe I'm lying unconscious in a hospital with tubes and beeping monitors attached to me, and none of this is real.*

Half-convinced it was all a grand illusion, a small but persistent voice in her head intruded into her logic.

This is all real. This is Meredith, not Earth.

This last thought caused her to jump to her feet and cry, "No! None of this is real. It's all a hallucination!"

The figure in the mirror copied her stance and words. The voice emanating from her lips rang with a rich, cultured quality, definitely not Mona's but that of a stranger. Still, it came from her/the woman's lips. On impulse, Mona snapped her fingers.

The *Mona* figure did the same.

Slumped on the bench, Mona sat with her head in her hands. There could be no other explanation.

I'm looking at myself.

CHAPTER 24

THE DAIRY FARM APPEARED THROUGH THE SWIRLING WIND AND rain.

As the column of winged horses neared the farm, Tal stiffened and stood up in the stirrups. A large force of mounted men and beastly creatures milled around the barn and farmhouse!

A savage thrill coursed through him. "There!" he cried.

"It seems your hunch was right, Sire," Lord Banebolt said. "*Storm Riders! Attack position!*" The winged cavalry wheeled and spread out in a V formation above the farm.

"I count some three hundred raiders," Bozar said. "Yet we have only a hundred Storm Riders. I suggest we alert the nearest garrison for support."

"We have the advantage of surprise, First Advisor. However, your suggestion is wise."

The cavalry leader took three large brass rings from his saddlebags and tossed them into the wind. Instead of falling, the brass rings hovered and kept pace with Banebolt, while the formation sped toward the raiders. The rings spun, slowly at first, then faster and faster until they merged as one. The clear visage of a rugged and weathered man appeared.

"Lord Banebolt," the grizzled image said. "To what do I owe the pleasure on such a surly night?"

"We are on the hunt, Lord Graveback. Three hundred odd raiders have surrounded a farm homestead, and we number but one hundred."

"Position?" Gravelback asked crisply. Banebolt gave him their coordinates.

A carnivorous smile grew across the garrison commander's face. "No doubt they will head away from the Watch Tower southeast of you and run north. We will be coming from the north and will be sure to give them a warm reception."

Gravelback added, "Keep me apprised of their position, Lord Banebolt. We have winged cavalry but none like yours which can ride on a night like this. Buy us as much time as possible so we can move into position to cut the vermin off. They must not be allowed to escape through the Veil!"

"Understood, Lord Gravelback. Banebolt out." The rings stopped whirling, and the cavalry commander dropped them back into his saddlebag.

"Gravelback has a reputation for being a fierce fighter. Does he have ancestral lands near here?" Bozar asked.

"Aye, that he does, First Advisor."

Tal, his attention riveted on the ravagers below, perked up at the comment. "Didn't Lord Gravelback lose his wife and son to the Veil raiders?"

Lord Banebolt, voice edged with bitterness, answered, "Aye, Sire. It is a sad tale familiar to all who live in this region of the cursed boundary. The raiders struck in broad daylight and overran a small village near the Gravelback summer estate. The Lady Gravelback and her young son were at the village market when the raiders attacked. They quickly overran the township's small defense force, took what captives they could, and killed the rest. Lord Gravelback's wife and son were among those killed in the fighting. He has not been the same since and blames himself for their deaths. He lives now only to hunt down and kill marauders."

Bozar shook his head. "A sad tale, indeed." His gaze fell on Tal, and he added, "Hatred and revenge brew a bitter cup of retribution. We must remember to not sink to the level of the enemy—unless someday we become a pale imitation of the self-same foe."

Silence greeted the first advisor's comment. Rain hissed through the wind, and the storm horse's wings beat through the air.

Finally, Tal's voice cut through the tempest. "We will help Lord Gravelback settle accounts tonight."

A red rage, fueled by the tale of the murder of Gravelback's wife and son, simmered within him. He pulled his sword from its scabbard and held it high.

"Soldiers of the Empire! Tonight we engage the enemy. May your aim be straight and your sword arm strong! When your courage ebbs, and your strength flags, remember all the innocents killed by the murderous Veil scum. Remember their names. Remember their faces. Let their memory add to your courage and strength!"

He brandished the sword. "For Meredith!"

"*For Meredith!*" a hundred voices roared into the night.

Bozar's lips pressed together in a thin smile. Tal, stubborn like his father, Mathias, also inherited his father's charismatic leadership ability. Even Banebolt joined the battle cry. A natural-born leader, Tal's men would follow him even into the face of death.

"Let us hope he doesn't also repeat Mathias' mistakes...and go to his own death as well," Bozar whispered to himself.

The Storm Riders swung into final position.

An ethereal image flowed from the drainage pipe and into the ditch.

It coalesced and wavered, then formed into a solid shape.

Pulpit blinked, shook his head, and discovered he stood in ankle deep water. Spent, the monk collapsed on the lip of the ditch, too drained even to lift his feet from the muck.

The de-corporeal spell, one of many he learned as a monk apprentice, was particularly exhausting. Although there were hundreds if not thousands of various spells he and his fellow apprentices could have chosen to learn, individual choice and affinity determined the novice monks' selections. Voluntary membership was a bedrock principal of the White Order. The Creator called the monks, who either answered the summons or not. The Masters—who taught Pulpit and his fellow novices—would never presume to substitute their judgment for the Creator's.

Pulpit learned the de-corporeal spell for reasons even now he could not pinpoint. He had been *drawn* to it as he had to various other spells. In every case, his attraction to an enchantment became readily apparent. None of his fellow novices would even attempt the de-corporeal spell. Extremely difficult to weave, one misspoken word, one wrong gesture, and an apprentice monk could spend the rest of his mortal life as a wraith. Yet Pulpit, under the watchful eyes of his instructor, had successfully produced the incantation the first time he attempted it. His body, reduced to a ghost-like facsimile, flowed safely under a solid door to an adjoining room before re-constituting into his old self. The spell left him spent, and his teacher found him collapsed on the floor.

Unfortunately, there were far simpler spells Pulpit couldn't come close to mastering. It would have been confusing in the extreme had not all monk apprentices simply accepted it as the will of the Creator. Regardless, every enchantment came with a cost, the only difference being the degree of the physical and mental toll.

The monk would like to have rested more, but time was something he didn't have. With a groan, he rose and trudged toward the Kings Road.

After a time, Pulpit felt his strength return, and his step quickened. While he walked, he scrutinized the ground before him. His efforts were rewarded when a short time later, a pair of footsteps appeared. By their faint glow, he could see the trail led away from the farmstead and toward the Kings Road. The monk added this twist to the enchantment he weaved for Caleb and Samuel, and it allowed him to follow their path.

He took a certain risk using the spell. No ordinary person could see the pale footprints, but the dark mages *could* sense the magic and follow it. He was buoyed by his conviction the Dark Brothers were incompetent and sorely inexperienced. The simple charm he placed on the barn doors, instead of being nullified within minutes of discovery, took the idiots time and effort to bash in instead.

The rain started to come down harder, and the monk picked up his pace.

Periodically, lightning flashed and illuminated the countryside. Otherwise, the night remained pitch black. Pulpit wasn't worried about the boys becoming lost. Caleb, having grown up in this area, could find his way around practically blindfolded. Once they reached the Kings Road, the way would become easier since the road, like the footprints he followed, glowed with a faint illumination. Magic woven into the fabric of the highway was part of the system of Watch Towers.

His main worry concerned *who* or *what* would be sent after them. However raw the sorcerers of the raiding party might be, the monk harbored no illusions about the raid leader. The Veil King and Queen did not easily grant such a position. Hard earned, only the most successful of the Dark Ones' minions were raised to such a lofty status. Therefore, Pulpit could only assume the leader of the marauders to be an experienced and dangerous foe.

Pulpit hurried, splashing through the rain. He tracked the boys' footsteps and eventually came to the roadway. Although he didn't know how far ahead they were, he suspected Samuel would begin to tire when his shorter legs couldn't keep pace with Caleb's longer stride. With that in mind, he jogged even faster.

He eventually stopped to catch his breath and searched for their sign.

Nothing.

His head swiveled back and forth. Hands on hips and breathing hard, Pulpit studied the ghostly illumination of the highway stretching into the darkness and rain. Convinced the boys' trail had merged to be undistinguishable with the shimmering road, Pulpit's continued on, heart in his throat, until he spied footprints in the muddy ground.

Good boy!

As instructed, Caleb stayed out of sight and used the thick cover of the trees and bushes alongside the road.

With a sigh of relief, Pulpit had one more trick to buy the boys more time to safely reach the Watch Tower. He grabbed the *haloub* from his belt, twisted the knob, and the magical implement telescoped to six hands in length. The monk used the staff's tip to draw a line completely across the highway. Words of power tumbled from his lips, and a blue line pulsed where the *haloub* touched the paved stone. After a moment, the stripe faded and disappeared.

Pulpit continued up the Kings Road. After traveling some distance, he repeated the process. The monk wagered their pursuers did not include a mage. He felt certain the raid leader would keep them with him. If wrong, his ruse would easily be discovered by these evil practitioners of magic.

The charm he weaved—another of the odd enchantments he had learned as an apprentice monk—caused directional confusion when one came in contact with the spell. It created a compulsion a traveler journeyed in the wrong direction. Many times, the person or persons actually reversed direction to go back the way they came.

Pulpit prayed this would be the outcome for their pursuers.

At worst, the raiders would mill around in confusion and interrupt their pursuit. Although Pulpit wanted to hurry after the two boys, he had to be sure the spell worked. If not, he planned to delay the Veil raiders some other way. Unfortunately, the monk was totally spent. Although his skill with the *haloub* was unquestioned, spell-weaving exacted a toll, and his limit had been reached.

Hidden in the rain-soaked weeds a short distance from the road, Pulpit, if need be, would ambush the raiders. Even if the spell didn't work as hoped, it would still give him a chance to strike. Outnumbered and his magic exhausted, the monk retained no illusions he would survive the impromptu ambush. He *could* strike quickly and fade back into the murky night, but he was determined to see Caleb and Samuel to safety—no matter the cost.

Pulpit tensed at the distant clatter of hooves. A short time later, five horsemen appeared at full gallop. The monk parted the tall grass to see when the horsemen reached his spell-lined portion of the road. He stifled a chuckle at the sight of the riders stopped and milling about the dimly luminous road. Snatches of conversation told him they were arguing. Pulpit drew his dagger and readied himself. If the raiders gave even a hint to continue down the Kings Road, he would attack while they were still disoriented.

Finally, the leader of the horsemen pointed in the opposite direction. The monk heaved a sigh of relief when they turned and charged back down the highway. Once they disappeared from sight, he emerged from hiding and picked up the boys' trail.

With a deep breath, he began to jog after them.

CHAPTER 25

MONA REMOVED HER HANDS FROM HER FACE AND FOR THE FIRST time, studied her reflection.

A stunning woman—perhaps the most beautiful woman Mona had ever seen—stared back at her.

She pulled and prodded her skin, still not quite convinced the flesh was hers.

The image in the mirror did the same.

She leaned closer. Her flawless complexion, creamy with a hint of rose blush, curved gently across smooth cheeks. Delicate eyebrows formed symmetrical arches above thick, long lashes framing eyes of soft, velvet blue. Mona tilted her head to view a perfectly proportioned nose, slightly upturned, perched on her face. Full, sensuous lips formed her mouth. Her slightly parted lips revealed perfect white teeth, beneath which, a strong, yet subtle chin extended. Thick, luxurious hair, the color of spun gold, flowed halfway down her back. In fact, the only imperfection Mona could find was an ugly, purple bruise located just above the right temple. Although obvious her new persona took a blow there, she had no way of knowing how or why.

Mona stood to continue the examination of her body. Tall and statuesque, she wore a thin robe belted loosely at her waist.

She untied the belt.

The robe fell open to reveal she wore only a pair of silky underwear. Red-faced, she quickly jerked the robe shut. A nervous laugh escaped from her lips at how foolish she was acting. *This is me—the "new" Mona Parker!* A smile tugged at her mouth, and she released the robe a second time to let it fall to the floor.

She posed before the mirror and turned from one side to the other.

Her legs were long and shapely. She ran her hands across a trim, flat abdomen that segued into an hourglass-shaped waist. Slim, tanned arms stretched from her shoulders to end in hands tapered with long, elegant fingers topped by glossy, manicured nails. She twisted to admire the sight of firm, muscular buttocks. Finally, she cupped her breasts, and a wide smile appeared. Large, full, and perfectly proportioned—like the rest of her body.

Mona picked up the robe. Conflicting emotions roiled inside her. Happiness, disbelief, and guilt waged a battle for supremacy in her mind. Part of her wanted to shout and celebrate, while another part stubbornly clung to her new appearance as a hoax, an illusion, with nothing good to come from it.

Mona stepped away from the mirror and studied herself again.

She estimated her height at well over six feet tall. *No wonder my body felt so strange and clumsy when I first got out of bed. After all, I'm barely five feet two inches.*

It struck her then just how peculiar the whole situation was.

I think of myself as short, but now I'm actually tall. She shook her head and struggled to align her thought processes with the obvious evidence of her eyes. *Everything is upside down.*

With a deep breath, she did a slow pirouette, her eyes narrowed in concentration at her reflection.

While the *new* Mona appeared to be a young woman in her early twenties, the *old* Mona would be eighteen on her next birthday. In fact, the woman in the mirror represented the opposite of everything Mona despised about herself. All the flaws she cursed her body over—acne, bushy wild hair, stick legs, and flat chest—every one replaced by physical features she could only dream about.

Mona knew firsthand the experience of being homely and plain. It gave her a perspective an attractive person could never appreciate. A chuckle escaped from her lips.

Take that, Lady Anne! You can't hold a candle to me!

Numb, Mona sat down on the bench...then leaped up. Arms stretched to the ceiling, she crowed, "I'm beautiful! You hear that world? I'm gorgeous!"

Joy filled her. *This isn't a dream or an illusion. My body is real, and I'm real!*

Mona hugged herself and laughed until tears of happiness spilled from her eyes. Although in a strange place, possibly even a different world, it didn't matter—*because I'm beautiful!*

Still giggling, Mona trekked to the old-fashioned toilet and relieved herself. When she stood, the commode flushed automatically. Mona paused. Nothing during the whirlwind tour of Meredith, courtesy of her angel, indicated technology like electricity worked on this planet—or that any technology existed at all. Instead, he had talked nonstop about magic. *Did an electric eye cause the toilet to flush? Could it have been caused by magic? Am I even on a parallel world at all? It's all so confusing.*

Mona searched high and low for electrical outlets or cords. Determined, she got down on her hands and knees to look under and behind the cabinet.

Zilch.

She found nothing even vaguely resembling an outlet, cord, or conduit. She craned her neck to study the lights hanging from the ceiling. Encased in globes of bulbous glass, they were arranged in circular groups of three. Too high for her to reach, Mona instead went to a brightly lit lamp positioned on the bathroom cabinet. She removed the delicate glass shade and discovered a spherical, blunt-shaped bulb. Larger than a *normal* light bulb, a ceramic fixture attached it to the lamp. When Mona tried to unscrew it, the bulb didn't turn. Instead, it popped out into her hand. She juggled the object and caught it. Cool to the touch, it was heavier than she expected.

Very peculiar.

But even stranger, the glass bulb *still glowed*! Mona frowned and popped the light back into the lamp and replaced the shade.

She cast about, and her eyes lit up at the sight of an enormous sunken tub.

A hot bath!

Although not dirty, her feeling of distortion would not go away. No doubt body-swapping did that to a person. *Maybe I will think more clearly after a warm bath.* Decision made, Mona stepped to the tub, only to stop and purse her lips. She could locate no plumbing fixtures except for the familiar drain at the bottom of the tub. *Where is the faucet? Where are the hot and cold water knobs?*

Mona made a circuit around the bath, then sat on the steps that led into it. Head tilted, she studied it. She noticed a slot located high on the inside of the tub she hadn't seen earlier. Five inches long and about one-inch wide, polished brass framed the opening. Pale blue tile covered the sides and bottom of the bath. She leaned closer and discovered the tile on either side of the slot appeared a darker shade of blue. Brow furrowed, she bent forward until inches from the brass aperture. The act caused her to place a hand on one of the darker tiles to brace herself. Water immediately erupted from the slot, hitting her directly in the face. Spluttering, Mona lost her balance and fell back.

Soaked, she climbed out as fast as she could to stand dripping while water continued to pour into the tub. An idea occurred to her, and she knelt beside the bathtub. She discovered by passing her hand over the darker tiles, she could control the flow of hot and cold water. After some experimentation, she got the water temperature regulated and went in search of a towel.

A thorough examination of every drawer revealed no towels. Instead, she discovered a flask of aromatic bath oil. After a sniff, Mona poured some into the water. Soapsuds immediately foamed. While the tub filled, Mona continued her search. The wall next to the bath was also tiled, and upon closer examination, she discovered a series of receptacles cleverly recessed into the tiled wall. Opening one, she discovered neatly folded towels. A cursory search of the other drawers revealed more towels and soft washcloths.

Shrugging quickly out of her wet robe and underwear, Mona sank into the bath. The water felt glorious, and she let it run until the bubbles reached her chin. Head back against the lip of the tub, Mona relaxed in the hot water. Eyes closed, she let her mind drift.

"M'Lady! Why are you out of bed?" an anxious voice asked.

Startled, water and suds sloshed wildly as Mona attempted to sit up. The sudden movement caused her to slip on the slick ceramic, and she slid under the water. Coughing, she surfaced, a cascade of foamy bubbles sliding off her face. Mona rubbed the soapy water from her eyes, then searched for the source of the voice.

"I'm sorry, M'Lady. I didn't mean to disturb you."

Mona homed in on the speaker. A pretty dark-haired girl stood next to the bath wringing her hands.

"You won't tell the Duke will you, M'Lady?" she pleaded.

Mona stared at the girl. *What Duke? Who is she talking about?* Tears formed in the girl's eyes as she took Mona's silence as proof of the reproach she would receive from this Duke person.

At the girl's obvious discomfort, Mona croaked, "Er...no, I will not tell, um, this Duke."

Palpable relief washed over the girl's face. "Thank you, M'Lady, thank you! Do you want me to scrub your back?"

Mona tried to get her lips to move in response, but all she could manage was, "Huh?"

While she tried to untie her tongue, Mona looked down and discovered she was sitting up—her exposed breasts jutting from the water like prows on a boat. *"Erk!"* she squeaked and sloshed back into the tub, the suds and bubbles again up to her chin.

"Uh, no, I don't need you to, er, wash my back."

The girl bowed and pulled the bench from the cabinet. She sat patiently while Mona finished her bath.

Mona studied the girl over the mounds of bubbles. She wore a freshly pressed …uniform? The girl's dress and blouse were simply adorned but obviously made of a rich fabric. A crest of some sort was stitched onto the blouse right below the girl's right shoulder. *She must be a servant in regular service to…me? Or whoever I am supposed to be here on Meredith?*

It occurred to her she was in a precarious situation. *I need to find out exactly who I am and quickly!* While the girl sat demurely, Mona decided to talk to her and get some information.

She cleared her throat. "Um, Miss? Can you tell me your name?"

"Not Miss, M'Lady, just Darcy." With a look of concern, she added, "Don't you remember? I have served M'Lady for the past seven years."

"Ah, no, I don't—"

"Of course! The blow to your head! It must have robbed you of your memory, M'Lady! I have an uncle who owns a stable. He once received a kick in the head by one of his horses and couldn't remember his own name for over a month. That's what must have happened to you!" Pleased with herself, Darcy sat primly on the bench.

"So is this what happened to me? Did I get kicked in the head?" Mona asked.

"Oh no, M'Lady. Your horse was spooked by a covey of gantry quail, and you were bucked off. You hit your head on a stone." Darcy giggled at Mona's wrong assumption, her laughter having a pleasing musical timbre to it. Mona decided she liked her.

"When did this happen?"

"Over a week ago, M'Lady. You have been motionless in bed ever since. The Duke's physicians could not bring you out of your sleep, and they feared you would not recover."

Mona mulled this over before asking the next really important question. "Who am I? What is my name?"

"You *did* take a hard fall, M'Lady! You are Alexandria DeChane Duvalier."

"You are the Duke of Wheel's daughter."

CHAPTER 26

CALEB AND SAMUEL STRUGGLED THROUGH THE WET UNDERBRUSH alongside the Kings Road. Doggedly, they slogged along, slowed by the rain and darkness.

Caleb figured they had traveled only half the distance needed to reach the Watch Tower. If they could have safely traveled on the highway itself, they would have long since reached their destination. Though he didn't doubt the wisdom of Pulpit's warning to stay out of sight, they had yet to see or hear any signs of pursuit. Concerned with his brother, he waited while the little boy stumbled along and struggled to catch up. Already tiring, Caleb knew Samuel's smaller body couldn't keep up the pace.

Their progress slowed to a crawl as Caleb made frequent stops to help Samuel or wait for him to catch up. Worry about his family ate at him, and Caleb was anxious to reach the Watch Tower and give the alarm. He debated whether or not to leave the safety of the roadside vegetation for faster travel on the luminous thoroughfare…then had the decision made for him.

The faint howl of a wolf cut through the night.

His mouth went dry. Caleb grabbed Samuel by the arm and pulled him onto the Kings Road.

"Why are we on the road?" Samuel asked. "Pulpit said to stay off it and out of sight."

"Did you hear the wolf howl? If it's the werewolf Pulpit warned us about, it could be after us. We have to hurry and reach the Watch Tower before it finds us!"

A flash of lightning revealed Samuel's fear-filled face. Caleb squeezed his small hand. "It's all right. We just have to hurry. Last one to the Tower has to clean out the milking stalls for a week!"

With a yelp, Samuel took up the challenge and darted down the highway. Caleb jogged to catch up, smiling at his little brother's sudden burst of energy.

They kept up the pace for half a league until Samuel slowed to a walk. Caleb picked him up and carried him piggyback until his own exhaustion forced him to a stop. Drenched and thoroughly winded, he bent over, hands on knees. While he caught his breath, he listened intently.

He heard only wind and falling rain.

A glance up and down the Kings Road revealed no threat. Its dim radiance displayed nothing but puddles of rainwater. Holding Samuel's hand, Caleb began to jog again.

Caleb, his entire focus centered on running and breathing, lost track of time. Exhausted, he had long since lost his bearings and the distance they traveled, when he heard Samuel shout. He whipped his head up and saw the spire of the Watch Tower. *We are almost there!*

"Hurry, Samuel! We've almost made it!"

Gamely, Samuel tried to run but managed only a short distance.

Caleb bent to pick him up for another piggyback ride when a bloodcurdling howl split the night. His breath caught in his throat as the howl echoed in the storm-ravaged air. *The werewolf is right on top of us!*

Before he could react, another howl originated a short distance up the road. Slowly, Caleb turned and looked.

The werewolf stood in the middle of the Kings Road.

Upright on two legs, the seven-foot beast sniffed the air and caught the scent of the two boys. Coarse black fur covered the creature, and its red eyes glowered at Caleb with malevolent intent. Snout pointed upward to bare sharp, gleaming fangs, the lycanthrope bayed again.

Caleb carefully lowered his brother and whispered, "Samuel, I am going to try to draw the werewolf's attention. While I'm doing that, run as fast as you can to the Watch Tower. You know what to do once you get there."

Tears formed in Samuel's eyes. "But what about you, Caleb? What are you—"

"Don't argue! You do what I tell you. Run and don't look back!"

Caleb didn't wait for a reply. He backed away and made for the other side of the highway, away from Samuel. The werewolf turned and tracked Caleb's progress. With a shout, Caleb sprinted for a large, dead tree thrusting upward alongside the road. Gray, skeletal branches reached upward into the night, and the tree leaned drunkenly. Launching himself onto one of the tree's lower limbs, Caleb climbed in frantic desperation.

The shape shifter reacted instantly. It dropped to all fours and raced after Caleb.

He scrambled up the tree as fast as he could. The beast leaped and swiped a massive paw at Caleb. The blow hissed past his left ankle, and the claws scored deeply into the trunk. Fear-induced adrenaline propelled him up the trunk in a frenzied attempt to escape. Aiming another blow at Caleb, the werewolf missed again, and its paw shattered the supporting limb beneath his legs. He desperately clutched for the branch above him, snatching it just as the limb broke with a loud *crack* and fell to the ground. Using his momentum, Caleb swung onto another nearby bough. This produced a rotten, cracking sound, and he immediately reached another above him, pulling himself up.

Before he could completely gain the branch, the werewolf appeared on the limb below snarling in rage. Caleb redoubled his efforts, a feeling of doom settling in his stomach. Suddenly, the bough beneath the lycanthrope broke.

Both werewolf and branch plummeted to the ground.

Samuel watched Caleb run away with the werewolf in hot pursuit. He turned and scuttled up the road toward the Watch Tower, sobbing until he could run no more. He slowed to a walk to catch his breath. Eyes red from constantly wiping them clear of the rain and tears, he almost missed the wide graveled path angling from the Kings Road to the Watch Tower.

Samuel paused, wide-eyed at the monolith in front of him. He had never seen the magical structure this close up before. Like the Kings Road, it produced a soft ambient light. Although the massive pinnacle was hundreds of paces down the path from him, its vast edifice filled his vision.

He continued and stumbled down the path.

The murky night made it hard to see, and Samuel tripped over a fallen branch. Arms wind-milling, he fell onto the gravel lane.

A huge shape hurtled over him.

As he lay prone on the ground, the werewolf sailed past him to crash into small trees and undergrowth. Samuel jumped up and bolted for the Tower.

Snarling, the shape shifter struggled to extricate itself from the underbrush. Finally, it broke free and gave chase. Samuel looked back over his shoulder and tripped again, this time to sprawl face first into the gravel. Heart pounding, he rolled to his knees. With a bubbling growl, the werewolf bunched its muscles and prepared to pounce on its helpless prey.

From out of the darkness, a long silvery loop of light appeared and lashed out at the beast. It struck the lycanthrope across the chest, to leave a ragged and smoking trail. Jaws snapped in pain and rage, and the werewolf whirled to face the source of its agony. It lowered itself to all fours and with a snarl, advanced toward a cloaked figure standing a short distance away.

"Samuel, get behind me."

Open-mouthed, Samuel stared at the man next to him. Recognition lit up his face, and his heart leaped for joy.

Pulpit!

A whip-like extension sprouted from the top of his *haloub*. Glowing with a silvery incandescence, the rope of light appeared transparent and vaporous—Samuel could see right through it— and it twitched and moved with a life of its own.

He scrabbled to his feet and darted behind the monk.

CHAPTER 27

MONA SHOOK HER HEAD. "DUKE? I-I'M SORRY. I DON'T KNOW what you are talking about."

Darcy sighed in disappointment. "The Duke will not be pleased his only daughter has no memory of him."

Mona decided it might be wise to steer the conversation in another direction. She waved her arms. "So, where are we? I mean, where is *here*?"

Darcy put her hand to her mouth. "Why, M'Lady, you *did* take a hard blow! You are in Wheel, the capital of Dalfur, and this is the Duke's estate. Would you like me to go fetch the Duke's physicians? Perhaps they can help you retrieve your memory."

"No!" Mona blurted. "That won't be necessary. I'm sure over time my memory will improve. In the meantime, you can help me by telling me what I need to know."

Darcy perked up. "Oh, I shall be very glad to do so, M'Lady."

Mona slumped into the tub, relieved. The last thing she needed was to be poked and prodded by what passed for doctors on...*Meredith*? Darcy's information added to what she already suspected—*this isn't Earth, but a whole new world.*

The revelation came with good news and bad news. If Wheel is the location of the Duke's estate, and by association, on the world of Meredith, then it proved she wasn't crazy. It explained her new body and her feeling of disorientation. But it could also mean she was trapped *behind* the Veil, an area ruled by a malignant evil according to Mr. Finkle.

Mona shivered despite the hot water. The happiness she experienced earlier over her new appearance evaporated like an early morning fog. In its place, a cold fear crawled up her spine. The tub—suddenly too confining—felt like a coffin, and now she just wanted to climb out of it.

Darcy's hand went to her mouth, and she stood and approached Mona. "Are you all right, M'Lady? Your face is frightfully pale. Perhaps I should fetch the physicians?"

Mona waved her off. "No, no. I'll be okay."

"In that case, will M'Lady allow me to wash your hair? It is wet and full of soap." Anxious to get Darcy's mind on something besides finding a doctor, Mona nodded.

The servant girl hummed to herself as she produced a flask of an aromatic shampoo and lathered Mona's hair. Despite her anxiety, Mona relaxed under Darcy's skillful fingers massaging her scalp. She repeatedly rinsed her hair until all the soap and shampoo sluiced away.

Darcy waited while Mona emerged from the tub, then wrapped a towel around her. While Mona rubbed herself dry, she retrieved another towel and expertly wrapped it around her damp hair. All the while, Darcy kept up a constant chatter.

By the time they returned to the main bedroom, Mona had learned more from the cheerful gossip about her own situation and about the ducal family. While Mona sat, Darcy expertly combed out her long hair and continued to fill her in.

Her *father*, the widowed Duke, Alton Duvalier, remarried ten years earlier. The new Duchess, Dorothea Duvalier, Mona's (*Alexandria's?*) stepmother, apparently exercised a great deal of influence over the Duke. However, she was neither well liked nor trusted by the Duke's closest advisors. Some, in fact, had retired (or been forced to step aside Darcy whispered) and replaced by advisors close to the Duchess. One of the first acts of the new

Duchess had been to replace Alexandria's governess with one of her own choosing. Mona could tell from Darcy's tone of voice she did not like the Duchesses' choice.

"The woman never smiles, M'Lady. It's like she swallowed a sour palm fruit."

"Why does Alexandria—I mean why do *I* need a governess anymore, Darcy? I'm old enough to take care of myself."

Darcy giggled, "You should be at twenty and one years, M'Lady. However, the Duchess says you are impulsive and need a strong hand to guide you. At least until you are married to Lord Regret," she added.

Mona bolted to her feet. "What?"

"Oh, M'Lady! I forgot about your memory. You wouldn't know about Lord Regret, would you?"

"No, Darcy, I wouldn't!"

With relish, Darcy told Mona the tale of Lord Rodric Regret, a powerful noble with landholdings far to the north of Wheel, who until ten years earlier, had been a virtual unknown.

"It is said Lord Regret appeared from nowhere and rode into the thick of a battle between the Duke's army and that of the Veil King and Queen. The Duke's army, sorely pressed and on the verge of defeat, was joined by Lord Regret's forces and together, they routed the Dark Queen's host and sent them fleeing. In celebration of this great victory, the Duke rewarded Lord Regret with a place at his Court."

Darcy leaned closer. "He spotted you at Court, M'Lady, and became immediately smitten. Lord Regret has been a frequent visitor ever since. He has not formally asked your father for your hand yet, but everyone expects the time is soon. Most think he will ask the Duke at the Midsummer Festival."

Mona, mouth open, sat back and stared at the wall while Darcy resumed combing out her hair. *I can't believe this is happening to me!* On Meredith for less than a day and already practically engaged to be married. Brow furrowed, she recalled Mr. Finkle saying how closely Meredith paralleled Earth, including a twenty-eight hour day and a three hundred and seventy day year.

"What season is it, Darcy?" she asked.

"Early spring, M'Lady," Darcy answered.

After a quick calculation, Mona estimated this meant mid-summer to be about five months away. *I need to learn as much as I can before then. A lot more!*

Darcy laid out underwear ("delicates" she called them) and a dress on the bed. The delicates looked vaguely similar to the panties and bras worn on Earth, and Mona had no trouble until she got to the *bodice* as Darcy called it. Mona's former bosom—practically non-existent—had been the work of seconds when dressing.

Her situation was *very* different now.

She couldn't just slip on the bodice, and it had laces and stays to adjust as well. Observing her struggle, Darcy jumped in and helped Mona finally get the bodice on. Cheeks flushed from the effort, Mona didn't object when Darcy also helped her into the dress. With a plunging neckline, the dress exposed an impressive amount of cleavage, and Mona was uncomfortable with it immediately. It felt like something Lady Anne would wear, which, in turn, heightened her distaste of the gown.

"Is there something…less revealing?" she asked.

Darcy gave her a strange look. "I thought—I mean, this is one of your favorite dresses, M'Lady." Mona shook her head, and Darcy darted back to the spacious closet to retrieve another dress.

While helping Mona change, the servant girl remarked, "You are different, M'Lady—in ways other than just your memory." Mona struggled to appear nonchalant, and managed a nod while Darcy helped her into the more modest gown.

If you only knew how different.

Once dressed, Mona waited while Darcy opened two large doors hidden behind floor-length gauzy curtains. This revealed a garden terrace, and as Mona walked outside onto the paved flagstones, she gasped, palms pressed to her cheeks.

A riot of color greeted her, composed of flowers, bushes, and small trees. Constructed of multiple tiers, fountains tinkled merrily at strategic locations on each stair-stepped terrace. A stream flowed across the dressed stone to feed small waterfalls, which, in turn, spilled into water gardens below. Tables and chairs were scattered about on each veranda with benches placed beneath the shade of the ornamental trees. A large gazebo dominated the middle of the first terrace. Vines ran up the sides of the gazebo and covered the pergola with a profusion of tiny yellow flowers. The flowers filled the air with a honeyed scent.

When Mona looked up, her breath caught in her throat at the sight of the vista that stretched from the edge of the balustrade and into the horizon.

Perched on the highest point of a plateau, the castle/estate of Duke Duvalier overlooked the city of Wheel. A river divided the city into two halves, the waterway a placid, meandering ribbon glinting in the morning light. The difference in the river's gentle flow through the city and from the highland where Mona stood couldn't be more stark. Wild, churning water spewed from the lip of the plateau to cascade in a spectacular flume, which fell hundreds of feet to the streambed below. Mist rose from the thundering cataract and created miniature rainbows of refracted light.

"It's so beautiful," Mona whispered.

She walked to the edge of the stout railing. The shear drop to the frothing water and moss-covered rocks below caused her to take a cautious step back. Arms crossed, she continued her observation.

Situated on a gentle knoll on the otherwise flat upland, the manor had a bird's eye view of the city below. Bordered on the west side by the treacherous river gorge, a bridge arched over the chasm to connect the castle to the plateau. A high, fortified wall circled the castle on the east side to end at the cliff facing. A massive, metal-studded gate dominated the wall, and a well-maintained road ran from Wheel to the gate.

Vast, Wheel spread for as far as Mona could see in all directions. She guessed it must be the home of more than half a million inhabitants. From her distant perch, the sprawling metropolis didn't appear to suffer from the building density so prevalent in big cities back on Earth. *Maybe the inhabitants of Wheel like their elbowroom.*

Mona moved to a table shaded by a tree and enjoyed the view. It was midmorning, the weather perfect for an early spring day. A feeling itched at her, one she couldn't quite identify. When it finally came to her, she gripped the arms of her chair.

The calm before the storm.

CHAPTER 28

THE WEREWOLF, CROUCHED ON ALL FOURS, LEAPED AT PULPIT.

Holding the *haloub* with both hands, Pulpit snapped the silvery loop at the lycanthrope. It met the beast in mid-air with a loud *crack*, catapulting the shape shifter backwards. Slammed into the bole of a large oak, the stunned werewolf lay at the foot of the tree. Driven to his knees by the brutal force of the strike, the monk struggled to find his feet.

The werewolf staggered upright.

Hoarse gasps came from the monk. "Samuel, my reach with my staff is not unlimited. The beast will ignore me and go for you if you try to make a run for it. Our best chance is for me to kill it—a task easier said than done. So, stay close. If I falter, *then* flee for the Watch Tower. Do you understand?" At the boy's nod, Pulpit took a deep breath.

He planted his feet and faced the werewolf.

The lycanthrope moved with caution after tasting the sting of the undulant whip. Beast and monk circled each other, neither taking their eyes off the other. With sudden motion, Pulpit snapped the *haloub* forward. The silvery cord scored a long, smoking gash on the werewolf's flank. The smell of burnt fur filled the damp air. The lycanthrope yelped in pain and bounded away. Pulpit, with Samuel pinned to his robes, carefully backed down the path to the pinnacle. Tense minutes passed as they slowly moved closer to the magical edifice.

The nearer they got to the Tower, the more agitated the

werewolf became. Finally, with a yowl so loud it hurt Pulpit's ears, the beast made a gargantuan leap completely over the monk. The swing of the incandescent cord at the soaring form proved too slow, and he missed. The werewolf's jump brought it onto the path…directly between them and the safety of the Watch Tower. The beast growled in triumph and fixed Pulpit with baleful eyes.

To advance any further, they now had no choice but to go through the creature.

Pulpit motioned for Samuel to change position behind him and away from the lycanthrope. After Samuel scrambled to obey, Pulpit said, "It looks like we must do this the hard way."

Without taking his eyes off the shape shifter, Pulpit whispered to the boy, "I'd hoped we could reach safety by going around the beast. Now, however, I *will* have to kill it…and the only way to do that is to remove its head. This means getting close enough to do even more deadly work. I'll have to draw the beast to me by enraging it to the point it disregards all caution and moves in to attack."

Pulpit risked a glance at Samuel. "When I engage the wolf, watch for your chance to flee. Don't worry about me…*and don't look back.*"

Pulpit smiled at the wet, bedraggled, and thoroughly tired little boy. "I am very proud of you, Samuel. You have already accomplished much this night. However, one more task awaits you. You must activate the Watch Tower."

Samuel squared his small shoulders. "I can do it, Pulpit. I can do it!"

Pulpit risked taking a hand away from the *haloub* and ruffled the boy's hair. "I *know* you can." He took a deep breath. "Are you ready?" At Samuel's nod, the monk firmly gripped the staff.

He advanced on the shape shifter.

Red, feral eyes tracked the monk's movement. The lycanthrope stood on two feet to its full height and snapped its slathering jaws.

With a blur of motion, Pulpit whipped his staff at the werewolf, and the sizzling light struck its shoulder before the beast could leap aside. With a yowl, it dropped to all fours and backed away from the monk.

The next time, Pulpit feinted a movement while actually snapping the searing lash in the opposite direction. The werewolf took the bait and sprang away from the feint—straight into the blow. The silvery loop struck the shape shifter full in the face. The lash burned through one eye and sheared off a protruding ear. The ground shook with the werewolf's roar of pain. Pulpit allowed the beast no relief while it rolled back and forth in agony. Relentless, the monk flicked the lash to strike the lycanthrope again and again. Finally, it could endure no more and rolling to its feet, sprang directly at Pulpit.

"*Now!*" Pulpit shouted at Samuel.

The little boy didn't hesitate and darted for the magical pinnacle.

Pulpit timed his next strike perfectly. The rope of silvery light looped around the shape shifter's neck, and like a snake's coils, began to constrict. The odor of scorched fur filled the air. Fat and gristle vaporized, the sound like bacon frying as the radiant cord ate through the werewolf's flesh.

Its snarls reduced to a low gurgle, the monk strained to hang on to the staff while dodging the shape shifter's desperate blows. The beast began to convulse, its struggles weaker and weaker. His own stamina flagging, Pulpit put all his energy into one last effort. Teeth clenched, the monk pulled with all his might. The greasy sizzle and pop echoed louder as the noose bit deeper into the werewolf's neck.

In a final act of desperation, the werewolf gripped the *haloub*'s silvery extension with its paws and despite the pain, tried to pull the garrote from its neck. The staff, almost wrenched from his grasp, dipped and bobbed while Pulpit clung to it with dogged determination. The aroma of cooked flesh permeated the air, the monk nauseated by the stench.

The *haloub* continued to buck and gyrate. More than once, the werewolf's struggles almost succeeded in ripping it from Pulpit's hands. Close to exhaustion, the monk labored to keep his grip.

The strain on his staff ceased abruptly, and Pulpit tumbled over backwards from the sudden release of tension. Blind to the position of the werewolf, he scrambled to his feet and wildly swung the *haloub*. Heart pounding, his eyes darted in every direction until he finally located the beast.

A head lay on the ground at his feet—the searing loop had burned completely through the werewolf's neck.

Pulpit, gulping air, leaned on his magical staff for support. He prodded the remains with his foot.

The beast's flesh melted away before his eyes. In its place, the body and head of a man emerged. Sightless eyes stared, the mouth slack, the tongue protruding. Studying the face and the slight build, Pulpit bit back a curse. Not a man at all, but rather a youth about Caleb's age. The boy—probably captured and carried through the Veil—then made to be deliberately bitten by one of the Dark Queen's creatures. Once in the throes of the werewolf's bite, he became a minion and slave of Marlinda. The poor soul never had a choice as to his fate.

The same lot awaited Caleb and Samuel had they been captured.

Completely drained, Pulpit groaned as he knelt by the body. He moved his hand to the boy's face and gently closed his eyes.

"May your soul find peace," he whispered.

His expression hardened.

"And may the hell the Creator prepared for your tormentors be exquisite indeed."

CHAPTER 29

MONA SHIVERED.

The intuitive sense of trouble refused to go away. Darcy thought her chilled and hurried to retrieve a cloak. She didn't immediately return.

Worried, Mona decided to go look for her. She stopped when voices came from the direction of the open doors. Moments later, two women and a tall, dark-haired man emerged onto the terrace. The servant girl followed a few steps behind, head down and eyes downcast. Both women were richly dressed, but one wore costly jewelry and carried herself with a regal air. Her companion sported no ornaments at all and carried a pinched expression on her face.

Based on Darcy's information, Mona guessed the woman with jewelry to be her stepmother, the Duchess, and the other woman, the governess. The gown worn by her stepmother had a starched collar giving her a stiff, stern look. Jeweled combs on the Duchess's head elaborately arranged her pale, blonde hair. Of medium height, her features underscored an austere beauty, while ice-blue eyes reflected a cold aloofness. The governess followed a step behind in obvious deference.

The tall, dark-haired man, while handsome, had a pallid complexion as if he avoided the sun. He wore a purple tunic of rich material buttoned from neck to waist. Pantaloons of a similar plush material were tucked into highly polished, calf-high boots. Dark, piercing eyes regarded the veranda over a long, hooked nose. Thick, black hair pulled back into a severe ponytail gave his face a predatory look. Full sensuous lips were set in a smirk, as if he enjoyed a secret joke. He leered at Mona and returned her attention with the scrutiny of a diner at a restaurant picking the choicest lobster from the tank.

She shivered anew.

The little group approached Mona and stopped next to her table. "My dear, you don't know how relieved we are that you have recovered from your fall," the Duchess purred.

Her eyes flashed. "We would have come sooner, but it seems your handmaiden neglected to tell us." Ashen-faced, Darcy clutched the cloak in her hand tightly, not daring to look up.

"Yes, Alexandria, you gave us all quite a fright," the governess said, her voice devoid of warmth. "When the physicians could not bring you from your swoon, we feared for your life."

The dark-haired man approached and grasped her hand to bring it to his lips. At his touch, a sensation akin to the rasp of a snake's scales filled her. Revulsion caused her to gasp and jerk back her hand like it had been scalded. The man flashed a cruel smile at Mona's reaction.

"Alexandria! Is this how you greet Lord Regret? What has gotten into you?" the governess admonished Mona/Alexandria.

"Now, now, Adelina," Lord Regret said. "Remember the handmaiden said she suffers from memory loss." He reached over and stroked her hair. "Do not be too harsh on her."

Mona clutched the chair with a white-knuckled grip and managed to not flinch a second time at his touch.

Adelina stepped closer to examine the purple bruise on Mona's forehead. "Is this true, Alexandria? Have you lost your memory, child?" She then placed both her hands on the bare skin of Mona's arms.

A ticklish sensation appeared in Mona's head like the caress of fingertips on her consciousness. Suddenly, a blinding light flashed from within her eyes, followed by a roar in her ears. A gate slammed shut with such force in her mind, it temporarily disoriented her. When the dizziness faded and her vision returned, Mona saw the governess with her hands held before her—hands blistered and burned.

"Wh-what has happened to you?" Adelina whispered. "I-I can't read you."

Stunned, Mona clutched her throat at the sight of the governess's scorched flesh. Lord Regret's eyes narrowed to black, flinty points at the sudden turn of events. Speechless, Mona could scarcely process what just occurred. It happened so fast.

The dark looks thrown her way by Lord Regret and the Duchess galvanized her into action. She had to say something, or they would draw their own conclusions...conclusions that could make things worse for her.

"I-I'm sorry. I-I don't know what happened," she stammered. "Wh-when I woke up, my head hurt, and I didn't know where I was. I don't know who any of you are. Even though Darcy has tried to help me, I still don't remember anything."

Mona had so far told the truth, but she was not about to tell them everything...especially the part about being Mona Parker from the Planet Earth. *Let them continue to think I suffer from amnesia.* As for the governess's hands, she had no idea what had happened. All she knew was Adelina's touch caused her to react in an instinctive, uncontrollable way. Like a light switch, something *clicked on* within her and then just as suddenly, *clicked off.*

The Duchess studied Mona for a long moment. Finally, she motioned to Darcy and demanded, "What happened when you discovered Alexandria? How did she appear and act?"

"It-it as M'Lady said, Duchess Duvalier," Darcy responded in a quavering voice. "M'Lady did not know me and even asked about her own name. She asked many questions about herself and the ducal family. I-I believe M'Lady truly lost her memory."

The Duchess dismissed Darcy's comment with a wave of her hand. "What would a slow-witted servant know about the difference between truth and fiction?"

Mona, a frequent recipient of condescension from others, became angered by the treatment of Darcy. The poor girl, scared to death of the trio before them, still dared to speak up for Mona's honesty. This anger gave Mona the courage to speak despite her own fear.

"It would seem she knows quite a bit, *stepmother*," Mona remarked, "because she tells the truth...as I have."

Lord Regret chortled. "Ho, ho, it seems the new Alexandria has a bit of the old left in her!" Duchess Duvalier's face turned a purple-red to match the bruise on Mona's temple.

Acid dripped from her voice. "You may have lost your memory, but it seems you still retain the sharp tongue we are all *so* familiar with."

A smile, like that of a feral cat, appeared. "Because we are concerned with your health and well-being, *stepdaughter*, then I know you won't mind an examination by the Duke's physicians...a *thorough* examination."

Mona couldn't hide the dismay on her face. Dorothea's smile grew wider.

"I shall send for them immediately. Oh, we shall expect you at the Duke's table tonight for the evening meal. He will be relieved to see his daughter whole again. The ducal advisors will be there, and it is important they see you whole as well. This won't present a problem will it, *stepdaughter*?"

Mona knew she made a mistake by openly defying the Duchess, but she didn't care. *I'm tired of getting stepped on and bullied. The Duchess is just the stand-in for Lady Anne in this world.*

Surprised by her sudden courage, she didn't know where it came from. *Could it be my change of appearance from ugly duckling to a beautiful swan?* She couldn't be sure. Regardless, she *did* know one thing.

She would have to be more careful.

There were more people involved here than just herself. Looking at Darcy's tear-stained face, Mona knew these people would hurt her for no other reason than to send her alter ego, Alexandria, a message.

Mona chose her next words carefully. "I apologize, stepmother, for my unseemly behavior. I am not myself. I shall gladly submit to an examination by my father's physicians. My head *still* aches." In truth, the drumbeat of pain started up again in her skull from the emotional intensity of this first meeting with the Duchess, Lord Regret, and the governess.

Mona dared to take a quick glance at the Duchess to see if her words had any impact. Her stepmother appeared somewhat mollified, but still wore a suspicious look. The smirk had returned to Lord Regret's face, while the governess continued to look queerly at her.

She is afraid of me, Mona realized with sudden insight. In the larger scheme of things, this might seem trivial to another person, but to Mona, it represented a triumph, a rare victory for someone who, too often, occupied the losing side. This new feeling infused Mona with a sense of confidence she so often lacked. She fought to keep a smile off her face.

"Very well, Alexandria. It is obvious you are not yourself. Go back to your bedroom and confine yourself there until the physicians have a chance to examine you."

The Duchess began to walk away with Adelina close behind. Pausing, she turned back toward Mona.

"Time has a way of revealing all things, Alexandria. I would keep this in mind should the temptation to be less than *truthful* ever strike you." The Duchess whirled on her heels and with skirts flying, marched off.

Regret stood his ground a moment and flashed a vulturine smile. "I shall see you soon, my love. Very soon." Boot heels clicking, he ambled after the Duchess.

Although fear gripped her heart, Mona rose and went to Darcy, who still trembled from the rebuke she received. Thoughts bounced about her mind like a rubber ball.

Regret is the man I'm to be betrothed too? My skin still crawls from his touch! Can I convince the Duke to stop this marriage? There is so much I still don't know or understand.

Taking Darcy by the arm, the two young women returned to Mona's quarters.

CHAPTER 30

ULPIT JERKED HIS HEAD UP AT THE SOUND OF A SHOUT.

A flash of lightning revealed Samuel gesturing frantically from where he stood on the trail to the Watch Tower. He opened his mouth to ask the boy what was wrong, when another jagged flash illuminated a huge shadow looming over him.

His monk-trained reflexes were all that saved him.

The ogre swung savagely at Pulpit with its huge club. *It must have been drawn to the sound of the battle with the werewolf,* he realized in the milliseconds that followed.

With catlike quickness, Pulpit moved the *haloub* to block the club. Able to only partially deflect the blow, the massive cudgel glanced off his left shoulder. Jolted off his feet and into the air, Pulpit catapulted into the brush bedside the gravel path. The undergrowth softened the monk's landing, but as he rolled to his feet, he gasped in pain.

His left arm hung limply at his side.

Shoulder numb with pain, he realized his arm wouldn't move. Pulpit brought the staff up to a defensive position with his good arm, the movement causing daggers of pain to course through the injured shoulder. He gritted his teeth to stifle a moan, while the ogre advanced toward him roaring and swinging the club in arcs around its head.

Staggered by shock and pain, Pulpit could barely stand, much less properly hold the *haloub*. The monk knew he would be as good as dead once the ogre prepared to bludgeon him to a pulp.

Abruptly, another cry rang out from the direction of the Kings Road.

The ogre paused.

Head cocked, it peered into the rain and mist. Pulpit, his weight balanced on his magical staff, used the momentary distraction to make a run for the safety of the Tower. The creature's attention immediately returned to the monk, and with a snarl, swung a mighty blow at Pulpit. Helpless, the monk knew he wouldn't be able to dodge the truncheon.

A low-lying limb from a tree saved Pulpit.

Obscured by the rain and darkness, the club struck the limb to become entangled in its thick leaves and branches. Dripping water and leaves cascaded onto Pulpit, and while the ogre struggled to extricate the club, Pulpit deactivated the *haloub* and thrust it in his belt. He gripped his useless arm with his good one and ran for his life, splashing down the path to the safety of the magical pinnacle. Ripping the club free, the ogre took a few steps in pursuit when another shout again distracted the slow-witted creature.

Samuel, jumping up and down, pointed, "It's Caleb!"

Pulpit paused in his flight to look over his shoulder, and sure enough, there was Caleb. The boy stood in the middle of the luminescent road yelling at the ogre. Relief filled him at the sight. *Caleb had survived.* This relief was short-lived when the monk realized Samuel had stopped to watch his battle with the werewolf.

The Watch Tower was no closer to being activated…and they were all still very much in danger.

"Hurry!" he shouted. "Sound the alarm!"

The ogre hesitated. Its large head swung from Pulpit to the shouting figure on the road. Its dull brain finally registered the man and boy were already halfway to the safety of the Tower. With a roar, the giant turned from Caleb and took off in pursuit.

Tree trunk-sized legs pumping, the ogre quickly gained ground on Pulpit and Samuel.

Pulpit glanced over his shoulder. The gray-skinned giant ran with a distance-eating stride nothing short of amazing for a creature so big and ponderous. The ground shook with each step as the ogre continued to close the gap. The monk measured the distance left before he and Samuel reached the Watch Tower.

It would be a close thing...too close.

Pulpit came to a quick decision and peeled off the path to draw the ogre away from the boy. His heart sank when the creature hesitated only briefly before it ignored the monk and continued after Samuel.

"Run, Samuel, run!" Pulpit screamed. *"Activate the Tower!"*

Fear galvanized Samuel.

The little boy strained to reach the magical edifice. He skidded to a stop at the base of the Watch Tower and craned his neck to study the massive structure. Twenty stories high, the top of the turret seemed to touch the night-darkened sky. His papa had drilled in him and the whole family the procedure to follow if they were ever forced to flee from the bad people and monsters. He knew the Tower sounded the alarm, and the bad people feared its magic. Papa explained the Kings of Meredith had built hundreds of Watch Towers all along the Veil boundary to protect them.

His thoughts went to his family he and Caleb had been forced to leave behind. *If I can trigger the Watch Tower, will it be in time to save them?* A tear slid down his cheek at the thought it might already be too late.

Samuel had never been this close to a Watch Tower before,

but he knew what he was supposed to do. His heart pounded as his eyes darted up and down the rounded base in search of the activation plate. *Where is it? Where is the door papa said is supposed to be beside the square piece of metal?*

Before Samuel could search further, a club appeared out of the dark flying like a javelin. Missing his head by mere inches, the bludgeon struck the tower's stone facing and shattered, showering him with splinters.

Samuel yelped as some of the shards of sharp wood pierced his skin. He fled around the corner of the fortification, the growl of the ogre close behind. When he rounded the curvature, he spotted a door, and sure enough, located next to it was a blue-gray metal plate. He sprinted for it and reached the door. He stood on his toes and stretched with his hand. He aimed a desperate slap at the activation plate, missed, then tried again. He was too short. Despair shook Samuel.

I can do it, Pulpit! I can do it!

The words Samuel spoke to the monk flashed through his mind, and a calm determination filled him. *He could do it.* He *would* do it!

Samuel took a few steps back, then ran and launched himself into the air. He stretched his arm as far as he could, and the cold, smooth surface of the metal panel slid under his fingers. The little boy pushed with all his strength before he crashed into the hard stone exterior. Samuel fell and lay stunned just as the ogre rounded the base of the tower.

Nothing happened. Samuel, groggy from the impact into the hard facade, staggered to his feet. The ogre roared in triumph.

With a snarl, it reached for Samuel with spade-sized hands.

CHAPTER 31

"WHAT DO YOU THINK, MY DEAR DUCHESS?"

Rodric walked beside Dorothea as they approached her residence within the large estate. He absently stroked the hilt of the rapier sheathed at his waist while he waited for her reply.

The Duchess considered her reply. "She has changed, there can be no doubt. Her memory has been altered, and I believe her when she says she has no recollection of herself as Alexandria. What I *don't* believe is that she told us everything about her *present* self. Look what happened to poor Adelina!"

She stopped and took hold of the governess's hands to examine them. Blisters, large fluid-filled pustules, covered her palms. The Duchess closed her eyes, and a faint glow of magic flowed from the Duchess into the hands of the governess. The blisters disappeared, replaced by pink, healthy skin.

Dorothea dropped Adelina's hands. "What happened?" she asked bluntly.

"I-I don't know. I have always been able to read Alexandria's emotions, and, as you know, I have also been able to influence her thoughts and actions. When I attempted to do so this time, it was like I ran into a wall and behind it, a different person existed."

Dorothea whirled and gripped Adelina's neck. She pulled her close and hissed, "I meant what happened to your hands, you fool!"

"I-I tried to force my way into her mind, and my connection

broke off suddenly. When I pressed harder to reestablish the mental bridge, it released a backlash of power so intense it burned me."

Rodric snorted. "You would have us believe not only did Alexandria lose her memory, she somehow acquired a new personality at the same time? More likely, it's due to your incompetence when using mind tricks on a woman recovering from a head injury."

"I tell you she is different!" the governess blurted. "I can't explain it because the mental link broke off so quickly. But in that brief time, I saw the thoughts of someone...*someone who is not Alexandria.*"

"Perhaps you would care to refine that for us, Adelina," Rodric sneered. "Does this mean her favorite color is now red instead of blue? Does Alexandria now prefer roast fowl to fish? Or perhaps she now prefers to use her left hand over the right."

"It is not like that and you know it!" Adelina retorted. "I know my ability, and I am confident she has changed."

"I know nothing of the sort!" Rodric spat. "And I have no confidence in this ability you bleat about. A more plausible explanation is you clumsily forced your way into Alexandria's injured mind, and *you* triggered the reaction, not her."

"Enough!" Dorothea barked before the governess could speak. "This bickering serves us nothing. We know Alexandria has tremendous latent ability—which so far we have been able to keep hidden. Even Alexandria isn't aware of the power she possesses. No one at Court or on the Ducal Council must discover she has this power, and there can be *no* more displays of her talent. Questions will then be asked, and they will point to us. I will not see our plans fall into disarray before we can use her."

Dorothea spun to face the pair. "She is the *key*. She is the means to the final victory over the remaining loyalist forces in

Dalfur. More important, *she will allow us to move beyond the Veil!*"

Rodric slammed his boot heel onto the floor with a loud *thump*. "Precisely," he snapped. "And what if this fool has compromised all we have worked for? My mother will not be at all pleased with these developments and my father even less so."

Dorothea scowled. "Let me remind you, Rodric, this is my task given directly to me by the Veil King and Queen. I have faithfully carried out the plan to infiltrate and compromise the ducal family. *I* poisoned the Duke's late wife, and *I* took her place. *I* have had to endure sleeping with the old fool, and it is *I* who has slowly poisoned him to the point that *I* now make his counsel. If you question my judgment, then by all means, take it up with the Dark Queen."

"Now, now, Dorothea," Rodric chuckled. "I seem to have struck a nerve. I have no quarrel with you or the plans we have so painstakingly carried out."

He cast a venomous look at the governess. "In light of what has happened, perhaps it would be wise to shake up our *new* Alexandria. Fear has a way of making malleable even the most stubborn of minds."

Dorothea nodded. "Very well, Rodric. If you have a plan to make Alexandria more pliable to our wishes, you have my permission to proceed. However, be sure you don't go to the excesses you are so renowned for," the Duchess warned.

The Duchess paused. Deep in thought, she tapped her lips. "*Hmm*. It might be best to accelerate the timetable for your betrothal to Alexandria. The sooner you wed her, the sooner we can put our final plans into play. Unfortunately, the Duke has been obstinate with me on this point. He will not even consider a wedding before the Midsummer Festival."

Dorothea smoothed her skirts. "In the meantime, I will suggest to the Duke we station guards to keep a round-the-clock watch on Alexandria. If she protests, we will say her injury is too severe to leave her unattended. There will be *no* more secrets or surprises."

Rodric snickered. "The doddering fool is clay in your hands. I'm sure you'll find a way to have him agree to an earlier marriage date. Now, if you'll excuse me, I must go to prepare my own little *surprise* for our Alexandria." With a bow, Rodric sauntered off.

"Remember," the Duchess called after him. "Whatever you have planned, I insist you exercise good judgment. I warn you again, nothing in excess."

Pausing midstride, Rodric turned and laughed. "Oh, you can count on me to use *good* judgment. Never fear, the message will be delivered, and our dear Alexandria will hear it loud and clear. I will see you at the Duke's table tonight."

Rodric's response did not reassure her, and Dorothea immediately regretted giving him the authority to chasten Alexandria. His cruelty often got in the way of his common sense. However, as the son of the Veil King and Queen, he knew the stakes and how much rode on the success of their plan—and the plan *must* include Alexandria to succeed. If that didn't temper Rodric's worst instincts, nothing she could say would make a difference anyway.

She gestured to Adelina, and they continued to the Duchess's chamber.

CHAPTER 32

THE OGRE'S FINGERS CLOSED AROUND SAMUEL...THEN THE WATCH Tower began to toll.

The creature clapped both hands over its ears and moaned in pain. The metal disk suspended within the turret's belfry shivered, each pulse growing louder.

Gong, Gong, Gong.

A cobalt light erupted from the pinnacle's spire to illuminate the night, followed by the door at the tower's base whisking open.

Samuel sprinted for safety inside.

Caleb approached at a dead run.

He stopped and bent over, gasping for breath. Finally, he looked up, and his eyes widened at the sight of the activated Watch Tower.

Cerulean light streamed from its spear-shaped peak. Like water, it flowed to spew upward in a torrent before cascading down around the magical edifice. The night sky ignited in an explosion of blue luminosity and spread in all directions. Even though wind and rain continued unabated, they had no effect on the resonance and radiance produced by the Watch Tower.

Blood oozed between the fingers clasped to its ears, and the ogre screeched. The creature tried to flee, blindly careening off the side of the Watch Tower before blundering into the night.

The giant traveled only a short distance when the quicksilver light from the spire caught up to the ogre and curled like fog around its thick feet and ankles. Wherever the luminous haze came in contact with the creature's skin, it began to eat away the flesh like a corrosive acid. The giant's shriek was of such intensity, Caleb's own ears rang in pain at the wail. Within seconds, only the gleaming bones of the ogre's feet and ankles remained.

An odd *click, click, click* came to Caleb's ears.

Puzzled, he realized the sound came from the ogre. From the knees down, only its skeleton remained, yet the creature continued to try and flee on legs and feet reduced to white, naked bone. A sickening *crack* like a dry branch breaking reverberated in the air. The skeletal ankles and feet broke and caused the giant to topple over and into the blue fog. The bright mist blanketed the ogre. Horrible screams erupted until, mercifully, they ebbed away to a gurgle. Finally…only silence.

The pulsing alarm, *Gong, Gong, Gong,* continued to toll as Caleb cautiously approached the fallen giant. He reached the ogre and peered down at the creature.

The bluish fog swirled and eddied. It thinned to reveal a gruesome sight.

All that remained were bones, scoured clean of flesh and gleaming a dull white in the murky night. His stomach heaved, and Caleb fell to his knees and vomited. Wiping his mouth with his sleeve, he stood.

Caleb jumped when a hand gripped his shoulder. He spun away, ready to fight, then recognized Pulpit beside him.

"I am sorry you have to see this. The power of a Watch Tower is a terrible thing to behold." The wispy radiance swirled harmlessly around their legs as it continued to thin and dissipate.

The monk kicked the skeleton. "However, these evil creatures from the Veil deserve their fate. Were it in my power, I would make their suffering linger even longer."

The vehemence in Pulpit's voice shocked Caleb. Even in the murky light, the rage displayed by the normally placid monk was something he had never seen before.

A happy cry interrupted Caleb's thoughts. He looked up to see Samuel hurtling toward them. Whooping for joy, the little boy skidded to a stop, his hair plastered to his head by the rain.

"Did you see me, Caleb? Did you see me, Pulpit? I did it, I did it! I activated the Watch Tower! The ogre ran off somewhere. Where is he? Is he dead?"

Caleb motioned at the huge skeleton by his feet. An enormous sense of relief filled him, while his little brother, apparently unharmed and no worse for wear, danced and jumped around the giant's remains.

"The ugly old ogre is dead! The ugly old ogre is dead!" Samuel shouted in glee. Infectious, his happy energy soon had both Caleb and Pulpit chuckling.

Caleb grabbed his brother and squeezed him tight. "Since you got here first, I guess I have to muck out the barn stalls for a week."

"Yippee!" Samuel shouted, then wriggled out of Caleb's arms and launched himself at Pulpit. The monk grimaced in pain at the happy embrace, unable to prevent the cry of pain which spilled from his lips. Caleb frowned and noticed for the first time his left arm limp at his side.

"What happened?"

"The giant managed to land a blow I couldn't completely block," Pulpit replied. "In fact, if you hadn't distracted the ogre, I would probably be dead by now and just a bloody spot on the vile creature's club."

Pulpit tried to flex his injured arm. Needles of pain shot up the arm, but his fingers moved without difficulty. Gingerly, he rotated his shoulder. After several moments of cautious and painful experimentation, he breathed a sigh of relief. "It's sore and bruised but thankfully, not broken."

Pulpit looked at Caleb. "How did you end up here just as we were attacked by the ogre?"

Caleb shook his head. "I'm lucky to even be alive, much less to arrive when I did." He recounted how, trapped by the werewolf, he had distracted the shape shifter by climbing a tree to allow Samuel to escape.

"I waited for the werewolf to climb up after me, but it never did. When I heard it howling in the distance, I knew the shape shifter had left me to go after Samuel. So, I scrambled down and ran to catch up. I arrived here about the time the ogre attacked you.. All I could think to do was shout."

Caleb grinned. "I figured I could just go up another tree if the giant came after me."

Pulpit gripped Caleb's shoulder. "You showed great courage tonight. Not once, but twice. You saved the lives of both your brother *and* myself."

Caleb shrugged, embarrassed by the monk's flattery. Suddenly, a thought struck him. "What happened to the werewolf?" Pulpit narrated the battle with the lycanthrope and how he had killed the creature with the *haloub*.

"C'mon, I'll show you." Samuel signaled for Caleb to follow and ran down the path. He pointed at the gruesome sight of the now mortal remains of the former shape shifter. A severed head lay beside the body, and Caleb quickly averted his eyes.

I've seen enough death and evil tonight.

With a sigh, Caleb collapsed on a fallen log. "What do we do now?"

"We wait," Pulpit replied. "There are provisions in the Watch Tower. The Empire's soldiers will soon be here from the garrison nearby. Then we will ride with them back to your farm and family. I pray they have found favor in God's eyes as we have tonight." He took a place on the log next to Caleb.

Bathed in the light of the Watch Tower, they waited side-by-side.

CHAPTER 33

ONA ENDURED THE THOROUGH EXAMINATION BY THE DUKE'S Chief Physician, Elton Fifer.

A small man, he fussily went about his business with little or no small talk other than to ask questions like "Does it hurt here? There?" before finally closing his small instruments case at the end of the examination.

"I can find nothing physically wrong with you, Lady Alexandria," he admitted. "However, it is not unusual to have memory loss with a head injury such as yours. Whether temporary or permanent, only time will tell. I will report as much to the Duke and Duchess. Unless you have any questions, I will take my leave." When Mona shook her head, the diminutive physician bowed and left.

Mona retreated to the terrace and sat on one of the comfortable chairs within the gazebo. She needed to think, and Darcy found her there several hours later.

"It is time to get ready for the evening meal, M'Lady."

Distracted from her thoughts, Mona nodded and allowed Darcy to lead her back to her room. After several tries, she settled on a suitable dress for dinner. So many clung to her figure like a second skin, which made Mona uncomfortable. However, what the dresses *exposed* bothered her the most. Numerous gowns were cut so low her breasts practically fell out, while many of the skirts, slit scandalously high, displayed her long legs almost to her crotch.

As Mona of *Earth*, she never considered provocative clothes… she had nothing to display. Who wanted to ogle a skinny girl in second-hand clothes? However, plenty of girls at school wore the latest designer fashions. Many were friends of Lady Anne and gleefully joined in when she carried out her cruel bullying crusade against Mona.

Mona refused to be anything like them—regardless of which world she occupied.

A thought struck Mona while Darcy adjusted the gown pulled from the department store-sized closet. With no figure to speak of, she always envied her curvy classmates. Now after *hitting the jackpot* in the boobs and legs department, she did her best to cover them up. It struck her as so funny, a chuckle escaped her lips. Soon, unrestrained laughter followed, and tears streaked her cheeks. Darcy, unable to resist, joined in, and they collapsed on the bed, giggling so hard they could barely catch their breath.

Hand to her chest, Darcy gasped, "M'Lady, what is so funny?"

Mona sat up and wiped her eyes with the back of her hand. "I just thought of something funny." Another snort threatened to erupt and start the wild laughter all over again. She clamped her mouth shut and managed to pat the girl's hand. "Th-thank you for laughing with me."

"It is nothing, M'Lady." Darcy paused. "M'Lady, please do not take this amiss, but I think…I think you *have* changed. You are so different. I have served you for almost seven years now, and you were, I mean you used to act…" Hesitant to continue, her voice trailed off.

Mona squeezed her hand. "Go ahead. Finish."

"It's just that M'Lady has always been demanding and…and quick to temper. And M'Lady *always* wanted to wear dresses designed to quicken men's hearts. Y-you are none of these things now," Darcy finished in a rush.

Mona smiled. *If she only knew how different.* "People change, Darcy. Sometimes for the good. Sometimes for the bad. I have changed too. Maybe a good knock on the head is what I needed."

"Yes, M'Lady." Darcy lowered her eyes. "I-I like this change."

Mona hugged the servant girl. "I am glad you approve. Now let's get ready for dinner!"

A short time later, they left the palatial suite and went to the Grand Hall where Darcy said dinner would be served. While the handmaiden led the way, Mona studied their route to familiarize herself with the strange surroundings. Finally, they came to an ornately decorated chamber which looked more like a banquet hall than a dining room.

A huge table, at least forty-feet long and five-feet wide, dominated the room. Plush chairs with cushioned seats and backs were arranged around the table. A series of chandeliers suspended from the ceiling illuminated the room. A fire blazed in an enormous hearth at the far end of the Grand Hall, the heat chasing away the chill of the early spring evening. Smaller serving tables were arranged alongside wood-paneled walls, the rich tones gleaming in the light. Fresh-cut flowers in large vases stood sentinel at intervals around the room.

A succession of portraits of past Dukes and Duchesses hung from the walls. Mona studied them and noticed one that looked remarkably similar to Alexandria. *Could this be her (Alexandria's) mother?*

Servants placed silver platters of food on the table. Steam rose from tureens of soup to mingle with the aroma of a variety of roasted meats. A steady stream of cook's assistants laden with dishes issued through the kitchen doors into the dining room.

A large knot of men congregated at the far end of the Grand Hall and sipped from glass snifters. One, a large bear of a man, broke away from the cluster to make his way to Mona.

Sliver-blonde hair matched a beard clipped close to his face, while his twinkling blue eyes blazed with unmistakable joy at the sight of Mona. He walked with a limp, and when he reached her, he paused to catch his breath, the raspy gulps of air closely resembling a blacksmith's bellows.

He wrapped her in a warm hug. "Alex," he wheezed, "I feared so much for you. The damnable physicians could tell me nothing about why your condition would not improve. But I knew you would recover. I knew! We Duvalier's are tougher than we look. It takes more than a fall from a horse to keep a Duvalier down for long."

He gripped her shoulders and looked Mona up and down. "How are you, daughter? Are you well?"

"Fa-Father?" Mona stammered, unsure of the man's identity.

The Duke looked like a knife had been stabbed through the heart. "Is it true, Alex? Have you lost your memory? My own daughter does not recognize her father?"

Tears appeared in his eyes, and the Duke whispered, "Tell me it isn't true."

Mona's heart broke at the sound of the Duke's anguished voice. He obviously loved his daughter dearly, and she couldn't bear to say anything which might deepen his anguish. Having drifted from foster home to foster home, Mona never knew her own parents. *What would it have been like to have a father love me like the Duke loves Alexandria?*

Tears threatened to leak from her eyes as she struggled to reply. "I'm sorry, Fa-Father. I have no memory of myself or my life here." *Only a partial lie,* she guiltily told herself. *I really don't know anything about Alexandria.* "But I am sure over time my memory will return. I know I will especially remember you."

She paused. "After all, I am a Duvalier."

The Duke's stricken look softened. Mona, after a moment's

hesitation, gave her *father* a hug and kissed him on the cheek. The Duke clung to her like a drowning man. He wrapped his arms around Mona, his cheeks red with joy.

"Welcome back...*my daughter.*"

Applause broke out in the Grand Hall from the assemblage of advisors, servants, and members of the court. Energized, the Duke led Mona to the place of honor beside him at the head of the table.

The Duchess, governess, and Lord Regret managed to enter the room with little or no fanfare during the reunion. They took their places and joined the applause with a decided lack of enthusiasm.

"A toast to my daughter, Alex!" the Duke cried. "For she has returned to us!"

Cries of *here, here* reverberated throughout the dining hall, and dozens of glasses clinked. The old Duke took his seat, followed shortly by the assembled guests. Wine flowed, and the food courses began. Mona, although hungry, ate just a bite or two from each dish. Dessert followed, and Mona discovered it too was served in courses. Though she limited herself to only samples of the sweet confections, even this soon left her full to bursting.

Mona's nibbling allowed her to observe the other assembled guests. With little surprise, she noted the Duchess's placement next to the Duke, with Lord Regret and Adelina seated beside her. Although occupied with eating and animated conversations, many of the guests found the time to cast curious glances her way.

Far down the table from her sat a group of men in military uniform. Dressed in blue pants tucked into polished black boots, they wore gold tunics with braided shoulder bars. Each wore a winged crest on their lapels.

One in particular seemed to take an inordinate interest in Mona.

He appeared quite young, and Mona guessed him to be about her, or rather Alexandria's, age. His hair, sun-bleached to white-blonde, was cropped short. Pale blue eyes gazed at her from a tanned, lean face. Mona boldly stared back, and red-faced, the young soldier looked away. Mona smiled at the reaction.

So this is what it's like to be pretty…people notice me.

She folded her napkin and cupped her chin in one hand. When the young officer glanced her way again, she crooked a finger and wriggled it at him. He froze, his face now an even deeper shade of crimson.

The Duke stood to give her admirer a reprieve. The act caused him to stumble, and a nearby servant caught his elbow and helped steady him. Flaccid jowls hung from the old Duke's face, and his rich clothes hung loosely from his frame.

Mona bit her lip. *Is he sick?*

Waving off the servant, the Duke motioned for Mona. He linked his arm in hers, and they exited to a drawing room, followed by a number of the assembled guests.

Spacious like the other rooms in the estate, chairs, couches, and tables populated the chamber. Thick woven rugs covered the hardwood floor, and a wainscot of burnished wood decorated the walls. A long mural completely encircled the chamber. The fresco depicted hunting scenes. Mona recognized some of the animals, but some of the panoramas portrayed creatures she had never seen.

Two fireplaces, located on opposite ends of the room, blazed away to provide a comfortable warmth. Mounted above each mantle, the trophy heads of a variety of animals cast frozen stares at the gathering. Some displayed truly unusual features. One creature resembled a furry rhinoceros with a trio of small horns on its snout. Another appeared to be an eagle, except it possessed small, catlike ears and a head the size of a lion. By far, the most bizarre trophy looked humanoid in shape. Mottled green skin stretched across its face, while large tusks protruded from the lower jaw and past a set of blubbery lips. Beady eyes peered from under a thick brow, and a yellowed horn protruded from the middle of its forehead.

Mona felt her knees weaken. The alien nature of the beasts hammered home the finality of her situation. She lived in a new world on a completely different planet. *This is my life now.*

And I'll never see my home again.

CHAPTER 34

RAZOR SAT ASTRIDE HIS HORSE, IMPATIENT TO BE OFF.

He couldn't shake the presage of danger, which continued to itch like a particularly bad rash. This feeling—like a mouse which blunders into a trap—grew stronger with each passing minute.

I'm not going to wait a second longer for the trap to spring.

His booted heels dug into the horse's flanks, and he sped up and down the ranks of his raiders. With threats and curses, the veteran leader urged them to make haste. Annoyed the Boarog still continued to straggle, he ordered the *horde* to move out without the laggards.

They could either catch up or be left behind.

Satisfied they were at last on the move, Razor relaxed a bit. He wanted nothing more than to put this place behind him and make for their rendezvous at the Veil. The last of the Boarog finally joined the *horde,* and a sigh of relief escaped his lips. He galloped to the head of the column.

This respite proved to be short-lived.

The toll of a Watch Tower rang out like a clarion, followed by a burst of cerulean light in the southeast horizon. The night sky lit up like a giant beacon.

Gong, Gong, Gong. The pulse filled the air.

Razor's blood ran cold. Of all the fears shared by Veil raiders, the sight and sound of a fully activated Watch Tower trumped them all.

Even at this distance, he felt the corrosive effect of the bastion's magic, and his ears burned and itched. Quickly, he shouted orders to his lieutenants to change direction to the north, and away from the searing magic. Spurred by fear and pain, the marauders firmed up their formation and headed away from the enchanted pinnacle.

Hope blossomed within Razor's breast. For the first time, his *horde* performed with the cohesiveness he expected. Now they just needed to reach the Veil ahead of the pursuit—which undoubtedly must already be on the way. Once there, he would trigger the Artifact draped around his neck, and they would be safely through the magical border.

This optimism evaporated seconds later.

A hail of arrows fell from the sky to rain down upon the *horde*. Within moments, bodies sprouted arrows, and the air resonated with screams of dying men, horses and Boarog. Razor snatched the buckler at his saddle and raised it above his head.

"Shields!" he bellowed.

Even as the raiders struggled to obey, a second volley of shafts cut through the night. Those slow to react found their screams joining the dead and dying, their bodies a pincushion of bolts.

Colley approached Razor at a hard ride, his own leather and wood buckler held over his head, while arrows continued to pepper the raiders. He pulled up and cried, "How could they have reacted so fast? The accursed Tower tolled only moments ago!"

"A better question is who triggered the damn thing?" Razor shouted back. "The monk must have escaped the party we sent after them."

He peered under his shield, the flash of feathered bolts still thick. "This must be a roving patrol, and we had the bad luck to be in the wrong place at the wrong time. We need to break free and flee north to the Veil before we are all crow food. Where are the Dark Brothers?" Colley gestured toward a wagon carrying the three sorcerers and the captured girl, who lay bound and gagged in the back of the cart.

Razor raced to the cart, arrows glancing off his shield. "Do something!" he screamed.

In response, one of the mages chanted and gestured with his hands. The wind picked up and blew in violent gusts. The arrows continued to fall on the raiders with deadly accuracy, unaffected by the windstorm the mage conjured up.

Razor edged his horse closer. "These are Storm Riders, you fool! They are shooting *charmed* arrows not affected by wind or rain. Place a protective buffer over us to deflect the shafts...now!"

Black rage filled the raid leader. His hands itched to throttle the mage for his stupidity. If he didn't have to hold the shield over his head, he could not have stopped himself from strangling the Dark Brother.

"Order our archers to return fire and cover our retreat," he managed to bark at Colley. "Start moving out."

Razor pointed at one of the Dark Brothers cowering in the wagon. "You! Go with Colley and make sure the defensive barrier extends to the front and back of the *horde*." White-faced, the mage nodded and climbed onto a horse tied to the wagon. Seconds later, he galloped off to join the horde leader's lieutenant.

Razor eyed the trussed girl and made a decision. He gestured at the two remaining sorcerers to hand her to him. Quickly, he slashed her bonds and lifted her onto the front of the saddle. No doubt she would hamper his movements if it came to battle. However, she would also provide protection from bolts should the screen the bungling mages created fail. The Storm Riders would have to be very careful with their arrow fire while he held an obvious captive. At any rate, he had no faith in the Dark Brothers' ability to maintain the buffer. Teeth clenched, mouths stretched into a thin line, the strain already showed on their faces. If they did not reach the Veil soon, the magical barrier would not hold.

Yes, a little extra protection wouldn't hurt at all.

He galloped to the front of the column to organize an orderly retreat.

The formation of Storm Riders made a third pass over the Veil raiders. Each horseman fired at will at the fleeing formation of men, horses, and Boarog.

Once his shafts began to bounce harmlessly off the screen of magic, Tal shoved his bow back into its oilskin sheath. "What now, Lord Banebolt?" he asked, impatient to rejoin the battle.

The cavalry leader barked an order to cease firing. "We drive them north, straight into Lord Gravelback's welcoming arms," he replied. "They will be trapped with no way to escape."

"What if they veer east and toward the Veil?" Tal persisted.

"Then we will have no choice but to engage and hold them until Gravelback arrives. However, in view of their situation, I would think it highly unlikely, Sire. That would take them near an activated Watch Tower. It would be nigh impossible to open a doorway through the Veil in such close proximity."

Unhappy even a small opportunity existed for the raiders to escape, Tal asked, "Why take a chance at all? Let me attempt to destroy this shield of magic they have created. At the very least, I should be able to punch holes in it. *They cannot be allowed to escape!*" Banebolt stiffened at the young Prince's outburst.

Bozar quickly interjected, "Surely you do not want to put Lord Banebolt's men at unnecessary risk, Tal. So far everything has gone as scripted. With a little patience, we will have the marauders trapped and forced to face an overwhelming numerical superiority. Why sacrifice this advantage?"

Tal struggled to reign in the intense desire to continue the attack. *I want none left alive!* However, the logic of Bozar's advice left no room for argument.

"My apologies, Lord Banebolt. Once again, my *Eldred* speaks with a wisdom I appear to lack."

"No need to apologize, Sire. We have all suffered losses. None want to see a single raider escape without doing everything in our power to prevent it."

Tal glanced in Bozar's direction, and embarrassment crept into his voice. "I-I know, Lord Banebolt. Once again, please forgive my impatience."

Tal adjusted his communication Artifact so only Bozar could overhear him. "I am trying, my *Eldred*. You know I do not want any unnecessary deaths."

Bozar's reply appeared in his ear. "Every journey starts with small steps. You could have insisted we press the attack regardless of Lord Banebolt's advice. Instead, you deferred to his judgment. I simply nudged you closer to a conclusion you would have eventually come to anyway."

Tal sighed, relieved to have the matter behind him. Both returned their attention to the fleeing host below.

"Are we to shadow the Veil raiders then?" Bozar asked Banebolt.

"Aye, First Advisor. If they are content to flee North, we will do nothing but harass them. They are running straight into the jaws of a trap. Why cheat them of the opportunity?" The cavalry leader's teeth flashed in the night.

A cloud of missiles rose to reach the Storm Riders. A few struck the *qurille* on the underside of some of the winged horses, only to bounce off. Unwilling to take a chance on a lucky hit, Banebolt barked, "Storm Riders, fly higher!"

He added, "Sire, would you like to cast a net of enchantment beneath our formation to snag their missiles? In fact, if you *bumped* their shield with your magic, it might cause them to scamper even faster to their doom."

Tal's impulse was to launch an immediate assault on the shield. Instead, he glanced at Bozar. The First Advisor inclined his head.

"Of course. Let's see if we can speed the filth on their way." Eagerly, Tal closed his eyes and drew power to him.

With slow, even breaths, he let his senses expand and flow. Farther and farther they traveled until they fetched up against the buffer of the Veil raiders. He *felt* the magic of the barrier, much like a blind man would grope an object with his fingers. He *tasted* its makeup in the same way. When he opened his eyes, the bubble of magic appeared like a beacon on a dark night. Within seconds, he had the measure of its enchantment and knew he could tatter it to shreds.

Mindful of Lord Banebolt's request, instead of destroying the screen, he weaved a shimmering wave of magic beneath the formation of Storm Riders. The enchantment expanded until it jarred against the raiders' bubble.

Tal smiled. *That ought to shake them up.*

"It is done," he called to Banebolt.

"Very good, Sire," the storm rider commander replied.

"Now, let's see how fast the rats scurry for their hole."

CHAPTER 35

ONA HELPED THE OLD DUKE REACH A CIRCULAR ARRANGEMENT of furniture, where he collapsed onto an opulent couch. He wheezed in relief and motioned for her to join him. She sat next to the grizzled Duke, while the rest of his invited guests filed into the room. Most eventually seated themselves, although a few chose to stand, including Lord Regret.

"This room is one of my favorites," the Duke remarked with a wistful expression. "I have always been able to think here." His eyes took on a faraway look while he reminisced. Abruptly, he shook his head.

"Right. Forgive the ruminations of an old man, Alex. My mind has not always drifted so. At any rate, we have other business at hand. It occurred to me your memory loss requires a reintroduction to the Ducal Council. They stand before you now." He swept his hand at a nearby group.

The Duke pointed at a reed-thin man whose age appeared close to his own. "This is Alabaster John, the Court Grand Master."

A blue sash of office, embroidered with bolts of lightning, encircled a robe that hung loosely from the Grand Master's shoulders. Untidy hair, shot with gray, swept back from the high forehead of the Court Magister.

Gray eyes appraised Mona, and with a bow, he stated warmly, "A pleasure."

The Duke continued and nodded toward a tall man who held

himself with a rigid posture. "This is Lord Randolf Ruffin, my chief military advisor." From the earlier dinner, Mona recognized the distinctive winged crest on the soldier's tunic.

An ornate saber fastened at Ruffin's waist rattled when he bowed. "Also a pleasure, Lady Alexandria."

The young officer who observed Mona with such keen intent, stood close to Ruffin's shoulder. He flashed Mona a crooked smile and nodded when Lord Ruffin finished his formal introduction. She felt his gaze linger after the Duke moved on to other members of the court.

The introductions went on for some time.

All received her cordially, with two exceptions. The Duke's First Advisor, Finneaus Spark, and the Keeper of Accounts, Orel Hawks, both greeted her coolly. While every member of the Duke's inner circle greeted Mona, it wasn't until the presentations of these two men that she felt any unease. Unsure why they treated her with such aloofness, an uneasy premonition tickled the back of her mind.

When the Duke finished, he waved Regret over to his side. "Dorothea tells me you met Lord Regret earlier today. If not for Rodric, I might not be here with you today. The story is an interesting one but perhaps better reserved for another time. I consider him an honored member of my Court. I think it fair to say he has had an *active* interest in you for some time now." Polite laughter erupted at the none-too-subtle jest.

Mona did not join in.

Unperturbed, the Duke continued. "You may not remember Rodric, but you seemed quite fond of him before your accident. It is my sincere hope that over time, your fondness may be rekindled."

With a sinking feeling, Mona realized the Duke's speech to be confirmation of what Darcy told her earlier—*I'm supposed to marry this scary creep!* A cold tendril of fear traveled up her spine.

Preoccupied with this unimaginable prospect, she didn't notice Rodric move to her side and place a hand on her shoulder. Mona flinched at the unexpected touch.

A murmur arose from the assembled advisors at her reaction.

She looked up to see anger flash across Rodric's face. Like a chameleon, his expression quickly transformed from cold rage to a warm smile. Dead eyes, however, continued to bore into her. A cold knot of fear formed a lump in her stomach. Mona knew she had made a terrible mistake.

This man is not someone you make angry.

"Duke Duvalier, you are too kind," he effused, with no hint of the brief rage he had displayed. "My small contribution to your rout of the Dark Queen's army does not bear the significance you seem to place upon it. *I* am the one honored to be part of your Court...and I'm deeply indebted to you."

He stepped behind Mona and placed *both* hands on her shoulders. "You see, had I not been extended your generous invitation, I would have never met this vision of loveliness—your daughter, Alexandria."

Mona reacted better than she thought she would. Fingers dug into her palms, she managed not to flinch again. She even forced a small smile onto her face.

Polite applause followed Lord Regret's gallant comment. Shortly after this, servants appeared and began to serve drinks from crystal decanters. This signaled an end to the night's formalities, and the assemblage broke apart and drifted out of the drawing room. A few lingered to chat a few moments longer until they too bid the Duke and Duchess good night and took their leave.

In an attempt to remain inconspicuous, Mona remained motionless in her seat. Nevertheless, many of the Duke's friends and advisors made it a point to personally give her their goodbyes before they left. One of the last was Alabaster John.

The Court Magister bowed. "We celebrate your return to us, Lady Alexandria. It has been a boon to Alton. I have not seen him so full of energy since...well, since before your good mother died."

At a loss, Mona finally stammered, "Th-thank you, Grand Master. I-I would like to see my, um, father happy."

"Please call me Alabaster, Alex. There is no need to stand on formalities between us. Your father and I are old friends, and to me you have always been Alex—as I have always been Alabaster to you."

"Yes, yes, of course...Alabaster."

The Grand Master studied Alexandria. "What about *your* happiness? Are you happy?"

Puzzled, Mona looked up at the Court Magister. *What is he fishing for?*

Suddenly it struck her. *Regret! Like everyone else, he saw my reaction when Rodric touched me. He knows I don't like him.* Alabaster John's powers of deduction appeared to be every bit as sharp as his skill in observation.

Her reply would have to be a careful one. "Although I have been robbed of my memory, I consider myself lucky. I'm surrounded by a wealth of family and friends no amount of riches could match. In time, I know they will fill in all the gaps and blank spaces for me."

Alabaster John smiled. "Well said, Alex, well said." He paused, a finger at his lips. "You seem to have acquired an appreciation for family—if I might be so bold—the *former* Alexandria Duvalier didn't hold quite so dear."

He squeezed Mona's hand. "You are always welcome to visit me. I would be delighted to help fill in some of the *blanks* for you." The Grand Master bid her a good night.

Relieved she faced no more questions from Alabaster John, Mona turned back to the old Duke...and caught the Duchess's suspicious stare. *She must have followed our entire conversation.*

Mona swallowed. *What is it about these people? Nobody trusts anyone.*

The room, almost empty now, contained only the Duke, the Duchess, Lord Ruffin, and his young aide. A handful of servants moved about cleaning up. The governess and Rodric were nowhere to be seen, a fact Mona found odd. Rodric in particular seemed the type who liked to enter and leave a room with as much fanfare as possible.

A shiver gripped her. *What could he be up to now?*

Dorothea motioned to Mona. "Alexandria, come here. We have something to talk to you about." Mona pushed herself up and walked over to the Duke and Duchess, who stood by the door to thank their departing guests.

The Duchess came right to the point. "We feel it is in your best interest to post a guard near your quarters until you make a complete recovery from your memory lapses."

Her face dripped concern. "After all, we wouldn't want you to wander off and get lost or worse, suffer a relapse." She patted her hand. "We are *just* thinking of your safety."

Mona couldn't believe her ears. *So now I'm a prisoner? She isn't interested in my safety. She just wants to keep tabs on me.*

Mona's stomach churned. *What is this all about? It's like she can't trust me, or rather, Alexandria, out of her sight.*

Somehow, in ways she did not understand, an equilibrium the Duchess worked hard to establish became upended when Mona awoke to find herself on Meredith—and replaced the *old* Alexandria with a far different person. *But how? Why? What is it about herself, the new Alex, the Duchess finds so disturbing? There must be something which involves Alexandria...something somehow tied to Dorothea's plans.*

Another name drifted into her mind. *Rodric! He must be involved with whatever the Duchess is up to as well.*

The problem was that Mona didn't know anything about Alexandria's previous life. She couldn't even make an educated guess. If only she knew more, maybe some of these questions could be answered.

Frustrated, she decided she wasn't going to be pushed around without a fight. The old Mona, the meek and passive girl who never stood up for herself, stepped aside, and in that brief space of time, a subtle but profound shift occurred. Like the cascade of sand in an upturned hourglass, Mona felt her personality shift and evolve grain by grain…into something new.

A door opened in her mind. It beckoned to her.

Mona knew if she stepped through, she would be forever changed. Strangely, this prospect didn't intimidate her. In fact, she welcomed it. Her core being—her Mona persona—would always be present, always the most important part of her. But an instinct, powerful and persistent, gripped her with a feeling she could be more.

So much more.

Could this be what Mr. Finkle meant when he said I could make a difference? That something dwells within me?

This same instinct sounded a warning bell ever since she awoke upon this planet…and the omen was clear. In order to survive, she could no longer be part of two worlds, one of Earth, the other of Meredith. The two must merge as one. Her angel's last words came to her.

Trust your heart, Mona. Always trust your heart.

The time had come to follow his advice. A peace settled within her, and she knew what she must do. The decision made, she closed her eyes, a hint of a smile on her lips.

I must think of myself as Alexandria, play her role, even discard my name from all thoughts so in all things I am her. From this day forward, I am no longer Mona.

I am Alexandria.

Mona stepped through the door...and Alexandria of Meredith was reborn.

CHAPTER 36

RAZOR, PREOCCUPIED WITH KEEPING HIS RAIDERS MOVING AT THE utmost speed, didn't notice the Dark Brother until he rode up beside him and began to speak. Irritated, he turned to see the mage quaking in his boots.

"What in the Nine Hells is the matter with you?" he barked.

"The—the Storm Riders have created their own screen so our arrows do not reach them."

"So? In their shoes, I would have done the same."

The Dark Brother's voice quavered. "But...but you don't understand."

"Enlighten me then and stop wasting my time!"

"Their enchantment jarred against our own. It-it is filled with such power!"

For the first time, Razor took an interest in the sorcerer's blathering. "Explain yourself. What do you mean?"

"This magic comes from a power that we have only studied and heard about during our training in the Dark Queen's caverns. It *must* come from a member of a noble family—one of high birth. There can be no other explanation!"

"A noble family of high birth? How high?" Razor demanded.

"Perhaps a member of the royal family itself."

A Royal?

Stunned by the news, it took a few moments for the implications to sink in before Razor's mind finally engaged. Prince Talmund, known to be a frequent visitor to the Veil, was also known to be an active participant in patrols of the enchanted barrier. Encounters with the young heir—often deadly affairs—left few raiders alive to tell the tale. Although there might be other explanations, Razor knew them to be unlikely.

They could not face the Blood Prince with any hope of survival.

If the Royal knew how inexperienced his Dark Brothers were, an all-out attack would already have been launched. He didn't realize this...yet.

It might be the only thing working in our favor on this accursed night.

He could use this cautiousness to their advantage and buy the time needed to reach the Veil border. Muurch would be monitoring their progress and, upon their arrival, have a portal prepared to open for them.

However, he would have to stay close to the bungling mages and stiffen their spines. Their only chance to escape lay in the defensive magic they provided.

The *horde* made good time. The Storm Riders sporadically fired arrows to test their charmed shield, but other than a few cautious magical thrusts at the buffer, it proved to be nothing the Dark Brothers couldn't repel.

In light of their predicament, Razor should have been pleased. However, the ease by which they were allowed to flee bothered him. It didn't smell right, and he learned long ago to trust his nose. Going with this instinct, he risked sending a small party of outriders to scout ahead along their path of escape. He included a mage with the party to provide protection from the enemies' arrows. No doubt the Storm Riders would straightaway notice the departure of the outriders, but he didn't care. He *knew* what was above him. Now, he wanted to know what was in *front* of him.

The scouting party had been gone only a short time when a shout came from the front of the column. Razor urged his horse into a gallop and thundered to the head of the formation. He pulled up at the sight of his scouts racing back at breakneck speed. They had an additional horseman with them, who leaned drunkenly in the saddle. The group pulled up to Razor, and his eyes widened at the extra rider.

Winston—the man he sent to intercept the monk and his charges before they could reach the Watch Tower!

The cause of Winston's unsteadiness protruded from his ribs—a broken shaft, his tunic stained red. A number of questions ran through Razor's mind. *How had the monk managed to escape— and where were the shape shifter and ogre?*

Face grim, he growled, "Report."

Teeth gritted, Winston answered, "We ran into a large party of royal cavalry while we searched for the monk."

He shook his head. "We-we lost our bearings somehow on the Kings Road. I swear I don't know how we got so turned around! By the time I realized we were going the wrong way, the cursed Tower began to toll. We rode hard to return to the *horde* but traveled only a short distance when the garrison outriders attacked us."

The raider coughed, and bright red blood sprayed from his lips. "We never had a chance. The first volley of arrows cleared our saddles of men, and I took an arrow in the chest. I-I don't think any survived but me, and I rode my horse near into the ground to warn the *horde*. Lu-lucky I ran into the outriders. Do-don't think I could have made it back without their help." He glanced at Razor, and a grim look passed between the two men.

The *horde* leader dismounted. Two raiders supported Winston, and he walked toward them. He placed his hand over Winston's heart. The raider shook off the two men and stood unsteadily.

Razor gripped his shoulder with his other hand. "You are a good raider, Winston. You have fought well...and I will see that you die well."

In a blink, he whipped his dagger from its sheath and slipped it between Winston's ribs and up into his heart. The marauder stiffened, and his breath left his body in a *whoosh*. He went limp in Razor's arms.

Gently, Razor lowered Winston to the ground. Wiping the dagger on the dead raider's tunic, he observed the men and Boarog around him.

"Winston died a death worthy of a raider. Now get back in formation. We ride for the Veil."

Remounted, Razor turned to leave when a voice called out, "What of our brother? Are we to leave him here?"

Razor snorted. "What, did you think we would place him in a crypt and mouth endearing words over his remains? He was a raider and would have expected nothing less. In battle, you, me, *all of us*, will lay where we fall, our bodies left to the worms, wild animals, and scavengers. It is the price a Veil raider pays. *Now, move out!*"

Razor moved to the front of the *horde* and led them due east. He motioned for Colley to join him. When his lieutenant reached his side, he said, "We cannot afford any more mistakes—*nothing* can be allowed to slow us down. We must make straight for the Veil."

"Aren't we still too close to the Watch Tower?"

"Probably, but we have no choice." Razor searched the landscape in front of them and added, "There is a good chance we will not survive the night."

Colley greeted this comment with silence. Finally, he asked "What are your orders?"

"Deploy the Boarog to our rear. There is a royal garrison north of here, and no doubt their cavalry will engage us soon. Then the Storm Riders will strike. It is obvious now we are being led into a trap. I want the Boarog to attack and hold the royal cavalry as long as possible."

"You mean to sacrifice them? Why?"

"It is a matter of logistics. The Boarog are on foot, and we need to move quickly. Fierce though they are in battle, the Boarog are slow-footed and cannot keep up with men on horseback. We need time to reach the Veil, and the beast-men are going to provide us with the time."

Razor looked up, sheets of rain still falling. "The storm riders will continue to attack, of course, but without the garrison's soldiers, we won't be outnumbered. We might be able to fight our way to the Dark Queen's enchanted wall and escape through a portal."

The veteran raider paused. "I will listen to a better plan if you have one."

Colley's silence provided the raid leader with his answer.

"See to the deployment of the Boarog."

Colley rode off to carry out his orders.

CHAPTER 37

WHEN ALEXANDRIA OPENED HER EYES, ALARM COVERED THE Duke's face, while the Duchess studied her with suspicion.

The Duke gripped her arm. "Are you well? Do you feel faint? You did not speak for several moments, and your face took on a peculiar look."

The calm Alexandria felt earlier evaporated like an early morning fog. *You can do this. Don't be like Mona! Remember, he is no longer the old Duke, he is your father.*

"I'm fine, Fa-Father."

She turned to face the Duchess. "In fact, I feel better than I have since I awoke this morning."

Alexandria crossed her arms and chose her next words carefully. "Am I to be treated like a child then? To be guarded like a witless fool?" This provoked an emphatic response from the old Duke.

He flapped his hands. "Of course not, Alex! We think only of your safety. You yourself admitted you have no memory of even me."

"That may be true, Father, but I have Darcy to help should I need it. Besides, how am I to remember anything if I am kept under lock and key? Shouldn't I get out to meet our people and rediscover the city and the places in it? This could help my memory and all that has been lost to me."

The Duchess answered before the Duke could speak. "You

199

assume we want you to be confined to your room, Alexandria. Nothing could be further from the truth. We want you to get out, explore your home, and regain your memory. Besides, no member of the ducal family goes anywhere, even in Wheel, without an escort of guards. These are dangerous times and is customary procedure. The *old* Alexandria would have known this."

The Duchess paused to let her words sink in. "As for Darcy, she is a simple handmaiden with limited usefulness. *And* she does not stay with you all day and all night. A guard *will* be posted at all times, just in case you have need."

Alex knew the argument lost when Dorothea pointed out the former Alexandria would have known she needed an escort anytime she left the castle. This served to reinforce the Duke's fear that her lack of memory could prove dangerous—just as the Duchess intended. Hence, she needed *protection*. However, Alex had one more card to play.

"So it is a question of regaining my knowledge...and the routine a daughter of the Duke and member of the ducal family would follow?"

"Yes. That would be a good start, Alexandria," the Duchess responded.

Alex turned to the Duke. "Then can I expect once I have proved myself competent, there will be no need to be guarded day and night—and this is just temporary, Father?"

Alex dangled the bait and hoped the Duke would bite. She knew the insinuation she was being kept a *prisoner* bothered him.

Dorothea's face fell.

This time her father spoke before the Duchess could make a comment. "Of course it is temporary, Alex. You know better than to think I want you watched day and night like a common thief."

Wounded by the very thought, the Duke's chin trembled. Alex, while happy at his response, felt badly for her father. The last thing she wanted to do was hurt or upset him.

This is Dorothea's fault. She'll do anything to keep me under control. Anger smoldered deep within her.

"I know, Father," she managed to say. "It has been an eventful day, and I am very tired. Do you mind if I retire early tonight?"

"Of course!" Concerned, the Duke placed his hand under her elbow. "We may have rushed you too soon from your bed. Do you feel weak? I can summon the court physician."

"No, no. I am just tired. Please don't summon Lord Fifer. I have been poked and prodded enough tonight."

Relieved, the Duke hugged her. "Have no fear, daughter," he chuckled. "We shall have no more *poking* and *prodding.*"

Alex returned the Duke's hug, but before she could pivot and leave, Dorothea cleared her throat.

"Eh? Oh, of course. So forgetful of me," the Duke chided himself. "Alex, you have already met Lord Ruffin. However, you haven't met his adjunct officer. This is Tell Tollett." Waiting a discreet distance away, the young man stepped forward and bowed formally.

"Lord Tollett comes from a long line of cavaliers. There isn't a breed of horse his family hasn't owned, bred, or broken to the saddle. In addition to being Lord Ruffin's aide, Lord Tollett commands a squad of winged cavalry from the Flying Legions of Wheel. Until you have *fully* recovered, he will be in command of the detail assigned to guard—I mean watch over you."

Alex cast a cool glance at the young officer. "Very well, Father. If that is all, may I retire?" The Duke nodded, and Alex walked out of the trophy room and back to her room.

It *had* been a long day.

Rodric left the Duke's feast early and returned to his room, where he shut and bolted the door.

He wanted no disturbances.

Still fuming over the slight from Alexandria when she flinched at his touch, he noted *twice* today she reacted in like fashion to his physical contact.

How dare she! Never shy before, she had always invited his caresses, and not just from him! Alexandria made it a point to act and dress in a provocative manner whenever and wherever possible. Her reputation to stir a reaction among any man was well-known. He wasn't sure what had happened to her since the fall from her horse—nor did he care. But she *would* pay for this insult to his pride. Dorothea warned him to do nothing in excess.

Well, he could be *very* flexible on the meaning of *excess*.

Rodric wore a cruel smile on his face as he began his preparations. He was determined Alexandria would remember this night—regardless of whether or not she remembered anything prior to it.

He placed a stone bowl in front of him, then he used a leather glove to lift a small copper pot from the embers of the fireplace. Melted wax floated within the vessel, and he poured it into the stone bowl. While it cooled, he retrieved a stoppered vial filled with a crimson liquid he prepared for just such an occasion. He pulled out the stopper and poured a tiny amount into the liquid wax. It hissed, a sound much like a human moan arising from it. A rotten, putrid odor assaulted Rodric's nose. Ignoring it, he took a small leather bag and shook out the contents to join the mixture within the bowl. The bag consisted of hair, dander, fingernails, and even bits of thread and cloth Rodric obtained earlier from Darcy.

The Duke himself could lay credit to the ease by which he obtained the necessary ingredients for the *encarthus* spell. The feast to celebrate Alexandria's apparent return to the living made it easy to sprinkle a sleep powder on the food sent to Darcy from the kitchen. Tasteless, the sorceress concoction was slow acting but powerful. The handmaiden would pass into unconsciousness which closely resembled a deep sleep. Once in her enchanted stupor, he stole into her room and procured the necessary ingredients.

The *encarthus* spell would now give him control over her body.

The smile on his face grew wider while he carefully stirred the potion. *Alexandria will feel my touch again tonight...and I'll make sure she doesn't cringe from me this time!*

He stopped stirring and prepared to perform the final steps to complete the spell.

He placed the potion in front of him and recited the words of power to activate the incantation. When finished, he took a deep breath and blew onto the brew. At first, nothing happened. Then the wax began to twitch and move. Tendrils rose from the bowl. Rodric stood with eyes closed, arms by his side and the palms of his hands turned outward.

Within minutes, a thin film of wax formed a transparent sheet in front of him. It shifted, bubbled, and stretched until it took the shape of a woman. The figure grew until it duplicated Rodric's size. Finally, it drifted onto his frame, and settled on his head, face and torso. The film adhered to his body with a wet *slurping* sound.

Then it was over.

Rodric opened his eyes to find he lay on a bed in a darkened chamber. His face split with a triumphant smile. *It worked!* This was Darcy's vision and her room!

When he attempted to sit up, he almost fell over. His Darcy-body responded sluggishly, so he practiced walking around the room. After sitting and standing a number of times, he felt sure he could move without losing his balance.

He studied his or rather, Darcy's, image in a mirror over her small dressing table. Her eyes wore a hypnotic, trance-like look. He walked his Darcy-body to the door.

Time to begin tonight's festivities.

With a spring in his step, Rodric made his way to Alexandria's room, where he would wait for "M'Lady."

CHAPTER 38

HIGH ABOVE, TAL OBSERVED THE FORMATION OF FLEEING RAIDERS. A large number peeled off and deployed to the rear of the main force. They spread out, while the mounted portion of the marauders raced toward the direction of the Veil.

Banebolt cursed. "It looks like the filth smelled out our trap before we could spring it. They have deployed Boarog to cover their retreat. Gravelback can't afford to leave them at his back. If he attempts to go around and attack those on horseback, his proximity to the Veil would be too close. He would be pinned against the barrier and then outnumbered if the man-pigs fall on him from the rear. His best chance is to engage them and try to kill them off as fast as possible."

Banebolt's words no sooner faded when Tal spotted the first outriders from Gravelback's force crest a knoll half a league from the Boarog.

The commander's voice rang in Tal's ear with a renewed sense of urgency. "We must attack the mounted raiders before they reach the Veil. Otherwise, they will escape before Gravelback can break free to join us."

He signaled his men. Mighty wings beat the air, and the storm riders wheeled away in pursuit of the raiders already disappearing from sight.

The winged riders rapidly closed on their quarry. A forested region appeared on the horizon. The mass of trees stretched for leagues in all directions. Abruptly, the fleeing column of horsemen altered course and made for the forest.

Banebolt's oaths reached an earsplitting level.

"They make for the Farthering Forest. It will take them close to the Veil, and we will lose them!"

"Is there a likely area they will emerge from the trees, Lord Banebolt?" asked Bozar.

"It would be strictly guesswork, First Advisor. They could emerge a half a league from us. By the time we discovered them, they would be safely through the Veil."

Tal followed the exchange with keen interest. "Why haven't the trees been cleared this close to the accursed wall? It provides cover for raiders coming and going through the Veil."

"It wasn't considered necessary this close to a Watch Tower, Sire. Apparently, we were wrong."

"Recriminations can wait. We must make haste," Bozar said.

"Aye," Banebolt agreed. He barked orders, and the storm riders streaked with even greater speed through the blustery wind and rain.

Although Tal's own mount surged past the rest of the formation, he knew they would not reach the marauders in time. Powerful wings beat the air, and the storm horse knifed forward through the treacherous wind and rain. Giving his steed its head, Tal pulled his bow from the waterproof case attached to the saddle. He quickly strung the bow and nocked an arrow. Now in range of the marauders, he took a deep breath and let power flow to him.

Once again, his senses expanded until they fetched against the defensive shield maintained by the dark mages. Tal clenched his fist...then plunged it downward as if to strike some unseen object. Through his enhanced awareness, he felt the buffer quiver from the blow. A low *boom* echoed from the collision of the competing magics. Again, Tal drew power and struck the buffer.

Again, it shuddered from the blow but still managed to hold. This time, Tal's senses detected a spider web of cracks, much like a cracked pane of glass. He knew the shield would fall with his next magical blow. Eagerly, he prepared to strike when the protective sphere suddenly disappeared.

The reason soon became apparent...the main body of horsemen had reached the forest. Only a few stragglers remained. Black rage filled Tal, and he pulled the bowstring to his cheek, sighted, and released the shaft. The arrow struck true. A raider screamed and fell from the saddle, the riderless horse galloping off into the night. Tal pulled and released another shaft before his first target hit the ground. Another raider pitched forward and toppled to the muddy soil.

By this time, the rest of the storm riders caught up with Tal and reached the edge of the forest. A thicket of arrows filled the air. Any marauder caught in the open lay either dead or dying. Tal ground his teeth in frustration. *We almost had them, but most still managed to escape!*

Forcing himself to become calm, Tal analyzed the few possibilities left to them. A thought crept into his head. "Lord Banebolt, is the forest as dense as it looks from here?"

"Very thick if memory serves me correctly, Sire. Why?" Banebolt asked.

"Because it will take the filth a long time to negotiate a strange woodland without knowledge of the pathways through it. They don't have a lot of time and are desperate to reach the Veil before we discover them. In their shoes, I would be tempted to use a pathfinder spell to locate a way through the trees. Their magic will leave a trail we can follow."

"To meet the unpleasant surprise we will have waiting for them," Banebolt added with a fierce grin.

"There are ways to cloak magic. How can you be so sure

they will not try to hide the pathfinder spell?" Bozar asked.

"Time, my *Eldred,*" Tal answered. "They must find the portal to take them through the Dark Queen's wall quickly. From my probes of their buffer, I do not believe they have seasoned mages. Because they lack skill and experience, they won't try to cloak the pathfinder spell—it will take them too much time."

"Let us hope you are right, Sire," said Lord Banebolt.

"I am certain of it."

"Then I shall apprise Lord Gravelback of our strategy." Through the communication rings, Banebolt passed on the change of plans to the garrison commander.

The thick canopy of pine and hardwoods made it impossible to see anything with the naked eye, so Tal concentrated on probing the woodland below with his magical senses. He directed his storm mount to follow a deliberate, circuitous route over the Farthering Forest. He fought his normal impatience to carefully scan every inch of the canopy.

He felt a tingle.

Excited, he homed in on the trace of magic. *There!* Like a beacon, a glowing line of enchantment snaked its way through forest.

"We have them!" Tal cried. "Signal Lord Gravelback we will soon give him a final position." Tal snapped the reins and turned his storm mount. The horse shot forward, its wings beating a fierce staccato in the air. Wind and rain whistled past Tal's ears.

"Follow me!"

CHAPTER 39

ON HER WAY BACK, ALEX TURNED THE WRONG WAY ONLY ONCE. She retraced her steps through the labyrinthine hall, pleased she didn't need assistance to put herself back on the correct path.

When she turned down the final corridor to her palatial suite, she stopped at the sight of sentries already posted outside her room. The *click* of bootheels echoed from behind her. Turning, she discovered Lord Ruffin's aide, Tell Tollett, hastening to catch up with her.

Alex crossed her arms. "Lord Tollett, I see you wasted no time in carrying out your assignment to *watch* over me. As you can see, I am more than capable of finding my own room, thank you."

Lord Tollett displayed the same embarrassed smile he'd worn when caught looking at Alex at the Duke's banquet table. "I assure you, Lady Alexandria, I understand your feelings on this matter. I would ask you understand mine. I did not ask for this task, and I'm simply following my orders. Also, please call me Tell. My parents are of minor nobility, and I find the title of *Lord* to be somewhat confining. I want no title I did not earn because of the accident of birth."

The young officer's brashness brought a smile to Alex's face, and she found herself liking him despite herself.

"Then accept my apologies, *Tell*. It seems you have no more choice in this matter than I do. And since we are to dispense with formalities, please call me, um…Alex." She liked the name *Alex*. It seemed to fit her better than Alexandria.

Relief washed over Tell's face. "I will make sure my men and I are as unobtrusive as possible, Lady—I mean, Alex," he stammered. The flustered young officer shifted from foot to foot.

Alex stifled a giggle. *He looks like a lost puppy.* On impulse, she whirled and kissed him on the cheek.

"Good night, Tell."

Mouth agape, Tell watched Alexandria disappear into her suite.

With a muted *boom*, the doors closed behind her. His hand crept to the cheek Alex kissed, the skin still tingling from her soft lips

He fought to bring his jumbled thoughts back into focus.

Finally, he tugged at his tunic and attempted to regain his military bearing. Focused again on his assignment, he turned to the soldiers stationed outside Alexandria's room. They quickly averted their gaze. Heat flamed across his face.

They witnessed the entire thing.

Tell marched to the guards and examined each one in turn. Both sentries struggled with limited success to keep smiles off their faces.

Cheeks afire, Tell barked, "Had enough amusement for one night? Perhaps you would like stable duty instead? A week of mucking out stalls should do wonders for those idiotic grins. Now back to your station before I put you on report!"

Alex giggled at the sound of Tell's angry voice.

His tirade carried past her doors. It ended with a *thump* of boots and pikes striking the floor as he ordered the guards to attention. Still giggling, she walked to a series of gilded dressers that contained underclothes and nightgowns.

My first crush!

As Mona, boys only noticed her when they laughed or made fun of her. She thought of Brock Stanton, his face purple with rage. *What would he think if he could see me now? What would be his reaction to beautiful Alexandria?*

She already knew the answer.

He and all his friends would run over each other to reach her side first. Being attractive and desirable instead of plain and homely—like everything else on this world—would take time to adjust to.

It occurred to her while she dug through the underclothes for a gown that Lady Anne and the former Alexandria were much alike, their lives a parallel to one another. Lady Anne *also* benefited from a privileged upbringing and *also* used her good looks as a weapon to manipulate others.

Of course, her Mona experiences couldn't be more opposite. She and Joe had no advantages and often skated on the edge of poverty. However, although poor and on the low rung of the social ladder, they still had a chance for happiness. But the pain, cruelty, and hopelessness inflicted by Lady Anne so deeply scarred her, she had no doubt if Mr. Finkle had not showed up at her bedside, one day the unthinkable might have happened.

I would have taken the pills.

She shook her head. Brock seemed so shallow and unimportant now. Could young Tell be just like him? Mesmerized by her physical appearance and not knowing—or caring—what lay beneath?

A mirror hung above the dresser. She studied her appearance, silky hair a golden pool around her face. A thought struck her and chilled, she turned and hugged herself. *What if I can never love someone—because I know they don't really love me?* Just a few short days ago, it wouldn't have mattered—Lady Anne saw to that. But the prospect of a loveless existence shook her...yet another curse which came with her new life as Alexandria.

Frustrated, Alex pulled a nightdress from the drawer and slammed it shut. *I don't care. I won't ever take my looks for granted, and I will never use it to hurt others...even if it means I can never fall in love.*

Immersed in her thoughts, she failed to notice the figure in a shadowed corner of the room.

Rodric observed Alexandria through Darcy's eyes.

Lust burned within him as he watched her undress. His eyes roamed over her creamy skin, taking in every detail of her half-naked body. However, his lust warred with another emotion...the desire to inflict pain. Fear and pain were as strong an aphrodisiac to Rodric as the sight of Alexandria's bare skin and full breasts. His lips stretched into a cruel smile.

Why choose when I can satisfy all my desires? A good rape should do the trick. But how to accomplish this with the servant girl's body?

His lips stretched wider. *Alexandria has many interesting objects in her rooms.*

I'll just have to improvise.

CHAPTER 40

RAZOR THOUGHT THEIR LUCK HAD CHANGED.

When the thick forest appeared providentially, hope bloomed in his chest. He knew it extended to only a short league or two from the Veil. The thick canopy would protect them from the Storm Riders' arrows and make it impossible to follow their progress from the air. Although accompanied every step of the way by the maddening pain from the toll of the nearby Watch Tower, he considered it a small price if they could use the dense woodland to sneak back through the Veil.

As he feared, the Blood Prince attacked the magical shield before his entire host was safely into the forest. The Dark Brothers, to their credit, managed to sustain its integrity through two onslaughts before he ordered them to dissolve the spell. By then, most of his men were into the thick woods. He made no attempt to save the few left when the enchanted buffer fell. The loss of a handful of men was not worth the risk of losing one of the mages. Besides, he felt sure he would need them again before the night was out.

Now, his initial optimism proved to be premature.

The deeper they fled into the forest, the thicker and more difficult to travel it became. Progress slowed to a crawl, and he decided to call a halt. Water-logged leaves dripped on their heads and turned into a cascade when a man or horse brushed against the foliage.

Razor motioned for the Dark Brothers to join him. They

had abandoned the slower wagon and now rode horses, with one mage riding double with the captive girl. Even in the gloom, Razor could see faces still pale from the encounter with the Blood Prince.

He wasted no time. "I need a way out of this accursed forest, and I need it now. What can you do to get us out of here?"

"We can conjure a pathfinder spell, *Horde* Leader," one of the sorcerers volunteered.

"Good. Then get to it."

The Dark Brothers dismounted and huddled. One took a vial from his robes and poured its contents onto the ground. It formed a small puddle that quivered and gyrated. Another took a thin wand of metal etched in strange runes and pointed it at the tiny pool. A beam of jade light flared from the rod to strike the puddle.

It produced an instantaneous reaction.

The fluid burst into a blinding green light. Gelatinous, finger-like filaments twitched and moved, then grew and spread from the radiant puddle. The filaments joined and raced into the gloom of the woodland, leaving an oily, luminescent streak behind.

Satisfied, the Dark Brother turned to Razor. "It is done, *Horde* Leader." The veteran raider acknowledged the mage with a curt nod, then motioned his men to follow him.

As fast as the thick, damp forest would allow, they followed the shimmering path.

The trail of magic produced by the mages' spell appeared to Tal like a vivid beacon.

Unlike the Veil raiders, forced to negotiate through the Farthering Forest, the storm riders could fly unencumbered...

and Tal led them straight to where the pathfinder spell exited the woods. Arriving well ahead of the raiders, the storm riders circled high overhead and out of sight.

Tal discussed their next step with Lord Banebolt and Bozar, and the decision was made to allow the entire force of raiders to exit the forest before attacking. Once clear and in the open, the storm riders would swoop in from the treetops and attack from the direction of the forest. This would prevent any retreat to the safety of the woodland and trap the marauders between the Veil and the storm riders. A small force led by Lord Banebolt himself would be held in reserve close to the Veil…just in case the raiders tried to open a portal and escape through the enchanted boundary.

"Sire, it is time to give Lord Gravelback our position," Lord Banebolt said.

Tal agreed, and Banebolt retrieved the communication rings. The image of Lord Gravelback appeared.

"What news?" Gravelback asked breathing heavily.

The sounds of battle could be heard in the background. The squeal of a Boarog was cut short when Gravelback cleaved a bloodstained sword through the creature's skull. He continued to gallop through the mêlée looking for other man-pigs to engage.

"We have found the exit point the raiders will use to flee the Farthering Forest," Banebolt explained. "Prince Tal traced the magic they used in their spell. We know where the cowardly scum will leave the forest."

"Well done! Give the Prince my congratulations on his resourcefulness." He waved his gore-spattered sword. "This shouldn't take much longer, and then we will join you. Tell me where the raiders plan to make their exit." Banebolt relayed the information, and Gravelback acknowledged he knew the area well.

A lone Boarog staggered out of a band surrounded by the attacking cavalry. Gravelback smacked his lips, a smile of delight on his face. Turning his horse, he raised his blade and bore down on the man-beast.

"Save me some of the murderous reavers!" he cried and ceased communication.

"Lord Gravelback seems...*overly* anxious to engage the enemy," Bozar commented.

"Aye. He has never been shy about killing the soldiers of the Dark Queen," Banebolt said. "He lives to avenge his lost wife and son. But don't judge him too harshly. Those who live in the shadow of the accursed Veil know only too well how he feels."

"A point well taken, Lord Banebolt. However, at some point, there must be healing or closure. I have found revenge to be a fruit which spoils over time, and if allowed to fester, it can poison the soul."

"Aye, you may have the right of it, First Advisor. But the *knowing* of it doesn't make the *doing* of it any easier."

Bozar chuckled. "A condition I'm afraid we all suffer from." Soon, both men wore grins of amusement.

Tal shook his head, amazed at how easily Bozar could relieve the tension with a simple word or phrase. Not for the first time, he wished he could acquire his *Eldred's* skill.

These thoughts flew from his head when a lone rider emerged from the tree line. The marauder stopped, stood up in the stirrups, and looked around for a long moment. He turned and signaled. Hundreds of mounted men broke silently from the forest to join the scout. When the last raider exited the safety of the thick trees, the horsemen spread out and made for the Veil at a fast trot.

A savage thrill filled Tal, and he looked at Lord Banebolt. With a nod at the young Prince, Banebolt gestured with his hand

and flew off to lead a small group to take up position along the enchanted barrier.

The storm had lessened somewhat, and while lightning and thunder still flashed and boomed, the heavy rain settled down to a steady drizzle. Tal raised his arm to signal the formation, then swooped toward the rear of the unsuspecting raiders.

Within moments, the storm riders reached the raiders, and Tal gave the order to shoot at will. Arrows hissed through the light drizzle to strike the horsemen with deadly efficiency. The screams of wounded men and horses rang into the night as the storm riders pressed their assault. Unable to retreat into the forest, the marauders urged their mounts to charge at full speed, while firing arrows blindly into the air above them. Only a handful reached the winged cavalry, to bounce harmlessly off the storm horse's *qurille*.

Within moments, a magical shield reappeared above the raiders and deflected the winged riders' shafts. Tal prepared to destroy the enchantment when it suddenly disappeared. After a moment of confusion, the storm riders resumed their barrage. More men pitched from their saddles as the deadly hail of missiles returned to take its toll. However, the lull in the action allowed the horsemen to steal ever closer to the Veil.

The protective bubble returned. Again, Tal prepared to destroy it, and again, it dissolved before he could assault it. This magical game of cat and mouse continued for some time, with the charmed barrier appearing and disappearing. Each time the shield vanished, the Veil raiders paid a heavy price, their ranks thinning as archers took out more and more of their number.

The survivors drew nearer to the enchanted boundary.

Tal ground his teeth. They did not have an inexhaustible supply of arrows to waste bouncing off of the magical barrier. More important, the tactic to deploy then dissolve the magical shield was working. Most of the raiders would die—shot off their horses each time the barrier disappeared—but some would survive and escape through the Veil. Banebolt would, of course, try to stop them, but unless Gravelback arrived soon, the odds favored a few of the ruthless bandits would slip through their fingers.

No doubt the leader of the murderous band would be among the survivors.

Bozar noted Tal's clenched teeth and twisted lips. "Their mages monitor your magic, then wait until they sense you drawing power to disengage the buffer. They know they cannot stand against your power. Target these evil spell weavers. Do not let them employ this stalling tactic any longer."

Tal felt his face warm. Of course, Bozar was right—he allowed himself to be baited into allowing the cruel filth to draw closer to the Veil. "Apologies, my *Eldred*. I have stupidly played their game."

"Do not be too hard on yourself. Remember, you discovered where the enemy would exit the Farthering Forest. Without this knowledge, the raiders would have escaped unscathed."

A bitter taste filled Tal's mouth.

"Because of my foolishness, they may *still* escape."

CHAPTER 41

ALEX JUST FINISHED PULLING THE NIGHTGOWN OVER HER HEAD when she noticed Darcy approach her. She moved with a strange, stilted, and jerky gait.

"Darcy! I didn't know you were here. You surprised me." When Darcy made no comment, Alex said, "As long as you are here, would you mind combing out my hair?" Her handmaiden remained mute.

"What is the matter with you?" Alex asked, irritated at her continued silence. "You act like you are the one who lost her memory."

Alex huffed at Darcy's lack of a response. She whirled and retrieved a brush from the vanity, then sat and unpinned her hair. With a shake of her head, her hair fell in a golden rush about her shoulders. As the bristles ran through her gossamer tresses, Darcy came up behind her and took the brush from her hand. *It's about time.*

"Ow!" The brushstrokes were uneven and painful. Before Alex could take another breath, her hair was yanked, and a hand clamped down hard over her mouth.

"How do you like my touch now?"

The disembodied voice came from Darcy but carried an oddly flat masculine inflection. The hair on Alex's neck stood on end at the realization it wasn't Darcy speaking.

She fought to free herself from the iron grip. The Darcy-creature reacted with a jerk of her hair so sharp, it brought tears to her eyes.

The voice hissed, "Resisting will do you no good, but I *do* so enjoy the challenge!" Paralyzed with fear, Alex stopped struggling.

"Good! You are not as big a fool as I thought you were."

The servant girl's image appeared above her in the mirror. Eerie, vacant eyes stared, and when she talked, the words were not synchronized with the movement of her lips—much like a poorly dubbed movie.

Alex trembled, and she found it hard to breathe. *What kind of creature is this? What am I going to do?*

The dread realization that she was helpless and at the mercy of whatever occupied Darcy's body coursed through her. Her mind shrieked, *What am I doing here? I'm not of this world!*

Her earlier conviction that she could merge her Mona persona within Alexandria to survive on Meredith evaporated. It was foolish naiveté. *Why did I listen to Mr. Finkle? What possessed me to ever think I could make a difference?*

Her quivering increased, and the creature chuckled. "Yes. You do well to fear me."

The Darcy-puppet removed the hand from Alex's hair to run it up and down her neck and spine. Her skin prickled, and her quaking increased to the point her whole body shook. An even louder chuckle issued from the bewitched handmaiden. The sound, an evil rasp, grated against her raw nerves with painful intensity.

Fingers trailed from her back to the bare skin of her abdomen. Reaching forward, the creature roughly cupped her breast.

"What a shame you have lost your memory, *M'Lady*. But rest assured, you will remember *everything* tonight."

Her breast was twisted savagely, and Alex screamed from behind the hand clamped to her mouth. Only a muffled sound came out, and tears of pain cascaded from her face. Lips whispered in her ear, "Oh, this is only a taste. The fun is just beginning."

The hold on her mouth relaxed somewhat, while the hand clutching her breast moved to her neck. Her terror spiked to a new level at the knowledge of what came next. *I'm going to be choked!*

A small voice within her rang like a clarion. It fought to penetrate her suffocating fear. *"Fight!"* it cried. *"Fight for your life."*

A calmness settled about her. She slumped in submission, hopeful it would convince the bewitched servant she had given up. The ruse might give her a chance to escape.

The hand around her mouth relaxed.

Tensing, Alex lunged back and threw her elbow into the Darcy impersonator's stomach. A satisfying *whoosh* followed as air left its lungs. She ripped the hands from her body, then stumbled to her feet and ran to the doors. Frantic, she pulled with all her might.

They refused to open.

The fiend occupying Darcy's body had locked and bolted them.

The creature attacked before Alex could make a move to unlock the doors. It knocked her to the ground with a powerful backhand, then grabbed a fistful of hair and dragged her across the floor. With a strength belying Darcy's slight build, it picked Alex up and threw her onto the bed.

Her screams shook the air.

Knocking on the doors resulted immediately, and insistent voices called out. Alex tried to scream again, but a hand clamped over her mouth. She bit down hard on the fingers, salty blood filling her mouth. A hiss of pain erupted from the Darcy-puppet— apparently it could feel pain—and it jerked its hand away. Mouth free, Alex screamed with raw-throated intensity. The guards shouted, and the persistent knocking quickly transitioned to pounding. Alex managed to roll off the bed, get to her knees, and crawl toward the doors.

"Help me!" she cried, "Help—"

Suddenly she couldn't breathe. An arm like an iron bar clamped across her throat. Alex kicked and bucked frantically, but to no avail—the pressure on her windpipe never lessened. The Darcy impersonator wrestled her back onto the bed and then, straddling her, forced her legs apart with its knees. A deep *boom, boom, boom* reverberated from the doors. Dust floated to the ground, shook loose by repeated strikes from a heavy object.

The creature chuckled at the sound of the assault. "Never fear, Alexandria. The doors are solid. They will not get here in time to save you. In the meantime..."

It reached down and tried to rip off her nightgown. Desperate, Alex managed to free an arm pinned under her. She hit the Darcy-mimic so hard it numbed her hand. An animal-like grunt of pain came from the creature. Eyes dark with insane hate, it placed both hands around her neck and began to squeeze the life out of her. The creature's façade dropped, and a familiar feeling returned to Alex. For the second time since awakening on Meredith, her skin crawled with the sensation of reptilian scales rasping and sliding over her skin.

Rodric!

The realization caused her to struggle even more fiercely, and she fought to bring air into her lungs. She choked and wheezed as too little air tried to make its way through her constricted windpipe.

Frantic, she tried to pry the steely grip from her throat. Although smaller than Alex, the creature in control of Darcy's body displayed an unnatural strength. Despite her best efforts, Alex couldn't loosen the fingers, much less remove them. Spots darkened her vision. She had only a few moments left before she would pass out—and then she would be as good as dead. Deep inside her, Alex raged against the unfairness of it all. *So I'm to be killed my first night on Meredith? Like this? To a foul creature like Rodric?*

Her anger sharpened her determination, and she redoubled her efforts. In her mind, she felt something...*open*, like a door or gate swinging slightly ajar. She sensed a *ripping* inside of her like a fabric stretched beyond its limits. A power gushed from the torn opening and spewed out in a rush. Eye-searing white light exploded from Alex's body to strike the creature. Hurled high into the air, the mimic struck the ceiling with a bruising impact and ricocheted off in a rain of broken plaster and tiles. It fell back onto Alex's bed and bounced off.

Darcy's body lay motionless on the floor.

Barely conscious, Alex struggled to breathe, but her bruised and constricted airway refused to function properly. With a *crack*, the door flange snapped off, and the door hurled open.

Tell's worried face appeared. It swam in and out of focus while he massaged the paralyzed muscles of her throat. The sound of shouted orders came to her ears, but it was as if he were at a great distance instead of by her side.

He pointed at a sentry. "You! Secure the area! And you!" he bellowed to the other guard. "Fetch the physician, then find Alabaster John and bring him here—now!" The guard ran from the room.

Tell tilted her head back, and her strangled breaths became a bit easier. Then he resumed rubbing her bruised neck. "Breathe, Alex, breathe," he pleaded.

It was the last words she heard before blackness overtook her.

CHAPTER 42

A SHIMMER RIPPLED IN THE DISTANCE. TAL ESTIMATED THE RAIDERS were now within a league of the Veil. He clenched the reins.

No! They must all die.

He fought to bring his emotions under control. He took a breath, then another. Calmer now, the young prince expanded his magical senses and searched for the vile mages. With ease, he traced the source of magic to three figures on horses racing toward the accursed boundary. A second individual rode double with one of the sorcerers. Because Tal could sense no magic in this person, he reasoned it might be a hostage. Taking no chances, Tal concentrated on the other two mages.

As a Blood Prince, Tal's magic had long been a powerful and natural part of him. Like any practitioner of magic, he needed training to refine and control this raw power. However, the *mastery* of it came easily. While others practiced and studied for years to harness the power of weaving magic, it flowed within him from the moment he took his first steps as a toddler.

With practiced ease, he drew the power he needed to attack the mages.

He opened his palm, and blue energy crackled in his hand. He reached back and flung the ball of explosive magic at the Dark Brothers. Like a comet, it streaked toward them.

They sensed the magic too late.

One sorcerer managed to partially deflect the pulsing ball

with a hastily cast defensive spell...losing only part of an arm in the process. Cleanly separated at the elbow, the severed arm—nerve spasms causing the hand to clench and unclench—cartwheeled into the air to land on the muddy ground. The mage screamed in agony, his stump still smoking and burning from contact with the sphere of magic. Somehow, the Dark Brother managed to stay on his horse. He swayed drunkenly, the pommel of the saddle gripped with his good hand.

His brother mage, not as lucky, took the full force of the spell. Blue lightning crackled up and down the sorcerer. Within seconds, his body was reduced to a pile of ashes.

The battle progressed to within half a league of the Veil. Arrows rained from the Storm Riders, and more marauders fell to join the trail of their fallen comrades. No buffer of magic appeared this time, but the torrent of missiles slowed when the cavalrymen began to run out of arrows.

Methodically, Tal picked his targets and shot until he had only one arrow left. He sighted on a fleeing raider, determined to make his last shot count.

Twang.

He released the shaft, and moments later, the horseman screamed and tumbled onto the rain-soaked grass. With a shout, Tal pulled his sword and swooped down. Bolts fired by the raiders hissed by him, one passing so close, he felt the wind of its passage.

Then, like a wolf among sheep, he was upon the marauders.

A raider's head toppled off his shoulders with a single swing of Tal's blade. He chopped and slashed, the *ring* of metal against metal a shiver in the air. With a hard pull on the reins, the young prince soared up into the air to circle back for another assault. Wings beat the air, and Tal's mount fought to gain altitude. Meanwhile, the other Storm Riders had followed Tal's lead and plunged in to attack the Veil raiders. Shafts rose to meet the aerial cavalry, and several struck home. One winged mount took a bolt through its eye. The horse gave a terrible scream and plunged to the ground. A sickening *crunch* signaled the impact of horse and rider into the ground.

The battle raged all the way to the Veil, where the raiders, finally brought to bay, turned and grouped for a last stand. Tal and the other storm riders flew high above. Like raptors, they circled and looked for the best avenue of attack.

Although greatly diminished, the *horde's* numbers still made them a formidable foe. By now, Lord Banebolt had rejoined Tal with his small group. Since no portal of escape opened at the Veil, they would be at full force when they began their final assault.

A loud *buzz* rang out, and a protective blister reappeared around the marauders. Tal immediately attacked the shield, battering it with repeated magical blows. A drumbeat of *boom, boom, boom* resonated with each strike. However, this time the barrier appeared different—much stronger and resilient.

Tal bared his teeth. "What happened?" he asked Bozar . "Even though I have killed one mage and disabled another, the filth's magic is even stronger. I can destroy the enchantment, but it will take time, and the murdering scum may escape while I'm at the task!"

"It is the proximity to the Veil, Tal. This close, its malignant power has the effect of magnifying the sorcerers' magic. They can draw from it to strengthen their shield."

Jaw clenched, Tal asked, "What can we do?"

Bozar tapped his lips. Finally, he said, "Instead of trying to destroy the entire sphere of protection, why not concentrate your efforts on a small part of it? Once you force an opening, your magic can rip it apart like fabric in your hands."

Tal's eyes opened wide. "That's it! My *Eldred,* your talents are wasted as a First Advisor. You should be Head Master at the Royal

Academy of Magic in Meredith City."

"Not totally wasted, I hope," Bozar remarked with a dry smile.

Laughing, Tal urged his horse to the ground. He landed a short distance from the magical shield. Bozar joined Tal a moment later. The drum of hooves shook the ground, and Tal looked over his shoulder to see Lord Gravelback and a large force of cavalry pound toward them from the north.

"It seems Gravelback completed his unfinished business," Bozar observed.

The garrison commander pulled up moments later and leapt from his horse. He knelt before the young Prince and made the age-old Meredithian sign of fealty from head to heart.

He stood and growled, "It seems you have our prey at bay, Sire."

Gravelback's eyes burned with a fierce intensity. Blood and gore covered him, which the rain had been unable to wash away. A small gash on his cheek leaked blood, while he looked at the raiders huddled under the bubble of magic. He studied them like a customer in a butcher shop selecting a choice cut of meat... then licked his lips in anticipation of the violent confrontation to come.

A glimmer of empathy struck Tal. *This is what my Eldred meant when he referred to the poisoning of the soul.* Some people could be alive physically but dead as a corpse if hatred ruled their lives. Tal repressed an involuntary shudder and forced himself to concentrate on the situation at hand.

"You've arrived at an opportune time, Lord Gravelback. I will attempt to tear open the filth's protection. Have your men prepared if I succeed."

"Have no doubt. We will be ready, my Prince."

Tal nodded and turned his attention to the sphere of dark

magic. Arms stretched high, he cleared his mind and visualized the process. Tendrils issued from his fingertips to curl up and around the bubble. Invisible to all but mages and fellow weavers of power, the wisps, thin and threadlike at first, wound about one another. The thick cord of enchantment grew ever larger as more and more threads merged. Bozar, a Master Weaver in his own right, nodded with approval.

Finally, the cable of magic pulled back, much like a rapier preparing to thrust. Darting forward, it struck the charmed shield. The competing magics collided.

The air shivered with a resounding *thump*.

CHAPTER 43

ALEX AWOKE TO WARM SUNLIGHT STREAMING THROUGH THE OPEN windows of her room.

She struggled onto her elbows and looked around with bleary eyes. Two men sat by the fireplace engaged in an animated conversation. She immediately recognized them as Alabaster John and Tell. She opened her mouth, but her bruised throat could only produce a *croak*. The men turned and, seeing Alex awake, hurried to her bedside.

When Alex attempted to speak again, Alabaster John put a finger to her lips. He poured an amber liquid into a small goblet and gave it to her.

He patted her arm. "Drink this. It is honeyed mead, which will help sooth your throat."

Gratefully, Alex took the goblet from the Grand Master and sipped. The drink went down easily and, as promised, eased the pain.

"Wh-What happened? How-how long have I...how long have I been out?" Alex rasped.

The Court Magister pulled a chair beside the bed. "All good questions. Your second question is easier to answer—you have been unconscious since last night, and it is now late in the morning. Why don't you let me tell you what we do know, then you can ask any questions if you like." Alex nodded, and the Grand Master continued.

"You were attacked by Darcy. However, it wasn't really Darcy but someone who placed an *encarthus* spell upon her. This enchantment gave the spellcaster possession of Darcy's body. Very difficult to do even on a corpse, much less a living person. I have seen this spell successfully used only one other time in my life. Most weavers of magic will not even attempt it because of the risks involved. If not cast with absolute perfection, it can turn the user into a lifeless phantasm. However, we know it *was* successfully used on Darcy."

Alex clasped her hands to her chest. "Is she injured? Is she okay?"

The Grand Master patted her arm. "Your handmaiden is in the infirmary under Elton Fifer's care. Besides an assortment of bruises and a rather nasty bite on her hand, she should recover."

Alex slumped and a pent up sigh escaped her lips. *Poor Darcy.*

Alabaster John continued. "Apparently, she was given a sleep draught, probably slipped into her food or drink. With all the activity in preparation for the Duke's banquet, it would have been easy for someone to tamper with her food. The powdered Maidens Root in the draught is commonly used for sleep disorders and can be obtained from dozens of Apothecaries in the city. Anybody could have procured it with no one the wiser."

The Court Magister shook his head. "Although the ingredients needed for the *encarthus* spell *are* rare, I hold little hope we will find evidence of the potion any time soon. Duke Duvalier's castle is large and filled with a vast assortment of nooks and crannies. It could take years to search every one of them. In addition, the spellcaster was clever enough to ward the magic...there is no way to trace its spoor to an individual."

Alabaster John sighed. "In short, while the investigation is ongoing, I expect nothing to come of it. I have reported as much to Duke Duvalier."

Tell stepped forward. "We think while your handmaiden lay

unconscious, the personal ingredients—like her hair—were obtained to bind her body to the spell. Once in control of Darcy's body, the spellcaster went to your room and lay in wait."

He gave a bitter shake of his head. "Thanks to my negligence, you know what happened next."

Alabaster John clucked his tongue. "I fear Lord Tollett is being modest and hasn't told you the entire story. He was inspecting the sentries when he heard your screams. Although unable to batter the doors open, his quick thinking led to the flange being pried from the hinge with a soldier's pike and the door forced open. He found you half-alive and straightaway summoned Elton Fifer and myself. He managed to squeeze enough air into your lungs to keep you alive until help arrived. Lord Tollett's quick actions saved your life."

Tell fell to a knee and grasped Alex's hand. "It's my fault! I should have searched your room before I ever let you enter. Please forgive me, Lady Alexandria." Miserable, he hung his head.

The Grand Master stomped his foot. "Rubbish! As I have already explained to young Tell, Lord Ruffin, and the Duke numerous times, there is nothing he could have done to prevent the situation. No training or procedure could have stopped the spellcaster. It is simply too rare and risky a spell."

Although she hurt in a dozen places, Alex's heart ached for Tell. She placed her hand under his chin and forced his blue eyes to meet hers. "You saved my life. Thank you...and remember, we decided no formalities. It's Alex, not Lady Alexandria."

Tell stirred and he stood, back rigid. "I failed you, Alex...but it will not happen again. I give you my oath I will not rest until I find the twisted bastard who did this. When I do," he fingered his sword hilt, "I will take care of the problem—permanently."

Alabaster John raised an eyebrow at the young officer's bold outburst.

Alex leaned forward and placed her hand on Tell's chest. "I know you did the best you could. But if it will ease your mind, then I accept your oath."

Tell hesitated at the press of her warm flesh. His hand slipped off the sword hilt to intertwine with hers. "My pardon. You are right, and we must move on."

When neither one moved, Alabaster John cleared his throat. "Yes...now, Lady Alexandria, can you please tell us your version of what happened?"

Alex blinked and snatched her arm back. "What? I mean, of co-course." Quickly, she related the sequence of events after she had entered her room. Unable to add little more to what the two men already knew, she deliberately left out the explosion of silvery light and how it hurled the Darcy-creature away from her. Still uncertain about what happened, for the time being, she wanted to keep this to herself.

The Grand Master studied her. "Are you sure? Is there anything you might have left out or missed?" Alex shook her head.

Alabaster John tapped his lips. "Strange. An enormous discharge of magic took place here, the power of which I have never encountered before. The air still reeks of it. Another mystery is the matter of Darcy herself. We found her unconscious with bruises that can only be described as *unusual*—like she had been slammed against a solid object."

Alex's heart fluttered. *He knows. He knows I haven't told him everything.*

She managed to shake her head. "I-I don't know what else to tell you. I don't know anything about this magic or how to explain the bruises on Darcy."

Although true enough—Alex *didn't* know how it all happened—it still felt like a lie. She hated to withhold the entire truth from Alabaster John and Tell, but what choice did she have?

If I tell them everything, they will think I'm crazy. Won't Dorothea love that! I'll never be allowed out of this room again!"

Nor could she dare reveal the identity of the person who placed the *encarthus* spell on Darcy.

Rodric.

She was sure of it. When he first touched her on the terrace, the same creepy-crawly feeling had scrabbled across her skin. She doubted Alabaster John or Tell would believe her, but even if they did, she had no way to prove it.

And what happens then? What happens when Rodric finds out I named him as my assailant? It could anger him enough he might attack me again.

She stiffened at an even worse thought.

Tell.

The young officer vowed to *take care* of the man who did this, and he might be impetuous enough to go after Rodric! It could get him killed, and it would be her fault.

No. Nothing good would come from revealing Rodric as her attacker.

She shivered, concerned for Tell on the one hand, but also fearful one day she would be forced to endure Rodric's scabrous touch again.

"Lady Alexandria, are you all right?" Alabaster John asked, concerned. "Your face has gone pale."

She took a deep breath to calm herself. "Yes, I-I'm fine. It's just thinking again about what happened last night is difficult. It frightens me when all I really want to do is forget it." Alex hoped her explanation satisfied the skeptical Grand Master.

"Of course. Forgive me for being so insensitive. I'm sure you have told us all you can remember." He wore a pleasant smile, but Alex couldn't shake the sense he was buying none of it.

Tell spoke up. "We are finished, at least for today, Alex. There is no need to replay your terrible experience."

Alabaster John stood. "We will take our leave. The Duke has asked to be updated on your condition, and I am sure he will want to see you now that you are awake."

"A moment please," Alex pleaded. "Could I see Darcy first? If you will allow me to get dressed, I would like to visit her in the infirmary. I can be in and out quickly, and I promise to be back in time for Father."

The Court Magister frowned. "The Duke was quite insistent...and Alton Duvalier rarely minces words when he directs something to be done." He paused, "However, there are a few stops I need to make before reporting to the Duke. That should give you sufficient time to make a short visit."

"Thank you," Alex said. "I will be back before Father arrives."

"Then it is decided." The two men turned and made their way out.

Alex crawled out of bed and was reaching for her robe when Alabaster John called to her.

He stood beside the broken door, now propped against the frame. "The night can sometimes hold terrors we can scarce comprehend. If you ever need someone to talk to, I am always available."

The weight of his words remained fresh on her mind long after he disappeared.

CHAPTER 44

AZOR WATCHED THE TINY HOLE, A PINPRICK AT FIRST, BEGIN TO expand.

The opening being drilled through the shield of magic by the Blood Prince's relentless assault, sparked and sizzled. Lightning forked from the competing magics, the widening hole creating strobe-like flashes of light.

The surviving Dark Brothers struggled to maintain the integrity of the shield. Sweat poured from their pale faces, while the maimed mage with only half an arm looked near to passing out.

Razor knew they could not win this contest.

When attacked after emerging from the forest, whatever doubts he had about whether they faced a Blood Prince were put to rest. Only a Royal and perhaps half a dozen Grand Masters could have tracked the magic of the pathfinder spell so quickly. Now their doom inched ever closer.

Damn Muurch! Where is the portal?

He activated the Artifact to return them through the Veil as soon as they exited the treeline. The Gatemaster should have had plenty of time to calibrate their position and open a bolthole for them. The proximity of the Watch Tower could cause a delay— this close to the accursed pinnacle, its magic would scramble a normal portal opening—but Muurch never failed him before. Regardless, he *was* certain of one thing.

If an escape portal didn't open soon, they were all dead men.

Razor assessed his remaining forces. Fully a third of his men had fallen to the Storm Rider's assault. Another third reeled in their saddles, with wounds that ranged from mere nuisances to mortal injuries. Not a single Boarog appeared, no doubt wiped out by the cavalry garrison from the north. He wasted no time on regrets of their demise—they had served their purpose to buy them time.

His eyes came to rest on the Dark Queen's *specials* huddled near the mages. By some miracle, most were still alive. Both centaur-like creatures survived, as had an ogre, the remaining shape shifter, and even the melded creature whose arms were writhing snakes.

An idea came to him.

"Colley," he called. "Have the men ready. I am going to have the Dark Brothers briefly drop the buffer. Shields should be up to stop arrows."

Colley looked askance at the *horde* leader. "What purpose will it serve to leave ourselves open to more volleys of missiles?"

"I need to let something out. If all goes according to plan, the barrier of protection will be back up before we can be attacked."

"What will happen if this plan fails?"

"Then be prepared to die as a Veil raider," Razor replied with brutal honesty.

His lieutenant hesitated only a moment before he turned and shouted orders to the remaining raiders.

Razor looked down at the Dark Brothers who had dismounted when they reformed the bubble of magic. Near collapse, they leaned on each other for support.

"Listen to me carefully," he told the wilting mages. "I want you to dissolve the shield at my command."

"But then we are certain to be killed!" said the one-armed mage through clenched teeth.

"I am not finished, you fool! I want the shape shifter ready to attack the Blood Prince the second you collapse our protection. When the lycanthrope launches its attack, immediately reform the shield. If we're lucky, the beast might wound or even kill the Royal. If not, the Prince will have his hands full and stop gnawing at our screen of protection…which gives Muurch more time to open a portal we can escape through. Do you understand me?" Both mages nodded.

"It just might work!" the whole Dark Brother exclaimed.

"It had better," Razor growled. "Because we are out of options. At any rate, if the Gatemaster doesn't open a portal soon, our doom will only be delayed. Prepare yourself!"

The hole opened by the Blood Prince inched wider and wider. Razor studied the young Royal and could see his total concentration was on the destruction of the protective barrier. The timing would never be better. With a nod, he signaled the Dark Brothers.

The werewolf surged to the edge of the buffer.

CHAPTER 45

FTER LEAVING ALEX'S ROOM, ALABASTER JOHN AND TELL traveled down the wide corridor until they passed out of earshot of the guards. The Court Magister stopped and looked Tell in the eye.

"Keep a close watch on Lady Alexandria. I am convinced she knows something she is not telling us. Whatever it is, it has terrified her to the point she dares not speak of it. I want to know what disturbs her so."

"I shall not let her out of my sight!" Tell vowed.

The Grand Master leaned closer. "Trust no one. There are things afoot here I do not understand, yet somehow these strange occurrences must be related." He leaned back and tapped his lips.

"You are new to Wheel, but I have known Alex since birth. She has been a spoiled, petulant child in all that time. Now, however, since suffering her accident, she is a different person. In fact, *different* doesn't do this change justice. *She is completely the opposite of what she used to be!* Then, of a sudden, she is attacked via an *encarthus* spell. A coincidence? I think not. This carries the stench of the Dark Queen, but for the life of me, I know not how."

Alabaster John swallowed his frustration and studied the young officer. He revealed more than he would have liked. He hoped his confidence in him was not misplaced.

Tell shifted from foot to foot, clearly uncomfortable. "Although my family has long supplied the military with horses, I have only been to Wheel twice—the ink on my commission is still drying as we speak. However, it is hard to imagine Alex—I mean Lady Alexandria—ever being *different* in the way you describe."

He looked up. "Forgive me, Grand Master, but her personality and everything about her seems natural, not forced—the way it *should* be. If she is acting, then she must be the greatest actress the stage has ever produced."

The young officer shrugged. "However, your words are wise, and I shall heed them."

Alabaster John favored Tell with a smile. "I would have expected nothing less." The mage turned to leave, but Tell called to him before he had taken two steps.

"Grand Master! You said trust no one, yet you appear to trust me. Why, when I am someone you have only just met?"

Alabaster John chuckled. "A fair question, Tell Tollett. You see, you wear your sentiment for the Lady Alexandria like a medallion on your chest. Were you part of any *plot* to harm Alex, you could not show such feelings."

Red-faced, Tell asked, "Is it that obvious?"

Still chuckling, Alabaster John answered, "I am afraid so." His face took on a sober countenance. "But be careful, Tell. Alex is a beautiful woman—the kind of beauty that causes men to forget whatever they are doing and take notice. So, while I view your *interest* in Alex as natural, there are others who might view your attentiveness with far more suspicion. Do not wear your feelings so openly."

"Y-yes, Grand Master," Tell stammered.

Alabaster John placed a hand on the young officer's shoulder. "Just keep a sharp eye open. Let me know if you observe or see anything unusual." With that, both men parted and went on their way.

Alex foremost in their thoughts.

Two figures walked about in a secluded garden adjacent to the Duchess's chambers. Dorothea was beside herself.

"You stupid, stupid fool! You almost killed her!" she raged.

Rodric's hand flew to his chest. "My dear, Dorothea. Are you not concerned for my own welfare? I could have been killed by the backlash of power from our *harmless* Alexandria."

"Would that she succeeded!" the Duchess snapped. "It would have made things far simpler."

A sardonic grin appeared on Rodric's face. "That almost sounds like a threat, Dorothea. My good mother and father surely did not have this in mind when you were chosen to carry out their plan in Wheel."

He furrowed his brow. "Let's see, what were the words you used? *Hmm*, ah yes, *This task was given directly to me.* Well, *I* am part of the plan lest you forget, so the *task* involves me as well!"

He paused, "By the way, where is my favorite governess, that cow, Adelina?"

"Adelina has been sent away. She left for the outer provinces early this morning," the Duchess snapped.

Rodric crowed and slapped his knee. "So I was right. *She* triggered Alexandria's power!"

"I never said that! Alexandria has behaved strangely ever since she fell from that cursed horse. However, because Adelina lost her control over Alexandria, it would be hard to justify the need for a governess *and* a posted guard!"

With a smug expression, Rodric asked, "Does it pain you so much, Dorothea, to admit I was right?"

"You don't get it do you, Rodric? Do you understand what you have done? Do you realize how much is at stake here, and how you may have jeopardized years of planning? This is not a game where you move pieces at a will. *You almost killed Alexandria!*"

"The whore flinched from my touch! She who flaunted her body at every man, from the baker's apprentice to pink-faced squires, didn't like my touch! She needed to be taught a lesson, and I was just the one to teach her! I need no lecture from a Dark Sister who owes her position to the generosity of Marlinda!" Rodric snarled.

Dorothea began to laugh.

"What, pray tell, do you find so amusing?" he scowled.

"Generosity you say? Oh, Rodric, you've been *far* too long from the Dark Queen's caverns. There is no generosity, only success or failure. You are rewarded with the former and sent to the breeding pits for the latter. I worked my way up from novice to master and was *never* afforded generosity! Do you think you are immune from the Veil Queen and King's anger? Do you think your position is secure because you are their son? You are a means to an end, Rodric, as I am. The penalty for failure is death, swift if you are lucky, long and agonizing if not."

Rodric went pale at Dorothea's reminder. This did not go unnoticed by her.

She nodded with satisfaction. "Good! It seems I finally have your attention. Now let me tell you what your little stunt has cost us. First, it has drawn Alabaster John into the fray. He has been a thorn in my side since I married the Duke and has never trusted me. He has a suspicious nature which I can assure you will be doubly so now. He will not rest until satisfied of the hows and whys of this attack on Alexandria. If he turns up even one thread of evidence that ties you to the *encarthus* spell, we are finished!"

Sullen, Rodric asked, "Why not just kill him and be done with it?"

"You mean besides the fact he is a Grand Master and would be hard to kill, or managing that, the small problem of how to explain his death?"

Rodric waved his hand. "Bah! It could be made to look like an accident."

"Don't think I haven't considered it. However, there have already been too many *accidents*. The old Duke is no fool, and neither is his Council. They might suspect his death no accident at all and once again, begin a search for evidence. Whether they found anything or not, the heightened scrutiny would bring a close watch on all of us. Our plans would be delayed indefinitely."

Rodric offered no comment, content to glower.

"Now, thanks to you, we can be assured Alexandria will be so heavily guarded, a mouse couldn't steal into her room unnoticed."

Dorothea stopped beside a stone bench draped with soft cushions. She sat down.

"*That* is another reason I sent Adelina away. I couldn't afford another reaction from Alexandria at her touch. If he caught wind of this, Alabaster John would have Adelina in his chamber for questioning before the ink dried on her arrest papers."

She pounded a fist into a cushion. "Damn you, Rodric! I wanted Alexandria watched but not so closely *we* have no access to her!"

She stood and pointed at him. "But the most damaging result of your cruel stupidity is to possibly estrange Alexandria. The Duke dotes on his daughter, and if she digs in her heels against marrying you, I may not be able to change his mind this time."

"I had nothing to do with her reaction to me!" Rodric spat. "I tell you it was Adelina's doing! *She* frightened Alexandria, and *she* caused her to act the way she did!"

The Duchess studied Rodric. "And you are sure she did not know it was you who attacked her through the *encarthus* spell?"

"Yes," Rodric lied.

"Then here is what you are going do. You will leave Wheel to visit your lands and estates. I will make up some pretext to give to the Duke. I will send for you when I want you to return."

Rodric's eyes narrowed. "Leave so suddenly? Why? Shouldn't I at least visit Alexandria before I go? Won't I appear a callous buffoon if I don't present a show of concern for her well-being?"

Dorothea stomped her foot. "No! I don't want her to lay eyes on you at all. *You* say she doesn't know you were the one who assaulted her, but I am not so convinced. To see you may jog her memory or worse, cause another disastrous response. How will we explain *that*? No, it is best if you leave and the sooner the better—this very morning if possible. I will give the Duke your apologies."

Rodric threw up his hands. "As you wish."

The Duchess fixed him with a baleful stare. "When I summon you back, you will do everything in your power to woo Alexandria. You will take her on trips, visit shops in the city, talk with her, and have intimate dinners. In short, you will *charm* her. Most importantly, you will do *nothing* to cause her to fear or reject you."

"Oh, I am good at charms," Rodric quipped, his dark humor returning. "And I will act the perfect gentlemen. She will be unable to resist me, never fear."

"*Fear* is something you specialize in, Rodric, particularly in helpless women," Dorothea retorted. "However, I don't care what you do once we have Alexandria under our control and have used her for our purposes."

Rodric flashed a wicked smile. "Oh, you can't imagine all the fun I have planned for our dear Alexandria."

His eyes glinted with malice. "And she will learn a whole new dimension of fear then."

He licked his lips. "Oh, yes indeed."

CHAPTER 46

OZAR TENSED AS THE HOLE IN THE CHARMED SCREEN YAWED wider and wider.

He gripped the reins tighter. *It won't be long now.*

The First Advisor turned his attention to the enemy within the buffer. A large man on horseback, undoubtedly the leader of the Veil raiders, appeared to speak with a pair of cloaked figures beside him. One displayed a scorched sleeve and a blackened stump. He nodded. *The vile Dark Brothers.*

A flicker of movement caught his eye.

A naked man hurried to the edge of the protective shield. Puzzled by the odd sight, Bozar's mouth dropped when the man's flesh bubbled, and shifted and he transformed before his eyes. A cruel snout thrust from the mouth, and paws with vicious claws replaced hands. Within seconds, an enormous werewolf stood where a man once existed.

Bozar blinked. *What madness is this?*

Too late, comprehension dawned on what the raider leader's plan must be about. Before he could shout a warning, the magical shield collapsed. The abrupt decompression between the two competing enchantments created a shock wave that slammed into Bozar and the mounted men around him. Ears ringing in pain, men clapped hands to their heads, while horses reared and bucked in terror.

Into this confusion came the werewolf.

The lycanthrope streaked toward Tal with preternatural speed, sharp fangs snapping in anticipation of tearing into the young prince's flesh.

Tal's reflexes saved his life.

In a blur of motion, he threw himself backward, the *snap* of slavering jaws passing just inches from his throat. The werewolf recovered and leaped again. Unable to dodge the creature this time, Tal brought his shield arm up and clubbed the werewolf with his mailed fist. With a *thump*, he connected with the shape shifter's chest. His arm shivered from the impact, like he had struck a rock wall, but it deflected the werewolf enough to cause the sharp fangs to miss again.

Tal rolled to his feet, drew his dagger, and twisted to face the shape shifter.

The lycanthrope's paws found purchase, and clods of wet sod flew into the air as it turned and sprang. The young prince didn't attempt to dodge away this time but instead, held his ground until the last moment...then sidestepped. The beast missed, and when its momentum carried it past Tal, he grabbed the werewolf from behind.

They tumbled over and over, with Tal plunging his dagger repeatedly into the shape shifter's chest. Howls of pain split the night, and the werewolf attempted to bite Tal's hand. He slipped an arm around the werewolf's neck and held the beast in a savage headlock, then moved his dagger arm out of reach of its fangs.

Cordlike muscles in Tal's arms stood in sharp relief, while he increased the pressure on the shape shifter's neck. The beast began to gag and wheeze, then grabbed his arm in an attempt to break free, its claws scrabbling impotently over his mail.

With a sudden shift of his weight, Tal rolled over on top of the werewolf. He pinned one knee on the beast's back, and with his arm still locked around the werewolf's neck, pulled with all his strength. The shape shifter's spine bent backward like a tightly strung bow.

Then it broke with a loud *crack*.

Tal picked up the disabled werewolf before its bones could re-knit. He lifted the creature high over his head and with a primal scream, threw it down onto the ground.

The lycanthrope lay stunned. Tal drew his sword and plunged it through its chest. Such was the force of his thrust, it skewered the werewolf completely through its body and into the muddy soil.

The Blood Prince spoke words of power.

Waves of magic coursed through the sword and into the wound cleaved by the blade. An agonized yowl erupted from the werewolf, which ended when the beast's body disintegrated into smoke and ash.

Tal pulled his blade from the charred remains and shouted in triumph. He turned and faced the Veil raiders.

The shield of magic reappeared.

Before he could renew his efforts to rip it apart, Bozar stepped in front of him. "Hold a moment, Tal."

Bozar removed a staff of *Kaba* wood from his saddle and planted it on the ground beside Tal. From Kazir, an equatorial string of islands and Bozar's birthplace, the staff represented his favored Artifact to channel magic.

"Now you may continue. I will be ready for any additional foul tricks the Dark Ones may conjure up."

Tal nodded, and once again, wisps of magic flowed from his fingertips and toward the screen of magic.

This time he would destroy it!

Within the buffer, Razor prepared to die.

He positioned his remaining men the best he could. They knew no mercy would be shown at the hands of the Empire's soldiers. Although green and inexperienced, like cornered animals, they would fight to the death.

The death of the lycanthrope cost him the element of surprise, so it would be pointless to dissolve the shield and send another *special* to attack the Blood Prince. Besides, he made short work of the werewolf, an amazing feat and one that he would not have believed had he not seen it with his own eyes.

His plan—the *last* before his certain death in battle—entailed the Dark Brothers maintaining as long as they could. When they wavered, he would order them to drop the screen, and the *horde* would attack first. He hoped the action would catch the Meredithians off guard, and they could take a few more of the Empire's soldiers with them before being wiped out.

A small consolation, but all he had left.

The hole punched through the shield grew wider. Razor gauged its progress and decided the time had arrived to have the Dark brothers dissolve it. He raised his arm to give the signal to attack, when a commotion occurred behind him.

He turned to see his men pointing at the Veil. The normally invisible barrier glowed and sparked with thousands of tiny discharges of light. The kaleidoscopic illumination revealed a cloudy wormhole—directly to the rear of the raiders! Within the portal, foggy mist twisted and swirled.

Grim despair transformed into hope in Razor's chest. A doorway finally opened for them! They just needed a little more time for it to fully coalesce.

"Hold!" he shouted at the Dark Brothers. "Hold, damn you!"

The uninjured mage nodded. The one-armed mage, slack-jawed and with eyes glazed in pain, did not acknowledge him. It mattered not to Razor, just so long as the Dark Brother gave his last to hold the integrity of the shield.

A few minutes more, that's all I need.

He just might make it out alive after all.

CHAPTER 47

LEX FOUND DRESSING MORE OF A CHALLENGE THAN SHE anticipated.

Weak and lightheaded, her neck still throbbed from Rodric's throttling. The thought of food nauseated her, and she pushed away the breakfast tray next to her bed. Fortunately, Alabaster John left the flask of honeyed mead, and she helped herself to it. Fortified somewhat, she found the energy to continue.

Her bodice, with its hooks and stays, provided her biggest challenge. Frustrated, she almost cast the undergarment aside and dressed without it. However, modesty aside, another reality stopped her. Her former Mona figure could get away without the underclothing, but Alexandria definitely could not. The last thing she needed was scandalous whispers in the Duke's ear—although she suspected the *former* Alexandria had provided plenty—and more pretext for interference in her life from Dorothea.

Alex picked the easiest dress from her cavernous closet to squeeze into. It fit tightly and exposed too much cleavage, but she needed to hurry. Alabaster John promised her time for only a short visit with Darcy, and she didn't intend to spend it trying on clothes.

A few brushstrokes later, her hair fell in a golden avalanche about her shoulders and back. *Just another advantage of being Alexandria—hair that cooperates all the time.*

Alex sighed and checked her reflection in a large oval mirror mounted on a wooden pedestal near her vanity. Purple bruises on her neck now matched the one above her right temple. When she leaned in for a closer look, she discovered odd symbols carved into the mirror's circular wood frame. Also interspersed on the frame were words in an unfamiliar language. The entire piece reeked of antiquity.

A bout of dizziness gripped Alex, and she reached out and grabbed the mirror's pedestal.

Immediately, the engraved words began to glow.

She snatched her hand away and rubbed her eyes. When she looked again, the mirror appeared normal.

What?

Hand to her mouth, Alex stared. All she saw was her reflection. She shook her head. *Now I'm seeing things.*

Alex didn't have time to puzzle it out further. She needed to check on Darcy.

She turned to leave, only to discover a carpenter hard at work repairing the broken door. The now *four* guards snapped to attention as Alex walked out.

Tell waited in the corridor, his eyes widening at the sight of her. He gulped at the sight of the curves the tight gown revealed.

Sore and tired, Alex snapped, "Do you like what you see?"

Tell's face turned scarlet. "Yes! I mean, no! I mean..." His voice trailed off.

The young officer swallowed. "My pardon, Alex—I mean Lady Alexandria. May we just go?" he pleaded.

Alex kicked herself for being so short. *What kind of reaction did you expect in this dress? Get used to it!*

She hooked her arm in Tell's. "Of course we can." A sigh of relief gushed from his lips, and he led her to the infirmary.

Two guards fell in behind, and Alex had a sinking feeling this was to be her lot for the foreseeable future. No matter where she went, soldiers would shadow her every step of the way. She tightened her grip on Tell—and hoped he would forgive her rudeness.

She needed every friend she could get in this place.

Tell led them through a maze of halls and intersections before they finally arrived at the infirmary. Although she tried to pay close attention to their progress, after the first half-dozen twists and turns, she became hopelessly lost.

As they entered the medical ward, they walked past guards posted inside and out. Alex spied the facility's lone occupant, the miserable, huddled form of Darcy on a corner bed. Her handmaiden quickly looked away, fear on her face.

Alex sat down next to her. Before she could speak, Darcy blurted, "I am so sorry, M'Lady! I-I didn't know. They told me I attacked you, but I don't remember anything. I fell asleep and awakened here. They-they will tell me nothing more. Please believe me, M'Lady!" Head in her hands, she wept.

Putting her arm around her shoulders, Alex hugged her. "Of course I believe you. The Grand Master and Lord Tollett have explained it all to me. You needn't punish yourself so."

When Darcy peeked from between her hands with red, tear streaked eyes, Alex threw her arms around her. Soon both women were crying.

Alex wiped the tears from her cheeks and stood up. "Come, Darcy. You are leaving with me."

The servant girl's face transformed from misery to hopeful joy. "Yes, M'Lady," she responded. She leapt from the bed and put on her slippers. "Can we go now?"

"We *are* leaving now aren't we, Tell?" Alex said to the young cavalry officer.

"As you wish, Lady Alexandria," he replied.

However, when they turned to leave the infirmary, the guards by the door moved to block their progress. "I'm sorry, sir," the guard nearest the door said. "Lord Ruffin has ordered the girl detained until further notice. She is not to leave without his permission. He was *very* explicit about this, sir."

Tell stepped forward, his face inches from the guard's nose. "The investigation, while still technically open, has concluded the servant girl innocent in complicity to harm the Lady Alexandria. This was confirmed by no less a personage than Alabaster John himself," he snapped. "Now remove yourself before I put you on report!"

The guard didn't flinch. "I'm sorry, sir. As I said, we have our orders."

Anger flashed in Tell's eyes. *This is not going to end well*, Alex thought.

Before he could react further, she quickly interposed herself between them. She turned to the guard and smoothed her skirt. "Do you know who I am?"

The sentry, a young man who looked to be about Tell's age, answered, "Of course, your Ladyship. You are the Lady Alexandria."

She moved closer and purred, "Who is my father, soldier?"

The young sentry struggled to keep his eyes straight ahead. "Your father is Duke Duvalier, Lady Alexandria," he replied.

"Good. Then I want you to know I *am* taking my handmaiden! If there is any question about your previous orders, you will take it up with my father. She is tired and frightened, and I am *not* leaving her here!"

Alex kept her tone polite but at the same time, made sure it contained a sternness which would brook no argument. The guards looked at each other but remained motionless, and Alex feared they would not let them pass. Then, the young sentry signaled the other guard, and they stood aside.

"I will have to report this, sir," he warned Tell.

"I understand," Tell assured him. "Conflicting orders are an unfortunate part of a soldier's life. I will make sure your superior understands this situation."

Alex thanked the sentries. "I will explain everything to my father and ask that your actions be commended. I hope this helps you with Lord Ruffin." Relief washed across the guard's face.

Alex turned to Tell and grasped Darcy's hand. He led the two young women back to her rooms. Once there, Alex planned to draw a hot bath and soak. She had a lot to think about.

And it was only the start of her second day on Meredith.

CHAPTER 48

TAL, HIS ENTIRE CONCENTRATION ON DESTROYING THE MARAUDERS' magical shield, was startled by Bozar's shout.

"A portal opens! If you do not rip the screen apart soon, they will escape!" The first to spot the telltale swirl of a gate appearing in the opaque Veil, his normally unflappable First Advisor now urged Tal to redouble his efforts.

Tal spared only a nod and brought all his power to bear against the barrier of magic. The smell of ozone filled the air, the *crackle* of magics popped and hissed.

The hole grew wider.

Tal forced the gap wide enough to gain the purchase he needed to tear the shield of enchantment in two. He strained, the veins in his neck bulging with the colossal effort. Suddenly, a *tinkle* like shattered glass resonated, and Tal, manipulating the magic with his hands, jerked them apart. With a *roar*, the Dark Brother's enchantment collapsed into a million diamond-like shards that flared and winked out.

Spent and exhausted, the young prince fell to his knees.

Bozar stood over his young charge, while his sharp eyes scanned for any threat. Dimly aware of the sounds of fighting, Tal staggered to his feet.

Gravelback's men attacked immediately upon the collapse of the magical barrier. They were soon joined by the Storm Riders, who alighted onto the ground, dismounted, and waded into the fight. Their storm horses were too valuable to risk in close-quarter combat—in fact, their wings put them at a disadvantage when grounded—and it was too risky to remain airborne and continue to shoot arrows at raiders fused in a hand-to-hand struggle with Gravelback's cavalry.

Tal ripped his sword from its sheath, only to find himself restrained by Bozar's hand.

"A moment. Recover your strength first."

Tal grit his teeth. All around him, the sounds of battle played a bloody symphony. The ring of swords against shields reverberated in his ears, the coppery smell of blood mingling with men's curses and cries of mortal agony. Flashes of lightning produced a strobe-like visual to the knots of men locked in mortal combat.

The young prince could take no more.

He shook off Bozar's arm and raced to join the fray. A mammoth figure emerged from the struggle. Swinging a huge club in an arc much like a farmer would wield a scythe, the ogre cleared the ground in front of it of living men. Maddened by pain, a score of arrows pierced the creature's tough skin, while green blood trickled from multiple wounds inflicted by Meredithian swords.

One of Gravelback's men attempted to charge the ogre and impale it with a javelin. The huge creature roared and with a mighty swing, smashed both horse and rider into the ground. A crimson pool spread from the inert bodies. More shafts sprouted from the ogre as prudent cavalrymen chose to shoot from a distance, rather than engage the creature at close quarters. Driven into an even greater frenzy, the giant charged a line of cavalrymen.

Tal screamed a challenge and before his First Advisor could stop him, sprinted after the ogre.

The giant paused at the sight of the young prince. It reversed course and with a bellow, tried to crush Tal with one blow. He dodged nimbly to the side, and the club pounded the rain-soaked ground, to shower him in mud and grass. Before the ogre could ready another blow, Tal swung his sword in an overhead strike at the arm holding the club. Bone and sinew parted, and the ogre's hand flopped to the ground, severed at the wrist from the ferocious blow.

The giant stared at the stump, green blood spurting from the horrible wound. Before the creature could recover from its shock, Tal reversed his sword thrust and drove the blade under the ogre's ribs and deep into its heart. The ogre swayed, a blank expression on its face. Death finally registered in its dull brain, and the giant fell to its knees and rolled over on its back.

Sightless eyes stared at the night sky, while Tal wrenched his sword free, and cleaned it on the ogre's tunic. He looked up to discover the battle rapidly drawing to a close. Scores of raiders lay dead and dying, with only a few left to carry on the battle. One, a large man, lay vigorously around himself, his sword cutting down one cavalryman after another.

Bozar pointed to the Veil. "Tal, look!" he cried.

A portal now coalesced behind the mass of struggling men. Resembling a large tunnel, it consisted of an amorphous gray-white matter that corkscrewed into the distance to disappear from sight.

A shout went up from the few surviving raiders at the sight of their possible salvation. Given new vigor, they redoubled their efforts to cut themselves free and flee through the door.

A riderless horse trotted near Tal. He picked up a discarded shield and launched himself into the saddle. Heels dug into the horse's flanks, and he urged the horse toward the fleeing raiders.

Razor spotted the Royal coming.

With a brutal thrust of his sword, he skewered the cavalry-man in front of him through the chest. Blood fountained from his opponent's mouth. By the time he ripped his sword free, he realized he could not break away in time to make it to the portal. Razor turned to face the charging Blood Prince.

The shock from the Royal's blow to his shield numbed his arm almost to the point of uselessness. He shook the arm to get some feeling back, then hacked at the Blood Prince's thigh, oblig-ing the Prince to block the blow with his own sword. The ring of steel upon steel echoed as the two blades clashed again and again.

The *horde* leader quickly changed tactics and risked an open-ing in his defense to strike a mortal blow at the Royal. Bent low over the saddle, he feinted with his shield—as if he was about to land an overhead slash of his sword. Instead, when the Blood Prince brought his own shield up to counter the expected blow, Razor thrust his sword *under* the Prince's guard at his exposed ab-domen.

The Royal's remarkable reflexes saved him.

Instead of delivering a killing strike, the Blood Prince man-aged to bring his shield down quickly enough so the edge caught the sword thrust...just enough to have it skitter harmlessly across the mail beneath his tunic. Razor cursed. Had his parry landed true, even armor would not have saved the Royal from being gut-ted.

Because Razor left himself exposed with the desperate gam-bit, the Prince's return parry slashed the *horde* leader across the chest. Fortunately, the Royal could not put his full weight behind the blow since he had been forced to lean away from Razor's at-tack. Still, a red line formed where the sword parted chain mail and bit into his soft flesh. The *horde* leader cursed anew. Teeth clenched in pain, he broke away and urged his horse away from the young Prince.

Razor's feverish eyes darted left and right. *I won't survive another encounter with the Royal.* Only a handful of his men were left, and the Dark Brothers lay dead, their bodies a forest of shafts. The headless torsos of the two Centaurs—one with hindquarters still kicking—lay near the sorcerers. Remarkably, the snakeman still lived. Nimble enough to avoid sword blows, his long serpent arms continued to strike at the soldiers and keep them at bay.

Then his luck ran out.

The swordsmen moved back, and arrows sprouted from the meld's body. Even in death, the arms continued to writhe and hiss.

Shafts began to rain around Razor. Realizing he was one of the few targets left, he bent low in the saddle and urged his horse to a swerving gallop. Out of the corner of his eye, he spotted the young girl they captured from the dairy farm. She stood alone and struggled to free herself from her bonds. The *horde* leader sawed the reins, turned his mount around, and galloped toward the girl.

With one hand on the pommel, he lowered himself to the side of his horse and snatched the girl around the waist. In one smooth motion, he swung her onto the saddle with him. Her wild struggles ended with a blow to her head from the hilt of his sword. Unconscious, her head lolled from side to side.

As he hoped, the deadly flight of missiles stopped when the Meredithians feared hitting his captive. Even so, his spine itched. With the girl held in front of him, sooner or later an impatient archer would take a chance and target his back.

Razor's head swiveled side to side. The gateway through the Veil lay tantalizingly close...so close.

But he would never make it.

Already a number of the accursed storm riders had returned

to their mounts and took flight. They would be cut off long before they reached the gateway. A plan born of desperation leaped into his mind.

"To the portal!" the *horde* leader roared and raced to the safety of the swirling wormhole. The few surviving raiders broke away and followed the *horde* leader.

Moments later, Colley pulled up beside Razor on a lathered mount. Covered in blood, the raid leader couldn't distinguish if it was his lieutenant's or the enemy's. However, there could be no mistaking the shaft which protruded from his shoulder.

"Think we'll make it?" Colley cried through clenched teeth.

Razor didn't answer and instead looked ahead. The garrison cavalry made no attempt to follow them, and seconds later, it became clear why. As he feared, storm riders already circled the area above the gateway...and their only avenue of escape.

Razor lifted a hand in salute. "You have been a good raider, Colley."

He pulled on the reins and let his men pound past him. Then he turned his mount and at a full gallop, angled away from them.

And away from the Veil.

CHAPTER 49

THE DUKE VISITED ALEX NOT LONG AFTER SHE RETURNED TO HER chambers.

His eyes widened at the sight of Darcy. "Lord Ruffin assured me she would be detained."

"Father, I *couldn't* leave her," Alex said. She explained why she insisted her handmaiden come with her. The Duke did not protest and promised to speak with Lord Ruffin on behalf of the guards.

The old Duke hugged her and repeatedly squeezed her like a plump fruit. "Are you sure you suffered no further injuries?" he asked over and over again.

"Yes, Father," Alex replied patiently. The relief on the old Duke's face both lifted her spirits and saddened her. The love he felt for his daughter and only child warmed her heart—yet it seemed a stolen love, unfit for an imposter.

Stop it, her inner voice shouted. *You are Alexandria, so you must receive and give love. You cannot think like Mona!*

Reminded anew of the dangerous ground she tread on, Alex leaned forward and kissed the Duke on the cheek. "Thank you for being so concerned about me."

He released her and stepped back. "Of course, daughter. What kind of father would I be otherwise?"

About a thousand times better than the drug-addled parents I had back on—Alex quickly squelched the Mona thought.

The Duke's face grew dark. "Whoever did this to you will be

dealt with severely. I have the entire resources of the Dukedom dedicated to the search for this-this...*fiend.*"

Alex bit her lip to stop from shouting Rodric's name. Without proof, her father wouldn't believe her. Worse, he might think her mind still muddled from the attack.

The Duke interrupted her thoughts. "An emergency has taken Lord Regret back to his ancestral lands. Although I assured him you have recovered and are whole, he apologized profusely for not being here at your side." He leaned forward and winked. "He seemed most anxious to conclude his business so he could return to you."

Alex forced a smile. *Rodric's afraid I might identify him as my assailant.* She repressed a shudder. *I'm just glad he's gone.* Had she seen him so soon after he tried to throttle her, she wasn't sure how she would have reacted.

An uneventful dinner followed that evening, attended by just the Duke, the Duchess, and Alex. No mention of the attack on her came up, for which Alex was grateful. She did not want to relive the experience ever again. Her father spoke of the Dukedom and some small affairs to be dealt with, while Dorothea contributed little, except to interject a comment here and there.

Her behavior seemed rather odd. Alex's first impression of the Duchess—a domineering woman quick to interject her opinion—yet she now appeared to take great pains to keep a low profile.

A suspicion crept into Alex's mind. *Could Dorothea somehow be complicit in Rodric's assault?* She tried to dismiss it as paranoia; however, it stubbornly clung to her thoughts. This made her already lukewarm appetite disappear, and she picked at her food.

Pleading exhaustion, she asked to be excused. The Duke readily acquiesced, then embraced Alex and wished her a good night.

Halfway to her chambers, Alex came to an abrupt halt—her guards almost running into her—when a thought struck her.

Darcy made it clear Alexandria has a reputation beyond shameless flirtation, much of it for being difficult. This has to change. I need friends and all the help I can get. Maybe I can start with the guards.

She pivoted and went back to the kitchen. The cook and staff, just cleaning up, gaped at her. Moments later, Alex had the guards pushing a food-laden cart toward her room. At the doors, the two sentries snapped to attention. She directed her escort to take the warming cloth off the food. The wonderful aroma of fresh-baked bread and meat-filled pastries wafted in the air.

"I thought you would like some hot food to eat on your watch tonight," Alex told the foursome. "It must be tedious to stand watch over me all night and then provide escort wherever I go."

The guards looked uneasily at each other. Finally, a soldier with a triple chevron on his uniform's shoulder spoke. "You are more than generous, Lady Alexandria. But we are on duty and are not permitted to eat or drink."

Alex shrugged. "Nonsense. There are four of you...more than enough to keep watch on me. I can't believe some good food would compromise my safety. Besides, if you are hungry, you might worry more about an empty belly than about me."

From the keen looks at the food, Alex could tell the soldiers agreed with her. The sentry with the chevrons chewed his lip, unsure what to do.

Alex decided to help him with his decision. "What if I sit here while you eat?" *That* seemed to satisfy him, much to the relief of his fellow soldiers.

One of the guards retrieved a chair for her, and she sat and watched them attack the food. She chatted amiably with them and learned their names were Henric, Rickert, and Arlo. The squad leader's name was Billet, although the other sentries called him Bill.

Three of her guards—fresh-faced, lanky, and fair-haired—could have passed for brothers, while Bill, shorter and stocky with a muscular build, had dark eyes and a swarthy complexion. He was also the oldest and the only married one among them.

The food soon disappeared, and the soldiers helped Alex clean up the plates and stack them back on the cart. Alex wiped her hands on her skirt.

"Perhaps one of you can return the cart to the kitchen?" She winked at Bill. "No reason to trouble anyone further I should think." A grin split the stocky squad leader's face. He motioned, and Rickert disappeared with the trolley.

While Alex waited outside, Henric and Arlo conducted a thorough search of her suite and the terrace outside—standard procedure from now on an apologetic Bill explained.

He cleared his throat, "Er, Lady Alexandria. We, ah, we, *ahem,* we would just like to thank you for the meal and all that," he stammered. "It were…it were a nice thing to do for me and the boys."

Alex waved her hand. "It was nothing. I enjoyed our conversation and learning more about each of you. Perhaps we can do it again soon." The guards nodded eagerly.

Moments later, Arlo emerged from her suite to declare all was well. Alex bid them goodnight and closed the door. She leaned back against the smooth wood and smiled. Their faces reflected a mixture of friendliness and, more importantly, *respect*. Only a small step, but still, an important one.

Alex drew the hot bath she had promised herself, and while immersed in the silky heat, reflected on the events of the past two days—her appearance, her future, her *life*, all changed in less time than it took to take a breath.

Alex glanced at her body, skin a reddish hue in the steamy bathwater. She shook her head. *Only days ago I woke up looking like this...but now it seems like years.*

She thought of the guard at the infirmary and how when she moved closer, the struggle he had to keep his eyes off her voluptuous figure...yet another reminder of the power her beauty held over men.

She turned this over in her mind and finally came to a decision.

Although she told herself she would never be like Lady Anne and use her looks to bend others to her will, occasions could come up when she might need to fudge on this...like survival. *Like life and death.*

Alex sighed and stepped from the water. She studied her dripping figure in the mirror. If circumstances ever forced her to use her body as a weapon of enticement, one thing was certain.

She possessed a formable arsenal.

CHAPTER 50

RAZOR RISKED A LOOK OVER HIS SHOULDER.

His remaining men, having cut themselves free from the Empire's cavalry, charged toward the Veil and open gateway. This gave the waiting storm riders a clear line of fire. A withering flight of arrows met the survivors, and they dropped like stones.

Soon, only one man remained—Colley. His lieutenant, although pierced by numerous shafts, still rode hard for the portal. As he watched, more arrows sprouted from Colley's body, and he toppled from the saddle.

Razor was the last survivor.

He turned away and thundered for the treeline ahead. His men's sacrifice bought him some time, but he had only a momentary respite before the Empire's soldiers took notice and resumed the chase.

He dug his heels into his mount, but the horse faltered, the weight of two riders taking a toll on the beast. If not for his hostage, he had no doubt he would have already suffered Colley's fate. Now, however, the girl was a burden he could no longer afford.

He flung her from the saddle.

His mount's speed immediately increased, but as he neared the forest, arrows whistled by him. One struck his mount's flank. By the time he got the wild bucking under control, the shafts had thickened to a deadly swarm. So close now he could make out leafy boughs, the safety of the forest beckoned.

Just a few more paces, just a few more…

He pounded into the trees, branches whipping his face and hands. The *zip, zip, zip* of arrows followed his progress for a short distance before the thick canopy stopped them.

He rode hard for several more moments, then pulled up. His pursuers would soon be upon him, so he had little time. He flung himself off the steed, then walloped its hindquarters with the flat of his sword. The horse reared and bolted into the thick under-brush. The raid leader bared his teeth.

That should keep them busy following a false trail.

He concealed himself within a dense copse and waited. His patience was rewarded when a short time later, the first of his pursuers appeared. Forced to dismount, the thick foliage obliged the men to scatter while they searched for him.

Perfect.

One of the cavalrymen wandered close to where Razor lay hidden. He studied the soldier and decided while a little smaller than him, he would have to do. Soundlessly, he left his hiding place and crept up behind him. With a sudden lunge, he leaped forward to place both hands on the soldier's head. Razor twisted and was rewarded with the *snap* of the cavalryman's neck. Taken by surprise, the soldier died soundlessly.

Razor dragged the dead man back to his hiding place and quickly undressed. He rolled his clothing and weapons in a ball and buried them under a layer of dead leaves and forest debris. Then he stripped the uniform off the body. Although a tight fit, he managed to get into it. Last, he reached for the chain around his neck and the Artifact that dangled from it and concealed it under the uniform.

Loud voices, accompanied by the noise of soldiers moving through the trees, came to his ears. He covered the body with shrubbery, then slipped from his hiding place. The dead caval-ryman's horse stood nearby cropping grass, and he grabbed the reins.

Pulling the horse along, Razor joined the search.

Helpless, Tal watched the fleeing *horde* leader disappear into the trees.

The murderous scum cleverly used the girl to shield him-self from arrows, and then at the last moment, hurled her to the ground to escape unscathed.

Gravelback's men poured into the forest. For a moment, he considered joining them, then dismissed the idea. One more would make little difference. Maybe they would get lucky and find the filth, but the odds were long. The Farthering Forest cov-ered an enormous area, and an army could search for years with-out success.

Disgusted, Tal turned away. His eyes fell on the Veil...and he froze.

The wormhole continued to swirl and undulate.

His mouth fell open. By now, it should have disappeared, ei-ther closed by the Veil Queen's sorcerers or from the magic of the nearby Watch Tower.

Yet it remained.

Bozar rode up, and the young prince pointed. "What do you make of that?"

The First Advisor stared. Finally, he said, "Most...curious."

The raid leader forgotten, Tal studied the amorphous vortex. "It's almost as if the gateway is stuck—unable to fully open or fully close. Have you ever heard of such an occurrence?"

"Never," Bozar stated flatly. "And there is little about the Veil

I don't know."

"What do you think it means?"

Bozar took so long answering, Tal feared he had not heard him. Before he could repeat the question, his First Advisor replied.

"In truth, I do not know. It could be nothing, an anomaly that will disappear before the sun rises."

He turned his horse to face Tal, eyes aglow. "But it could be significant. Perhaps the Dark Queen has finally made a mistake."

Tal's heart leaped. "You mean—"

"Organize a search for the missing raider! Use every man and send for more, even if it strips every garrison from here to Meredith City. We must find him!"

Tal had never seen his *Eldred* so animated. "Of course, but—"

Bozar interrupted him again. "We must not tarry!"

Tal ran to his storm horse and leaped into the saddle. A singular thought percolated through his mind.

A way through the cursed barrier might finally be at hand.

CHAPTER 51

RIGHT SUNSHINE WARMED ALEX'S FACE.

She stood in a large meadow covered with a profusion of yellow wildflowers. Bees buzzed in abundance, drawn to their honeyed scent. An enormous oak stood sentinel in the middle of the field. Moss-covered boughs, thicker than a man's torso, drooped toward the ground. They looked perfect to climb upon and sit. Drawn, Alex walked to the tree, her long legs parting the sea of flowers.

As she drew near, she noticed a young man seated underneath the oak, his back against the gnarled trunk. Turned away, she couldn't see his face. However, the closer she got, the more detail she could make out. Ruddy-brown hair fell untidily past the nape of his neck. Long legs stretched out before him, while his tunic revealed arms bronzed by the sun. When he moved to place a grass stem in his mouth, corded muscle rippled beneath his skin.

Alex stopped, her heart beating a tattoo in her chest. Desire gripped her with such ferocity, it took her breath away. *I must go to him!*

She pulled the hem of her dress higher and started to run.

Alex woke with a start.

Disoriented, she sat up with great wheezing gasps. Hands clasped to her chest, longing burned within her. Slowly, it faded, and she collapsed back onto the pillows.

What…was that?

Never had she felt such an attraction. *To feel his arms around me, his warm skin against mine—*

"Stop it!" she cried out loud.

She threw the covers off and leaped out of bed.

Bleary-eyed, Alex peered into the murky darkness and sighed in relief. No meadow, no oak tree, and no…young man. Just the same spacious rooms and furnishings as before.

Alex shivered and, despite her mental and physical exhaustion, found herself wide awake. The events of the previous day, her near death at the hands of Rodric, and now *this*. She hadn't even seen the stranger's face in her what—*dream/vision?*—yet she still yearned for his touch. With a sigh, she crawled back under the covers and tried to sleep.

She tossed and turned for another hour before finally throwing her hands up and climbing out of bed. She grabbed her robe, slipped it on, and then stepped past the terrace door and into the night.

The early spring air held a chill, and Alex pulled her robe tighter. She picked out the nearest chair, a chaise replica with soft cushions, and sat down. Eyes closed, she leaned back and listened to the sounds of the night. Crickets chirped, a night bird of some kind hooted, and over it all, the thunder from the nearby falls. The sweet fragrance of flowering vines filled the air, and Alex breathed in their scent.

She opened her eyes and gazed at a sky filled with stars. Endless in number, they formed baffling patterns and constellations, none of which she recognized.

However, the most telling evidence Alex was no longer on Earth were the moons…all *three* of them. High in the sky, they gleamed with a silvery luminescence. Strung out from largest to smallest like pearls on a necklace, the moons chased each other across the dark sky. Moved by the astral beauty of the universe, Alex couldn't tear her eyes from the cosmic display.

One of the stars flared and separated from the others. Her eyes narrowed, and she sat up. The point of light arced closer and closer, and she soon could make out the unmistakable appearance of a man *walking* toward her. Alex recognized him immediately.

Thaddeus Finkle.

He pulled up a chair beside her and waved a hand at the sky. "The heavens are bright tonight, are they not?"

Speechless, Alex stared. Finally, she sputtered, "That's it? That's all you have to say? The stars?"

Her Angel shrugged. "You seem upset, Mona. What did you want me—"

"How about, *glad you're alive, so happy you weren't murdered your first night on Meredith*! You could have warned me. You could have told me where I was going, and I would be trapped behind this, this, *veil* thing you showed me. And mostly, you could have told me I would wake up as Sleeping Beauty!"

"Now, Mona, I did warn you. I told you that you would face dangers—"

"Only in the most general sense! You gave me no details...at all. And, thanks to you, the name is Alex, *not* Mona!"

Mr. Finkle clapped. "Bravo, bravo. You passed the first crucial test. You transitioned with minimum prompting from Mona to Alex. Well done!"

Alex's eyes bulged. *"Minimum prompting?* Are you crazy? I was almost choked to death by a monster inhabiting the body of a poor servant girl! I have never been so scared in my life—and if that wasn't bad enough, I'm going to be forced to marry the man behind the attack."

"But you *did* survive, and you have shown remarkable

resiliency." Furious, Alex didn't reply.

Mr. Finkle clucked his tongue. "Come, come, Alex. You haven't even commented on your new appearance?"

"You mean going from ugly duckling to beautiful swan? Again, you could have told me."

"There is much I couldn't share with you, Alex, and recall I did mention the wonder *and* the perils of Meredith. Besides, aren't you pleased with your new appearance?"

Alex threw up her arms. "Yes. Yes, I like it, a dream come true. Is that what you want to hear? Awkward, ugly Mona replaced by the elegant and gorgeous Alexandria Duvalier? It's what *every* girl must dream of."

Mr. Finkle cocked his head. "*Hmmm*. Snippy, are we? I'm rather surprised you don't appreciate the new *you* more. Would you like to see if I can change you to a more ordinary appearance?"

Alex blinked. "No! I'm okay with my, um, *looks*. It's just that it has taken some getting used to. People—*men*—notice me now. As plain, skinny Mona, I could pass through a room, and no one would know I was ever there. But now, I have boobs and hips, and I have to be careful what I wear, what I say, and…it's all very confusing."

Alex shook her head. "I'm not even sure how I feel about it now."

The chill of the night deepened, and she hugged herself. "I always dreamed of being pretty, to have boys flock around me. I thought it would make me the happiest girl in the world. But now…it just feels shallow."

She turned to the angel. "I'm still *me*, but no one will ever know who I really am. How can I ever share my life with someone if they only care about how I look? I'm less of a person now than when I was Mona."

Mr. Finkle frowned. "Ah, yes. It is a puzzle. Reconciling to your new appearance does take time."

He leaned closer. "However, you were never ugly. Splendor comes from within one's heart and is far more valuable and durable than outside appearance—and yours shines like a beacon during the darkest of night. The *me* you refer to will endure, while beauty, no matter how stunning, eventually fades away."

Her angel paused. "Be patient. I think you will discover there will be others who see what I see...and the notice you receive will be for all the *right* reasons."

Mr. Finkle's words managed to still her anxiety, and her thoughts turned to a question on her mind since she woke up on Meredith.

"What happened to the *old* Alexandria? She couldn't have just disappeared."

Mr. Finkle stood and clasped his hands. "Some questions are best left unanswered. *You* are Alexandria now, and that's all you need to know. For better or worse, the die is cast."

Face hard, he turned back to her. "Heed these next words carefully, Alex, because your very survival depends on it. The life you knew as Mona, the one you lived in Texas—it's gone. Your life now is what you make of it. Embrace it, and don't *ever* look back."

Silence reigned, the dull roar of the mighty cataracts the only sound. Subdued, Alex finally spoke. "So, what do I do now?"

Mr. Finkle snorted. "Well, I could say something grandiose like, 'go and fulfill your destiny' or some such nonsense, but instead you simply carry on as Alexandria Duvalier."

Alex shook her head. "You make it sound so easy. Why go through all of *this*," she said arms stretched wide, "if all you need me to do is pick up where the life of the former Alexandria ended?"

The angel flashed her a humorless smile. "An astute observation...and of course, there is far more here than meets the eye. All I can do is repeat what you already know. You are a wild card, one that can make a difference—but as Alexandria Duvalier not Mona Parker."

Alex sat up and pointed at Mr. Finkle. "What difference? How? You've told me *nothing*."

"Unfortunately, you must discover these answers yourself. I wish I could tell you more, but this is the path you must tread."

Mr. Finkle took a few steps away from Alex and stared at the sky, hands clasped behind his back. "I understand the confusion you must feel. But it *must* be this way. Of your own free will, you made a choice which in turn led you to Meredith. Now, by this same free will you must see where this leads you...I am forbidden to be more specific."

He pivoted and returned to stand beside her. "However, I can give you *some* information that might help you find your way. It includes a little history lesson."

He rubbed his hands together.

"On how magic works on Meredith."

CHAPTER 52

THE GROANS OF THE WOUNDED AND DYING GREETED THE RISING sun.

Blackened pools of congealed blood dully reflected the early morning light. The new day revealed the totality of the slaughter inflicted on the Veil raiders. Dead bodies of marauders and horses lay scattered by the hundreds across the battlefield. A makeshift pyre took shape as cavalrymen stacked bodies in preparation to burn them. The moans of wounded raiders abruptly ended as they were put to the sword, their bodies added to those already on the pyre.

The coppery tang of blood saturated the entire area as Tal inspected the site of the battle. Bozar walked by his side, while the young prince took in the entire scene with a keen eye. The rain had stopped, and blue sky began to break through ragged patches in the cloud cover. Tal found it eerily silent after the frantic chase and clash with the *horde*.

They both stopped and looked at the churning portal in the Veil.

"Any news?" Tal asked.

Bozar shook his head. "Gravelback's men are scouring the forest, while Banebolt's Storm Riders search from above. Nothing so far."

Tal's lips formed a tight line. "About what I expected. Unless we have a stroke of good fortune, we may never find the murderous scum." He turned to his *Eldred*. "I'll send word to Waldez we need every soldier they can spare."

Bozar shook his head. "Let us not be so hasty. For now, we need to study this phenomenon before we alert the entire Empire of its existence."

Tal frowned. "What? Last night you wanted to strip every garrison within hundreds of leagues to join in the search. Now you want to wait?"

His First Advisor smiled. "My assessment has changed."

"But what about the raid leader?" Tal pointed at the portal. "He must have something to do with this, or you wouldn't have wanted to find him so badly."

Bozar inclined his head. "You are correct. He may carry the Artifact that caused it to appear."

"But everyone knows the cowards have the means of creating escape holes through the Veil. This is nothing new."

"True, but remember, it is a two-step process. A Gatemaster must open a doorway, but the Artifact signals the location. One without the other is useless."

"But then how..." Tal paused and scratched his chin. "The gateway should have closed long ago."

"Exactly." Bozar moved closer. "The portal shouldn't be here, shouldn't have opened this close to a Watch Tower, and certainly *should* have disappeared by now."

Tal pursed his lips. "So, the Dark Queen and her minions think the portal closed..."

His eyes widened. *"They don't realize it is still open!"*

Bozar looked around, then pulled Tal closer. "Not open, but *caught*—somewhere in between!" he whispered. "The magic of *this* gate has been compromised, and if so, we may finally be able to force a way through."

The enormity of the First Advisor's comment settled on Tal's shoulders like a tremendous weight. For over a thousand years, a succession of Kings and Queens had used every means possible to find a way through the Veil...and all failed. Now, at long last, redemption for all these past failures might finally be at hand.

His knees weakened at the prospect.

"We must tell the Queen, have her assemble the Crown's advisors, plan an invasion—"

"No!"

Tal blinked. "I don't understand. Why not?"

Bozar shook his head. "The Empire is infested with the Dark Queen's spies. If Marlinda is made aware of this anomaly, she will close the portal, and our one and only chance in a millennium will be gone! In fact, not one cavalryman or soldier from the garrisons can be allowed to leave here. They have *seen* the gateway."

Tal spread his hands. "So, we just stay here and stare at the wormhole?"

Bozar rubbed his hands. "First, we continue the search for the *horde* leader. If we find him, we find the Artifact to fully trigger the portal. Next, I'm going to send for an expert on the Veil, Artemis Thurgood, an old colleague of mine. He teaches at the University in Meredith City. Since the odds of catching this raider are slim, we will need other options to fully open this doorway. He may be able to provide us with the means on how to do this."

Bozar turned to Tal. "You will collect him from Waldez and bring him here. I don't trust anyone else with this task. *No one* must know the real reason why you are there. Once we have his report, I'm certain we will have enough information to plan our next move. *Then* we contact Celestria and have the Queen assemble her counselors."

The First Advisor squeezed Tal's shoulder and made his way to a line of picketed horses.

"Where are you going?" Tal called.

Bozar paused and looked back. "To break the news to

Gravelback and Banebolt."

He swung into the saddle. "And tell them their men need to settle in for a long stay."

He looked longingly at the vortex embedded in the Veil. *Close enough I can almost touch it.*

Razor grabbed the legs of a dead raider and with the help of another soldier, tossed it onto the growing pyramid of bodies.

He pulled at the neck of the snug uniform and stifled a curse.

When he emerged from the forest the previous evening, he joined the cavalrymen employed in the grisly task of disposing of dead bodies. Spattered with gore, so far no one had given him a second glance, but he knew his luck couldn't hold. In the aftermath of battle, a period of chaos and disorganization always reigned. However, sooner or later, a roll call would be taken, and his disguise revealed. Worse, word had been spread among the cavalrymen they would not return any time soon to the garrison. There would be no opportunity for him to slip away while en route.

Razor figured he had only days left before his ruse was discovered.

He looked longingly at the vortex embedded in the Veil. *Close enough I can almost touch it.*

The *horde* leader fingered the Artifact beneath his tunic. In all his raids, he had never seen a portal act in such a way. They opened. They closed. They *never* looked like this. The only explanation must be the proximity to a Watch Tower...it had to have caused the phenomena. If so, this meant he needed to get much closer before the Artifact's magic could successfully be employed.

I can open it. I just need a chance to sneak away and fully trigger the gate.

He shook his head. Right now, it might as well be a thousand leagues away. A single soldier approaching the Veil would draw immediate notice. He would be discovered and then dead long before he could escape.

With a grunt, he picked up another body. His eyes widened in recognition. *Colley.* So many arrows sprouted from his second-in-command, he more closely resembled a hedgehog than a man. He carried the lifeless body to the pile and added it to the pyre.

Jaw clinched, he wiped his hands. He had no choice but to bide his time and wait for an opportunity.

When it came, he would leave this place far behind.

CHAPTER 53

Mr. Finkle seated himself next to Alex.

"First, you need to understand that Meredithian culture is permeated with magic."

He steepled his fingers. "Magic is routinely practiced here and affects all aspects of life. It is used in the construction of homes, cultivation of crops, growing trees for lumber, practicing medicine, even for communication. The list is endless."

Alex nodded. After what she had seen and experienced, nothing surprised her.

"You will find no computers, cell phones, or flat screen TVs here. They're not needed. Magic works here in the same way technology works on Earth."

With a sheepish smile, Alex recalled the fruitless search for an outlet when she first woke on Meredith...and the cordless lamps with the unusual *light bulbs*.

"This practice of magic is called *weaving* because the inhabitants of Meredith believe magic is 'weaved' much like you would knit a tapestry on a loom. It is in *how* you intertwine this tapestry that determines its pattern and, as such, the configuration of magic."

Mr. Finkle stood and began to pace. "Much like an athlete, the skill level of these weavers varies from practitioner to practitioner, with some more accomplished than others. However, regardless of ability, this magic falls into three general categories: Elemental, Locomotive, and Artifice."

He paused and turned to face Alex. "Now, Elemental uses materials, substances, or ingredients to make magic work—potions or powders for example. Locomotive is the use of mental imagery and energy to produce magic. Often the hands and mind are used in conjunction to practice this form of magic. Finally, Artifice produces *Artifacts* or objects of magic. A staff, sword, or ring—any solid object—can be infused with magic and turned into an Artifact."

Intrigued, Alex sat higher. *Magical objects like a flying carpet or Gandalf's staff?* Her interest level took a leap forward.

"Since Artifacts are easily created, Artifice is the most common form of enchantment. Lodestones are often embedded in these objects because they absorb and store magic. When the Artifact is in use, the lodestones release magic."

Brow furrowed, Alex asked, "You mean they are like batteries?"

Her Angel inclined his head. "Excellent. A good analogy."

Pleased, he continued, "Each kind of magic has its advantages and disadvantages. For example, practitioners of Elemental are limited by the materials they have at hand. If a key substance is missing, it limits the enchantment, while Locomotive requires mental discipline—the magic fails with any break in concentration. Finally, the weakness in Artifice is that without the Artifact, the practitioner is powerless. There is complete dependency on the charmed object."

Alex rubbed her temples. *Everything is moving too fast. The events of the past two days and now this. It's too much. I don't understand it all.*

Finally, she looked up. "So everyone on this planet is a what? A magician?"

Mr. Finkle shook his head. "Everyone *uses* magic, but not everyone *weaves* magic. And remember, even among these practitioners of magic, there exists different levels of skill."

Alex crossed her arms. "You said that before. But what does it mean? Some are better at it than others?"

"Precisely. In fact, the independent practice of magic is forbidden except for those who have undergone formal training—and even they must begin their tutelage at an early age. The selection process is vigorous, and few have the stamina and necessary skill to be successful."

He began to pace again. "The first or lowest proficiency is called the Apprentice level. This is basic magic at its most rudimentary means, a hard and demanding task, and many fail. The next level is Adept. An Adept is competent enough to weave basic magic without close supervision but has limited options outside of simple enchantments. This is followed by the more difficult proficiency of Master. Masters, or *Magisters*, have attained complete yet *specialized* competency in only one kind of magic. They have little skill in other forms of enchantments. For example, a Master of Elemental has scant ability in Locomotive."

Mr. Finkle returned to stand beside Alex. "Finally, the highest and most powerful level of magic is that of *Grand Master*, one who has attained proficiency in *all* types of magic. These individuals are rare and few in number. Only nobles—those born of royal blood—can rival a Grand Master in terms of their power."

Alex's mind churned. She could scarce absorb everything she had heard. It was like being trapped in a digital game, one with certain rules which *must* be followed. Even Mr. Finkle *himself* was an unexplainable phenomenon. But the attack on her by Rodric via Darcy's body provided the clincher. The rules *did* matter, and ignorance of them could have lethal consequences.

Knowledge of this didn't make it any simpler to wrap her mind around. Too many questions were still left unanswered. "You mentioned nobles. What exactly is a noble? Is it like a King or a Queen?"

"Ah, an excellent question. Nobles are those who can trace their lineage to the original founding of the Meredithian Dynasty. These descendants have genetic advantages which give them a natural affinity for magic not enjoyed by the general population. While the Empire's citizens are a long-lived race, nobles have life spans that easily exceed the century mark. They also possess physical advantages of being stronger and faster. The Kings and Queens of Meredith, in particular, have unmatched physical and magical strength."

Alex chewed her lip. "So, these nobles rule, and everyone else has to do what they say? Sounds pretty backward to me."

Mr. Finkle shook his head. "Not at all. Again, you must think like Alexandria, not as Mona. On Meredith, royalty is revered, and the population looks to the King and Queen for protection and leadership. Unlike Earth's experiences with feudal societies, here the nobility has a close, organic connection with the people they serve, and this relationship has endured for thousands of years."

Alex pulled her robe tighter. It was Alex's, or rather *Mona's*, experience that people with wealth and privilege—like Lady Anne—could and *did* take advantage of people they thought beneath them. *Could this society be different?* Her head and her heart seemed pulled in different directions, and the beginnings of a headache throbbed at her temples.

Mr. Finkle placed a hand on her shoulder. "You are of two worlds, Alex, no matter how you choose to reconcile this in your mind. The instincts of one contradict the other. Realize the best part of you is, and will always be, the Mona of Earth, whose unselfishness and compassion gave back to help others—just like your compassion as Alexandria moved you to insist your handmaiden be released to you."

A crooked smile appeared on his face. "You see, when you

think about it, the two aren't really all that different. Only the circumstances change."

Mr. Finkle crossed his arms. "Now it's time to share some history with you. In particular, you need to know how the Veil came to be created." He gave a slight nod, and a book materialized on a small table beside Alex's elbow.

"I strongly recommend you do a little reading. I think you'll find some of your questions will be answered."

Alex picked up the book. No title or text appeared anywhere on the spine or facing. Bound in soft brown leather, it looked unremarkable. She started when it expanded to twice its size in her hands. "What—"

"It is a tale of Man's passions, love, jealousy, and ultimately... *murder*."

The angel bowed. "Now it is time to take my leave. Fare thee well, Alexandria." He started to walk away, his image shrinking.

"Stop!" Alex cried. Mr. Finkle paused and turned back.

"You-you can't just...*disappear* and leave me here. Not like this! I-I don't know what to do."

Her angel inclined his head. "All will be revealed in the fullness of time. In the meantime—as I told you before—follow your heart. It has led you true so far."

His tone rang of a finality in Alex's ears. "I won't see you again, will I?" she whispered.

Mr. Finkle cocked his head. "Why, Alex. That all depends on you." His image continued to shrink until it disappeared.

One more point of light among the myriad of stars.

CHAPTER 54

TAL YAWNED AND STARED AT THE BROWN PORRIDGE IN THE WOODEN bowl.

The pyre had burned all day and through the night. Although reduced to a pile of grey ash, the smell of scorched flesh still filled the air.

He pushed the bowl away.

Bozar pulled aside a flap and entered the tent. Tal's *Eldred* made no move to join the line of soldiers being served the porridge by the camp cook. Instead, he pulled up a stool and sat at the canvas table next to the young prince.

He looked carefully to his left and right, then leaned forward. "I have sent word to Meredith City for Artemis. When I receive confirmation, you will take a picked squad of storm riders and collect him at Waldez."

Tal nodded. As he started to speak, an approaching soldier interrupted him. A tall, cloaked figure with long white hair followed beside the cavalryman. He blinked at the sight of the silvery hair and the *haloub* tucked at the man's waist.

A White Monk.

The soldier carried Lord Gravelback's sigil on his tunic. He stopped and saluted palm to head and heart.

"Sire, we found this man at the Watch Tower, along with two boys. He insisted we bring him to you."

Tal stood. "Greetings." He studied the monk. "Were you the one who activated the Tower?" Before a reply could be offered, a shout came from behind them.

"Pulpit! Have you found Ellie yet?"

Tal looked up to see a young boy burst through the tent flaps, a larger lad in hot pursuit.

"Samuel! Stop! Pulpit told us to wait with the soldiers!"

The small boy came to a breathless halt before Tal. With an apologetic smile, the monk said, "Sire, let me introduce you to the person who *did* activate the Watch Tower. This is Samuel Ledbetter. The lad running after him is his brother, Caleb." Caleb skidded to a stop just as Pulpit finished his introductions.

"Aw, Pulpit," Samuel chimed. "You killed the werewolf and fought the ogre long enough for me to get away. After that, it was easy."

Tal smiled and squatted beside the small boy. "I have never heard the word *easy* used to describe the activation of a Watch Tower...much less the slaying of a shape shifter or a battle with a giant."

Caleb stood close by and stared, his mouth agape. "Y-you are th-the..." he stammered, and his voice trailed off.

Pulpit grasped Caleb by the shoulders and pushed him forward to face Tal. "Sire, I can assure you the boy is capable of speaking in complete sentences. He is just a little...*surprised* to see one of your personage here."

"*You are the Prince!*" Caleb managed to blurt.

Tal chuckled. "So it would seem." He raised an eyebrow at the White Monk. "Is it true you fought and killed a werewolf? That you fought an ogre?"

"He did it!" Samuel cried. "I saw him!"

Pulpit coughed. "We do what we must, Sire." At Tal's urging, he recounted the attack on the farm, their subsequent flight to the Watch Tower, and how Samuel had activated it.

"Sire," Pulpit said, "I beg your pardon, but we are concerned with Caleb and Samuel's sister, Ellie. We believe she may have been taken captive. Would you know of her whereabouts?"

Looks of dread appeared on both boys' faces. Tal reached out and ruffled Samuel's hair. "Your sister is sore and bruised but otherwise unharmed. She is in the infirmary. Come, I'll take you to her."

They left the cook's tent and walked a short distance to the hastily erected field hospital. Low cots filled either side of the pavilion, many filled with wounded men. Soft groans greeted them, along with the smell of astringents. Tal led them to an isolated bed near the corner of the tent. The young prince stopped and nodded at the figure in the bed. A young woman lay with her eyes closed, a bandage about her head. Numerous abrasions marked her arms and face.

"Is this your sister?"

"Ellie!" Caleb cried. He fell to his knees and hugged her. Samuel soon joined his older brother.

Ellie's eyes fluttered open, and she smiled through cracked lips at the sight of her brothers. "Caleb, Samuel! How did you get here?" She spied the monk beside the bed. "Pulpit!"

Ellie sat up. She looked around and frowned. "Papa, Mother! I don't see them. Are they—"

Pulpit interrupted her. "Hush, child. They are safe and back at the farmhouse. However, I am sure they are terribly worried. They don't know what has happened to any of you. We must get back to let them know you are safe."

Ellie nodded...then became aware of the other figure beside the monk. Her eyes widened, and a squawk escaped her lips. She pulled the sheet up to her chin.

"What's the matter with you?" Samuel asked. "It's just the Prince. We told him all about what happened."

Tal chuckled at the small boy. He knelt, then took one of

Ellie's hands and kissed it. "It is a pleasure to meet you."

Ellie stared at the prince. "I must...I must look a fright," she stammered while trying to brush tangled hair from her face.

"For what you have been through, you look—"

Ellie's scream stopped Tal. Her face had gone white, and she pointed a trembling finger at the entrance to the hospital.

"It's him," she whispered in a ragged voice.

Tal sprang to his feet. A commotion ensued outside the pavilion. Shouts and the clash of steel rang in the air. A cry of pain ended in a moan.

Tal pivoted back to the young woman. "Who?" he demanded. "Who did you see?"

Ellie's breath came out in strangled gasps, her lips quivering.

"The raid leader. The one who captured me."

CHAPTER 55

LEX STARED AT THE SWEEP OF STARS IN THE SKY.
She never felt so alone, the night suddenly cold and sterile. Tugging her robe tighter, she picked up the book and hurried back to her room. The hearth still flickered with the remnants of a fire, and she picked a nearby chair and collapsed into it. With a wave of her hand, a lamp flared to life.

She opened the book...and blinked.

The first page held the image of a woman with an infant in her arms, a man seated beside her on the bed. Then, like a streaming video, the frozen figures on the page moved and spoke.

"We will call her, Sonja," the man said. "A beautiful name for a beautiful daughter and one to proudly carry on the Salterhorn lineage."

Alex almost dropped the book when, suddenly, the pages flipped by in a blur. When they stopped, an adolescent girl appeared. Slender, her pale blonde hair fell about a face creased in concentration. She stood in a room with a large table. Spread on its flat surface lay a map. Scattered about were ink pots and various tools for wood and metalworking, each with lodestones embedded in them.

A stylus hovered over the map. When the girl moved her fingertips, the instrument matched her motion. A streak of golden light flared from the tip, and the girl drew a rectangle in the air. The bright square drifted motionless, and when she pointed at the map, a stream of incandescence shot from the rectangle to connect with the chart. Whispers—like the rustle of fabric— scratched the air, followed by the scene of a hamlet within the bright lines. A horse-drawn wagon moved along a cobbled road, while villagers strolled by.

A man entered the room, and Alex recognized him as the father from the first page. He wrapped the young girl in his arms and hugged her.

"Sonja, are you still at it? Your mother said it's time for supper, so you'll have to tear yourself away long enough to eat."

Sonja giggled, then pushed herself away and pointed at the hovering image. "Do you see it, Father? It's the village of Atherton. I opened a gate to Atherton!" She twirled and danced. "I did it, I did it!"

Her father chuckled. "Well done." He squinted at the sight. "Although only a mouse or small bird could travel through your gate."

Sonja sighed. She picked up a round object from the table and held it before her. It looked to Alex like a smaller version of a baseball. "I know. I haven't worked out the mechanisms of time and space yet. But someday...someday I will."

Sonja's father shook his head. "You have learned all the tutors here can teach you. Your mother and I have talked, and we intend to enroll you in the Academy at Locus. Because it is so far away, at the foot of the Blue Teeth Mountains, the decision has not been easy for us. However, there you can receive the instruction you need to further your Talent."

Tears appeared in his eyes. "We will miss you...terribly."

Sonja held the sphere before her. "Don't worry, Father. I am going to find a way where home is only a breath away. Distance will no longer matter."

The pages whisked forward, and another scene presented itself. A young woman stood again at a table, this one larger and far more sumptuous. Tools and implements lay scattered everywhere.

Alex recognized Sonja immediately. The former adolescent girl now possessed soft curves and, in her womanhood, had grown tall. Her golden hair was pulled back by combs, and eyes of cerulean blue studied a spherical object held in her hand.

At first, Alex thought it to be the same circular piece she had seen earlier, but upon closer examination, changes became apparent. Delicate scrollwork covered the entire sphere, its surface now chased in silver and gold. Tiny lodestones were embedded in the four cardinal directions, while each half of the sphere contained a series of small panels or doors.

A knock on the door signaled a visitor, and a sallow-faced young man entered. Painfully thin, he ran his hand through greasy black hair. "He-hello, Sonja. Missed you at the noon meal today."

Sonja flew to the young man and hugged him. "Jack! It's finished! I've completed the orb. I couldn't have done it without you." She embraced him again.

Jack, face red, shuffled his feet. "Go-good. Wh-what will you do now?"

Sonja clasped her hands to her chest. "Have you heard the news? I am to be betrothed to Will Martinvale, the son of the Lord Governor of Dalfur." She laughed and dropped the orb in the pocket of her dress.

"Can you believe it? I met him when Father hosted the Lord Governor at our manor overnight. When I saw Will, I almost swooned. He is tall and handsome, with brown eyes so clear…"

Sonja clutched Jack's shoulder. "The betrothal ceremony will be here at the Academy Ballroom tomorrow night. You *must* come as my guest."

Jack's mouth worked, but no sound came out. Finally, he

stammered, "Be-betrothal? You are to be married?"

"Yes! Isn't it wonderful?"

"But what about me?" Jack's face twisted. "What about *us*?"

Sonja touched his arm. "Don't worry. We will always stay close friends. You will—"

She cried out when Jack grabbed her hand and wrenched it. "Friends? You think I am satisfied with being friends? You are mine. *You were always meant to be mine!*"

Sonja jerked her hand back. "You're hurting me!"

He ignored her protest. "I shelved my own projects, neglected my studies, all to help *you*! I-I thought you loved me too."

Sonja stepped back. "I do love you, Jack. But as a brother. A friend."

Skin flushed, he jabbed a finger at her. "You used me, made me believe you returned my love, just so you could finish that cursed orb. Well, damn you, and damn this Will Martinvale!"

He rushed from the room.

"Jack, stop—"

The door slammed in Sonja's face.

Alex, hand to her mouth, put the book down. Curiosity got the better of her, and she picked it back up. The pages flapped forward and stopped. She leaned forward.

Jack sat alone in a darkened room. The cubicle looked as disheveled as he was. Books teetered on a table and chair, while others were stacked wherever space allowed on the floor. Rumpled blankets lay on the unmade bed, while soiled clothes formed lumps on the ground. A growl suddenly issued from his mouth.

He jumped up and dashed out.

A whir of pages sped by and stopped, presenting Alex with the sight of Sonja seated beside an open window. She appeared lost in thought, when a pounding at the door broke her reverie. When she opened it, Jack rushed in. He grabbed Sonja and threw her to the floor.

"No one will have you but me!" he shrieked. He pummeled her and began to rip off her clothes.

A muffled cry escaped from Alex's lips. *He is going to kill her!*

Sonja fought back, her screams mixed with Jack's maddened cries. A short time later, the rumble of booted feet could be heard, and several young men rushed into the room. They spotted the struggle and ran to pull Jack off Sonja. Other students appeared, and they joined the melee. Kicked and punched senseless, Jack's head lolled on his shoulders.

Alex dropped the book in her lap, her breath coming in short gasps. It was too reminiscent of what Rodric had tried to do to her.

I don't want to see anymore.

But Thaddaeus Finkle wouldn't have given her the book if he didn't want her to finish it...*all* of it. With shaking hands, she picked it back up.

Faster now, the pages whisked by. A new scene presented itself. This one showed Jack in a chamber of some sort. Stout iron bars covered the front, while solid brick covered the windowless back fortification. Jack sat with his back against the wall, his head between his knees.

A flicker of light appeared before the cell. Lines of a golden hue blazed and grew into a rectangular shape.

Through this door stepped Sonja.

She carried a bag in one hand, the orb in the other. Jack looked up, and a cackle escaped his lips. The sound carried a tinge of madness.

"Come to gloat? To see your pet rat imprisoned?"

Sonja's eyes were puffy, and a dark bruise adorned one cheek. "I never wanted this."

Jack leaped to his feet and rattled the bars. *"Liar!"* he screamed.

Tears streaked Sonja's cheek. "My father, Will, and the Lord Governor will arrive tomorrow. I-I am afraid what they might do once they discover what you...what you tried to do. I can't bear the thought of any further harm coming to you."

She moved forward a step and placed the bag at the foot of the cell door. She nudged it against the bars with the toe of her slipper. Jack snatched the satchel up and pulled it between the iron rods. He eyed it suspiciously. "What's this?"

"Food and a water bladder. It should be enough to last you for several days."

Sonja held the orb before her, and one of the tiny doors opened. A shaft of golden light streamed out and into the dungeon cell. A blazing line raced from floor to ceiling. When it met, tall evergreens, dense brush, and a small stream appeared within its parameters. A tiny meadow was situated in the midst of the trees, and the babble of a stream, birds warbling, and other forest sounds formed a gentle cacophony.

"I know you remember this... our special place. We stumbled across it our first year at the Academy. We would come here and talk for hours about our hopes and dreams."

Jack's face softened at the scene, and he clutched the iron bars. "It's where I fell in love with you. I beg you...don't marry anyone but me."

Sonja started to reach for him and stopped. She slowly pulled her hand back. "Don't you see? Neither one of us is the same. We were so young and so far from home then...and we made a terrible mistake. We've changed, and we—we can't go back."

Sonja wiped the tears from her cheeks with the back of her hand. "You should recognize the foothills that lead up to the mountains. I am certain you will be pursued, but this at least gives you a head start."

Jack bared his teeth. "So, I am to be hunted and run to ground like a stag?"

"Please," Sonja sobbed. "Step through the gate and flee."

Hot eyes bored into Sonja, then Jack twisted away and paced back and forth. Suddenly, he pivoted and stepped into the doorway. He stopped and looked back. A harsh smile grew across his face.

"One day we will meet again…I promise."

He took another step, and the gate closed behind him.

CHAPTER 56

RAZOR'S LUCK FINALLY RAN OUT.

Assigned to stand guard at the entrance to the field infirmary—a posting he was glad to take—it offered a respite from carting dead bodies and a chance to think of a plan to steal away and escape through the portal.

When the Royal walked by him to enter the medical pavilion, it took every ounce of self-control to stay his hand from his sword. However, he *did* turn his head and follow the Prince's progress.

A costly mistake.

Moments later, the Royal's little group stopped at a wounded patient's bed, and a young woman sat up. Before he could turn away, she looked up, just a casual glance at first, but then returned to him. Her eyes widened.

It was the young woman he had taken captive.

He didn't wait for her reaction.

His life now measured in minutes, and her scream followed him as he ran toward a line of picketed horses. He ignored the storm mounts and made for those of Gravelback's garrison. Although the winged horses offered the fastest means to the beckoning gate, he had no experience riding them.

Several bored sentries stood nearby, posted to watch over the horses. Razor slowed down and approached the nearest one with a friendly smile on his face. When he drew close enough, he snatched the dagger from his belt and slashed the surprised guard's throat in one fluid motion. The sentry gargled, his blood a fountain in the air. Razor ignored him and turned to engage the next soldier.

The guard fumbled for his sword and managed to draw it before Razor attacked. The clash of steel echoed as both men slashed and parried. Razor threw a glance over his shoulder and saw the other soldier running toward him.

Desperate, he hacked and chopped then pressed closer for a killing strike. His opponent's blade skittered off his sword and scored a long slash on the exposed flesh of his right arm. Blood gushed from the wound. Razor cursed and brought his hilt up to collide with a solid *thud* on the guard's chin.

He dropped like a stone.

Razor pivoted, flipped the dagger's blade into his hand, then flung it at the charging soldier. The blade sank deep into cavalry-man's chest. He cried out, dropped his weapon, and clutched the blade. The sentry sank to his knees, then toppled over.

Quickly, Razor picked out a sturdy horse and leaped onto its saddleless back. He cut the picket line and began shouting and hitting horses with the flat of his sword. Within moments, scores of panicked horses stampeded out of the camp. Bent low, the horse's mane firmly in his grasp, Razor followed the stampede. Clods of dirt and grass mixed with dust flew about him.

Wind whipped by his face, and Razor risked a look back. The camp looked like an overturned ant hill. Soldiers ran back and forth, confusion evident in their rudderless actions. No one had attempted to even catch a horse and take up the chase.

The horde leader turned away and chuckled. Even if one of the storm horses took flight, by the time a storm rider saddled his mount, he would be safely through the Veil. He lifted his head and screamed in exultation.

Razor thundered closer and closer to the cloudy, whirling

vortex. He ripped the neckline of the stolen uniform, buttons popping, and pulled the Artifact from inside his tunic. It bounced and dangled, and he caught it with his free hand. His fingers slipped inside the grip, and he closed his fist. A *buzz* emanated from the Artifact.

The turbulence inside the wormhole stilled. Slowly, it clarified into a tunnel, whose bottom and sides remained cloudy and gray. Pinpricks of light, too innumerable to count, embedded the channel and marked the way.

Without slowing down, he charged into the tunnel and disappeared through the magical door.

CHAPTER 57

ALEX SAT BACK AND RUBBED HER EYES.

Numb, she tried to make sense of what she had seen...a young woman, a young man. Unrequited love followed by jealousy, hatred, and even madness. Then a magical orb is introduced into this convoluted mix to produce...what? *Why did Mr. Finkle want me to see this? It doesn't make any sense. What good is only part of a story—*

She sat up.

Because it isn't finished!

Alex fumbled for the book in her lap and opened it. Jack stood frozen in the middle of a wilderness...then he started moving.

░

Jack's hair, tangled with leaves and briars, whipped about his face.

With continual looks over his shoulder, he climbed higher up a steep slope populated with fir and pine. His breath came in explosive gasps. Rivulets of sweat formed vertical lines on his dirt-encrusted face. In the distance, the deep bay of hounds wafted in the air.

Jack climbed faster, babbling as he went.

"I'm on a holiday, la, la, la. Nothing can touch me, la, la, la. Sonja is mine, la, la, la." Hysterical laughter followed each outburst.

Jack scrabbled onto a plateau and bent over, hands on hips. He straightened, and crazed his eyes surveyed his surroundings.

Thick vegetation covered most of the granite outcroppings of rock. The yelp of hounds sounded again, closer now.

Jack flinched, but before he could resume climbing, a thick screen of vines and brambles wrapped upon the rock facing trembled and parted.

To reveal the mouth of a cave.

Jack's eyes widened. He pointed and cackled at the sight, then stumbled into the grotto.

The book's pages remained fixed, frozen on the mouth of the cave.

"What? Where did he go?" Alex mumbled to herself.

Curious, she leaned forward. Her nose only inches from the page, she peered at the cavern entrance. A tug pulled at her shoulder. Startled, she looked up.

Nothing.

Then another heave gripped her. Finally, as if a giant invisible hand closed about her body, the pull grew stronger and more irresistible.

With a cry, she disappeared into the page.

Alex gasped. Wild-eyed, her gaze swiveled left and right.

Rock walls, slick with moisture, arched over and around her. Water dripped from the ceiling to form shallow puddles at her feet, the cool air heavy with a musty, stale odor. A line of sconces fixed to the walls held torches which sputtered to produce an eerie illumination. The hollow passageway undulated before her in curves and angles, like a coiled snake.

She blinked. *Wha-what is this? Some sort of cave?* It took only seconds to make the connection she no longer viewed the narrative in the book.

I'm in it!

Movement caught her attention. She turned and stifled a scream. A man walked toward her.

She spun and searched for a place of concealment. The tunnel stretched away from her, to disappear behind a bend of solid rock. On either side, sheer walls rose from the cave floor. Silhouetted in the middle of the passageway, dread realization struck her.

There's no place to hide.

Before Alex could turn and make a run for it, the man looked up—right at her! Paralyzed, her breath caught in her throat as the stranger continued on his way...and brushed by with no acknowledgement of her presence. Her eyes widened in recognition, and she clapped a hand over her mouth to smother a gasp.

It's Jack!

But he ignored her. He walked right by her like she wasn't there. He couldn't have missed her. She stood right in the middle—

Illusion. This is all an illusion produced by the book's magic.

She shook her head, and a shaky laugh escaped from her. *None of this is real.*

But why?

It occurred to her this had to be by design. Mr. Finkle left nothing to chance. Apparently, it wasn't enough to see or hear the story. She needed to be *in* the tale and experience it as well.

Alex turned and followed Jack.

She drew closer, shocked at his appearance. His tunic, torn in numerous places, revealed ribs protruding from a gaunt frame. Black, matted hair, greasy and unkempt, grew in wild profusion from his head, while dark, black eyes peered from his dirty face.

The flickering torches led them into a large cavern. Several spacious chambers were carved out of the sides of the enormous cave. Jack stopped and surveyed the vast hollow. He turned and made his way to one of the excavations.

Alex followed and stopped when inside the quarried room. A large table took up most of the space, while the walls of the chamber held shelves filled with all manner of jars, bottles, tools, implements, and books. Some of the *things* inside the containers stirred in response to Jack's presence.

He picked up one of the jars that contained what looked to be a pickled snake. The serpent suddenly spun around within the container, the preservative fluid frothing. Without warning— mouth open wide to display serrated rows of teeth—it struck at Jack. The jar shook in his hands, and Jack almost dropped it. He set the vessel down and backed away.

Her attention focused on Jack, the squeak of a chair came to Alex's ears. She turned, and her mouth dropped. At the far end of the table, concealed in shadow, a cloaked figure sat. The sound alerted Jack, and he pivoted as well.

He stared, then a snicker escaped his mouth. "Who are you?"

The individual remained mute, the cowl disguising his features. A copper bowl sat on the table, and the shrouded figure passed hands over it, muttering words in a strange language. Abruptly, the man straightened.

"Welcome, Brother. Sit next to me." The stranger acted like he expected Jack.

Jack's giggling took on a higher pitch. "Oh, yes. Of course." He sat down.

The man pulled back the hood from his head.

To reveal the face of a woman.

Jack huffed. Then peals of laughter erupted from his lips.

Alex shook her head. *He's crazy. He's truly mad.*

She turned her attention to the woman. Jet-black hair fell from her heart-shaped face. She removed her cloak and placed it on the table, revealing a striking figure. A thin gown accentuated her small waist and large bosom, while her eyes were every bit as dark as her hair.

These eyes, now fixed on Jack, were devoid of warmth or pity. "You are late, Jack Morley. I worried something ill had befallen you."

Jack's laughter settled to mild cackling. "L-Late?" he tittered. "Wh-What are you talking about? Who are you?"

"I am Marlinda Darkmoor. I beckoned you here to my mountain cavern."

Marlinda produced a hard loaf of bread and a steaming bowl of stew. She poured an ocher drink into a large goblet and then produced a small vial. She emptied its contents into the chalice and shoved it toward him. "You are no use to me in your current state, hungry, thirsty, and half out of your mind. The potion will help settle your wits. Now, eat and drink!" she commanded.

Jack fell onto the meal. A short time later, he pushed himself away, sated.

His eyes appeared clearer and absent the clouded tinge of madness. "You are right. My mind doesn't seem to be so...confused."

His words, calm and measured, also carried a clarity missing in his previous speech.

Jack regarded Marlinda warily. "You have told me your name, not *who* you are. Or how I discovered this grotto, one so cleverly hidden I could have walked by it a thousand times and never discovered its entrance."

"I've already told you. *I* drew you here. As for who I am..." She stood and spread her arms wide. "I am a practitioner of Wildling magic. It is why I must remain hidden in this dark hole, so the Empire's lickspittles won't find me."

She waved at the shelves crammed with the vessels filled with odd creatures. "How do you like my creations? So far, I have been forced to limit myself to small creatures, but melding them is no longer a challenge. I desire larger beasts...*much* larger and more intelligent."

Jack favored Marlinda with a humorless smile. "In other words, you are a *witch*."

Marlinda laughed, the malevolent sound cutting like a blade across Alex's skin. "Call me what you like. *Witch, Wildling, Sorceress*, it is all the same to me. My only desire is the freedom to practice magic as I choose without interference. *I need no one's permission!*"

Jack pointed at the pickled specimens. "Yet the Academy rules strictly prohibit experimentation—particularly the use of magic—on even the lowliest of creatures in any unnatural way. After seeing some of your *creations*, I can guarantee the Empire's authorities would disagree with you."

A mirthless chuckle spilled from Marlinda's lips. "Yes. I imagine they would. Tell me, is this the same Academy whose students beat you senseless and had you imprisoned? And is it not the Lord Governor, an officer of the Empire, who has directed you to be hunted down like a game animal?"

Jack's face flushed. "You know of this?" he demanded.

"Of course. I know *everything* about you. That's why I need you, or rather, the Artifact your colleague created."

Jack frowned. "What Artifact? What are you—"

His eyes widened. "The orb? Why? I can make—"

"Silence! All I need to know is can you control its magic?" She leaned close, ruthless, stygian eyes boring into his. "Can you manipulate the orb?"

Jack gulped. "I-I worked closely with Sonja, but I am no

match for her skill. However, with enough time, I'm confident I can unlock the Artifact's magic."

He ran a shaky hand through his lank hair. "Outside of Sonja, no one knows more about the orb than me. With proper supplies and your help, then yes, I can do it. Nevertheless, I will need time—"

"Done!"

Marlinda's smile revealed teeth clenched in a rictus of triumph. She tugged Jack to his feet. She pulled him close and rubbed her warm body against his. "We will be partners in all things and will share equally in the risks and rewards." She took his hands and placed them on her breasts. "And I'll make sure to fill your every desire."

Jack's breath caught in his throat, and he drew the wildling witch closer.

Her lips next to his ear, Marlinda breathed, "We will take the orb, you will unlock its magic, and I will build an army none will be able to resist. Together we shall conquer Dalfur. The land will run red with the blood of all our enemies."

A cruel smile appeared on Jack's face, and he licked his lips. "All?" he asked. "Including Sonja, her betrothed, and the Lord Governor?"

Marlinda purred, "Oh, yes. *All.* And we will begin with those who betrayed you."

Eyes bright with hate, he turned to the sorceress. "Then let's get started."

The exchange caused a cold chill to travel up Alex's spine. The malignant evil lay in the room like a blanket, suffocating and malicious.

Now I understand why my angel insisted I do more than just "see" this meeting between Jack and Marlinda. No description would do justice to this kind of wickedness with such potential for murder and death.

She took a long, shaky breath. *It can only be experienced...and I've been provided with a front row seat.*

Harsh laughter burst from Marlinda. Maniacal, the mirth was razor-edged with bloodlust and slaughter. Jack joined in, and it rose in intensity to reverberate off the walls of the chamber.

The copper bowl on the table rocked back and forth to repeatedly strike the planks with a *rat-a-tat*. A viscous fluid bubbled up from within the basin to overflow and spill out on the table.

Alex's hands flew to her mouth.

Blood!

Bright red, it spread across the table and dripped onto the floor. It flowed in an endless procession as pulsing gouts of crimson vomited from the bowl in a volcanic eruption.

Alex gasped and jerked back. "No," she whispered. "It's not real. None of this is real."

A dread and familiar sensation crawled over Alex. Her skin itched as if rubbed raw...the same sensation Rodric produced in her.

Without warning, Marlinda pivoted, her black eyes boring into Alex.

She pointed a talon-like finger and shrieked, *"You!"*

Alex screamed. She backpedaled, stumbled, and fell.

And kept falling.

CHAPTER 58

LEX FOUND HERSELF BACK IN HER ROOM AND LYING ON THE FLOOR beside the chair.

Her heart threatened to leap out of her chest, her breath, ragged explosions. The book, closed, rested beside her. She heard an odd sound like a soft keening. With a gulp, she discovered it came from her own lips.

She clamped her mouth shut.

Leaving the book where it lay, Alex pushed herself up and hurried back to her bed. Once there, she leaned back against the headboard, knees to her chest and blankets pulled up to her chin. Although not cold, she couldn't stop trembling.

"I want to go home," she whispered. *"I don't want to be here anymore."*

Life as Mona now seemed a wonderful prospect compared to her continued existence as Alexandria. *Wicked, bad, evil,* she understood all these terms. However, what she just experienced defied description. She *felt* it! The feeling so strong the evil took on a physical aspect, something you could hold or touch.

Mr. Finkle's words resonated in her mind. *The life you knew as Mona, the one you lived in Texas—it's gone. Your life now is what you make of it.*

There was no turning back. She had no place to go but forward.

Curled in a ball, she cried herself to sleep.

Tal rushed out of the infirmary, Bozar close on his heels.

"He was hiding in plain sight all along," the First Advisor said. "No wonder we could find no trace of him."

Tal pointed. "Look!"

Horses erupted in every direction. In their midst, a lone figure galloped toward the Veil. "He's headed for the wormhole!"

"He must have the Artifact. He's going to fully open the gate and escape!" Bozar cried.

The horrible implications staggered Tal. If the *horde* leader escaped with the Artifact, the portal would close and with it, the only chance since the Veil's creation to destroy it.

"No!" he shouted. He sprinted to the picket line and the storm horses. He slowed to a stop and looked for saddles and tack. A large canvas tent on his left stored the saddles and kept them out of the weather. Before he could run and retrieve the tack, a hand fell on his shoulder.

"Hold, Tal. It's too late."

Bozar gestured with his chin and Tal's heart sank.

The raid leader disappeared through the portal.

"*Nooooo!*" he howled. Desperate, he cast about, and his eyes came to rest on the fallen sentries. The sword of the one closest to them was streaked with blood.

Tal's eyes widened. He rushed to the sword and picked it up. He held it before him, gore dripping from the blade. "There may still be a chance!"

He raced to the equipment tent and emerged a short time later with a bow and quiver.

Bozar frowned. "What do you intend to do?"

Tal turned to his *Eldred*. "Kill the raider."

He drew power, the magic filling him with an audible crackling of energy. Tal's eyes glowed a luminescent blue as he placed a drop of blood from the blade on his tongue. His gaze turned to the Veil and like bread crumbs, spots of blood led to it. They sparkled like tiny jewels, clear evidence the fallen soldier managed to wound the *horde* leader.

The lifeblood of the enemy.

Tal snatched an arrow from the quiver and smeared its tip with the raider's blood. He nocked the shaft and pulled it to his cheek.

"*Seek. Seek the heart,*" he whispered.

The magic from Tal shimmered over the arrow and covered it with a thin film. It hummed and vibrated like a living thing. He released the shaft.

The missile streaked into the air.

Razor grinned as he thundered through the narrow twisted and curved tunnel of the portal.

Normally broader, the magic of the nearby Watch Tower had restricted its diameter—not that he cared. He had escaped… and with only a mere scratch!

He burst out of the gateway and into bright sunlight.

Arms raised high, Razor screamed, "Free!"

For the first time, he considered his immediate future. The Dark Queen would not be happy he had lost an entire *horde*. Anger filled his eyes.

It's not my fault! I never should have been sent on a mission with so many green and inexperienced raiders. It guaranteed disaster!

Fists clenched, the Artifact's grip dug into his skin. Immersed in his wrath, he forgot about the portal until a flicker of motion caught his eye. He looked up to see an object streak from the amorphous tunnel and bury itself in his chest. Razor looked down at the shaft buried up to the fletching in his heart.

It proved to be his last mortal sight.

He fell from his horse, dead before he even hit the ground, the Artifact clenched in a lifeless fist.

And the portal still open.

Preview of *Escape From Wheel*

Conquest of the Veil Series
Book Two
Coming Spring 2020

ℙROLOGUE

MUURCH TRIED NOT TO SOIL HIMSELF.

He obediently followed the guard who led him across a polished marble floor. The color of obsidian, the quarried slabs formed a path ending at a pair of massive doors embellished with gold and silver leaf. Fully twenty hands high, they shielded entry to an inner sanctum he had only heard rumors of.

The throne room of Marlinda Darkmoor and Jack Morley—the Veil Queen and King.

Spaced at intervals, hammered brass bowls lined their path. Held aloft by the outstretched hands of sculpted figures—some human, some animal, some a melding of both—all contorted in various poses of agony. Within these bowls, flames flickered to illuminate the way.

Muurch passed one of the carved busts, a naked woman with pendulous breasts and a sharp, hooked beak rather than a mouth. The licking flames of the braziers cast his shadow on the figure. It stirred, eyes following his progress.

The Gatemaster gulped. Terror filled his veins like shards of ice. The razor-sharp needles pricked him with every step.

Why have I been summoned?

Since escorted from his post at the Gateway, this singular question occupied all his thoughts. As a young acolyte, he trained in the Dark Queen's caverns and had spent years there before his posting as a Gatemaster. But that was half a lifetime ago, and never once in all this time had he ever caught a glimpse of Marlinda...or Jack.

Now he had an audience...*with both*.

Muurch glanced at his guide, the sentry which accompanied him from the Gateway. A reptile's head, large as the fabled dragon lizards of the Katros Islands, rested upon the muscular shoulders of a man's body. A forked tongue flickered in and out of the creature's mouth, the iridescent scales merging with pale flesh.

Muurch thrust trembling hands in the pockets of his robe to conceal his fear.

The colossal doors swung open silently at their approach. Once inside, they whispered shut. Two guards stood inside, each a *meld* even more menacing than his guide. One wore the head of a ram, a pair of matched horns curling beside its head. Cloven feet *clacked* on the floor while a shaggy, fur-lined hand held an enormous axe taller than Muurch.

Tawny fur covered the other guard's entire body. Wicked incisors spilled from its feline mouth, and a pair of vestigial wings sprouted from between its shoulder blades. A paw armed with sharp claws clutched an iron-shod spear.

Both sentries struck the floor with the butt of their weapons.

"Kneel in the presence of the Queen and her consort!" the ram-headed guard boomed.

Muurch fell to his knees.

"Ah, our faithful servant, Muurch. Welcome, Gatemaster. Come forward and be received."

Muurch stood and forced his balky legs to propel him toward the sound of the voice. Before him, seated in a glossy marble throne, the Dark Queen gestured with one hand. Beside her sat her consort. Both wore garments of black silk. The Queen's floor-length gown accentuated a tiny waist, while her bodice strained to contain her full bosom. Hair, the color of night, cascaded past her shoulders. Her consort wore a pleated tunic and breeches, a gold cape draped over one shoulder. His long hair, a match for the Queen's own stygian shade, tumbled past his neck.

The pair's physical stature appeared to be rather ordinary. Of average height and weight, they hardly presented an imposing sight. But when his gaze met their eyes, all semblance to *ordinary* disappeared.

They oozed a dark evil which made the black marble floor look radiant by comparison. Insatiable hunger burned in their eyes, an appetite no amount of cruelty, murder, or slaughter could satisfy.

Muurch forced himself to tear his gaze away.

Perched on their heads were circlets of gold. Embedded with lodestones, the crowns glittered in the light. The Queen held a scepter, tapered at one end and flared on the other. Runes etched its entire surface, but it was what the belled end held which caused Muurch's breath to catch in his throat.

The orb.

At first glance, it looked rather commonplace, just a spherical knob on the scepter, but its power was legendary. He had never seen it, and in all his long life, never met anyone who had.

The Queen motioned to King Jack, and both stood. She smiled at Muurch, but no comfort came from the cold expression.

"What do you think of our audience room? I designed it my-self." She tapped the wall behind the throne with the scepter. "I'm particularly fond of the façade."

The veneer thrust upward to the ceiling. Skulls of all shapes and sizes were fused to the bare rock. Other skeletal remains, mis-matched parts of yellowed ribs, leg and arm bones, appeared as well.

The sight chilled Muurch.

The Dark Queen leaned forward. "Vanquished foes, our enemies, all have taken their place here. Do you know why they occupy such a place of honor?"

Mute, Muurch shook his head.

"As a reminder of what happens to those who oppose us. This includes servants who displease us."

The Gatemaster's bowels clenched.

"Let me demonstrate." Marlinda inclined her head and the two guards stepped forward.

She pointed the scepter at one and then the other. With a *whoosh*, both creatures ignited. Within seconds, all that remained were ash and bones. The acrid odor of burnt flesh filled the room. Bile rose in Muurch's throat, and he fought to contain it.

With a flick of the scepter, the smoking bones of both sentries flew to the façade and with a *hiss*, merged into the rock.

The Dark Queen gestured at the Gatemaster. "Now, you must be thinking what our sentries did to deserve such a fate. And the answer is...*nothing*. They were loyal and wouldn't hesitate to give up their lives for us."

Marlinda stood and walked toward Muurch. Jack followed behind and the two flanked the Gatemaster. "And of course, that is the point. They were sacrificed so you would know just how important the task is we are going to set before you."

The Dark Queen's eyes bored into Muurch. "There *will* be no failure."

The Gatemaster's teeth chattered. "Of co-course. Wh-what is your pleasure, my queen?"

Her icy smile returned. "Good." Marlinda crossed her arms. "Were you aware a portal remains open?"

"Wh-what?" Muurch felt the blood leave his face in a rush. Now he knew why he had been summoned. His scorched bones would soon join—

"You must make sure it remains that way," Marlinda said, interrupting his thought.

Muurch's mouth opened and closed several times before he finally found his voice. "Ke-keep it o-open?" he stuttered.

Jack spoke for the first time. "Yes. At all costs, the way through the Veil must remain unobstructed."

"Bu-but, why? The Empire may discover it. They'll send soldiers and, *gurk*—"

A strangled gasp escaped from Muurch as the Veil Queen's paramour lifted him off his feet and held him inches from his face. "You were chosen for your expertise on portals, not to ask questions!"

The Gatemaster managed a nod and the Dark King released him.

Marlinda moved closer and straightened Muurch's crumpled lapel. "There, there, good Muurch. We are confident you will use your considerable skill to make sure the gateway remains open. Oh, and one more thing."

"Yes, my queen," the Gatemaster rasped.

"No one is to know we had this conversation or of your efforts to keep the wormhole unlocked. *No one!*"

"A-as you command, my queen."

Her face hardened. "Good. Because should this portal close or should even one pair of inquisitive ears become aware of it, your bones will join our collection...and it *will* be a prolonged process. You'll burn one inch at a time."

Marlinda waved her hand. "You are dismissed."

A guard escorted Muurch out, and the doors closed behind him.

His robe flapped like a bird in flight when he broke into a run.

CHAPTER 1

OROTHEA, THE DUCHESS OF THE DUCHY OF WHEEL, POURED water into a crystal bowl.

She muttered words of power and touched the liquid with the tip of her finger. A languid ripple appeared, and her reflection stared back to reveal a pale face with ice-blue eyes. More undulations disturbed the water, and then stilled.

Another face now stared at the Duchess.

Lord Rodric Regret flashed a cruel smile at Dorothea, ivory teeth displayed like a predator prepared to take a particularly juicy bite. Dark eyes cast a penetrating gaze from above a hawkish nose and narrow face. A crown of long black hair, plaited in a braid, looped across his collar.

"Dorothea. To what do I owe the pleasure? Especially since you banished me from Wheel less than a fortnight ago. Do you miss me already?"

The Duchess's mouth curled. "Your memory is as short as your self-control, Rodric. Or have you forgotten already your ill-conceived attack on the Duke's daughter, Alexandria? The very woman you are to be betrothed to?"

Rodric laughed. "Such fun, and yet my talents continue to be unappreciated."

"You are a fool!" Dorothea snapped. "However, I am in need of the very *talents* you boast of."

Rodric's eyes gleamed. "Oh, do tell. I'm all ears."

Dorothea snorted. "I'm afraid it doesn't involve torture or

pulling wings off helpless insects."

A disappointed sigh escaped Rodric. "Very well. What is it you need?"

"A shade. One I can use to track Alexandria's movements."

"Why? You already have guards posted at her door every night."

"Because the Duke has given her permission to roam the city!" Dorothea barked. "And because I don't trust her! Since recovering from her fall, she has behaved oddly...almost like she is a different person. She needs to be watched at all times."

Rodric tapped his lips. "Hmmm. I agree. She indeed seems changed. The Alexandria before the accident was more malleable." He leered and added, "And much more open to the concept of what it means to give *and* receive pleasure."

The insolent smile returned. "I'll decant a shade tonight. Be prepared to receive it by tomorrow."

Dorothea nodded in acknowledgement, and the watery image wavered and disappeared.

The Duchess pursed her lips. *"Don't ever try to match wits with me, Alexandria,"* she whispered. She picked up the bowl and hurled it against the wall where it shattered into a thousand glittering shards.

"Because you won't like the results."

Lost in thought, Alexandria Duvalier sat beneath an ornamental tree on the terrace. A cup of warm tea, untouched, sat forgotten near her fingertips.

Gardeners moved about the terrace pruning, pulling weeds, and tending to the numerous flower beds. She stirred and eyed them uneasily.

Outside of Tell and Darcy, I don't know who I can trust.

Since rousing from the accident on Earth which left her in a coma, everything about her life had changed in an instant. She found herself on a new world with a new body and a new identity.

And faced with *new* problems and threats.

Mona Parker—her *former* self—was a plain and homely teenager, a penniless foster child bullied to the point of suicide by a rich and arrogant classmate. Her guardian angel, Thaddeus Finkle, appeared one night with a proposition;

Exchange a life with someone else.

Faced with the cruel bullying paired with her otherwise drab existence, the choice seemed easy. *What did she have to lose?* The next thing Mona knew, she woke from unconsciousness to find herself on the world of Meredith as Alexandria, a beautiful woman and the daughter of a Duke complete with servants and riches. Her wildest dreams had come true.

Only then did she learn the cost of her bargain.

Trapped behind the Veil, a curtain of magic, the Duchy of Wheel was the last major province still unconquered by Marlinda, the evil creator of the Veil. The Dark Queen's brutal subjugation of the populace—ongoing for over a thousand years—was now almost complete.

But, bad as that prospect seemed, worse lay in store for her.

Attacked her first night on Meredith by her handmaiden, Darcy, the poor girl's body had been mystically commandeered by Rodric—the man her father, Duke Alton Duvalier, was determined she would marry. Via Darcy's body, Rodric's brutal assault almost killed her. Saved by a sudden explosion of power from within her—something she still couldn't explain—the experience even now, in bright sunshine, continued to chill her blood.

The final evidence of her dire circumstances came last night.

Given a magical book by Thaddeus Finkle, she found herself actually *pulled* into the volume. There she became part of a narrative where she witnessed firsthand the initial meeting between Marlinda and Jack. Now dubbed the Veil Queen and King, the poisonous fruit of this malevolent partnership became the magical barrier known as the Veil.

Alex reached for the tea and took a sip.

Still shaky from this surreal experience *within* her angel's book, she arose early and spent most of the morning lost in thought. No amount of meditation, however, could change her situation. Her only choice was to grab hold of her new life and move forward.

I am Alexandria Duvalier, heir to the Duchy of Dalfur...and I need to start acting like it.

No more "Mona" moments of indecision or fear of change. No more feeling sorry for myself. And most of all, no more dependency on Thaddeus Finkle...for anything! His last visit made clear, I'm on my own.

Her guardian angel—at times rude and condescending, and other times, warm and empathetic—never revealed more to her than snippets of what to expect.

Meredith is a world of magic and wonder where magic has replaced technology. But with dreams there are also nightmares.

He was spot on with his description...especially the nightmares. The fact he refused to elaborate further left her feeling she had been tricked into her decision to swap her old life for a new one.

Alex shook her head. *That isn't completely true. I wanted out of my old life...and I have only myself to blame if it didn't end in sunshine and roses.*

Frustrated, her fist struck the table and the teacup jumped and rattled.

The weather turned warmer, sunlight flickering through leafy branches. Clothed in a pair of tan riding breeches and a simple white smock she liberated from her sea of clothing, Alex felt comfortable for the first time since arriving on Meredith. Medieval ideas of appropriate women's attire prevailed here, and although sure to cause a stir among the Duke's stodgy court, she didn't care. She made a mental note to have the court seamstress make her more clothes suitable for riding.

Maybe I'll start a new fashion trend.

Earlier, she had sent Darcy to summon Tell, the officer in charge of her guard detail, so they could ride into Wheel. Since Rodric's attack with Darcy's hijacked body, the young lieutenant never strayed too far away. While waiting, she nibbled on a tray of scones.

On the table next to the sweet biscuits were books her hand-maiden retrieved for her. They chronicled the history of Dalfur, and contained maps of the entire region. Alex intended to pour over them at length until she knew the lay of the land and the rich history behind the Duchy. Although never a dedicated student back on Earth—she always considered history a dusty, pointless exercise—the stakes were higher now.

My life may depend on gathering every scrap of knowledge I can.

First, she needed to learn to negotiate the labyrinthian castle until she could find her way around without help. Next, read and learn everything she could about the region of Dalfur. Finally, she planned to explore Wheel, meet the city's people, and learn their ways and culture.

At the distinctive *click* of Tell's bootheels approaching the terrace, Alex rose from her seat. While she waited, the thought occurred to her that finding her way about the Duke's estate would be easy. The hard part lay ahead.

Determining who on this world I can trust.

Jaw clenched, Tal hurled the bow away from him.

The arrow disappeared into the gray tunnel. A desperate gambit, he had no way to know if the missile would strike the murderous raider or simply be swallowed up by the Veil's magic. If he managed to escape, the *horde* leader would close the portal and all would be lost…their only chance in a thousand years to finally penetrate the accursed barrier gone in an instant.

The Prince and Heir to the Empire of Meredith squatted and watched.

The gateway remained open.

Slowly, he stood, attention riveted on the Veil. Long moments passed.

The entryway into the enchanted boundary still lingered.

His eyes widened. Still no change.

The entrance beckoned.

Tal could stand the wait no longer. With a cry, he ran to a nearby horse cropping grass. He vaulted onto its back and grabbed the dangling reins. Ignoring the shouts of Bozar, he thundered toward the open doorway.

A dozen heartbeats later, he reached the tunnel…and charged into it.

Upon entry, a momentary disorientation came over him. Then just as quickly, it passed. Bent low on the horse's back, Tal steadied himself by squeezing his thighs against the beast's barrel. The smoky, swirling passageway flew past him. Although having the consistency of mist, the channel somehow still managed to support his weight and that of his mount.

Suddenly, he burst into the open. Bright sunlight assaulted his eyes and he blinked. When his vision cleared, he spotted a glorious sight.

The *horde* leader lay motionless on the ground, a shaft protruding from his body.

The last of the murdering scum from the Veil dead!

Tal slid off his horse and knelt beside the dead raider. A metallic flash at the edge of his vision caused him to turn. His eyes narrowed at the sight of a sprawled arm with the Artifact still clutched in a lifeless grip.

The key to the portal!

A commotion came from the gateway. Seconds later, his First Advisor, Bozar, galloped into the open with the garrison commander, Lord Gravelback, hard on his heels. They pulled up and stared at the sight of Tal beside the dead raider.

Tal grinned fiercely and pointed at the Artifact. "The vermin died before he could close the portal." Jubilant, he reached for the magical object when Bozar's cry stopped him.

"Hold!"

Startled, Tal looked up to see his *Eldred* gesture for him to step away. "Do not disturb the body! We must do nothing to cause the Artifact to move."

Frozen in mid-reach, Tal stared at Bozar. "Why?" he snapped. "What harm can come from it?"

Gravelback answered before the First Advisor could reply. "Because even a slight shift might cause the pressure on the Artifact to slip. The portal could close."

Both men dismounted and joined Tal. He backed away, hands against his chest.

"I-I didn't think."

He swallowed and felt his face flush. *The only opportunity in a millennia to penetrate the Veil and my foolishness almost cost us that chance.*

Bozar gripped Tal's shoulder. "Do not think ill of yourself. If not for you, the way would never have remained open."

Gravelback agreed. "Aye. Your quick thinking slew Marlinda's pet before the murderous bastard could close the doorway."

The enormity of the event sank in, and Tal felt his heart soar. He bounded into the air and shouted, "We did it! The way is open! The Veil is finally breached."

Bozar's normally stoic composure slipped, and laughter spilled from his lips. Even Gravelback lifted his grizzled face to the sky and crowed in exultation.

After more celebrating, Tal collapsed on a nearby knob of rock. The culmination of the events of the past day and night left him drained.

The running battle with the Veil raiders lasted most of the night to finally end with their defeat and total annihilation. Daybreak brought the realization the enemy's leader had somehow managed to escape. Too late, they discovered him hidden in their midst posing as a soldier of the Empire. By the time this ruse was revealed, the *horde* leader had stolen a horse, opened a portal, and fled through it—only to die moments later from Tal's hastily shot arrow. Then, the most important occurrence of all.

The discovery that the portal remained open.

Tal pulled his sword and held it before him, the sharp steel glinting in the light.

He chanted a familiar mantra, one he had mouthed countless times, "Blood shall be paid with blood. And one day, the Dark Queen's blood will paint my blade...this I swear."

He rose and sheathed the sword. *Much work lays before us...an invasion needs to be planned.*

The first step in the conquest of the Veil.

ABOUT THE AUTHOR

Michael Scott Clifton, a public educator for over 38 years as a teacher, coach, and administrator, currently lives in Mount Pleasant, Texas with his wife, Melanie and family cat, Sadie. An avid gardener, reader, and movie junkie, he enjoys all kinds of book and movie genres. His books contain aspects of all the genres he enjoys…action, adventure, magic, fantasy, and romance. His fantasy novel, The Janus Witch, received a 5-Star review from the prestigious Readers' Favorite Book Reviews, and he has been a finalist in a number of of short story contests with Edges of Gray winning First Place in the Texas Authors Contest. Professional credits include articles published in the Texas Study of Secondary Education Magazine. Clifton's latest book, The Open Portal, launches the fantasy book series, Conquest of the Veil. In addition, look for the YA novel, Edison Jones and the Anti-Grav Elevator, to be released soon. He can be reached at mike@michaelscottclifton.com. Follow him at www.michaelscottclifton.com.